DEATH IN ARAMEZZO

MURDER IN AN ITALIAN VILLAGE · BOOK 1

MICHELLE DAMIANI

RIALTO
PRESS

DEATH IN ARAMEZZO

MURDER IN AN ITALIAN VILLAGE · BOOK 1

RIALTO PRESS
P.O. Box 1472
Charlottesville, VA 22902
michelledamiani.com

CAST OF CHARACTERS

CASALE MAZZOLI

Stella	*arrives to Aramezzo to take over her family's bed-and-breakfast*
Mimmo	*the caretaker of Stella's bed-and-breakfast*
Ilaria	*the housekeeper of Stella's bed and breakfast*
Signor Severini	*Stella's first guest*

JOBS IN ARAMEZZO

Domenica	*owns the local bookshop*
Matteo	*the streetsweeper*
Cosimo	*the antiquarian and expert on local lore*
Romina	*owns Bar Cappellina, married to Roberto*
Roberto	*owns Bar Cappellina, married to Romina*
Marcello	*the mayor*
Victoria	*the mayor's wife*
Marta	*raises sheep, mother of Ascanio*
Leonardo	*an ex-racecar driver who now operates the family porchetta van*
Antonio	*the red-bearded baker*
Orietta	*the pharmacist*
Bruno	*the butcher*
Flavia	*the florist*

THE CHURCH

Don Arrigo	*the parish priest*
Cinzia	*Don Arrigo's assistant*
Enzo	*Cinzia's father*

THE POLICE

Luca	*police officer*
Salvo	*Luca's partner*
Palmiro	*the local police captain*

PART ONE

Stella clutched the phone against her ear, huddling away from the white-coated chefs banging pans as they called for flour or kitchen twine. Pulling the landline's cord as far as it reached, she whispered, "But you *told* me. You called it a lock, that the executive chef position was mine."

Before she could even finish the sentence, Martin's voice rushed across the phone line. "I know, I'm sorry—"

"And now it's . . . *gone?*" Her grip tightened until she wondered why the handle didn't snap in two like the *grissini* breadsticks she'd just been rolling.

Martin sighed. "Like I said, the silent partner—"

A sound exploded from her throat that vaguely resembled a laugh. The bustling kitchen paused. Hands stilled and eyes shot toward her. Vanessa, the apprentice at the fish station mouthed, "Okay, boss?"

Stella waved off the question and made a circling gesture to prompt the line of chefs to keep working. Not for the first time, she wished her cell reception reached this deep in the bowels of Lucky, the restaurant centered on food borne out of Italian immigration. But no signal could penetrate these walls. She rolled her body around the corner, away from prying eyes, the cord binding around her.

She adjusted her bandana lower over her cacophony of curls. People meeting for the first time Stella assumed she wore the bandana as an affectation, an attempt to create a signature look. As if she had the time. "The silent partner . . . it makes no sense. Tell me again. Slower."

Martin's words drifted over the line, slow and careful. "He said if you set foot into Farina's kitchen, he'd pull his funding."

"But . . ." she sputtered, desperately untangling the cord to get a few more feet. If only she could reach her office, this would all make sense. "*Why?* They came to *me*. The concept for Farina, that was *mine*. The whole—"

"Stella." Martin cut her off and then stalled, breathing uncomfortably on the other end of the line. "It's Chad."

At the name, Stella went cold. The answer formed in her head even as she asked the question. "What's Chad? Martin . . . *what's* Chad?"

She heard Martin's intake of breath, as if summoning the courage to say the words. "Chad. He's the silent partner. The one bankrolling Farina."

Stella tried desperately to slow her brain even as her thoughts darted like seeds in hot oil. She repeated, "Chad is the silent partner."

The phone cord unknotted along with the muscles behind her knees. With the extra few feet of line, she pivoted around the corner, onto the floor of her office. Not much of an office, more of a desk between vertical beams, cookbooks piled high, furry with scraps of paper marking pages. She hadn't even found time to hang her corkboard, now leaning against the wall beside her.

She slid to the floor, creating a draught that loosened a photograph taped to the cork (where were tacks when you needed them?). She picked up the photograph absently, trying to focus on Martin's words.

"I *told* you not to invest without a contract."

"You also told me it was a sure thing! That Richard said a good-faith investment would make them take me seriously. I cleared my bank account!"

"Listen, Stella, I'm sorry but—"

"No." Stella didn't want to hear it. She didn't want to hear Martin's I-told-you-so's about investing in Farina, and she couldn't bear it if his words turned to I-told-you-so's about Chad. She knew better than anyone that she shouldn't have let that *New York Times* reporter take her to lunch, to ply her with wine and a sympathetic ear. She tried to tell herself that outing the New York culinary scene's worst sexual harasser was worth it. At least women up and down the island would know, and maybe he'd be less likely to coerce fresh-faced apprentice chefs into the storeroom where his hands would—no. It didn't bear remembering. She tried to focus on the fact that someday the article would seem less of a sacrifice, rather than remembering that since its publication two months ago, doors had been slamming in her face, one by one.

As if reading her thoughts, Martin said, "Stella. You did the right thing. Someone needed to out that guy."

She mumbled, "Maybe it should have been someone with more clout. Who wouldn't have gotten blackballed."

His voice gentled further, a surprise given how much he and his girl-friend Heather had lamented her impulsivity over the years. "Like who? Stella, it had to be you. Only you had the guts—"

"Forget it. It's done. It doesn't matter anymore." She ran her finger over the edges of the photograph. Though she could barely make it out in the half-light, she had gazed on it enough to recognize those stone walls rising behind a grove of olive trees. Drawing in a shaky breath, she said, "I can't believe this. After that meeting. With you. With the investors. Drinking until three in the morning."

"Well, to be fair, we didn't start until two when you got off the line."

Stella ran on as if he hadn't said anything, "About how women restaurateurs work twice as hard, jump through rings of fire to be taken seriously. When mediocre men can step over a threshold and expect a crown of gold and a celebratory torch."

"Always with the colorful language."

3

Her voice felt far away, even to Stella. "Everyone seemed on board. And that was *after* the article. Even so, they talked about executive chefs who disparaged me in public while putting my ideas on their menus." She whispered, "I have nothing. *Nothing.*"

"What are you talking about? You have Lucky! Your brigade loves you, they nominated you for that mentor award. Even as sous chef, everyone knows you made that restaurant what it is—"

"Martin," she sighed. "I quit Lucky."

"You quit! Why—"

"Because I had this new venture. Farina. And it felt too good to stick it to Angus when he called me 'baby' for the fifteenth time during service and accidentally-on-purpose touched my behind in the walk-in."

"Oh, Stella."

The clattering of the kitchen filled her ears. Usually, she found it soothing, like how other people described the murmur of the sea. She never understood that—by the sea, you were left alone with your thoughts, your memories. Why would anyone choose that? No, give her the bruising action of a well-trained kitchen. But now...now the clinking forks dumped out of the Hobart, the call-and-response of dinner service on the cusp of starting, it all grated. Gunshots of memories of every leer, every insult.

She didn't want any of this drama. She just wanted to make food that people closed their eyes to savor. Belonging to the restaurant world had meant everything to her. Stella would never forget packing her knives before stepping out of her mother's kitchen, which had fed a community of New Jersey Italian immigrants. For that one brief moment, her mother's eyes shone with pride, rather than the grief that had blurred her expression since she lost her favorite daughter along with her husband. For that one moment, never before or since, Stella's mother cherished her.

"What are you going to do?" Martin's voice tore through the fragile veil of memory.

She closed her eyes and concentrated on breathing. When she opened them, her gaze landed on the photograph in her hands—the olive trees, which even in black and white gleamed like silver, the arbor of what looked like grapevines or maybe wisteria framing a *terrazza*, and the stone house rising naturally above the scene, windows open and merry against an expansive sky. "I guess it's time to move on."

His voice thrummed with false cheer. "That's the spirit! You always land on your feet. Maybe Manhattan is played out. At least for now. I have contacts in Atlantic City. They might not have read the *Times* article. Or, no, of course they have. It took the restaurant world and swung it by the tail."

"Martin."

"I'm just saying. You may have to move down the line. Give up on an executive chef or even sous chef position. Or work somewhere that will care more about your Michelin star than your outing a culinary giant."

She said nothing. Could she move back to Jersey? She'd sold the house when her mother died last year, and put the money into Farina. She shook her head to tamp down the useless anger. She winced as she heard a plate smash to the floor, followed by an apologetic voice bleating, "Sorry!"

She sighed. "Don't bother. I'll figure something out."

"What though? You can't work in New York."

She murmured to herself, her gaze fixed on the photograph. "Then maybe I'll leave."

"Leave? Leave for where? Stella, please, for once in your life, curb your impulsivity. Let's talk this through."

But Stella had dropped the phone and stood, holding the photograph with both hands.

As Stella sailed past the foreigners' line at Fiumicino airport in favor of the much shorter EU citizens' line, she sent up a prayer of thanks that even though her mother had nothing positive to say about her birthplace, she nonetheless made sure to register her daughters' births with the consulate and placed an Italian passport in their hands. The wheels on Stella's carry-on slowed momentarily as it occurred to her that perhaps it was her father that fought for citizenship for both Stella and Grazie.

After all, he never tired of showing off his family as his very own Italian art. His wife and daughters, all variations on a theme, with their refined features, eyes like a Madonna in a fresco, glossy hair tumbling in variations of waves and curls, their tiny frames so unlike his own bear-like width. Only Stella got what had to be a throwback to his Scottish heritage, in the form of a fall of freckles across her nose. She remembered how he'd parade his family into church each Sunday, so proud of their slightly exotic beauty. That is, until…

She shook her head and blinked back the easy tears that rose whenever she thought of her father, whose strong arms served as a refuge for those twelve years she had him. Now was not the time to dwell on the morose.

Anyway, whoever applied for that passport that allowed her to sail through immigration with no more than a "*bentornata*" from the bored officer, Stella had been the one to maintain it all these years. That passport had been her ticket to stage at restaurants in Milan and Florence and Bologna without fussing over work permits or visas. It occurred to her to wonder, with all those apprenticeships in Italy, she'd never taken a weekend to visit Aramezzo. Then again, she hadn't even known about the house until her aunt died two years ago and her mother shoved the photograph into her hands, announcing that she'd had her fill of that backwater town and now it was up to Stella to manage the bed-and-breakfast or sell it, as she saw fit. Her inheritance, her responsibility. Her mother had washed her hands of the property and Aramezzo years ago, though she never said why.

Leaning on her carry-on as she waited at baggage claim, Stella fingered the old black-and-white photograph in her pocket, wondering at the fact that she hadn't sold the property as soon as it landed in her proverbial lap. Obviously, she'd hopped online right away to investigate the property's potential, but had trouble even finding a listing. Finally, she stumbled on an obscure Italian website that included Casale Mazzoli. The photos of the house were good enough, though with the low light, it was hard to tell. The few reviews were decent. Her aunt had obviously taken good care of her guests, and Stella particularly noticed how much the guests appreciated the meals. It seemed Aramezzo wasn't exactly on the tourist trail. The only visitors trended toward bikers and people making pilgrimages to the town's chapel, though no matter how Stella searched, she couldn't figure out the chapel's draw.

Her aunt left behind a caretaker, Mimmo, who helped with odds and ends and, with her aunt's passing, had offered his services as property manager. Mimmo didn't have an email address, and indeed there wasn't one for the house listing. So she'd called him, hoping to get enough information to help her decide whether or not to sell. Mimmo seemed more full of assurances and platitudes than actual information. He promised to keep the bed-and-breakfast running and to deposit the proceeds into her Italian bank account. His oozy charm hardly proved comforting, so she'd poked around to look at property values, which seemed so shockingly low she soon gave up. She had too much to do to manage a sale. She decided to keep Mimmo on and be happy if she made a little extra each month off the enterprise.

Every once in a while, usually when she was a little tipsy and feeling sorry for herself, she hopped online to check the reviews, which grew worse over time. Though the listing boasted Wi-Fi, guests complained they were never able to connect. Even worse, meals of local cuisine and freshly baked breakfasts gave way to, and Stella could hardly believe it, *packaged pastries.* At the memory, Stella shivered, despite the hot airport. She had tried calling Mimmo, but he always seemed to be in the woods with poor reception, if he picked up at all. Finally, she decided to visit someday and sort it all out then. At some point, she had to have a vacation, right? Well, the vacation never materialized. Until now. If this could be called a vacation.

A rumble announced the start of incoming luggage and she did a double take as her tattered burgundy suitcase slipped down the track, unfamiliar in these new surroundings. Watching people unload piles of luggage, it occurred to her that this one suitcase held just about everything she owned in the world. Other than the pile of cooking books and wares she'd left with Martin and Heather.

Tugging the suitcase from the carousel, she waved off attempts of one man after another who tried to lift it off the belt and therefore allow their biceps to pop under their thin t-shirts.

"I got it," she told them in Italian, ignoring their widened eyes. Like every Italian she'd ever met, they assumed she was American. She didn't know why. Her skin was olive, if on the light side and with the faint fall of freckles, and it wasn't like there weren't Italians with grey eyes. Even her mother, almost in counterpoint to her father, had always sighed about the fact that Stella was all American. The comment rankled when, other than food and language, Stella's mother proffered crumbs of her culture only reluctantly. Without an Italian upbringing, of course Stella grew up on a diet of Britney Spears and Pepsi.

She passed the remaining families waiting for their luggage, her eyes scanning for the taxi she'd ordered. It cost too much, of course. Everything cost too much when one's bank account had cartoon moths twirling around it. But the thought of schlepping to Rome's main train station, then a train ride to Assisi, then waiting for the bus to Aramezzo . . . No, she needed to not arrive in her ancestral village *that* disheveled and exhausted. She also needed to arrive with an extra hundred euros in her pocket, but, ah well.

Stella ducked around the clutches of Italians smoking in relief after the long flight until her eyes landed on the taxi driver, holding the sign with "Mazzoli" scrawled across it. Even after all these trips back to Italy, it never failed to delight her to see her mother's maiden name spelled correctly. She'd learned from experience not to expect Italians to know what to do with "Buchanan." Her family name written easily across a white sheet of paper felt like all the welcome she could ask for.

Two hours later, she waved goodbye to the taxi driver, grateful that he'd taken the hint of her closed eyes and the jacket rolled between her head and the window. He hadn't irritated her with idle chatter, and in fact said nothing at all in the hours between the edge of the airport and a few minutes ago when he'd cleared his throat. "Signorina. We've arrived. Aramezzo?"

She knew, of course. She hadn't really been asleep. How could she be, when this road unspooled to her new home? Or her home for the moment.

No, she'd peeked from lowered lashes at the rolling Umbrian hills laced with fog, the lines of cypresses, the hilltop towns that resembled nothing so much as piles of stones glowing in the morning light.

She'd tensed as they'd left the highway, tucking into the wooded valley behind Assisi. It had been all she could do to not sit bolt upright and ask the driver questions as she peeked out at houses and arches so charmingly medieval they seemed straight out of a Disneyland version of the King Arthur story. But the sleeping charade had gone on so long, she didn't know how to break it and so waited until the wheels slowed to a stop.

And now, she shifted her weight, drinking in the town in front of her.

The woods lay mostly behind her, reaching up the mountain that must be Monte Subasio. In front of her rose Aramezzo. She knew from her research that, unlike most Umbrian towns, which ran along the spine of a hilltop, Aramezzo was laid out in concentric circles. Like a wedding cake, she'd thought to herself a week ago when she'd fought the internet for any kernels of information about this town that didn't seem to exist to the rest of the world.

It didn't look like a wedding cake now, though. From here, a rise of buildings blocked her view of the concentric streets, and Aramezzo seemed like nothing so much as a squat, upside-down ice cream cone. Made of stones in hues of honeycomb-gold and blush-pink. Pink? She blinked at the realization. That seemed odd.

At the top of the town, the chapel's steeple punctuated a sky so heavy with blue it seemed almost purple. A few thin clouds drifted, like tentative swipes of a brush barely dipped in white paint. Their presence only made the blue bluer. That must be Chiesa di Santa Chiara di Aramezzo, Aramezzo's lone church. The bells lay silent and still.

The entire town lay silent and still.

From the corner of her eye, Stella noticed a line of laundry, blue and green and coral swatches of color, vibrant against the stones, spangled from one window to another. Life. At last. Just as she had the thought, she watched an orange cat scramble to the top of a wall. All these outward-facing homes had gardens that rolled down like an apron around Aramezzo to the ring road she stood on. The orange tabby seemed to be standing guard on one of the few garden walls. His eyes glowed green as he stared at her from above the wall, the tip of his tail flicking.

Stella lifted her chin. *I will not be cowed by a cat.* She hated cats anyway.

The tabby turned away as if already bored by her, and Stella followed its gaze to the squat two-story building across the ring road from Aramezzo. It seemed to be a school, if the sign was current. If so, it would be a small one. Then again, how many children could live in a town the size of a large shopping mall? No more than fifty, surely.

The orange cat leaped nimbly down onto a structure Stella hadn't noticed, some sort of stone bath. No, two baths. Water bubbled into one side and then spilled over a dividing wall into the other side, before being piped away. A fountain?

Stella peered into the shadows of the structure and noticed old photographs, blown up and faded by time and the elements. Her thoughts whirred and clicked into place. Ah, this once served as the village laundry. Women washed clothes in the basin furthest from the incoming water and rinsed in the cleaner water at the spout of the first basin.

She smiled at the discovery. She always loved making sense of strange towns when she traveled. Her face stilled as she considered—for the first time in her travels, this *wasn't* a strange town. This was her home until she could sell the property for enough money to finance her own restaurant back in New York.

But Aramezzo was her mother's birthplace. Her grandparents' birthplace. *Their* parents' birthplace. If the documents she'd flipped through after her mother's death were any indication, there had never been a time when she didn't have family walking these circular roads, climbing the steps to that perilously perched chapel. Or doing their laundry, right here in these stone basins. Her eyes flitted over the women in the photographs, looking for any sign of familiarity.

In her mother's documents, she'd only found one photograph, of a severe-looking couple dressed in black with two daughters dressed in white lace—one in arms and one standing between her parents. The baby had been her aunt, the older one her mother, Stella the elder. Stella wished she'd carried that photo in her pocket as a talisman, rather than the faded photo of the house. She debated getting the family photograph out of her suitcase, to compare the cheekbones of her grandmother, the ferocious eyebrows of her grandfather, the rounded cheeks of the girls, to these women in the blown-up photographs stretched across the walls of the former laundry.

There would be time later. For now, she let her eyes scan the faces. None looked familiar. Just a random assortment of typically Italian faces . . . except. Stella paused and dragged her suitcases to look more closely. One of the women, perhaps two, it was hard to tell in the light, appeared to have eyes of two different colors. Strange.

Stella shrugged. Probably cataracts or something. In a remote village, medical care could never have been easy, especially before cars. Assisi must have been a few hours' ride away by horseback. And Stella knew from her research that the only other town in the vicinity was mostly abandoned, tucked even higher on the mountain. In Italian fashion, the town, Subbiano, was actually part of Aramezzo.

Stella looked at the cat, begrudgingly thanking it for this little window into the history of life in Aramezzo, but only caught its orange tail whisking behind a shed as it dashed away. Her eyes followed the cat and then gasped, wondering why it had taken her so long to notice—spreading out below Aramezzo, lay what to her sleep-deprived eyes seemed to be a frothing sea, sparkling and tossing waves of silver and green.

She blinked, and the view refocused into olive trees, following the lines of earth, down and away from Aramezzo like a glittering quilt. Stella swayed a little, mesmerized by the rustling light, interspersed with patches flecked with rows of vegetables or vines.

It wasn't like she'd never seen olive trees before. In Italy, they were as much a part of the landscape as those iconic cypresses and vineyards. Stella adjusted the bandana around her head to get the curls out of her eyes and realized that she'd driven through groves on her way to restaurant apprenticeships, but she'd never stayed silent and been surrounded, on all sides. Nothing but quiet and the drifting of boughs caught by a breeze she couldn't see or feel.

She clenched the handle of her suitcase as if to ground herself, but her hand merely slid, catching on the edge of the plastic. The suitcase fell to the ground with a bang that reverberated into the still air.

Stella groaned in frustration and hefted the suitcase upright, snatching the carry-on as well as she walked up the road, looking for the town entrance. She knew no cars were allowed in Aramezzo, but she wondered if the little three-wheel trucks, Apes, she reminded herself, maneuvered those circular streets, still hidden to her.

Where was the entrance?

She lifted her hand to shade her eyes from the rising sun that seemed bigger than the one in New York, closer maybe. She startled at a sudden whirring behind her. A biker, wrapped in yellow and black spandex, muttered "*salve*" as he passed, and then gave her a second look before slowing, resting a foot on the dirt road. He said nothing for a moment, no doubt taking in this stranger in a strange land, burdened with a suitcase that must weigh twice as much as she did.

"Do you need help?" the man asked in English.

She sighed. In Italian, she responded, "I'm looking for Casale Mazzoli. It's a bed-and-breakfast."

His eyes widened as she spoke. He nodded and responded in Italian. At least, she thought it was Italian. She couldn't catch some of the words, though they tugged her brain. Maybe her Italian wasn't as flawless as she thought. "*Come?*" she asked.

He smiled and spoke again, and this time she caught all the words. Thank God. She remembered that Italian towns all had their dialects. This man, his words were like her mother's. She'd just never heard anyone other than her mother blur her t's and g's that way. She almost lost focus, so distracted was she by the memory of her mother's voice. "You passed the town gate, it's behind you there." He pointed and she followed his finger and wondered how in the world she'd noticed a cat and a laundry but missed the rising arch that announced the town entrance.

He went on, "Casale Mazzoli is on the outermost street. So go up the steps, turn right, and follow the road around past the butcher shop." He appraised her suitcase. "But you may want to reconsider. I stayed there a year ago with my buddies for a biking weekend, and I wouldn't recommend it. There aren't any other bed-and-breakfasts in Aramezzo, but there's one not that far from here, on the road to Assisi. That's where I'm staying."

As her face stilled, he went on, as if trying to make sure she knew it wasn't a pick-up attempt. "Or stay elsewhere, there are loads of places, obviously, in Assisi. Casale Mazzoli is a dump. Cobwebs everywhere, the shower looked like it hadn't been cleaned since Mussolini. Not bad views, of course, but views I get for free." He patted the handlebars of his sleek bicycle before gesturing to the panorama in front of him. He looked back at her. "And don't get me started on the mess. What kind of B and B has boxes strewn around like moving day? My friends and I decided the whole thing felt like an off-brand horror movie." He shook his head. "Take my advice, Signorina. Go elsewhere."

She could barely get the words out. "I can't."

"Can't? But—"

Her eyes lit with more annoyance than resolve. "I own the dump."

The biker mumbled half apologies before pushing off to veer onto the white road with a sign indicating Monte Subasio.

Stella sighed.

Unless she'd just met an unusually fussy cyclist, she had her work cut out for her. How long would it take to turn Casale Mazzoli around so she could sell? Six months? A year?

Dragging her suitcases to the entrance arch, she bumped them over the steps that rose through the tunnel, up to Aramezzo. She winced as the wheels slammed against each step, and then echoed back through the surrounding stones, either blackened with age or shadows. Stella shivered.

What had she gotten herself into?

Basta, she berated herself. Stop it. She couldn't let the biker's words get to her. Messes could be cleaned up, bathtubs could be scrubbed, and of course the packaged *cornetti* would be the first things she'd change. One step at a time and she'd banish the ghosts.

She straightened her shoulders as she came out of the end of the tunnel, into the hesitant morning light. Quiet. So quiet. People lived in Aramezzo, didn't they? The internet had assured her the town had over two hundred residents. Then again, how often were these things revised? A tucked-away town like Aramezzo, maybe nobody had thought to update the websites after some sort of cataclysmic event, like a radon leak, or—

The sound of church bells broke through Stella's downward spiral, and she stopped to look up. She could barely see the top of the church from here, the view blocked by walls and rooftops. A horde of birds—crows—burst from the top of the bell tower at the sudden rending of the silent morning.

Murder, she reminded herself.

A group of crows is called a murder.

She shivered and wrapped her cardigan around her before snatching up her suitcases and turning right. As the bells continued, she saw shutters thrown open by disembodied hands up and down the street. The hands withdrew as quickly as they appeared, with no heads partnering to lean out the window and take in the morning.

A woman's voice sounded deep within the recesses of the house on the left, and Stella smiled a bit at the sound of the whining response of a child, no doubt reluctant to leave the comfort of bed to face the day.

Stella sympathized.

Stella knocked on the door of Casale Mazzoli, but though she could hear the raps echoing within, no footsteps hurried to the door. She sank onto the stone steps with a gusty sigh. Though she kept herself fit by jogs through Central Park, today had already winded her completely.

She fished for her phone in her overloaded handbag before remembering that she had no international plan and no SIM card and therefore no service.

Damn.

Or *cavolo*, she silently amended to herself. She might as well start swearing in Italian. Her cheeks flushed faintly, as they always did when anyone swore. Even herself, to herself.

Where was Mimmo? Was she expected to sit and wait? Would she have to go door to door begging for a phone to call him?

She peered up and down the quiet street, but only saw a trim older woman stepping out of her house with a brown plastic bag held away from her body. She dropped it unceremoniously where the steps met the street, no doubt for the trash men. Or trash women? Maybe in Italy, the gender gap had been taken down in ways it hadn't in the United States. Somehow, she doubted it.

The woman did a double take at the sight of Stella, perched on the steps leading to the door of her inheritance. The woman stepped forward, into the patch of sunlight filtering through an arbor draped with what looked to be grapevines on the wall above. Stella noted the pert slash of a red belt across the navy dress before the woman drew back as if burned. She wheeled around, darting back into the safety of her home, probably already reaching for her phone to call everyone she knew to report a stranger in town.

Stella sighed. Her mother never told many stories about Aramezzo, but those she did share all featured gossip and innuendo as their main characters. Stella had never noticed a culture of gossip at her Italian apprenticeships, but then again, those were in major cities, with plenty of entertainment. Unlike Aramezzo, where nothing happened, and the citizenry had no option but to sit around and watch their neighbor's every move. No wonder her mother left. Even though, Stella had to admit, the town appeared quite charming. Her mother had never mentioned the pink stone walls or the arbors laden with grapes or those olive trees stretching into the distance.

Anyway, within ten minutes everyone in reach of that lady's phone line would know a young woman with impudently curly hair sat on the steps of the old Mazzoli place. Stella stretched out her legs and leaned forward to unkink the cramp in her lower back, a holdover from the flight. She wondered how long it would take for someone to put her presence together with Mimmo's news of her arrival. Then again, if Mimmo was as absent from gossip circles as he seemed to be from his appointment schedule, it could buy her some time. For what, she didn't know.

As if summoned by her increasingly annoyed thoughts, she heard footsteps approaching. She looked up to see a man in jeans far too long and a shirt not lined up properly over his substantial girth. Even from this distance, she noted his pitted face and a nose that resembled an exploded cork. She thought for a moment that the man leered at her, but she blinked to clear her eyes and decided it was a trick of that filtering light. As he drew closer, Stella noted a coffee stain at his belly button. Certainly not the dapper Italian she'd expected.

She mentally checked herself. This wasn't Milan.

She rose to meet Mimmo, sticking out her hand to introduce herself, inadvertently slamming him in the gut as he reached to kiss her cheek.

He grunted before catching his breath. Mimmo pulled back to examine her face more closely. "You are Stella?" He asked in ponderous English.

Stupid, really, since she'd conducted their previous conversations in Italian. "I am," Stella answered, in Italian. "And you must be Mimmo." She drew out her phone again and pointedly looked at the time. He couldn't know that it was in airplane mode and therefore set to New York time.

He switched easily to his native language, ignoring her hint. He turned to the door with an enormous bundle of keys. "Yes, Mimmo. Your first time in Aramezzo, yes?"

"Yes."

He nodded, flipping through the keys before landing at what must be the correct one. "Your accent. It's different." He said "different" like she might say "poop-covered."

"I expect so." She didn't feel the need to fill Mimmo in on her backstory—the Italian learned first from her mother, and then from the customers who lined up in the back alley to buy her mother's bags of frozen homemade tortellini, her aluminum foil pans of baked pasta. Later, Stella's Italian improved from working for chefs all up and down the boot.

In a bored voice, he said, "Everyone will be looking at you. Not my idea of a good time, but you Americans like a show."

She decided not to respond to this strange assumption.

He flung open the door with a grand gesture. Stella stopped at the threshold, her breath caught in her throat. This was it. Her home, her birthright, the place where she'd lick her wounds, gather her strength for her next move.

Stella peered into the darkness, stumbling over the threshold. She turned back to Mimmo. "The light? Where is the . . . " She stumbled over the word for switch.

He understood, though his huff suggested annoyance that she would need something so first-world as light. Brushing past her, his body nudged hers to the side. She tensed, her bile rising. But Mimmo seemed unaware as he strode to the lamp in the far corner of the room, flicking it on. A weak light nudged the darkness. Stella looked around, her eyes growing accustomed to the dimness. "That's the only light for this room?

Why isn't there an overhead light?"

Mimmo shrugged, his pockmarked face growing hard. "I'm not a decorator. I'm a manager. And not a well-paid one." His raised eyebrow suggested what she should have anticipated. The man saw her as a money tree, ripe for the plucking.

"Hrmph." She made her way to the enormous window that would normally let sunlight spill across the stone floor, if only the sky hadn't turned suddenly overcast. Were Umbrian days always this tumultuous? Still, the view stalled her and she paused, gazing out over the rolling hills and the peaked mountains beyond. What had her mother thought when she stood here for the last time, wondering about her future in America? What had her grandmother wondered about as she contemplated the same view? Did she look at the olive trees below the window with fondness, or was she only ever counting them, calculating yield and profit?

Mimmo's impatient gesture at the doorway recalled her attention. At her blank expression, he grinned and waved his arm at the room. "A big room, set up for guests to have their breakfast." He strode past the bookcases without comment, though Stella couldn't help but let her vision linger here, her fingers running over the spines, looking for her twin passions of old cookbooks and old mysteries, or *gialli*, as they were called in Italy, after their trademark yellow spines. She did spy a patch of goldenrod, indicating that over the years the house had accumulated a selection of the mysteries. In Italian, no doubt, but she'd picked up Italian murder mysteries many times over the years, as a way to unwind after the heat and stress of the kitchen. She could see herself, curled on that sagging sofa with a book on her lap, the fireplace crackling. She looked up. "The fireplace, does it work?"

"Birds live in it." Mimmo shrugged, as if that were an answer. He cocked his head to the side and crossed his arms. "You said you're a chef." His words rang with accusation, like she'd lied to him.

"I am." She lifted her chin and tried to broaden her five-foot-two frame.

Mimmo snickered and shook his head. "You couldn't swing a pig."

She adjusted her bandana. Was this a regional insult? Or a crack about her size?

It must have been the latter the way he let his eyes run up and down over her body, muttering, "Not a lick of meat on those bones. What kind of chef can she be?"

Stella bristled. "I'm quite capable, I assure you."

With an indulgent smile, he said, "I'm sure you think so. But American food doesn't count around here."

She set her teeth but before she could formulate a retort, he walked through a doorway to the right of the living room, calling over his shoulder, "You can make your hamburgers in here."

The kitchen. Her heart skipped a beat.

She followed him, more awake than she'd been all day. Maybe all year. She amended her vision of reading by the fire to include the wafting scent of stew bubbling, rich with slowly cooked onions and fragrant with rosemary and red wine. Or maybe even just a simple mac and cheese.

The kitchen.

The kitchen would soothe her feathers, ruffled by the foreboding that began with the biker's warning, the dour silence as she walked through town, the woman hightailing it away from her, and the tumult of black birds like a tornado rising into the sky.

Stella stopped, her vision cracking as she took in the dining room table, rings in the varnish peeking out between piles of boxes. She took a breath and turned to the cooking area: the stove leaning against a yellowing refrigerator, across from a row of cabinet doors hanging at odd angles, and the grime of a thousand fish fries ground into the tile backsplash. The enameled sink was deep, so deep it must be original to when the house was a farmhouse, but other than that, everything looked too old to be modern and too new to be vintage. She wondered what could lie under the cracked linoleum. Stella ran her bottom lip between her teeth, taking it in. "It all works, I hope."

Mimmo stuck his index finger in his ear and turned it like a Q-Tip.

Something flashed past her ankles, with a sound like tearing paper. Losing her balance, she reached for the wall, and then pulled back as her fingers brushed against something prickly and moist. With a ferocious twist, she righted herself, following the flash of black and silver. A dog? A fox?

Mimmo snickered at her near collapse. "You'll want to do something about the cat."

"Cat? That was a *cat*?"

"*Sì.*"

"And it lives here, in this house?"

Mimmo frowned. "Who can say? It's always been here."

"Always? What do you mean, always?"

"Since I can remember. This cat, another cat that looks like it. Same kind of spotted fur. Always here." He shrugged in punctuation.

"Who feeds it?"

"*Boh.*" The classic Italian non-answer. He pushed the door open and didn't wait for her as he barreled back through the living room to the open door on the other side. "This is your aunt's room. Guests sleep upstairs."

She stood her ground. "I don't favor cats."

"It doesn't much matter. This cat doesn't favor anyone."

Stella looked around pointedly. "It got in somehow."

Mimmo stood silently, waiting for her to ready herself for a new topic. She sighed and joined him on the rest of the house tour. As he gestured to the bathroom added in the 1950s and then climbed the steps to the two guest rooms, Stella cataloged each hole in the floorboards and gap in the plaster. She'd have to plug up each one to keep out the cat. Or vermin, she realized with a start.

But as she took in the bare wires sprouting from the ceiling and the watermarks on the plaster, she realized the cat might well be the least of her problems.

A few days later, Stella felt like she'd spent more time in her cabinets, scrubbing, than in the streets of Aramezzo.

Stella yelped, her fingers pulled back as if she'd rested her hand on a hot griddle. She glared into the darkness of the kitchen cabinet, prodding the offending attacker with the edge of her sponge. No, not a bug this time. A trap. Ancient, by the looks of it. And thanks be for that, the rusted hinge snapped slowly enough to barely scrape her quickly withdrawn fingers. Stella tossed the sponge into the bucket in irritation. The water, already filthy after just a few passes over the shelf, sloshed onto the floor.

What did it matter? Far from being fussy, the biker had been generous in his assessment. This place was a sty. A legitimate comparison since she'd investigated the actual pig's house next to the terrace. Empty for years, it gleamed in comparison to her home. And why, Stella wondered, adjusting her bandana, did she find more chicken excrement in the house than in the chicken coop? Did Mimmo keep chickens in this kitchen? It couldn't have been her aunt. Her aunt's bedroom was the best-maintained room in the house. How it had avoided Mimmo's dereliction of duty, she'd never know.

Her aunt's bed was actually fairly comfortable. She'd slept better these last few days in Aramezzo than she had in months, even though it took her about forty-five minutes to fall asleep. How could quiet seem so *loud*?

After her bedroom, the guest rooms were the next least awful. The bedrooms weren't terrible, though each bed sagged in the middle like a weary plow horse. That view made almost anything forgivable, which could be why none of the reviews she'd read mentioned the stains on the walls or the splintering beams. Unfortunately, nothing would distract from the smell creeping from the upstairs hall bathroom. She hoped that she'd be able to find the source of the smell before her first guest arrived tomorrow. Not likely given how many excuses she found for not entering the bathroom. She shivered in dread and told herself that she needed the confidence boost of clean kitchen shelves and then she could tackle the offensive odor.

At a movement in the doorway, Stella startled, bumping the edge of the bucket with her heel, and sloshing water all over the floor.

"Miss! I'm sorry! So sorry!"

Stella barely took in the sight of a middle-aged woman in a black housedress and black apron before the stranger flung herself onto the floor to sop up the water, which Stella suddenly noticed smelled of fish. What kind of bacteria smelled of fish? Maybe fish bacteria. She had fish bacteria growing in her cabinets.

She put out her hand to forestall the stranger. "You probably did me a favor. I think I might be better off filling the house with water like a pool than this piecemeal process, which is getting me exactly nowhere."

The woman grinned.

Stella frowned. "What?"

"Your accent, Miss. It's ... "

"Yes, yes, I know, it's a patchwork." The guy at the hardware store had pretended to not understand her before chuckling as he walked her to the industrial solvents and lightbulbs. Though that didn't stop him from leaning across the counter to ask how old she was and why her mother left Aramezzo.

She had barely said a word to the young woman at the register at the little *alimentari* where Stella had picked up coffee and pasta and a bottle of wine her first day in town, but even so, the woman had furrowed her brow in a parody of confusion. Before she too decided that Stella's life was fair game, and Stella spent the next few minutes batting away questions about whether or not she was married.

Stella waited for the woman in the black dress to explain who she was, or at the very least, what she was doing in Stella's wreck of a kitchen.

With a start, the woman laughed awkwardly. "Ilaria, Miss. I'm Ilaria."

"Ilaria. *Piacere.* I'm Stella."

"Yes."

Stella waited. When no other information was forthcoming—Ilaria seemed a person perfectly comfortable with the long silences Stella abhorred—Stella prompted. "So, Ilaria. You are here because?"

"I'm the cleaner."

Stella looked down at the bucket now only half-filled with grayish, fishy smelling water.

Ilaria laughed again. "For the guest rooms, Miss. That's all Mimmo hires me for."

Stella nodded thoughtfully. "I see. Which explains why those are decent."

"Thank you, Miss. "

Stella hadn't realized it was a compliment.

Ilaria went on, "I've asked Mimmo, many times, if I can bring in my cousins to replace the plaster, patch the floors, but he always says no. The smell in the bathroom would be more difficult, but my husband—" Her voice trailed off and Stella noticed the sudden lines that had taken up shop on Ilaria's gentle face.

Stella didn't know what to say.

Ilaria sighed. "Mimmo, he always says no. So I change the sheets, scrub the bathroom, mop."

Stella gestured to the bucket, sluggishly dribbling more water onto the floor. "So the kitchen is never cleaned? Or the living room where the guests have breakfast?"

Ilaria's olive-toned skin flushed coral. "No, Miss. I did ask. But he said..." She looked down at the floor, blushing brighter. "He says he pays me enough as it is."

Numbers from the pile of papers Mimmo had handed Stella (not a spreadsheet in the bunch, just a bundle of scraps and receipts) clicked together in her mind, releasing understanding like garlic hitting warm butter. "How much is he paying you?"

Ilaria shifted uncomfortably. "It depends, Miss. On how often there are guests. I'm not meaning anything by this, but not many people stay here."

"Call me, Stella, please. So I can call you Ilaria." Ilaria nodded uncertainly and Stella went on, "As an estimate, would you say you get paid about a hundred euros a week?"

Ilaria's laugh seemed to take her by surprise. At Stella's frank expression, she stopped and rearranged her face into one of great seriousness. "No, Miss. I mean, Stella. More like ten euros a month."

"I see."

A look of concern flickered across Ilaria's face. "I work hard in that hour or two I'm here. If Mimmo told you different..."

"He didn't. He didn't even tell me you existed, other than the line in the bill for cleaning." Stella went on, "Look, I'm sure you have realized this place needs more cleaning than a couple of hours a month. I could do with the help, I guess is what I'm saying. I can't give you a raise, but I can give you more hours. If you have the time—"

"Oh, yes, Miss! I mean—"

Stella waved off Ilaria's apology. "Great. Can you start now? As you see, I'm out of my depth." She glared at the offending bucket. "And while it's been fine for Mimmo to give guests packaged *cornetti*, I'd like to make a proper breakfast and I can't while the kitchen is this filthy."

Ilaria started to nod, but then stopped. She held up a white paper bag. "I have to bring this to my husband. Blood thinners. He had surgery last week. For a blood clot after falling off a ladder. I only meant to come by and get the sheets to wash. But I can hurry and come back."

"Absolutely." Stella adjusted her bandana while glancing at Ilaria. "I hope he's okay? Your husband?"

Ilaria stared at the ground, her face suddenly taking on a patina of stone. "I hope so, too."

When Mimmo dropped by with the keys she'd asked for, she cornered him. "I met Ilaria."

His finger rose to turn in his ear again, his eyes fixed on Stella, waiting.

"Turns out, she does an excellent job when she's allowed to take the time." At Mimmo's blank expression, Stella went on. "We got the kitchen cleared of what seems to be centuries of random animal feces, and she called her cousin to get the stove hooked up because, Mimmo, it was not."

Mimmo shrugged, the gesture pulling the front of his shirt out of his pants.

"That's not an answer."

"*Boh.*"

"Neither is that."

Mimmo stared at her. "Don't worry about it. Everything is fine."

"Fine? Did you hear me mention the animal feces?"

Mimmo looked like a second-grader asked to do a calculus problem.

Stella shook her head. "I don't know what you've been charging me a hundred euros a month for, but it wasn't cleaning. I went back over the records, what I could make of them. Your record keeping is a joke. After going over it again and again, I realized you've been taking eighty percent of the profits."

"You have no right to question me." He squared his shoulders, his pitted face reddening. Then he handed her the keys as if to end the conversation. "I'll be back tomorrow to greet Signor Severini when he checks in."

She raised her eyebrows. "You won't though. Your services are no longer required. I can take it from here."

Scratching his head, Mimmo stared at a spot over Stella's left shoulder. She half wanted to turn around to make sure that cat wasn't about to leap on her shoulder. The beast had surprised her twice already by appearing where it seemed only darkness lingered. But she didn't want to give Mimmo the satisfaction. Her face hardened. "Mimmo? Are you hearing me?"

He leered. "Maybe the Smurfette's Italian isn't as good as she thinks it is."

It took Stella a moment to figure out what he said until she remembered the book her aunt had sent her for a birthday gift when she was in grade school. Right. *I Puffi*, Smurfs. No doubt he figured she wouldn't get the reference. "Could be. Let me try again. You're fired. Does that translate?"

Mimmo showed his teeth before lowering his gaze to her face. "You can't fire me."

"I can, actually. This place is a hellhole, you've been charging me for repairs and cleaning you haven't done, and perhaps worst of all, you've been feeding guests garbage." She shook her head. "I don't need to say more. Just give me your keys. I have an enormous amount of work to do before this guy comes from Australia tomorrow."

"Rome. He comes from Rome. How can you manage Casale Mazzoli if you don't know the difference between Rome and Australia?"

"You told me—" She shook her head. "It doesn't matter."

"Of course it matters!" Mimmo leered now. "What makes you think you can run this place?"

"Oh, I don't know. Years of running a brigade? If I can manage a thriving kitchen, I can certainly manage a guest once a month, which is all you've been able to book. You haven't even listed the Casale on Booking or Airbnb. Of course, nobody knows about it."

His gaze hardened. "Listen, little girl—"

"Get new material, Mimmo. Believe me, I've heard the bit about my height before. From you, actually."

"I don't know how things are run in Los Angeles—"

"New York City. Not the same."

"—but here we have our ways. You can't fire me."

"I believe I just did. Get out. And take that cat with you."

"It's not mine!"

She shrugged. "Worth a try."

He gawped like a landed fish. "I had a contract with your aunt!"

She held out her hand. "Show me the contract then."

He sputtered. "It wasn't written. It was understood."

"I think you understood that she was sick. An easy mark. I am not so easy. Leave your keys and go, Mimmo."

He glared at her. "You will regret this. I promise you that. You'll regret this."

She bit out a harsh laugh. "Give me your worst. I promise you, I've been through it and more."

A slow grin crept across his rough face. "You'll see."

"And this is your room," Stella waved Signor Severini into the space, watching for his reaction. Would he notice the baseboards that needed painting or the surly paintings on the walls that she hadn't been able to remove for lack of art to replace them? The cheap paint had been so discolored by sunlight she'd been forced to keep the pictures on the walls.

"Nice," he said dismissively. His eyes barely flicking over the view as he hefted his suitcase onto the bed.

"Once you're settled in, there's pastries and coffee for you in the sitting room downstairs."

Tugging at the zipper that appeared disinclined to open, he said, "I don't eat sweets."

She was glad he was so focused on his suitcase that he didn't notice her look of horror. Her mind raced. "I see. So for breakfast tomorrow, I had planned on house-made *cornetti,*" she couldn't help the pride in her voice, "but if you'd prefer—"

"It doesn't matter," he said, gritting his teeth with the effort of releasing his zipper. "I'll be leaving early, anyway."

"Leaving? But you said you'd be here—"

"Not leaving leaving. Just, you know, going. To Subbiano."

The guy sure did enjoy interrupting. She smiled at the knock-knock joke she and her little sister never tired of repeating, the one about the interrupting cow. Her father had always been game, forever pretending it was the first time he'd heard the gag. She bit her lip at the memory of her father.

Stella startled to find Signor Severini's gaze on her. She stammered, "Subbiano. That sounds nice, I haven't been there yet."

He narrowed his eyes. "It's a *frazione* of Aramezzo. They are under the same stewardship. How can you not have been there?"

She shrugged and tried to smile, remembering suddenly how much she hated dealing with customers. The kitchen was where she belonged. Not front-of-house. She never knew what she was supposed to be saying. "I'm new myself!" she grinned, trying for pep in place of confidence.

He shook his head.

"Is that where your business is? Subbiano?"

"Business?" he asked, coldly, studiously not looking at her as he removed a stack of neatly folded sweaters of some expensive material. Followed by three cell phones marked with different colors of tape across the back.

"You said you were here on business."

He closed his eyes as if fighting down annoyance before straightening to gaze levelly at her face. "Look, if you must know, I'm looking to put together a tourist package, and I'm trying to get the lay of the land. I'd do better without all this harping."

Stella recoiled as if slapped. "Certainly, sir, I apologize, I was just—"

"You can help by telling me where I might find Don Arrigo."

Don Arrigo? The name sounded familiar and suddenly she remembered Ilaria mentioning him in her litany of people Stella had to meet. "The priest?"

His rolling eyes were completely at odds with his highly tailored suit. "Of course the priest. I have some business with him." Under his breath, Stella heard him muttering about avoiding phone calls.

Her brain darted in different directions. How did hostesses maintain their composure in the face of entitled patrons? How was she supposed to know where Don Arrigo was? And what business could this fancy guy have with the village priest?

"I expect at the church—"

He sighed with barely controlled annoyance. "I know *that*. But where does he *live*?"

This guy wanted to meet with Don Arrigo where he slept and ate, rather than where he ministered to his flock?

Signor Severini flicked his hand into the air as if to dismiss her. "Never mind, I'll ask at the bar."

Stella pushed her bandana back over her curls. "Bar Cappellina? Do you need directions?"

His snort of laughter seemed response enough.

"Okay, I'll be downstairs doing some maintenance and repairs."

"Probably a good idea." He slammed the drawer closed and opened his briefcase before glancing up at her with ill-concealed impatience.

She nodded uncertainly and stepped to the door before realizing they hadn't discussed his payment. Stella winced at having to bring it up. But then, what did she expect, Signor Severini to arrive with his credit card outstretched? She turned, her mouth open to speak, when she caught the gleam of something chunky and metallic whisked into the drawer. A gun? Her blood went cold. But, no, it couldn't be a gun. Italian law made it awfully hard to own a gun. Unless this gun wasn't acquired by legal means. Who *was* this guy?

Stella stepped back into the hallway, every impulse telling her to get away, now.

Severini's voice recalled her back. "Hey! The Wi-Fi password?"

She closed her eyes briefly and turned to him with a smile. "We're experiencing difficulty with the internet, I'm afraid."

He straightened. "There's no Wi-Fi?"

"Not at the moment, no." Before he could argue, Stella went on, the memory of that gleam of silver making her words tremble. "Signore? There is the matter of payment?"

Signor Severini scowled. "I'll probably stay longer than a week, remember? It depends on how long my business takes to conclude. That's why I worked it with your associate—"

"Mimmo?"

"Mimmo, yes. We arranged that I'd pay at check out. You didn't discuss this with him?" He shook his head, regarding her with disdain.

"Oh yes, of course!" she said, backpedaling. Guests didn't leave glowing reviews for poorly run establishments. Especially guests with possible guns in their luggage. "I apologize, I don't know what I was thinking. Okay then, I'll leave you to it."

The corner of his lip twitched. In amusement or annoyance, she couldn't tell. She slipped out of his room, closing the door behind her.

Was this what running a bed-and-breakfast was like? If so, she had to get this place cleaned up and then sell it and get back to New York as quickly as she could. No amount of income compensated for this level of aggravation.

No, more than aggravation.

This guy, something about him seemed wrong.

She smelled it all over him. Like rancid oil.

Stella blinked at the sudden sunlight. Holed up in the house, scrubbing and baking like mad, Stella had enjoyed only brief forays out to collect provisions and, oh my blessed God, yet more cleaning supplies. Now that the guest was settled (if begrudgingly), she could take a breath.

She ducked into one of Aramezzo's tunnels, this one leading to the middle street that circled the town like a belt. Climbing through the final tunnel to the top of Aramezzo, Stella gazed up at the chapel. She still hadn't figured out the allure of this modest establishment to religious pilgrims, though the staggering view over the valley gave her pause.

Despite the church's open door, Stella decided against entering. She wasn't into churches and never understood why people felt so reverent in them. She wondered if she inherited this impatience with the church from her mother, who rejected Catholicism along with the rest of her family background. After Stella's father died, they'd never gone to church again.

Stella turned back through the tunnel to the middle road. She stopped outside the bar, her nose lifted to the scent of coffee. In such an out-of-the-way hamlet as Aramezzo, she expected the acrid, burnt scent of ill-managed bean grinding, but this was…chocolatey. Nutty. *Huh*. She shook her head and kept walking, glorying in the feeling of stretching her limbs and inhaling air free of solvents. She ran her hands along the feathery plants growing from the stone walls and then ducked back down to the lowest road, the thought of her destination quickening her pace, until she emerged from the tunnel and practically tripped over a man, hunched on the cobblestones.

A bum? But she hadn't seen any homeless people in Aramezzo. Her nose wrinkled at the pervasive scent of liquor, a tannic red wine, and, if her nose didn't lead her astray . . . hay? Grass?

The man rose unsteadily, and Stella realized that he'd stopped to tie his shoelaces but had made poor work of it. The laces themselves looked bitten off, and he'd more tangled than tied them. She wondered if she should help him, at least to tie his shoes properly. But before she could decide what to do, the man shambled away.

As Stella watched him go, a man exited the bakery beside her. Dressed in white from his t-shirt to his shorts to his sneakers, he resembled a member of a tennis-and-swim club more than a provincial baker in autumnal weather. He caught her eye and smiled until his mouth opened, his red-blond mustache twitching. "Don't worry, Signorina. Enzo will be fine, he always is."

Her gaze followed this Enzo as he tripped on a loose cobblestone and turned to yell at the cat watching from the stoop, before rounding the corner and disappearing. Stella turned to the baker. "Shouldn't someone help him? He looks so . . . wobbly."

"Looking at him now, I bet you wouldn't guess he was a champion wrestler in his day. But he'll land on his feet, make no mistake. He's almost home, and if he doesn't quite make it, his daughter will find him." He chuckled.

It didn't seem exactly funny to Stella, so she appraised the baker and noticed his ruddy cheeks and merry brown eyes. A man who found humor in everything, perhaps. "I'm Stella, I just moved into—"

"Casale Mazzoli. Finally!" He crossed his arms in a satisfied way, as if she'd presented him with a gift he'd hardly expected.

She smiled in return. "Yes."

The sound of yelling from inside the bakery startled him and he said, "Excuse me, Signorina—"

"Stella, please."

"Stella, then. I'm Antonio. But people just call me 'The Baker.'" The grin spread over his face until he looked like he was laughing. "Bread calls. Go on and don't worry about Enzo. He's been this way for years, nothing anyone can do."

Before she could ask him any more questions—and she did want to know if he had yeast on hand since the woman at the *alimentari* said she'd need to buy it from the bakery—he strode back into the bakery, pulling one of the workers into a headlock before letting him go with a song. The three assembled bakers, all in matching white attire (ah, that must be a uniform of sorts), erupted in laughter. Never mind, she'd stop in another time.

She pulled the paper from her pocket and turned it one way and then another, trying to orient the map Ilaria had drawn for her. It had to be around here somewhere. She looked up at the buildings, trying to find a number, then back at the sketched map with an arrow pointing to the bookshop. Stella squinted and brought the paper closer to her face.

Was that a *cloud* in the drawing next to the bookstore? Stella peered more closely. No, a sheep! Stella remembered now, Ilaria had said the bookstore was next to Marta's house, a woman with a young son and a herd of sheep. Examining the buildings in front of her, Stella finally noticed the word "Domenica" punched in iron over the door of a shop, next to a rendering of a pile of books.

Stella pushed open the door. A black cat whizzed past her ankles to the street, where it stopped to clean its backside, as if the close call with the strange American had sullied its pristine fur.

Cats! She couldn't escape them. Ilaria insisted she hadn't been the one feeding the cartoonishly big silver-spotted cat in Stella's house. The cat had probably been subsisting on the rodents in her cabinets. Well, her home wouldn't be a rat buffet for much longer. Then maybe the trespasser would take a hint. She was tired of having it hissing at her when she met it in the hallway.

Turning into the brightly lit shop, she passed a chair full of blankets and rags and inhaled deeply. The smell of books filled her. Old books, thin and papery, new books with lurid covers, and probably magazines judging by the pulpy scent. Ilaria was right, this place would have what she needed. She inhaled again at a smell she couldn't place. Old newspaper? She frowned, the provenance of that particular musty scent just out of reach.

Before she could identify the scent, a peal of laughter startled Stella. It seemed to come from the pile of rags. Which Stella now realized was not a pile of rags at all, but rather a woman covered in sweaters, shawls, and scarves. Stella waited for the woman to say something, but the laughter ended in silence and the woman said nothing, only brushed the iron-grey bangs out of her eyes. She settled deeper into her chair, peering more closely at the book spread across the desk.

Stella stepped toward her, noting the cat draped over the printer, though she didn't see any computer. Maybe it was a copy machine? "Excuse me?"

The woman, who must be Domenica, looked up.

Stella went on, "I'm looking for a book."

The woman stared at her, unblinking behind her overlarge glasses.

Stella fumbled. "Well, that is, obviously I'm looking for a book. I mean, I need . . . ." Why didn't the woman say anything? Stella tried again, taking her hand out of her pocket and holding out her phone. "My phone, I don't have service yet, and I want a recipe. I heard you had books here."

The woman gazed around at the floor-to-ceiling shelves, crammed with books. Her lip tugged up in a suggestion of a smile.

Stella groaned inwardly. She was making a hatchet job of this one. "Of course you have books. I mean, do you have *cookbooks*? I need one from Puglia, with pastries."

The woman cocked her head to the side, appraising Stella, her eyes wide.

Stella blurted, "Do you understand me? I know my accent—"

"You moved into the old Mazzoli place."

Stella startled at the change of landscape. "Yes."

"A big cat lives there, maybe a hybrid with a Subasio wildcat."

At Stella's confused expression, Domenica added, her eyes sparking with interest, "With a black chin."

As if that helped. Then Stella realized. "Oh! That stray I can't get to leave! He does have a feral look to him."

The woman's eyes narrowed before she shoved her glasses higher onto her nose and returned her attention to her book, her hand reaching to pat the calico cat on the copy machine. With a start, Stella realized she'd insulted a cat lover.

Stella cleared her throat. The woman didn't look back at her. Finally, Stella prompted, "Cookbooks?"

The woman pointed down a dusty hallway, lit by one hanging bulb. Stella hitched her bag higher over her shoulder and grumbled yet again about having no internet. This would be so much easier if she could google *fruttone*. Then again, having internet would deprive herself of all these *books*. She ran her fingers along the spines. Passing a room that looked painted in yellow, her breath caught. Mysteries! She forced herself to stay on topic.

Ah!

Stella stopped in front of a wall full of not only cookbooks but what looked to be newspaper inserts. She'd forgotten about these, recipe booklets that came with the weekend paper. That must have been what she'd smelled when she'd entered the bookstore. She wanted to pore over the shelves, but she needed to get back to start the pastries, and anyway, that Domenica woman failed to send out welcoming vibes.

Stella followed the spines until she found a battered encyclopedia of Pugliese dishes. The index was missing, but luckily the book was organized alphabetically. She flipped through the f's, noting a recipe for *faraona*, which included a warning about sourcing the pheasants from a reputable vendor since they, like deer and hares, could ingest poisonous foliage and live quite well even as their meat held the poisons. Apparently, a restaurant in Lecce had been shut down after a family got sick off pheasant cacciatore. She flipped forward to an entry on *funghi*. Though Stella loved mushrooms, she didn't stop to read it, only to note she didn't find *fruttone* between the entries.

She sighed and put the book back on the shelf. How ridiculous to get obsessive, to be intent that only one specific baked good would do. But she couldn't help it. Just the thought of working her way through the recipe, of pulling the little surfboard-shaped shortcrust pastries filled with almond paste and jam out of the oven and dipping the tops in melted chocolate, it soothed her nerves. Not to mention how nice it would be to bring a plate to Ilaria and her husband.

Ilaria had said little about her background but referred once to her ancestors that had emigrated from Albania, though both she and her husband had been born and raised in Puglia. Stella had noticed how thin the skin around Ilaria's eyes grew when she told Stella about her husband's illness, and how he'd missed so much work she wasn't sure they'd make rent.

The *fruttone* wouldn't help them with that problem, but if her work at her mother's elbow had taught her anything, it was the restorative power of a taste of home. So ... *fruttone*. And an afternoon project. She always did her best thinking while cooking, so maybe while she baked she'd finally figure out how to get the smell out of the upstairs bathroom. She and Ilaria had settled for directing Signor Severini to the other bathroom and filling the offensive one with air fresheners.

Luckily, she had better luck with the next book, which focused on southern Italian desserts. No *fruttone*, but she spotted a recipe for *sfogliatelle* that specified candying the orange peel before folding into the ricotta. She kept the book in her hand as she continued her hunt.

Halfway through a pile of inserts, she found one on Puglia. A quick flip through the pages and she nodded. Yes, there was a recipe for *fruttone*.

Stella walked up to the desk but didn't know where to set her purchases. The desk seemed positively stacked with books and magazines, including an open one gleaming with images of sleek motorcycles. Domenica sighed dramatically in irritation as she nudged the stacks of books out of the way, pulling Stella's selections toward her.

In the pause, Stella cleared her throat and gestured to the calico still snoozing on the printer, its orange, black, and white patches rising and falling with its gentle breaths. "Such a pretty cat."

Domenica humphed, her hand reaching seemingly without her knowledge to scratch the calico behind the ear. A rumble of a purr sputtered momentarily from the sleepy beast, and Domenica almost smiled.

Catching sight of Mimmo passing the shop, Stella jumped back behind the standing lamp that lit the desk. She chanced a look at Domenica, hoping she'd missed Stella's reaction. No such luck. The woman swiveled her head from Mimmo who continued to stride down the street belly first, to Stella. Stella straightened her clothing as if she'd simply had a wardrobe malfunction. It's not like she had any reason to hide. She wasn't afraid of Mimmo, despite his dire warnings.

Domenica regarded Stella's books with new interest. She flipped them over and backward. "Doing some baking, I see."

"Yes!" Stella nearly shouted, in relief to have a normal conversation. She checked herself. "That is, yes. Ilaria . . . do you know Ilaria . . . her husband is sick, I thought I'd make them something familiar, a pastry from Puglia. Do you know *fruttone*?" *Stop it*, Stella ordered herself.

Domenica regarded Stella over her glasses. "You made an enemy of Mimmo."

Stella shrugged, mutely.

Domenica harrumphed. "Welcome to the club."

Stella startled. "Club?"

Domenica peered at the numbers on the calculator, not inclined to continue the conversation. "That will be two euros, twenty. The second insert is half off."

Stella fished the money out of her pocket and tried to quell her babbling. Too late. "Oh, that's so nice, you know I'm new and—"

"Unsolicited advice?"

Stella stopped. "Yes?"

"Go to the bar. Have a cup of coffee."

"The bar? Which bar?"

"Little one, we only have one bar in Aramezzo. Bar Cappellina. Let the people see you so they can stop guessing what you're about."

"But I make my own coffee."

Domenica gazed at Stella levelly. "As you please."

"Thank you. For the books. And the advice." Spotting a long-hair white cat with a squashed face picking its way along the shelf of children's comic books, Stella added, "You have quite a variety of cats here!"

Domenica didn't bother answering.

"I don't suppose you want a silver-spotted one to round out your collection?" As soon as the words slipped from her mouth, she wanted to reel them back. She wondered how a woman as unflexible as herself could find so many ways to fit her foot in her mouth. Domenica straightened her scarf. Without raising her gaze, she said, "Get your house in order."

And here Stella thought that's exactly what she was doing.

Stella left the bookstore feeling unnerved. She tried to tell herself that she didn't care what Mimmo thought of her, but her impulse to become invisible bothered her. Then there was Domenica, who seemed to look into Stella's soul and find her wanting.

Her heartbeat settled as she drew her arms through her chef's coat. She felt her breathing even as she measured the almonds. Her thinking focused, sharpened. Domenica was just a bit of an oddball, no harm in that. And, if she thought about it, Mimmo was harmless. Just a yakking testicle really, and hadn't she dealt with plenty of those? All bravado, no substance. Well, she thought, as she slipped the almonds into the oven to toast, no substance until they took away the one thing that mattered— her restaurant. She dragged a flour-laced hand across her forehead. God save her from yakking testicles with too much power.

The smell of roasting almonds quieted her bouncing memories. Space grew between her heart and her thoughts, and she remembered gentler moments of her morning's errands. She'd enjoyed the Thursday market on the edge of town, against the old laundry. She'd found bowls, whisks, even a blender, and the woman said nothing about her accent. Yes, her son commented that Stella looked too young to manage a blender without help, but his open smile made the remark seem friendly. And the woman at the *alimentari* didn't startle at her entrance as she had the other times, and she didn't ask about Stella's marital status or her family connections. Instead, she'd asked with friendly curiosity what Stella was making as she bagged the chocolate, jam, and almonds. And then told Stella that her name was Cristiana.

Maybe it would be okay. Even if this guest didn't leave her a glowing review. She'd banked on the pastries sweetening his words, but true to his glowering character, he hadn't touched them. But more guests would come. Maybe ones lacking in both contempt and guns.

Once she had a car, she'd put up signs advertising the bed-and-breakfast in bike shops across Umbria. Once she had internet, she'd get on biking and hiking message boards and tout her establishment. She'd started from zero before, she could do it again. As long as nothing else went wrong.

Grinding the almonds with cinnamon and sugar, she felt her

shoulders unhitch. When Severini ponied up at the end of his stay, she'd be able to pay Ilaria's family for their rush job getting the kitchen hooked up. She'd get paint on the walls and figure out how to tile the bathroom. A piece at a time until it was done.

Stella's practiced fingers flew, folding the pastry cases around the almond paste and jam. She slipped them into the hot oven. She sighed in happiness and unbuttoned her chef's coat. Ilaria found it funny that Stella couldn't be in the kitchen without her white coat, but given how few clothes Stella had, she couldn't mess them up.

She put her hands at the base of her spine and leaned back, delighting in the satisfying pop. In the sudden silence that bloomed in the absence of her kitchen bustle, she heard a strange noise drifting in the open window. A bird perhaps? But the sound seemed too continuous, too musical. She stepped to the window that faced the countryside, but the music grew fainter, so she stepped to her front door, facing the street. No, not a bird, a thin, reedy flute. Stella breathed in the evening air, tilting her head back to catch a view of the stars spangled across the blue velvet sky. She let the haunting melody fill her. The last notes faded away and Stella waited for some acknowledgment of the music. Applause perhaps? But none came.

As she turned back to the house, her vision snagged on a rectangular hole in the exterior wall that she hadn't noticed before. She peered in to make sure there were no creatures inside, taking out her phone to shine a light into the corners (at least she didn't need internet for the flashlight). No mammals or insects, but she did spy a channel snaking up from the ceiling of the opening. She ran her hand along the bottom of the hole and brought her fingertips to her face to inhale. Ash. And . . . burned flour?

"It's a pizza oven," came a gravely voice from behind her.

Stella jumped back, her ashy hand clutched to her heart as she whirled around to face a priest. Or a man in a black dress. No, of course it was a priest. In New York, it could have been either, especially with hair that well-coiffed and cheekbones that pronounced, but here ...

The man nodded to the hole. "Most houses in Aramezzo have them. For cooking on sweltering days when villagers don't want to heat the house."

From the smell of the ash on her fingers, this one hadn't been used in a long time.

To her silent pondering, the priest said, "I'm Don Arrigo. You'll have heard of me, I expect." His grin shone white in the gathering darkness.

She had, but Stella bristled at the presumption. And bristled further at Don Arrigo's searching expression, seeming to drink in her visage. And did his eyes dip to her neckline? Sigh. Yakking testicles every one of them. She blushed a bit at the thought and, hoping he didn't notice the flush, said, "I'm Stella."

"Yes, I know. Small town, word gets around, right?" He smiled jovially, clearly expecting her to grin along with him. Could that be all he meant, a remark about the provinciality of Aramezzo, not an assumption that she must have heard of his vast and magnificent holiness? *Nah.* He was full of himself and assumed everyone was as smitten with his broad chest as he was.

The priest gestured to her shirt. *Here we go*, she thought. "Is that a band?"

She looked down at her Fermented Forest t-shirt, stretched thin across her chest. She pressed her lips together, wishing she hadn't unbuttoned her chef's coat. Clearly, this guy took any opportunity to check out a decent rack. The silence stretched. Finally, Stella realized she needed to answer. "A pickling company. Based in Jersey."

He nodded in what seemed an approximation of thoughtfulness, a hand resting on his cheek. "Pickling?"

"It's hard to explain." This was true. She'd long ago given up on describing the wonders of lactic acid fermentation to Italian chefs. Inevitably, they continued to assume she meant vinegar packing. As hard as she tried, she couldn't convey the difference between a cornichon and a pickle.

He narrowed his eyes as if debating whether or not to press her, but then seemed to decide against it. "Will I be seeing you in church on Sunday?"

"I'm not Catholic." Not strictly true, as all those old photographs of her in white gowns would attest, but how could he know?

He cocked his head to the side as if he found this hard to swallow. "Your mother, your family ... "

"No offense, Father, but my mother didn't think enough of the church to send me or my sister to catechism. We weren't confirmed. We never went at all." Again, not true, but also none of his business.

"Sister?" He looked behind her as if expecting to see a smaller double of Stella waiting in the wings. Perhaps one less immune to his charms, which Stella could see were formidable.

She had to stop herself from glancing over her shoulder for the sister who should be there. Who should have grown up and gone to college to be a vet like she'd declared she would as she took meticulous care of their stuffed animals. At the memory, Stella felt her eyes sting with unshed tears.

"She died," she said flatly.

"Ah, I am sorry to hear this." And he did indeed look sorry. Faking bastard. She felt suffocated by the pretended kindness softening the grating corners of his voice.

Stella lifted her chin. She wouldn't let this guy assume he understood her because he knew this one intimate fact about her life. "It was a long time ago. Another lifetime."

He raised his eyebrow before reaching to put his hand on her shoulder. She torqued her body away from him. His eyes widened, but he let his hand fall to his side and said, "You don't need to be brought up Catholic, Stella, to join us in worship. All are welcome at God's table."

Yeah, I bet, Stella thought. She'd been proselytized to at least once a week living in New York. In fact, she'd once joked, as she'd cuffed her chef's coat after a particularly trying interlude with a Jehovah's Witness, that she must stop wearing her perfume, *eau de heathen*. "Well, isn't that grand," she said stiffly. She'd learned not to engage.

He grinned again, his eye crinkling at the corners like she'd offered him a juicy confession rather than a stone wall. "So, I can count on seeing you Sunday?"

"Oh, I don't think so."

A shadow passed over his face. "Come on. It will be a great way to meet the villagers. After all, you're not meeting them at Bar Cappellina, right?"

Twice in one day? "Word gets around."

He shrugged easily. "As I said, it's a small town. Sharing stories is as much a feature of Aramezzo as appreciating the cats."

With great effort, she bit her tongue to avoid the impulsive retort.

"Come to church. You'll be glad you did."

Suddenly, Stella felt tired. Tired of being told what would make her feel better, what would solve her problems, what she needed to do for the sake of others. Tired. All she wanted to do was get the chocolate on the *fruttone* and go to bed with the mystery novel she'd started. She'd found a lamp in the shed and loved how it banished the shadows with a circle of gold. "Sure, whatever."

"Marvelous!" Don Arrigo beamed, lifting his arm as if to clasp her shoulder again, but then, no doubt remembering the previous gesture, thinking the better of it and letting it fall to his side. "I'll let Cinzia know to expect you."

"Cinzia?"

He nodded, a faraway smile plastered across his face. "My assistant. I can't imagine what I did before she came on board five years ago. She'll help you with the liturgy. Tell you when to sit, when to rise." Stella groaned inwardly. This sounded like her ninth circle of hell. Don Arrigo didn't notice the annoyance that flashed across her face. He was lost in imagining Sunday. "And all those old women, so anxious to meet you! Some of them will have memories of your mother to share with you. How about that?"

He smiled as if he'd proffered an enormous treat. But the realization that all these old biddies knew her mother, when she, who was birthed by the woman, had found her inscrutable, well, she realized, she'd been in error. *This* was her ninth circle of hell.

She stretched her mouth in an approximation of a smile. "Sure," she said, even as she swore to herself that the ancient Etruscan demon Orcus, who reputedly terrorized central Italy back in the day, couldn't make her go, on pain of dragging her to the underworld for breaking her word.

As she nodded goodbye, she felt the priest's eyes flicking to her chest again. The nerve of this guy. "Ferments, eh? Someday you'll have to explain that to me."

As he walked away, Stella realized he'd been one of the few people who hadn't commented on her tangled accent. Maybe, she decided, because he'd been too intent on noticing her other attributes.

Stella had rarely seen a man go soggy-eyed in the face of pastry, but Ilaria's husband did just that. Even now, on his third, he kept a running commentary on how these *fruttone* rivaled his grandmother's. Ilaria could only compare them to the bar in Lecce, where she'd grown up, since her grandmother learned to cook in Albania. Nonetheless, they had agreed that the chocolate dipped pastries rated a score of *dieci e lode*, ten and applause, but refused to take them all, insisting that Stella save them for Signor Severini. Ilaria hadn't met him, and so still labored under the misapprehension that he would love anything Stella prepared.

Stella knew she should trust Ilaria. The woman had quickly become indispensable, the way she organized teams of her relatives for the renovation, all while keeping the linens clean and tackling jobs like clearing the *terrazza*. But Stella couldn't help but worry that if she confessed that Signor Severini refused her offer of breakfast, Ilaria would tell a neighbor and thus inadvertently start a rumor that guests of Casale Mazzoli hated the food. So instead she accepted back a portion of the *fruttone* and confirmed with Ilaria when she'd drop by with her husband's new ideas for how to remedy the offensive smell. Ilaria's husband squeezed his wife's hand and declared the *fruttone* made him feel young again, so rejuvenated that soon he himself would fix the plumbing. Ilaria regarded his upturned face with such affection, it shot a pang of longing through Stella's heart.

Stella announced her need to get going, kilometers to go and all that. As she walked home, she paused in the *piazza*. She stood overlooking the view of the valley and noticed Signor Severini driving down the road that led to Subbiano in a car that resembled an electric blue panther, coiled to pounce. Did Italian tour guides make enough to afford such fancy vehicles? Stella didn't know a Fiat Panda from a Fiat Punto, but she knew enough to know that whatever kind of car this was, it was a feat of Italian or maybe German engineering.

As Severini turned into the parking lot, Stella noticed a Manchester United sticker in his back window. How odd. Nobody in Aramezzo decorated their cars with novelty plates or window stickers or other ways to announce their identity. And even though the amount she knew about soccer could fit into a rice bowl with room for a ladleful of stir-fried pork, didn't Italians root for Italian teams? She certainly did, the once-every-few-years that she bothered to notice that such a sport as soccer existed, and then, she had to admit, it was mostly because the Italian soccer team seemed to be made up of former Gucci models. Swoon.

She watched as Signor Severini flicked down the visor and checked his hair, shaking out the ends to curl carelessly against his collar. He turned his head this way and that, baring his teeth and smiling in turn. The man primped worse than a model during New York Fashion Week. He gathered up a pile of papers from the passenger seat and launched himself from the car. Stella wondered for a moment if he'd stopped by Domenica's. Yesterday, he'd asked her in passing about how to find old postcards of Subbiano, and she'd recommended the shop, but he'd sneered like this was a ridiculous notion. And maybe it was. What did she know?

Her thoughts turned to that flash of metal. She decided she must have imagined it since dwelling on it made her heart race.

Stella continued walking, but paused again outside Bar Cappellina, peering through the plate-glass windows. Should she go in? But she made perfectly serviceable coffee at home. And what did she care about meeting the locals? They'd only make fun of her accent (again) or ask her intrusive questions (again). Her mother had been clear that the worst part of Aramezzo was the people. Why should she get to know them?

Even if they were fabulous—*a big if*—all these people being in and out of each other's lives . . . that wasn't her style. Keep footloose, that was her motto. A small voice whispered that perhaps there were other reasons she avoided getting close to people.

She shook off the thought. No, better to maintain a shallow hold on life in Aramezzo. She was here only to get the property ready to sell, hopefully as a successful business, since the property itself seemed worth hardly more than the dirt it stood on. She'd sell and then move back to the States. Maybe Martin had been right that she couldn't ever return to New York restaurants, but there were other options. Philadelphia, maybe? The food scene there was picking up. Chicago, if she could handle the cold. Her father always joked that her Italian blood made her cranky in winter.

A shadow fell over her shoulder and Stella startled at the man who appeared beside her, regarding her quizzically. Without his uniform, it took a moment for her to recognize him as one of the police officers who patrolled the streets, swinging their batons, eyes scanning for trouble. Odd, when the only crimes in Aramezzo seemed to be loitering and trespassing, and those more in animal control's wheelhouse than the police.

At close range, she noted the man resembled one of the soccer players she'd just been remembering—with those broad shoulders and his dark hair swept off his forehead. Did Italian soccer players have that shading of stubble that made their cheekbones stand out like this guy? If not, they should.

The man seemed to be holding back a smile, and she realized she'd been not only staring at his Adonis-like features, but blocking the door. She stepped back, gesturing to the officer to go ahead. Now he grinned down at her, one dimple playing peekaboo with his cheek. An eyebrow cocked, he asked, his voice so deep it almost rang gruff, "Going in?"

She shook her head.

His full upper lip pressed against the lower one as he said, "Are you sure? The coffee is reliable. Though I can't speak to the company. Veronica is waiting to complain to anybody about the challenges of growing the most beautiful roses in Umbria. But if she's in there, at least Luisella won't be. As bad as Veronica is, at least she talks. Unlike Luisella who looks around stunned, a queen who has found herself among the unwashed hordes."

Despite herself, Stella turned to look through the window to the long bar. Was all this true? Could this much drama exist in a little town? So much that this young man picked up on it? It was as good as a Jane Austen novel!

Well, she didn't want to find out by becoming a character. She looked back at the police officer and shook her head, not giving him the opportunity to tease her about her accent. The ironic tilt of his eyebrow made him look ready to tease her about anything.

At her saying nothing, he shrugged easily. "Suit yourself." He swung open the door to a chorus of, "*Ciao, Luca! Come va?*" She heard a voice raised to praise the wealth of recent sun and another pontificate about how the wild greens would be excellent around now.

The door closed.

Stella looked down at her platter of pastries. She could take them into the bar, offer them. If it was one thing she knew, it was that sugar and butter were the keys to anyone's good graces. But she'd already told that mocking Luca guy she wasn't going in. Anyway, hadn't she already decided there was no point in making friends with the locals?

Yet, as the butcher passed her to open the door, she found herself staring at the villagers hunched around the bar. Luca might have spoken harshly of the Veronica he mentioned, but he seemed to already be deep in conversation with her. Beyond them, Stella noticed a peaked ceiling lined with curved, arching beams. She stepped back, taking in the building. Ah, no wonder the bar was named Cappellina. It must have been a chapel, deconsecrated long ago. That explained the pointed windows and the steep roofline perching high above the surrounding buildings. Also, the bar opened onto this *piazza*. Italian churches usually offered a space in front of them for parishioners to congregate. Stella had to admit that this *piazza* was prettier than most, with its sweeping views over rolling hills, the stone school with its tumbling children calling in glee while kicking a soccer ball, and, Stella squinted, were those snow-covered mountains in the distance? She shouldn't be surprised, she knew Aramezzo lay in striking distance of the Apennine mountains. It still thrilled her.

As her eyes lowered again to the bar, she caught sight of Luca's gaze on her. He raised his *espresso* cup with a smirk and she startled, clutching the plate closer to herself before hurrying away.

The cobblestone streets had quickly grown familiar. Not home, of course. Home could never be anything but tired steps leading to an old tenement building, teeming with the vitality that comes from a long history of immigrant communities. Every time Stella crested the stairs in any apartment she lived in, she swore she could smell boiled cabbage and fried garlic and red sauce steamed right into the walls.

So, no. This town, with its stodgy, continuous history, marked only by a flirting with Fascism and engagement in war theaters across the globe, could never feel like home. But...she could see the appeal. The curiously pink buildings seemed to glow, especially in the early morning or evening. But even now, at midday, they gave off an ethereal quality, gilding the air. She shook her head. Too much by half, as her mother used to say, and would probably say even louder if she heard Stella's admiration for this little town.

Nonetheless, Stella couldn't deny Aramezzo's charms, which, now that she thought about it, did bear some resemblance to the contrasts she loved so much in Manhattan. In Manhattan, those contrasts took the form of tumble-down apartments towered over by skyscrapers so tall they seemed to bend back down to earth. Here, it was those glowing stones coupled with the shadowy alleys that would be right at home in one of her mystery novels. On this walk alone, between the *piazza* which overlooked one side of the Assisi valley and her edge of town, which overlooked a valley with more grapevines and olive trees than people, she had discovered a shortcut that helped her skirt the main road, cluttered with villagers propped at their windows, ready to call out to each other or stare at a passing outsider, such as herself.

The shortcut took her through a serpentine alley, with quiet homes on one side and a wall that seemed to contain a garden, judging from the persimmon tree dangling its limbs over the path. And now, now came her favorite part of the walk, the part that filled her with a secret thrill. The path dipped down as homes continued above her head; the ceiling above the walkway crisscrossed with beams, what must be the floor of the house above. Darkness thickened here, the air drawing still, before the path suddenly turned up and into the sunlight again.

This time, as she crested the incline, she noticed more outdoor ovens built into the walls. These seemed more used than hers, which made sense since families occupied these houses, rather than passing guests. She paused beside an oven, surprised that she didn't smell yeast or flour, but rather the scent of crackling chicken skin. Faint, yes, but definitely there.

Images of summer evenings—when villagers crowded the streets, slipping pizza and bread and chicken into their ovens, calling over to each other to pour wine into squat glass tumblers—filled her mind. In a reverie, she turned the corner to her house and slammed into the silver-spotted cat streaking past her legs. She stumbled and watched, horrified, as the pastries arced off her platter in slow motion, splattering across the cobblestones.

The *fruttone*!

She'd turned each one with care, meticulously covered them with chocolate, and now they scattered like marbles. She sat down on the ground and tried not to cry. That damn cat! It stood now on the steps across from her house, hissing at her in a continuous snarl.

"Don't they have littering laws in America?" She looked up at the man in a public works uniform of blue pants and long sleeve top, florescent yellow stripes at the ankle, wrist, and around the bottom edge of the shirt. She couldn't see his face, backlit as he was, but his voice carried a grin as he said, "You don't remember our last meeting? I'm offended, truly."

Now she remembered. She'd dropped her canister of compostable trash at the step and he'd stopped her to say she could just leave the bag without the canister. She'd nodded, removed the bag, and tried not to feel self-conscious about dropping the leavings of her solitary meals right there on the street, for anyone to judge.

Stella smiled absently and kneeled to pick up the remains of her shattered pastries.

The man kneeled as well and said with gentleness, "Hey, *scherzavo*, I was joking."

She shook her head. "I can clean it."

The man sat back on his heels, looking like a cricket, with his folded long limbs, his expansive tanned forehead, and the curls that stood out on his head like antennae, threaded with premature silver. "She speaks!"

Stella started to bristle, but then noticed the man's friendly smile, made more friendly by the honest gap between his two front teeth. She tried to return the smile, but it felt more forlorn than cheerful. The man reached out and touched her wrist. "Everything okay?"

She shrugged and focused on picking up the shards of pastry caught between the cobblestones.

He studied her for a moment. "Well, if everything is not okay, you have only to tell me. Trash collectors in Italy, we're like priests. We know everyone's business and we don't tell tales. Because we know what few people do—no matter how neat someone's life looks from the outside, we all make garbage."

Despite herself, a laugh escaped Stella's constricted throat. She looked at the man with wide eyes.

He chuckled. "That's better. So what is this that's dirtied up my clean streets?"

"*Fruttone.*"

"*Fruttone?* What's that?"

"A pastry. From Puglia. Short pastry filled with almond paste and jam. These have quince. And then covered with chocolate. And then tossed into the street."

The man picked up a barely dented *fruttone* and, breaking off the side that had been on the ground, he popped the rest into his mouth. He closed his eyes and chewed.

Stella studied him. You could learn a lot about people by watching them eat. She hated people who rushed eating and looked for the check.

The man licked the crumbs from around his mouth. "I can't believe I've never had one of those before. Where did you get them?"

Now Stella grinned. "I made them."

"You *made* them?" He gave her a frank, appraising look. "That explains the smear of cream on your jeans. Are you a baker or something?"

"Or something." Stella went back to clearing pieces of crumpled pastry, watching as the man found another large piece and chewed thoughtfully. His long neck and curly ponytail reminded her of someone...who? Ah yes, her childhood best friend, Ernie. The two of them must have climbed every tree in their neighborhood before his family moved to Florida. She wished they hadn't lost touch; she only knew about him marrying his college boyfriend thanks to the photos on Facebook.

When the largest pieces of pastry were removed to the platter or to his mouth, he put out a staying hand to stall Stella, now reaching for crumbs stuck between the cobblestones. "No need, really." He stood. "The dogs will get it. Or the rain."

She looked at the street, hating to not leave it as she found it, a clean kitchen being part of her DNA. No matter how tired she was, she always, *always*, washed and dried and put away every measuring cup and wooden spoon.

"It's okay, I promise." He waved his hand over her head. "On behalf of the sanitation department, I give you leave to go."

She scanned the ground one more time before rising. "*Grazie.*"

He grinned. "No problem. I'm Matteo, by the way."

"Stella."

"I know."

She smiled. Effortlessly this time.

"So, are you starting a bakery, Stella? You'd give Antonio a run for his money."

"A bakery?" She snorted out a laugh and then covered her mouth in embarrassment.

He threw his head back and guffawed, a pleasing sound that reverberated through the streets.

She shook her head. "No, not a bakery. Just righting the reputation of Casale Mazzoli."

His laughter faded, but stayed in his eyes. "Well, that would do it. You have any guests?"

"Yes, one. A guy looking to put Aramezzo on a touring packet."

His face lost its animation. "Ah, he's staying here then. I'd wondered."

Stella didn't know what to say.

Finally, he went on, "Well, I'll let you get to it. Hope he's easy on you. You know those big-city folks."

She darted a look at him. Was this a remark about her New York City background?

But his eyes held a lilt of merriment, so she simply grinned in return before climbing the steps. At the sight of the cat, still sitting on the stoop across the street, she asked, "Matteo? That cat. Does he belong to anyone?"

He narrowed his eyes at the silver-spotted cat, now flicking its tail that had to be bushier than a normal cat's. "That cat? Sure. He's yours."

From the living room, Stella heard Severini on the phone. The tones emerged from behind his closed door, jabbing angrily. She tried not to listen, returning to her task of arranging olive boughs around her old photograph of Casale Mazzoli. How lucky that she'd found that box of frames! She only wished the frames hadn't been empty. So odd that she'd found not one photograph in the whole house.

Her head picked up as Severini's voice rose higher. She tiptoed to the foot of the stairs and leaned forward. She knew she shouldn't eavesdrop—it probably ground against some ethical rules for hosts—but she couldn't help herself.

The sounds muted again. She turned away, then startled at the sound of Signore Severini's growling, "I'll kill him. Or worse."

Her breath caught, and her mind turned to that flash of metal. Was this hyperbole? Or was Signor Severini intending to hurt someone? Or . . . kill them?

Who?

Not her, surely. He definitely said "him." And, anyway, what was worse than killing? The person on the other end of the line must have wondered the same because, though Severini lowered his voice, she heard him say, "I don't know what's worse, but it won't be hard to find. Those do-gooders always have a weak spot to exploit. And I think I know his."

Severini went quiet. All Stella could hear was the jackhammering of her heart. At the sound of his door opening, she hurried back to the mantle, to arrange the already arranged olive branches. She heard him jog down the stairs and she hesitated, suddenly unsure if she should tell him about the breakfast she'd made.

Before she could decide, the words escaped her mouth. "Good morning, Signore!"

He paused with his hand on the door. He shot her an accusing glance, as if wondering why a proprietress would presume to speak to a guest.

Good reviews, good reviews, good reviews, she chanted in her mind like a mantra. But . . . did members of the mob leave reviews? And when had she decided that he was in the mob?

Waving her hand at the dinette table laid out for breakfast, she rushed on, "I've made breakfast pizza for you, since—"

"Breakfast what?"

"Breakfast pizza. It has softly scrambled eggs, crisped prosciutto, a bit of basil. I figured since you don't eat sweets . . ." Her voice trailed off when she realized he stared at her as if she had laid the eggs.

"Pizza is not a breakfast food."

She attempted a laugh. "No, I know, of course I know, but I thought—"

In perfect British-accented English, he said, "You are mad as a bag of ferrets."

He swept out of the house, leaving Stella to stare after him. He spoke English? She guessed he must if he was in the tourism industry, but what a time to trot it out.

She nudged the breakfast pizza with a desultory finger before wolfing it down, barely tasting it. She tried to toss the dishes in the sink and walk away, but couldn't leave them there undone. So she tidied the kitchen before heading to the butcher shop.

Her spirits lifted as she walked into the sunshine. Well, if Signor Severini refused all her attempts to feed him, then it left her more time to put in light fixtures, make more phone calls to the Wi-Fi company, and figure out how to get a SIM card so she could start using her phone. Dealing with Italian bureaucracy was a full-time job and living with a landline was old before it began.

As she approached the stairs, she caught sight of Signor Severini. Stella ducked into a doorway, not eager for more insults. But wait, this couldn't be Severini. Yes, they looked similar, but this man called out to an older gentleman in a voice full of the sugar Severini claimed he hated.

Stella peeked her head out and watched as bizarro Severini caught up with the older gentleman. They chatted pleasantly in the street, and Stella started to come out of the doorway. But when his head turned in profile, Stella realized that this was indeed Severini, though she didn't recognize his expression, having never seen the man smile. The older gentleman looked familiar, and Stella realized she'd once seen him with Veronica, the woman Luca pointed out in Bar Cappellina. This older guy seemed rather posh, with his artfully styled hair and tailored suit.

The men walked together into the tunnel that led to the second road.

Stella withdrew further into the shadows and debated continuing to the butcher. But this new and improved version of Severini spurred her curiosity. She pressed against the walls and followed, listening.

What was it about the suited man that turned Severini into this genial, laughing, sport of a guy? She quieted her breathing to make out their conversation. She could only catch a few words. Severini seemed to be complimenting the suited man, saying that everything was just as described and, in a word, perfection. Well, he certainly couldn't be talking about Casale Mazzoli.

The suited man dropped his voice, so she didn't hear his response, but then Severini guffawed—Stella blinked at the sound—and said in a carrying voice that he didn't anticipate any trouble on that score. Stella shuddered at the icy vein underlying his words. The men paused in the tunnel in a spot where their words echoed, so Stella had no trouble hearing Severini when he said in a placating tone, "I'm honored by your support, Signor Sindaco, and I assure you, you'll be pleased with what I can do for you."

Sindaco? This guy was the *mayor*? Of Aramezzo?

Of course Aramezzo had a mayor, but it hadn't occurred to Stella to consider local politics. Even if she had, she hardly would have imagined a stylish guy like this one schmoozing with a waste of space like Severini. Then again, the Severini she knew was clearly different from the one the mayor was treated to. She paused in thought. Well, actually, this one seemed as insufferable, just in a different way. Who wanted their ass kissed like this?

The mayor, apparently.

As the men entered the tunnel to the chapel, Stella tentatively climbed the stairs, coming out into the middle street. She put her hand on the banister in the final tunnel. Should she follow them a little further? The word "Mimmo" carried down, the tones blunted by the angles of the tunnel so she wasn't sure which of them said it, but it was enough to propel her forward. What did Mimmo have to do with either the mayor or Severini?

She crept forward, carefully, hardly daring to breathe, but then the two men crested the stairs and disappeared into the chapel. What a weird time to pray. Then again, the role of the church in Italy was different, right?

She realized that when the men left the church, they'd head for her tunnel, so she hurried down the two flights of tunnel steps and turned right at the middle road, toward the butcher shop. She felt eyes on her, and imagined Severini and the mayor shouting, "Hey you!"

She met no more obstacles in her journey, other than Enzo stumbling across her path, his shoelaces still a mess. Nonetheless, she heaved a sigh of relief when she pulled open the *macelleria* door to find only one customer. The relief vanished when Stella recognized that customer as Veronica, who she now understood must be the mayor's wife. The woman held two gem-studded leashes that led to two tiny, long-haired dachshunds that wouldn't have been out of place on the Upper East Side.

Veronica gave Stella the once-over with a wrinkled nose as if she'd smelled something bad. Stella fought down ridiculous thoughts about how the mayor must have called to alert his wife to Stella's lurking. But why did Veronica have that expression? She didn't have to wonder long, as Veronica said, "I know you. The Mazzoli girl."

Stella nodded mutely, trying to nonchalantly catch her breath.

"Come to Aramezzo with your tail between your legs, I imagine."

Stella shot her an astonished look. Did villagers in Aramezzo read the *New York Times*?

Veronica shook her head as if in answer to Stella's silent question. "Your mother left in such disgrace, I never thought we'd see any of you again. In fact, I was stunned that your aunt decided to stay. But these things do blow over, I suppose. Luckily for your aunt."

Stella said, "How...what..." she had no idea how to articulate how little she understood the woman's meaning, even though to Veronica it seemed obvious as rain causing wet streets.

"Is that Italian? I can hardly tell." Veronica smiled. Not a nice smile, more of a grimace. "Don't worry, *cara*. Your aunt wound up being a credit to Aramezzo. I remember my children always ran to school on the days your aunt prepared the noon meal. And she did the best she could with Casale Mazzoli. Such a preposterous venture for a single woman. How could she think it would improve the town's standing? But we can't all be born as civic-minded as I, I'm afraid."

Was this woman speaking in tongues? Stella said, "I'm sorry . . . what?"

The woman let loose a tinkle of a laugh that caused the butcher to look up with a scowl from slicing Veronica's pork chops. Veronica delicately rested her fingers against her chest and said, "My word. How odd you are. I suppose I should have known. In any case, I hope you are taking good care of our dear Signor Severini. I have high hopes for him."

The butcher wrapped the pork chops and thumped them on the counter. Veronica cast him an approving look and said, "You've met Signor Severini, Bruno, surely?"

He humphed in a way that could have indicated something or nothing.

Veronica nodded as if he'd agreed with her.

Stella couldn't help herself. "You think adding Subbiano or even Aramezzo to one tour operator's list is going to change this town's fortunes?"

Veronica regarded her steadily for a moment before offering another tinkling laugh. "You do amuse me, I'll give you that."

Stella waited as Veronica slipped the parcel of pork chops into a reusable bag that seemed to be made of leather with little metal studs. Rather than paying, she rapped on the counter twice in thanks and then turned to Stella to offer a last, consoling look.

Stella watched Veronica sweep out of the *macelleria* with her twin sable-coated dogs.

The butcher cleared his throat. "Something I can get you, Signorina?"

Unlike the cartoonish descriptions of Italian butchers, she'd never seen Bruno smile. Now was no exception. Though she noted a new warmth in his dark gray eyes. She sighed. "What in the world was all that about?"

He shrugged. "Not for me to say."

It wouldn't do to push him, not when this was the most he'd said to her. Unlike the other villagers, the butcher had offered only an eyebrow raise on her first visit to his shop. And while he'd never been anything remotely chatty with her, he didn't seem loquacious with anyone. In fact, the only change she ever noticed in Bruno's expression was when the baker passed and he muttered angrily under his breath. No love lost there.

Stella stepped to the counter. "I wanted to ask you a question. The eggs I bought here the other day."

He stiffened.

"Where are they from? They tasted better than the ones I bought at the *alimentari*."

His shoulders relaxed, even though his face betrayed no shift of emotion. He harrumphed, "Those are good eggs."

"The best I've had, and I've worked in some discriminating restaurants." She noticed the butcher's eyes glaze over, so she rushed on. "Super rich eggs. I love the chive flower flavor."

He raised his eyebrows. "I get them from Marta. She lets her chickens forage so they eat worms and insects and greens."

He looked winded from saying so much at once. Stella nodded eagerly, "Yes! I've read about how a chicken's diet changes egg quality. But I always ordered farm eggs for my restaurant and they still didn't taste like these."

He shrugged. "This is Umbria."

"It certainly is," she smiled. "Which reminds me, I wanted to ask you about the sausage I bought."

"Which day?"

She thought back. "Thursday."

"Garlic and rosemary."

"Yes, that's it. But the garlic didn't have that sharpness. It was rounder, sweeter. Like it had been roasted, but not quite that caramelized."

He stared at her. "I confit the garlic."

"That's it! And the rosemary, that's different, too—"

"I fry it." He frowned. "Someone told you."

She laughed. "As you recently witnessed, I'm not exactly Miss Popularity around here." That probably didn't translate, given the blank look he gave her. She tried again. "No one told me."

"You couldn't pick up on all that. The eggs, the garlic . . ."

She shrugged. "Tasting is my superpower, I guess. Everyone gets one, right? Mine happens to work well for my job."

He nodded slowly, as if wondering if she was duping him.

"I'll be back next Thursday for that sausage. Exceptional. I wish I'd had access to them at Lucky. It would have made the Michelin star all the easier." Was he blushing? "What kind of sausage did you make today?"

"*Porchetta.* With fennel pollen, red pepper, and garlic."

"Is the garlic confited?"

"Yes."

"And I imagine you aren't relying on solely regular red pepper flakes."

He stammered, "No. I add Aleppo pepper to the chili pepper flakes."

She paused, ruminating. "I see, the Aleppo pepper adds—"

"Fruitiness," he supplied.

Just as she finished, "Fruitiness."

They smiled at each other.

"I'll take three."

It had become a morning routine of sorts. She woke up, made herself coffee, and took it out to the *terrazza*. Ilaria had managed to clean off the moss, as well as clearing the arbor of years' worth of dead vines, and Stella had figured out how to scrub the rust off the iron furniture she'd found in the pig shed. Well, she'd only cleared one chair and the table, but it wasn't like she had any company. One chair worked fine.

After she finished her coffee, she toured the yard, touching each olive tree as if in gratitude for their holy presence on her property. The gnarled and twisted forms must easily be a hundred years old, yet their leaves seemed tender as new rain. She noticed that her trees bore fewer olives than her neighbors', but they appeared to be ripening. There must be something she was supposed to be doing to help them along. Maybe she should look for a book at Domenica's. But for now, she limited her olive education to a daily walk around the ring road, checking for signs of olive activity on neighboring properties. So far, all the groves seemed devoid of action.

She stalled at the sound of voices approaching from the ring road. Looking down, she realized she was hardly in appropriate attire, with her pajama pants and the chef's coat and the Doc Martens. Stella swore to herself and ducked into the pig shed. Through a crack in the door, Stella spied Don Arrigo with a slight yet voluptuous woman, glossy waves cascading over her shoulders in ways that Stella would never experience, even if she spent hundreds of dollars for a designer blowout. And yet this woman looked like she'd tumbled out of bed with hair this effortlessly waving. Damn her.

As they neared, Stella heard their conversation.

"He's a pest, no doubt, but I can handle it." Don Arrigo's voice oozed confidence.

"You say that, but he's only growing bolder." Stella startled. She realized she'd expected the woman's voice to be high and nasally—monied, New Jersey housewife. Instead, her voice was rich and melodic.

"More desperate, Cinzia. Not bolder." Ah, this was the famous Cinzia, the secretary Don Arrigo couldn't do without. She didn't look like any secretary that Stella had ever seen. Except maybe the glamorous ones in *Mad Men*. How did this carelessly elegant woman wind up with a gig as assistant to a priest in a backwater Umbrian town? The two of them together, they looked like the cast of a movie about a village—one of those sweeping Hollywood numbers. Stella half expected one of them to break into song.

"It's getting out of control." The woman's voice rose in emphasis and she placed a manicured hand on the priest's arm.

The priest laughed easily and gazed down at Cinzia with great affection. He soothed in his gravely voice, "Ah, *cara*. You worry like a good daughter."

Even from this distance Stella could see the flash of darkness cross Cinzia's face. What was that about?

The couple swept past the pig shed. Stella needed to hear the rest of their conversation. She tiptoed from the pig shed and lingered outside for a moment to make sure the priest and Cinzia didn't look back, and no neighbors idled about. Then she darted to an oak tree and then to a large olive tree, using the rolling walk her father taught her when hiking so they wouldn't disturb the wildlife.

Hurrying a few steps, she caught more of the conversation.

"Arrigo, I think he knows."

Stella stopped still again. Knows? Knows what? She forced her feet to move, to keep up.

The priest's own steps faltered a bit, and he said, "He can't. We've been so careful."

"I don't trust him."

The priest chuckled. "Well, probably best not to trust criminals."

Stella couldn't hear Cinzia's response, only an exclamation hanging in the air. Or maybe an expletive.

The priest's voice grew chill. "I've dealt with his kind before."

"But what if he forces you—"

"He wouldn't dare."

From her vantage point behind a tree, Stella watched a figure round the corner up ahead. The priest must have noticed it too, because he shushed Cinzia out of the corner of his mouth. She looked at him in confusion, and he pointed with his chin.

Signor Severini.

Stella ducked into a chicken coop. The chickens looked up at her, surprised, before clucking lazily in welcome. She shushed them and found a knothole to peer out of, watching the interaction unfolding on the street.

Her houseguest hailed the priest with a hearty "*Buongiorno!*"

The priest responded with wide eyes at odds with his wide smile.

Severini ran his eyes appreciatively over Cinzia before ignoring her in favor of Don Arrigo. Stella felt a tug of sympathy for the strange woman. Signor Severini used the same high tones as his conversation with the mayor. "Don Arrigo. Just the man I wanted to see."

Could he not even say hello to Cinzia? Standing right there?

Apparently not.

Was Stella wrong, or did the priest's smile waver? "What can I help you with, Signore?"

Stella prayed no rattling, three-wheeled Ape passed at this moment to interfere with hearing the answer. Severini lowered his voice, his eyes scanning the ring road and luckily skipping right over the chicken coop that housed Stella, now furiously trying to calm the chickens that were pecking at her shoes, confused why she had entered without food. The chickens clucked with petulance and Stella went back to staring through the knothole.

"I'm on my way to Subbiano. Hoping I can interest you in coming along."

Don Arrigo shook his head and Stella almost missed his answer as she shook off a chicken that had decided her shoelace resembled a worm. "Not today, I'm afraid. Cinzia and I are on our way to Assisi."

Severini's smile grew. "Ah, come on. I know you have an interest in Subbiano. A *special* interest."

The priest exchanged looks with Cinzia, who glowered and then turned away to stare without interest at a puddle. "I'm a busy man, as I've said—"

Severini's voice lost all its oily charm. "You know as well as I do what's at stake."

Stella didn't miss the glance Cinzia shot the priest, who turned his head in a barely imperceptible "no."

The priest dropped his voice until Stella could barely make it out. "You have no idea what you're asking."

Signor Severini clapped the priest on the shoulder, his pinched face drawing close to the priest's aquiline nose. "Now, you and I both know that's not true. I'll be at your office tomorrow morning as planned. Don't bother trying to avoid me."

Stella's mind turned to Severini's threat and the gun glinting in his drawer. Could the village priest be his quarry? But... *why?*

Stella wondered if Cinzia also felt the danger. She watched in awe as Cinzia shrugged off her glowering expression. She rested a hand on Severini's arm, and he looked at her as if suddenly clocking her presence. Cinzia smiled, her face alight, and said, "Don't worry, Paolo. I'll make sure you get that meeting with Don Arrigo."

At the way Severini looked down at Cinzia's hand on his arm, Stella wondered if the woman had squeezed lightly. He leered, "Ah, Cinzia. Lovely to see you, as ever."

She looked at him through lowered lashes, quite the feat considering how much smaller she was than either man. "And you. Always a delight." She seemed to hit the word "delight" awfully hard. Stella heard her intake of breath before continuing, "I know an important man like you has heaps of things to do, so I'm terribly sorry to ask this, but I wonder if I might persuade you to move the appointment to the evening? If it's not too much trouble."

Severini frowned. "Evening?"

Cinzia's laugh tinkled like wind chimes. "Yes, my fault entirely, I'm afraid. Don Arrigo has a standing visit to the hospital on Tuesday mornings. I've double booked the priest, as it were. If you don't agree to the change, I'm afraid he'll be cross with me."

Don Arrigo frowned at Cinzia's worried pout. "Cinzia—"

She stalled him with a smile. "It's all right, Don Arrigo. I'm sure Paolo won't mind visiting us in the evening. Say at six o'clock? Right? Paolo?"

Severini looked a bit dazed, and Stella couldn't blame him. Cinzia certainly knew how to dazzle. Finally, he shook his head. "That's fine. I have to get paperwork in order first and for that I need Wi-Fi. My stupid B and B doesn't have it."

Stella had to clap her hand over her mouth to keep from shouting in protest that she was working on it.

Severini looked from Cinzia to Don Arrigo. "Tomorrow evening then. It's a date."

"Yes, it is," Cinzia breathed in soft tones Stella barely caught.

Severini's gaze lingered on Cinzia's neckline before he stormed toward the parking lot. Cinzia sagged in relief, her face pale. Clearly, the woman had not been prepared for the emotional weight of fascinating a tool like Severini. Don Arrigo put out a steadying arm as he said, "Cinzia? You know I visit the hospital on Thursdays."

Cinzia caught her breath. "Of course. But you need the time."

The priest gazed at Cinzia with a worried expression. "It's too much. We've talked about this—"

"Remember our arrangement? You handle the ethereal concerns, and I'll take care of the earthly ones." Her voice trembled. "It's what makes us work. Together."

"But Cinzia, I don't want you mixed up in this."

"I can handle men like Severini. Don't worry," Cinzia smiled tremulously at Don Arrigo.

Stella couldn't hear the rest as Cinzia ducked her head, and even the priest had to lean toward her to listen. He frowned and nodded and the two of them continued to the parking lot, just as Severini roared by in his electric blue sports car.

Stella watched until the pair walked around the bend and then waited until they, too, rolled out of Aramezzo.

Only then did Stella look down to find her shoes speckled with chicken excrement. She sighed and offered a prayer of thanks that at least Doc Martens were indestructible and that she'd chosen to wear them even with her pajama bottoms.

She slowly opened the door of the henhouse. Dashing back to her house, her mind buzzed as if over-caffeinated. What was all *that* about? She needed to get to the kitchen.

Stella's thoughts bounced around her brain like corn kernels popped in bacon fat. As she measured flour for the *sfogliatelle* she was finally baking from the book she'd purchased at Domenica's, her internal narrative quieted. By the time she slid the crackling pastries filled with ricotta and candied orange and spices into the oven, she noticed her breathing had returned to normal and she'd made three important realizations.

One, she was in danger of becoming a lurker. Seriously, these Umbrian grannies had nothing on her. Two, Signor Severini and the priest were up to something, something they were meeting about tomorrow, and the priest wasn't happy about it. Three, whatever they were up to, it had nothing to do with her. What happened in Aramezzo stayed in Aramezzo, as far as she was concerned. She made a vow not to eavesdrop on anymore conversations. No matter how scintillating and no matter how easy it seemed to flatten her frame and listen in the shadows. She had one job and one job only. To turn Casale Mazzoli around.

She exhaled happily as she took the *sfogliatelle* out of the oven. Poking them with a pinky, she could tell the layers would shatter beautifully. Stella blew on one and took a bite off the corner of the triangular pastry.

Yes.

Hearing the recycling truck making its way around the ring road, Stella hurriedly piled the *sfogliatelle* onto a platter, covered them with one of the embroidered linen napkins she had found in the armoire, and raced out the front door. Just in time to see the odd little truck approaching. She'd learned now that it had offset wheels to shuffle up the tunnels, straddling the stairs. Peering closely, she checked to see if—

Yes. It was indeed Matteo at the wheel.

Catching sight of Stella standing with a napkin-covered platter, he threw the diminutive recycling truck into park and leaped out of the cab. "Stella! How goes the proprietorship? Preparing yourself for worldwide B and B domination?"

She couldn't help but smile in return. "Hardly. My guest barely tolerates me. I may be categorically bad at this."

"But I'm sure your pastries will win over even the hardest heart."

"He seems to assume if he eats one, he'll turn into someone as lame as me."

He frowned. "He refused your baked goods?"

"He's up and out before I can catch him, usually. But even when I do, he turns his nose up at everything. The *cornetti*, the pizza—"

He put a hand over his heart and staggered backward. "Not the *fruttone*?"

"Yep, that too."

"Bastard." He shook his head. "Some people don't know what they're missing. And I suppose there go your hopes of him being bowled over by your hospitality and writing a glowing review."

"You get me."

"I'm trying." Matteo grinned, the gap between his two front teeth flashing. "So, where is he going every morning so early?"

"Subbiano, I think."

The grin dropped from Matteo's face.

"What is it?"

"Nothing. Probably nothing. I've just been hearing something about Subbiano lately, and now that I'm thinking about it, Severini was mentioned, too."

"Like in a bad way?"

He ran his hand down his long face. "Maybe? Do you know why he's going to Subbiano so often?"

"Yes, to see if it's worth adding it to a tour package."

"Huh."

"What?"

"Probably nothing. So who is this loser? What do we know about him?"

She shrugged.

"You didn't google him? Check him out on Facebook?"

"You forget I have no internet. I'm lucky Ilaria is keeping tabs on the listing for me and bringing by her phone when I need to respond to an inquiry."

Matteo reached into his back pocket. "What's his name again?"

Stella sidled next to him. He wasn't wearing cologne, perhaps that seemed a fool's errand when you worked in trash. But he gave off a clean, botanical scent, like ivy. "Severini. Paolo Severini. From Rome."

Matteo's thumbs flew across the screen. "Huh."

"What?" She leaned across him to peer at the screen.

"Well, he's not coming up." Slipping his phone back into his pocket. "I don't know. Refusing *fruttone*, leaving before breakfast, no internet footprint. Is this guy even Italian?"

She laughed despite herself. "I'm hardly one to judge."

He grinned. "You'll do."

Stella watched as Matteo started flinging bags of glass into the back of the truck. He held up her bag. "Wine for one?"

"I thought you accepted all people's garbage without comment."

"I never said without comment." Matteo smiled his sidelong grin, the silver-threaded curls that had escaped from his ponytail framing his face. "Keep careful, okay?"

"You think my glass of wine or two with dinner is going to do me in?"

His face grew still. "With this houseguest of yours?"

"*Ma dai*," she waved away his concern. "I think my ego can withstand his refusals of my pastry charms. I know this will come as a shock, but it's been known to happen."

"Not that. Something about this guy seems off. And I know I've heard something. I think he's mixed up with something with the mayor."

"They do seem tight."

"It's suspicious."

Stella silently agreed and wanted to run through possibilities with Matteo, but she hardly knew him and anyway, didn't she just make a vow to herself? "Honestly, I've decided that it's none of my business as long as I get paid."

He glanced at her, and she raised her hands with a naive grin. He laughed. "You're funny."

Am I? Stella thought to herself. She looked down and realized she was still holding the plate. "Oh! I made *sfogliatelle*. If you want—"

"*Do* I?" Matteo clasped his hands to his heart. "The day you arrived in Aramezzo was one lucky day."

Stella wondered.

Stella pulled the lemon scones out of the oven and smiled at the rich scent. One sheet was ready, the other needed another minute or two and they'd be perfect.

She knew she shouldn't have bothered, but ever since Severini had lashed out at her in British-accented English, she'd been playing with the notion that since he'd spent serious time in England, perhaps the way to his good side was through foods that reminded him of his travels.

The odds of him thrilling to a scone seemed slim at best, but if he didn't, she knew Ilaria's cousins who were coming to replace the tile in the second guest bedroom today would happily accept them. And Matteo would no doubt love a few.

Hearing a thump above her, Stella paused. Signor Severini? The thump sounded more like a dropped duffel bag than a man waking, but it must be him. It was long past his normal wake-up time. Then again, he'd gotten in so late last night she hadn't even heard him return. He must have gone somewhere after he met with Don Arrigo. She couldn't imagine that meeting could have dragged into the wee hours.

Just then, the cat galloped down the stairs. How had he gotten into the house? Ilaria's crew had blocked off every illicit entry, and yet here came the cat, with spotted flanks heaving and tail whipping from side to side. The cat stopped to clean a spot on his back and then trotted to the kitchen and sat down, staring at Stella, his black chin raised to sniff the air.

"What?" she asked, surprising herself by using English. As if the cat spoke either.

But he seemed to understand her, the way his eyes flicked to the cooling tray of scones, as if politely reminding her she'd neglected to offer him one.

Why was it her lot in life to be pestered by tenacious males who couldn't take a hint? She wagged her finger, "Not for you, you . . . whatever the word for mongrel is in cat."

The cat lowered his ears, his nose wrinkled.

She rolled her eyes. How would she get the cat out of here? She hadn't reckoned how lucky she was that as quickly as he arrived, he'd always left. His deciding she was no longer a threat wasn't exactly a positive turn of events. She slipped her oven mitt back on her hand and turned in time to catch the cat leaping onto the counter. He lifted a paw over a scone and let it hover. She waved at him and he glared at her, hunkering his black chin down and hissing.

"Get *out!*" she whisper-screamed, not wanting to wake Signor Severini, but needing to get the cat off her clean counter and far away from her cooling scones.

Not taking her eyes off the cat, she reached behind her for the broom, but the beast must have guessed her intentions. He whisked around, taking the flour canister with him as he leaped to the floor and raced away. Most cats wouldn't have been able to even budge a full container of flour, but this cat's enormous proportions made anything possible.

"Argh!" Stella moaned in frustration at the flour all over the counter and floor. And her scones. Flinging off the oven mitt, she wet a bundle of paper towels and began sponging off the counter, scooting flour toward the sink. She got onto the floor and pushed the flour into a pile and then scooped up what she could. Mopping could wait. Stella picked up a scone and brushed it off. Maybe a dusting of flour would be okay?

The scones! The thought smacked her just as an acrid scent accosted her nose. She gagged, never having been able to abide the smell of burning. She reached into the oven to pull out the offending tray of blackening scones and then squealed at the hot pan. In her haste, she'd forgotten the oven mitt. What a rookie mistake. As she pulled on the mitt, she fervently hoped she hadn't woken Signor Severini.

An hour later, the kitchen back in order and the offending scones tossed into the trash can, the salvageable ones sprinkled with cinnamon and sugar to mask the dusting of flour, she listened at the base of the stairs. Was he taking a day off? Sleeping in?

Though how he'd been able to sleep through all the ruckus was beyond her.

She crept upstairs and found his door wide open, revealing the empty bedroom, towels stacked neatly on the embroidered coverlet. Did the cat open the door somehow? Signor Severini left the door closed whether or not he was in, but admittedly, the latch was faulty. The cat could have pawed it open from the inside. As if in confirmation, Stella noticed the window cracked open enough to admit the entrance of a feline, and a tree limb conveniently brushing past the lower edge of the frame.

Well, that solved the mystery of the cat's continual presence. Hardly a satisfying conclusion. She'd have to get that limb pruned or the cat would invite himself in whenever any guest left the window open. A problem for another day, she reminded herself. It didn't look like that couple from Australia would stay after all, since she'd answered their question about a washer and dryer by sadly saying their only option would be the laundromat on the edge of town. She supposed bikers would particularly need access to laundering facilities, and mentally added "washer" to her never-ending list of upcoming purchases. Though how she'd pay for a washer if people who needed a washer wouldn't stay at her establishment seemed a problem.

She put a finger on her cheek for a moment and then her eyes widened as she realized a solution—she'd offer laundry service as part of the fee and haul clothes to the laundromat herself. It wouldn't cost much, only time. One more reason to hound the internet company to install

Wi-Fi so she could update the website.

Stella turned back to the stairs and stopped. Something about the room bothered her. Something...*the towels*. Folded on the made bed.

Yesterday morning, Severini had left with his laptop, no doubt to secure Wi-Fi. She'd walked to Ilaria's to drop off *sfogliatelle* and collect the laundered linens. On the way home, she popped into the butcher to see if pastry moved him and, though he'd harrumphed at the plate, he'd taken the last two, muttering that his wife came from Naples. By the time she got home, Severini had returned. She hadn't wanted to bother him with the towels, so she'd waited until he left for his meeting with Don Arrigo. Then she'd stacked the towels on the bed.

And the towels still sat on the bed where she'd left them. Yesterday evening. He hadn't moved them to the bathroom. He hadn't even moved them off the bed to sleep. She stepped farther into the room and turned slowly, looking for any other items out of place.

His briefcase and car keys rested on the dresser. So he couldn't have left Aramezzo. Unless he rode in somebody else's car. Could he and Don Arrigo have gone to Subbiano together after all? She remembered the zigzag road up the mountain. In the dark, it would take no more than a crossing fox to spook a driver to veer over the edge.

Stella bit her lip and stared at the towels for another minute before whirling around and jogging downstairs to fling open the door. She strode through town, hoping against hope to catch sight of Signor Severini. What she wouldn't give for even a taunting barb, just to know he was safe. There! She saw him...only when she rushed forward and put a hand on the sleeve, the man who turned bore no resemblance to Severini.

No sign of him on any of the three circular roads. She jogged down to the edge of town, ignoring the curious looks of old women and young men peering down at her from their windows. Her ears perked at the sound of merry shouting, and she turned into the park to find a group of men calling out insults at each other, syncopated with the sound of bocce balls knocking together, thwack after resounding thwack.

Arriving at the side of Aramezzo's bocce court, at the edge of the playground where children climbed a dilapidated slide and pumped their mini legs on tired swings, Stella raised her hand to her eyes to scan the players. No sign of Severini.

The muscles of her shoulders released at the sight of Don Arrigo sitting on the bench. She hadn't realized that part of her had worried that Severini had shot Don Arrigo and then fled. She wondered if she should check if the gun was still in the drawer. Though that seemed perilously close to snooping, which she'd resolved to stop.

In any case, Severini hadn't injured the priest. And if Severini had indeed left Aramezzo, it must not have been with Don Arrigo. Unless they left, returned, and Severini got lost on his way home. Hardly likely. She frowned. Could Don Arrigo have left Severini somewhere? Maybe Severini pulled his gun and Don Arrigo shoved him out of the car?

She started to turn away in thought when she noticed the men calling Don Arrigo to take his turn. The priest stood and tripped over his own feet. His normally animated face looked ashen, strained. The men pulled his arm, mocking his slowness, and Don Arrigo laughed along with them, but as the sound carried to Stella, it sounded hollow.

Stella jangled her keys as she turned away, wondering where to check next. She shivered, as if someone had walked over her grave.

PART TWO

Stella hadn't noticed the bell over the door at her first visit to the bookshop, but the sound of it rattled her now.

Domenica glanced up as Stella entered and returned to the pages in front of her. Stella couldn't identify the magazine, but as she stepped to the desk, she noticed a photo spread of camo-clad hunters in front of large African animals. Could Domenica be into killing animals for sport? She certainly didn't give off that vibe, what with her allowing cats to drape themselves over the books and printers.

Stella placed a plate of *sfogliatelle* in front of the shop owner. It had been a gamble . . . she had only a few *sfogliatelle* left and loads of scones, but Italians often turned up their noses at non-Italian food, and anyway, she couldn't feel good about that fine dusting of flour thanks to that infernal cat. So, *sfogliatelle*.

Domenica's eyes widened. "What's this for?"

"I wouldn't have been able to make them without you, so I wanted to bring you a few," Stella said, shrugging.

Domenica cocked her head to the side to study the platter before delicately lifting a pastry from the plate and biting off a corner. She laughed as the shattering pastry prompted a cloud of powdered sugar to explode in her face. And then she moaned as the ricotta cheese, warm spices, and candied orange peel hit her tongue. She chewed thoughtfully with her eyes closed and put the pastry back on the plate, almost reverentially. "Wow."

Stella smiled. All right then. Domenica was okay. A little weird about cats, but we all have our vagaries.

Taking a breath, Stella said, "Did Signor Severini come in here?"

Domenica leaned back in her chair, still chewing. She plucked up the long-hair white cat Stella hadn't noticed and placed it on her lap. As she stroked the cat, the beast curled into as tight a ball as its luxurious white fur would allow, purring like a Mack truck. Finally, Domenica said, "He did."

"Can you tell me when he came in?"

Domenica thought for a moment. "Monday I think? Yes, because I was closing for lunch to head over to Adele's. She serves green pasta lasagna with mushroom bechamel on Mondays. I never miss it."

Stella stopped. "She does? Who is Adele? Where, I mean which *trattoria* ?" She shook her head. Not the time. "Never mind. Have you seen him since?"

Domenica's grin spread slowly across her face. "Only one *trattoria* in Aramezzo, my dear. Trattoria Cavour, on the *piazza* across from Bar Cappellina. It's owned by Adele's husband, and she does the cooking. And serving. He lacks his wife's following, you'll find."

Huh. Stella hadn't even noticed a *trattoria* there. She'd seen people eating sandwiches at the tables, but assumed they had gotten them at the bar. She had noticed no plates of pasta, let alone green pasta.

As if reading her thoughts, Domenica said, "You have to venture within to ascertain worth."

Stella paused for a moment. Were they still talking about the *trattoria*? Why did this woman speak in riddles? Before she could stop herself, the words flew out of her mouth. "I don't understand you."

Domenica offered a faint shrug. "I'm an enigma."

Stella frowned.

Domenica took another bite of the pastry and said, "Now, why are you searching for your guest as if he's a little boy lost on his way home from school?"

Stella nodded, grateful to be back on solid footing. "He didn't come home last night."

Domenica stroked the cat's face until it leaned into her palm. "You must care very much about him to pay such close attention to his whereabouts."

Stella's laugh sounded like a bark, and the cat stopped its purr, glaring at her with narrowed eyes. "Hardly."

Domenica nodded as if to herself, soothing the cat until it began purring again. "You have a premonition that something bad has happened. Something that would prevent your guest from paying his bill."

"Premonition?"

"All the women in your family had the gift."

Stella stepped backward. "Gift?"

Domenica nodded.

"You knew my family?"

"It's a small town, my dear. We can hardly avoid running into each other."

"My mother, you knew my mother?" Stella could hear her voice tightening.

It occurred to her that this could be why the only people she'd bothered trying to get to know were too young to know her mother (Matteo) or too new to Aramezzo (Ilaria). She didn't want to be confronted with information about her mother before she was ready.

Stella's mother had been a study in contrasts. She'd declared that she'd been a fun and vibrant young woman until having Stella. And yet, in those rare times that Stella's mother discussed her youth, she described it as if jackals had surrounded her, nipping at her until she cowered in corners. Stella couldn't make sense of the competing stories.

Domenica shook her head. "No, your grandparents and aunt. I arrived after your mother left to marry your father."

At the mention of her father, Stella stared at her shoes, waves of grief she'd thought long settled crashing over her again. Grief for her father. Grief for her sister Grazie, who had filled each day with the love their mother denied Stella. Even grief for her mother, because as angry as Stella often found herself at the elder Stella, she never could help seeing her as a tragic figure, her heart closed and dark. And grief for herself, alone in this stupid town with a guest who somehow couldn't make his way home. Tears rose in her eyes and she felt like she couldn't breathe. Oh, no, not again. She thought these panic attacks were long behind her. She hadn't even had any when the story came out in the *Times*. But now, she gasped, like a landed fish.

Domenica studied Stella's wavering expression with a worried frown. She reached across the desk to take Stella's hand. "Breathe, my love. You're here now."

Stella tried to focus on the smell of the books laced with the spice from the pastry. The draught coming from the old windows. The sunlight slanting in. She felt her heartbeat slow. She nodded, embarrassed at her mini-freak out. What must this woman think of her?

Domenica prompted, "Now, tell me how you know your guest is missing and not just out for a jog."

The roar of thoughts cycloning through Stella's mind quieted further as she reached for an answer. "He-he . . . " She swallowed and tried again. "He didn't come down this morning. And I saw the towels I gave him last night were still on his bed."

"Who goes to bed with towels on the bed?"

"Right. You think that's strange, too?"

"I do. Though the police won't, if you're hoping to solicit their assistance."

It was, indeed, exactly what Stella had considered her next move.

"Do you suspect an accident? Or foul play?"

Stella's thoughts flitted to the gun, possibly still in the drawer, possibly on Severini, or possibly made up. "I don't know."

"Sure you do. You have a terrible poker face, by the way."

Stella said nothing. How to talk about her feeling that Severini had some dark dealings with citizens of Aramezzo without letting on that she'd been eavesdropping? She remembered her sojourn in the chicken coop. That might actually count as spying.

Domenica nodded as if Stella had answered. "You don't think he left for an excursion overnight? I know he's been taking almost daily trips to Subbiano."

Shaking her head, Stella said, "He left his keys."

"There's no place to stay overnight in Subbiano, anyway." Domenica thought aloud. "You've looked all over town? The women in the alley behind the church are often full of observations you wouldn't even think they'd be interested in. And the bar, of course. Someone there will have information."

Stella's face flushed. "I haven't been in yet."

Domenica's face grew still. "Sounds like you've found your moment."

Stella waited outside the bar. For what? An invitation? She shook her head in annoyance at herself. When the door opened, she backed up and craned her neck, staring at the roofline, pretending an interest in the pitch and cornices. That super svelte and elegant woman she'd seen on her first day glanced at her with mild curiosity but said nothing. The woman stalked away with precise, mincing steps. Stella watched her leave, adjusting her bandana in thought.

The sound of the bustle in the bar cut off suddenly as the door closed again, leaving Stella with the foggy landscape at her back, a crow cutting through the faded sky.

Pull your socks up! She ordered herself. But she'd never been good in groups of people. She always felt more comfortable on the margins, where she could communicate with one person at a time and social cues were less overwhelming. In groups, she often wondered what she was supposed to do with her arms.

Before she could talk herself out of it, she pushed open the glass door and stepped into the bar. She stopped still in the center of the room, feeling all eyes on her. Conversation ebbed away. Ignoring a whisper to her left that absolutely included her name, she lifted her chin and strode to the bar. "*Espresso, per favore*," she said to the owner behind the bar, a heavyset woman dressed all in white with hair to match, pulled back into a loose bun.

The woman cocked her head curiously.

It hit Stella suddenly, and she wished she could fish the words back as easily as a cheesecloth bag of seasoning from a soup. "*Caffè!*" she corrected herself. She'd momentarily forgotten that in Italy, coffee was *espresso*, just called *caffè*.

The woman pressed her lips together to fight a smile as she asked softly, "*Americano o . . .*"

"*No, no, Italiano.*" She did not want an *espresso* with water added to approximate American coffee. She shuddered at the thought. The woman's grin broadened at Stella's gesture, and she turned to the *espresso* machine to pull a shot.

Despite Stella's sinking worry about Signor Severini and the weight of what seemed a million eyes on her, she couldn't help but admire the elegant lines of the espresso machine. She tried to determine the brand, but then remembered her mission. She scanned the bar, looking for likely candidates to strike up a conversation. Never her strong suit in the best of situations, but desperate times and all that.

The assembled villagers ran mostly to farmers, judging from their clothing and work boots, but Stella noticed a woman with curly hair as wild as her own, but plaited into a series of braids that surrounded her head like a crown. The woman tipped a glass of freshly squeezed orange juice (judging by the almost green scent) into the mouth of a little boy with enormous brown eyes and a red and white spotted stuffed dog clutched to his chest. Stella heard him tell his mother, "Pimpa wants some, too, Mamma."

Pimpa... that sounded familiar. Stella remembered now a series of Pimpa comic books on a low shelf at Domenica's bookshop.

The young mother laughed. "Dogs don't drink orange juice, *tesoro*." As she moved to return the glass to the counter, Stella caught a whiff of lavender. Not lavender perfume or soap, there wasn't any thread of alcohol or carrier oil, the scent was purely floral. The woman stroked her son's cheek and Stella felt something behind her throat, like when she smelled rising bread. It seemed a sign.

As Stella accepted the coffee from the woman behind the counter, she turned and caught the gaze of the young mother. "*Ciao*, I'm Stella. Stella Buchanan. I own the old Mazzoli house on the edge of town."

The woman studied Stella's face for a moment before her face warmed in an answering smile. "Yes, of course. *Piacere*. I'm Marta and this thirsty boy is Ascanio." Marta... the name sounded familiar. Stella realized this must be the Marta with the sheep next to Domenica's.

"Ascanio." Stella smiled at the boy, swiping now at the counter to wrap his hands around the juice glass. She remembered an Ascanio related to some Trojan king. "Big name for a small boy."

"It was his father's." The woman's face tightened and Stella wished she'd kept her stupid mouth shut. But a moment later, Marta's face cleared, and she said, "If the gossip is correct, this is your first stay in Aramezzo?"

"Gossip is, in fact, correct."

"Well, it had to happen sometime," Marta smiled. "And you know the Americans, I suppose?"

"The Americans?"

"Yes, they live in the villa up the road. You don't know them?"

Stella shook her head.

Marta laughed good-naturedly. "I'm not sure why I supposed that all Americans must know each other. Now that I'm thinking of it, they leave with the summer."

The woman behind the bar pushed the container of sugar packets to Stella, who took a plain sugar and shook it before opening it with a satisfying rip. As Stella stirred, the woman behind the bar offered, "The Americans left in August. The girls start school before September and you know they take a while to get their closets together." Was it her imagination, or did Stella detect a note of amusement in the woman's voice?

Stella raised the diminutive cup to her lips and breathed in the nutty *espresso*. She took a sip and closed her eyes. Yes, Italian coffee was wonderful, but she just assumed that in a small town like this it would be lackluster. This was . . . well, this was the opposite of lackluster. This was sublime.

The woman didn't seem to notice Stella staring at her cup, dumbfounded. How had she been subsisting on moka coffee? That Domenica knew what she was talking about. If she'd meant the coffee, that is. The woman was inscrutable.

As Stella clinked the cup into the saucer, the woman behind the bar said, "Welcome to Aramezzo, Stella. I'm Romina."

Stella smiled. "*Piacere*, nice to meet you."

"And this is my husband, Roberto." She called across the bar to a lanky man leaning on the counter to talk to the farmers. "Roberto!"

He held a finger up to excuse himself from the group and patted the bar as he walked. "What's up?"

Romina gestured to Stella. "This is Stella. She's new to Aramezzo."

He gave her a frank look of appraisal. "Stella Mazzoli?"

"Buchanan, but yes . . . that's me." Stella hoped her voice sounded lighter than she felt.

He sucked his cheeks in as if about to say something and then clearly changed his mind. "How's the house?"

Stella laughed. "I'd say I've seen worse, but I wouldn't want to get off on the wrong start by lying to you."

It took him a moment and then he threw his head back and belly-laughed so loudly the entire bar turned to stare at him before shaking their heads and chuckling over their coffee and pastries. Everyone took it in stride, so Stella assumed Roberto often laughed like joy had caught him and swung him by the tail.

She went on, "Ilaria's family has been helping me with the safety repairs, but soon I'll need to update the place. I'm hoping income from the bed-and-breakfast will help with that." She hoped the segue was deft. "Say, speaking of, have you seen my guest wandering around? A Signor Severini?"

"You lost your guest?" Romina smiled. "Hardly a way to begin."

"Nothing like that." Stella forced a chuckle. Then improvised, "No, he had a call come in and I wanted to give him the message."

Her new friends—no, friends was too strong a word—the people that Stella now knew to call by their names exchanged glances.

"What?" she asked.

Romina picked up the empty juice glass and turned to deposit it in the sink.

Roberto said, "We're hoping he's not like your future guests."

Affronted, Stella asked, "Why? What's wrong with him?" She realized as she asked that she already knew the answer and her defensiveness was just that. Defensiveness. She held up a hand. "Never mind, I think I know. And believe me, I'm hoping the same."

Marta swiped up crumbs from Ascanio's breakfast. She seemed to choose her words as she answered, "Your Italian is good, obviously. Fluent. But there's a word we have in dialect you may not know. *Castrino?*"

"*Castrino?*" Why did that word register as familiar? Suddenly, Stella had a memory of her mother storming out of the funeral home in the middle of ordering caskets—one regular size and one child-sized. "*Castrino*," she'd muttered under her breath before shouting it over her shoulder. Stella had been left to negotiate with the funeral director, who pleaded that this was the very best price. She never forgot his oily smile.

Marta nodded. "It's not a very . . . nice expression. It refers to the men who remove an animal's . . . "

"Balls," finished Roberto. "So a *castrino* is a man who profits from removing innocent people from their money."

Stella thought for a moment. "I understand. And believe me, I get it. I'm not his biggest fan either."

Another exchange of glances.

Romina chose her words carefully. "He'd given Aramezzo to understand that you were helping him with a . . . project."

"Project? What kind of project?"

Roberto said, "Paolo Severini has been working with Marcello Bernini, Aramezzo's mayor, on getting Americans to move to Aramezzo and Subbiano."

To Stella's blank look, Roberto went on. "Subbiano is a *frazione* of Aramezzo, so all of its governing—from trash schedule to road repair—happens here."

"But why would Signor Severini be interested in what happens in Subbiano? And why would he say I'm a part of it?" She looked around at the faces watching her, including the farmers at the other end of the bar who had abandoned their conversation to listen. "Because this is the first I'm hearing of it, I swear."

Marta shrugged as she knelt to zip Ascanio's jacket. "It's all a bit hush-hush at the moment. I suspect Marcello knows the town might have some strong feelings, so he's keeping it under wraps. But we heard Marcello say you were going to work with them to get the right sort of

Americans into Subbiano. Those with Italian connections, that wouldn't just use the house as a vacation home, but would live here, like you do. Permanently."

Stella shook her head, confused. "I don't live here permanently."

Romina turned. "You don't? But—"

"I don't. I'm only here long enough to turn the bed-and-breakfast around and sell it before I . . ."

Romina patted Stella's hand as her words trailed off. "We'll see. Aramezzo has a way of turning visitors into residents. Right, Marta?"

Marta brushed a curl off her cheek and smiled. "Me and my sheep, yes. And my neighbor, Domenica. You never know where fate will take you. Maybe you'll stay."

Stella didn't understand why her eyes suddenly stung. She blinked rapidly and caught her breath before saying, "So I'm guessing the rest of Aramezzo isn't big on Signor Severini's plan?"

Roberto shook his head. "Marcello keeps trying to convince us that an influx of new residents will suit Aramezzo. But we're used to being a ways from the tourist trail, visited only by bikers and penitents. And we like it that way."

"I still don't understand why Signor Severini told people I'm helping him. He had to know that I would correct the record."

Romina leaned forward a touch before answering for them all, "*Cara*, I believe he counted on you not gossiping with us villagers."

Stella's face flushed, and in her embarrassment, she said without thinking. "He wasn't wrong. Domenica made me come in today."

Marta laughed. "The thing about a *castrino*, he often sees more than we wish. And preys on that."

Stella nodded. She sipped the last of her *caffè*, placing the cup back on the saucer before pushing it forward. "This is all very illuminating. But I still don't know where to find Signor Severini. And now I need to have a word with him before he sullies my good name. Or whatever good is left."

Marta said, "Aramezzo is small, he couldn't have gone far. But Stella? I don't know about having a word with him. I'm not sure he's ... well-tempered."

Judging by the look of concern Romina focused on Marta, Stella wondered if perhaps the young woman had had a run-in with Severini. Or maybe had a history she'd rather forget with a bad-tempered man.

Stella's face grew grim. "I'll be fine. I always am."

She reached into her pocket to pull out a handful of change.

Romina put out her hand, her eyes glistening. "No, you're covered. Consider it a welcome to Aramezzo."

Roberto nodded, though again, his eyes that flicked over her face seemed to hold some emotion she couldn't read.

Stella pushed her hand back into her pocket. "*Grazie*. That's very generous."

Romina grinned. "I think we can spare the ninety cents."

"Ninety cents! That's all?"

Roberto chuckled warmly. "You were expecting more?"

Stella shrugged. "I've only ever stayed in cities when I've been in Italy. Roma, Milano. Bologna."

Romina picked up her cup and said, "Well, I'm glad the price is agreeable because you'll be paying next time. And there'll be a next time?"

Stella smiled. "I'll see you tomorrow."

Emboldened by her fruitful trip to the bar, Stella wondered where she could pop into next. She stopped in thought. She guessed it wasn't fruitful, exactly. In fact, it raised more questions than it answered. Even so, something about it left her feeling ... better. In a way she couldn't articulate and truthfully didn't have time to figure out.

She needed to find Severini. The toad. No amount of money was worth this aggravation. She needed to get him out on his ear. The disappearing was one thing: she could summon concern at the image of him in a shadowy back alley with his foot twisted, or his head dented on a stone step. Cats milling about him. She shuddered. But this revelation that he'd been telling tales about her, either expecting she wouldn't find out or wouldn't have the stones to do anything about it, that was the limit. She was sick to death of men underestimating her.

Stella caught herself. It wouldn't do to paint all men with the same pastry brush. Matteo certainly seemed a decent sort. Like her old friend Ernie, Matteo seemed to see her as a person worth knowing, not as a "girl."

She stopped outside the *alimentari* and peered in. Cristiana unpacked boxes in an unhurried way. Stella stepped in and said, "Excuse me, Cristiana?"

Cristiana looked up surprised, and Stella realized this might be the first time she'd addressed her. No matter, she hurried on. "Has Paolo Severini been in today?"

Cristiana scratched her chin absently and then called into the back, "Papà!" Stella hadn't even known the elderly man who sliced prosciutto when the shop was busy was Cristiana's father. "Has that Severini guy staying at Casale Mazzoli been in today?"

"No," came a thin voice from the backroom.

Cristiana called back, "Not even when I was making deliveries?"

"You make deliveries?" Stella asked.

Cristiana gestured to her scooter waiting outside. "Some of the older villagers can't get here daily, or can't carry a six-pack of bottled water up the hill."

Stella had no idea. She wondered how the scooter made it up the stairs and then remembered cobblestone ramps flanked each side of the steps, which allowed service trucks to straddle the stairs and climb from one level to another and scooters to motor up the ramp. So many adjustments to life in a hill town.

Cristiana's father shuffled out of the backroom, straightening his apron. His hair swept back carefully from his lined forehead. "I haven't seen Signor Severini for days. Didn't he come in for a *panino* over the weekend?"

"That's right! Mortadella on *torta al testo* bread." Cristiana turned to Stella. "You've had it?"

She shook her head. "Not yet. I mean, I've had mortadella of course, but I don't know about *torta al testo.*"

"It's our local flatbread. We get ours from the baker. You must try it."

Stella smiled, the injunction feeling less hostile and demanding than it would have just an hour ago. "I will. But Signor Severini . . . "

"He always got that *panino.* But my father is right, we haven't seen him since Saturday. No, Sunday."

"Okay, thank you."

"You've tried calling him?"

"Yes. My cell isn't set up, but I called from my landline. Straight to voicemail. About a hundred times."

At the worry in Stella's voice, Cristiana pressed her lips together in thought. "I'll tell him you're looking for him if I see him. He passes by a couple of times a day since we're on the way to the parking lot."

Stella nodded in thanks.

Popping into the *fruttivendolo* proved as useless, though she hadn't been to the *fruttivendolo* before and couldn't believe her eyes at the shelves of gleaming produce. The greens alone . . . she found lettuces she'd never seen before and some sort of cooking green that made her mouth water, imagining those fresh leaves briefly boiled and dressed with garlicky olive oil.

Stella's stomach told her the hour even before she checked her watch. Almost noon. She headed home, stopping to watch Enzo, who seemed to have pulled his hair until it stood on end and had taken up walking in a circuit. He walked twenty meters in one direction, stopped, pivoted, and walked twenty meters in the other. The butcher, who must be on his way home for lunch himself grunted to Stella that Enzo must have forgotten his key. That didn't explain Enzo's wide eyes and lurching steps, but Stella realized there was nothing she could do, so she continued home.

She paused as she opened the door to make sure no silver-spotted tabby barreled past her legs. The house lay silent. She cut herself two slices of bread and used them to make a salami sandwich, chewing as she called Severini again. Voicemail.

As she swallowed the last of her sandwich, her thoughts returned to that mysterious gleam of silver. If nothing else, she needed to know. She wiped her hands on her jeans and nonchalantly made her way to the stairwell. Foolish, she knew. As if acting like she was not about to violate her anti-spying resolution effectively eliminated her transgression. She climbed the steps, one by one, listening for the sound of the front door opening. It would be just her luck to have Severini return home to find her rifling through his drawers.

She paused after opening his door, but the sight of the stack of towels fueled her into action. Stella flung open the drawer. Nothing but pants. She sighed in relief. She talked a good game, but she didn't know what she'd do if she stumbled across a gun.

Like exclamation marks appearing over a cartoon version of herself, she realized that if there *were* a gun, it was likely hidden. Listening out for another brief second, she hurriedly lifted each pair of slacks.

Nothing.

She opened the second drawer, her breathing shallow. She lifted a blue silk shirt and underneath it . . . a flash of silver.

The gun.

She almost dropped the shirt in surprise, her breath caught in her chest. Forcing herself to inhale, she peered more closely at the gun. Stella had no idea what kind it was, having always skipped gun descriptions in her murder mysteries. But she knew enough to know it was most definitely a gun.

She wasn't sure if she felt better or worse at the sight of it. Good to know Severini wasn't out on a shooting spree. But it didn't answer the question of why he thought he'd need a gun in the first place.

As she closed the drawer, her eyes caught on Severini's briefcase, leaning upright against the chair. Maybe something lay hidden in its depths... maybe a matchbook or a brochure from a place he frequented that might know how to find him. Silence roared in her ears and she opened the briefcase, pulling out a ream of papers. The first page seemed to be a legal document, which she'd always struggled to make sense of in English, let alone Italian. None of the names on the documents looked familiar. She frowned. Maybe these were templates? After all, wherever a monetary designation was mentioned, it read €1,00. No one would create so much documentation for a good or service worth only €1,00.

The next paper and the next, actually most of the following documents, all seemed to be variations on that theme, with unfamiliar names and no real money mentioned. One name, though, appeared on all the documents—Danilo Crespi. Stella adjusted her bandana in thought. Maybe Severini was a pawn in a larger scheme, one orchestrated by Danilo Crespi. Maybe this Danilo Crespi had something to do with Severini's disappearance.

The only other piece of paper in the briefcase was a handwritten list of addresses. Checkmarks dotted the far end of some listings, along with a date. She read more closely and realized that the dates were indicated as dates of death. She read the addresses more carefully, looking for some clue, and realized that all addresses were for homes in Subbiano. Quite a lot of them, perhaps forty in all. Was this akin to New Yorkers combing the obits to find a new apartment?

A creak sounded from the stairwell and Stella froze. Instantly, she felt sweat prickling her underarms. Could Severini have returned, so quietly she hadn't heard the door open? Had she been so distracted?

She hesitated. Her body wanted to fling the papers back into the briefcase and crawl under the bed, while her mind sprinted in all directions, searching for acceptable reasons for standing in her guest's room, her hands in his papers.

Another creak, closer this time.

What could she do? What did she have time for?

The cat sauntered in and Stella's breath released.

The cat. It had been the cat, climbing the stairs.

Still, it felt like a narrow miss. She needed to get out of the room that suddenly seemed to not contain enough oxygen. She straightened the papers the best she could and shoved them back in the briefcase.

Tossing a surly glance at the cat, who jumped onto Severini's bed and stood, staring at her, she left the room. She pulled on a sweater from the rack by the door and then stepped into the street. As she walked through town, she stopped every villager, even the ones she'd never noticed before, and asked if they'd seen Signor Severini. Most looked at her as if she was mad, but she cared less and less the more dire his absence appeared. At the top level of Aramezzo, Stella ducked into Chiesa di Santa Chiara di Aramezzo. Don Arrigo's bocce game must have finished by now and she needed to talk to him about his meeting with Severini.

Silence descended as soon as she stepped across the church threshold, like a velvet curtain across a baroque stage.

No one sat on the pews or loitered outside the confessionals. No one milled around the niches that held statues, paintings, and what looked like crypts. Crypts? She knew many Italian churches held relics of saints. Could the pilgrims to Aramezzo be coming for the sight of a saint's finger or uncorrupted remains? She'd read about a cathedral in . . . Gubbio, maybe? Some Umbrian town planted on the tourist network and thus with a guidebook entry. The cathedral boasted a saint that when exhumed years after burial, hadn't degraded at all. The awed villagers transferred the corpse to a glass coffin in celebration of the miracle. As many murder mysteries as Stella read, the very thought made her stomach turn over.

An illuminated niche at the far end of the church glowed, drawing Stella's eye. She glanced at the painting in the niche and then stopped. The image pulled Stella forward, her eyes fixed as if hypnotized. Unaware of her feet moving, the painting drew her in. Her eyes widened and all thoughts of Severini evaporated into the darkness gathered beyond the vaulted ceiling.

A Madonna and child, classic fare for Italian churches, big and small. But something about this one quickened her heart. The Madonna—her eyes, they were light grey. Like hers, like her mother's. An unusual color in central Italy. The cheekbones, too . . . high and prominent, making the face appear almost like a statue. But warmer than a statue, the painting exuded love, acceptance, delight. How could a painting be so like her mother, and yet so different? The Madonna caressed her baby's face, as Marta had caressed Ascanio's. A gesture Stella had never received from her mother, but somehow, the painting didn't fill her with familiar grief. She sighed, as a window opened into a part of her that felt filled, complete enough for this world.

"She's beautiful, isn't she?"

Stella jumped, her hand over her heart, now beating so harshly she could hear the blood thrumming in her ears. She glared at the man who had appeared beside her like an apparition. A slight man, though he seemed taller, with his white candy floss hair standing on end. Nevertheless, she was almost eye level with his face, close enough to notice that he had one blue eye and one green. Though perhaps that was a trick of the light.

"There's a lore about this painting," the man said with a soft smile, turning back to the Madonna. He seemed unaware of Stella's writhing annoyance. "A relatively unknown painter, but what we can find of his earlier work suggests that before this, he painted exclusively Roman, rather than Christian, iconography. Some say that this Madonna is actually Cybele, the mother of gods. The strands between Aramezzo and Cybele are strong indeed."

He stared unblinking at the painting, not noticing that Stella could parse no meaning from his words. It didn't seem to matter though, as she turned back to gaze at the Madonna's face, so familiar and yet so removed. She and the man stood together, in an easy silence that stretched, thickening around them, surrounding the strangers in a swirl of shared devotion.

A tapping sound like a tropical bird pecking in a rainforest shattered their reverie, and Stella glanced to the front of the church to find Cinzia slipping through a door off the main vestibule. That must be the hallway to the church offices. Right. Stella's destination.

She turned to the man, unsure if she owed him a farewell after their moments together. She found his eyes resting on her, a gentle smile lighting his face. "Stella of Casale Mazzoli, may I presume?"

She nodded, suddenly aware of the chocolate streaks on her jeans and a piece of dough she hadn't yet washed off her bandana.

"Pardon my familiarity. Given my history with your family, it feels like I'm allowed the indulgence. I am Cosimo."

"You knew my mother?"

"Not well, no. But I knew your grandparents since we were children. Fine people."

"I never met them." She frowned and gazed at her feet, suddenly ashamed of never having made the trek know her family, never even thought about them enough to ask her mother.

"No, I expect not."

She looked back up at him, and his smile remained, warm and intent.

Gently he said, "It's good you're here. It's been difficult to witness the demise of their lifetime of work. Not just the *casale*, but those groves, that garden."

"I hope I can fix it."

"I'm sure you can, my dear."

She shook her head. "I wish I had your confidence. It all seems overwhelming. What do I know about olive trees?" Why was she confessing all this to a total stranger? Was it the intimacy of the church? The man's confidential tones?

He patted her arm reassuringly. "One thing at a time. Your ancestors planted those trees when your great-grandmother was in pigtails. They can be patient a little longer."

She raised her hands. "I don't know how to begin. Not many olive trees in New York City."

"Isn't that the truth?" He chuckled and reached into his pocket to pull out a business card. "If you don't mind the older set, there's a friend of mine who helps locals with their trees. He's passionate about keeping tradition alive, so it's a volunteer project for him."

Relief flooded around Stella's shoulders. "You're kidding."

He patted his pockets. "I am quite serious, though I am sadly without a pen. I don't suppose . . . ?"

She held up her empty hands, but then remembered the pen she always kept in her pocket, a holdover from working in restaurants and needing to make frequent notes on recipes. She handed him the pen and he took it with thanks, writing a phone number on the back of the card.

"There's that, my dear. And on the flip side, you'll find my information. Stop by my shop sometime. We'll have tea."

She nodded, glancing at the card that read *Foro Antiquariato,* in what looked like type from an ancient typewriter. She looked up and asked, "Cosimo, have you met the guest staying at Casale Mazzoli? Paolo Severini?"

A shadow passed over his eyes. Though it fled so quickly, perhaps she could chalk it up to a simple look of consideration. Those eyes of two different colors—she was sure of that now—made it difficult to read. He offered her a small smile. "I'm afraid I have yet to have that pleasure."

She nodded, and turned her head back to the Madonna, as if in farewell.

"You are a Mazzoli, through and through, aren't you? The eyes, the tilt of the chin." He cocked his head before breaking into a grin. "And, as I've heard, quite the independent spirit."

She smiled weakly.

"Now, when you come to call, I hope you'll bring some of those pastries I've heard Ilaria raving about?"

She laughed now. "You can count on it."

"Excellent," he nodded. "Now, if you'll excuse me, the Madonna and I have more communing to do." He put his hands into the pockets of his baggy plaid pants and turned his attention back to the painting.

Stella opened her mouth to add something more, a goodbye, perhaps an appreciation for having met him in this fortuitous way, but something about the stillness that washed over his face, lit in profile, stalled her. She tiptoed out so as not to draw his attention from his meditations.

Pulling open the door, Stella's footsteps were immediately muffled by the deep carpet. Cinzia sat at the desk at the end of the room, in front of a glass door that seemed at odds with the ancient building. Stella stopped herself just as she was about to greet Cinzia, remembering they hadn't met. Their entire interaction had been more of the stalking variety.

Clearing her throat, Stella waited for Cinzia to acknowledge her, but the woman kept her eyes glued on the computer screen, her fingers flying across the keyboard. Finally, Stella said, "Excuse me?"

Cinzia jumped in her seat and then hastily covered up her gesture by straightening her scarf around her neck. She stretched her lips across her mouth in an approximation of a Miss America smile. She leaned across the table toward Stella as if to clasp Stella's hand. "Yes? Can I help you?"

Stella decided Cinzia must be an intense person. "Yes, we haven't met yet. I'm Stella Buchanan."

Cinzia looked unimpressed, and Stella suddenly remembered that she'd been avoiding the woman's calls and handwritten notes inviting her to join them at church. "I'm looking for Signor Severini. He, um… told me he had an appointment with Don Arrigo yesterday and I haven't seen him since."

Cinzia glowered. "What does that have to do with Don Arrigo?"

A very intense person. Stella tried for a casual shrug. "Not a thing." Remembering what she knew from the villagers, she tried for a conspiratorial tone. "Look, I don't like this any more than you do. This guy is like a burnt stew. You just can't get the smell out."

Cinzia's lip curled in a smile.

"But I have a message I need to get to him and I can't find him. I'm hoping you have ideas about where he went after his meeting with Don Arrigo."

At Stella's intentional look of innocence, Cinzia softened. "I wish I could, honest. But he left without saying anything."

"Do you know what time it was?"

Cinzia checked her watch and then laughed at herself. Obviously, the answer wouldn't be there. Stella laughed, too, adding, "I do the same thing when I'm asked about the time, and I don't even wear a watch."

Cinzia shook hers and held it out. "This one doesn't even work, I only wear it for the design."

Stella said, "So pretty, I love the silver rabbits around the edge."

Smiling, Cinzia said, "You like rabbits?"

Honestly, Stella had never thought about it, but she said, "Do I! I begged my mother for one when I was young, but she told me rabbits were only good for pasta sauce."

The woman looked horrified. "I would never eat my rabbits. Never!"

"Of course not!" Stella tried to backpedal. Cinzia seemed to feel about rabbits as Domenica did about cats. "My mother just didn't understand. She wouldn't even let me get a cat."

"Oh well, no loss there. Cats are always taking swipes at my rabbits."

Stella wondered if she'd finally found the single person in Aramezzo who cringed at the enormous cat population. She heard villagers joke about how there were more cats in Aramezzo than people, and she didn't understand how they could sound so cheerful about this dire situation. "Tell me about it. I sort of have one that came with Casale Mazzoli, and it's just the worst beast, clawing and hissing and making a general mess."

"I know that cat. I think his mission is to trip me whenever I walk down the street."

"Darting out of corners, that's got to be the same cat." Stella and Cinzia grinned at each other. Remembering the thread of the conversation, Stella went on, "So, do you remember when Signor Severini left?"

"It was dark. Maybe around seven?" A look of recognition passed over her face and Cinzia snapped her fingers. "I remember now! He said he needed to pick up a bottle of wine and asked where he could buy one."

Finally! Something to go on. "What did you tell him?"

Cinzia frowned. "That must be why I forgot. The owner of the wine shop is preparing for the olive harvest, so he closed the shop for the month. I mentioned Cristiana's, but when he left I remembered that they'd be closed, too. I'm not sure where he went. Maybe he drove to Assisi?"

"Maybe. But his car is still here."

"Hmm." Cinzia straightened the papers on her desk. "Well, I'm sorry I can't help you."

"Is Don Arrigo here? Maybe he has an idea of where—"

"I'm afraid that won't be possible." Cinzia's clipped tones surprised

Stella, who had thought perhaps Cinzia might successfully drag her to church after all. Maybe they could get coffee afterward, talk. Kitchens were so full of men, she rarely had the opportunity to meet other women.

"Is . . . is Don Arrigo not here?" Stella glanced toward the glass door. "I can leave a message or something."

Cinzia put down the papers. "Look, I don't mean to be rude, but I have a lot of work to do. So does Don Arrigo. Your houseguest demanded more than his share of meetings, which has meant Don Arrigo hasn't been able to tend to his flock. He needs time to catch up, comfort the sick, celebrate with the well. You'll understand?" Cinzia's beseeching tone softened the harshness of her words.

Stella remembered the scene on the street, how Cinzia bristled on Don Arrigo's behalf. The woman clearly felt protective of the priest. Stella smiled at Cinzia. If she kept walking the streets, she was bound to run into Don Arrigo somewhere. "No problem at all. I appreciate your taking the time. And I'd love to see your rabbits one day."

Cinzia softened again. "Well, I have enough rabbit fur on me to make a whole animal."

Stella followed Cinzia's gaze and saw her lap covered with strands of long fur. She laughed.

Cinzia shook her head in bemused wonderment, with an expression Stella noted on mothers complaining about their children's drawing on every available surface like da Vinci or whizzing through math books faster than Amazon would deliver new ones. Cinzia half-heartedly brushed her skirt, saying, "Hardly professional, I know, but I went home for lunch and couldn't find my lint roller. My father must have moved it again."

Nodding, Stella strove for a note of reassurance when she said, "There are worse things to have on your clothes than rabbit fur. As a chef, I happen to know this is factually true."

Cinzia grinned up at Stella.

It wasn't an offer of coffee, but perhaps there was promise here, after all.

Stella found Don Arrigo more quickly than she expected. In fact, she crashed directly into him as she rounded the corner into the tunnel.

He caught hold of her shoulders. "Slow down there, Stella. Aramezzo will teach you there is no medal for arriving out of breath. No matter what your destination."

Well, he certainly seemed to have found his serene countenance again.

"You look happy," Stella said, with a furrowed brow.

"Why shouldn't I be?" he laughed, hoisting his shopping bag. "It's chestnut season! I got a bag of them and some new wine, plus sausages from Bruno."

She stared at him, but he didn't notice and went on, beaming. "Ah, if there's anything in the world better than a fine meal, I don't know what it is."

This she did not know how to answer, as she happened to agree with him. Instead, she said, "I've stopped in to ask about Paolo Severini."

The priest's face froze. "Is that right?"

Stella nodded. "Cinzia and I had quite a cozy little chat."

Don Arrigo's eyes slid away from her.

Stella went on, "You see, Paolo Severini seems to have gone missing."

Don Arrigo's gaze snapped back to her. "Missing?"

"Missing. Do you have any idea where he could have gone?"

He shook his head. "I'm afraid I don't."

"He had a meeting with you before he disappeared."

"*Allora*," he shrugged. "It's a small town. I'm sure he'll turn up. He's probably already back at the house, wondering what to have for dinner."

"What was that meeting about, Father?"

"Meeting? What meeting? Oh! Last night. I'm afraid I don't remember."

Stella cocked her head to the side and pressed her lips together. "You can't remember. A meeting from last night."

"Actually," he corrected himself. "I do remember, but of course, what a man says to his priest must be held in the strictest confidence."

Her eyes widened. "He was confessing? To you?"

Don Arrigo's eyes flicked toward the church like he couldn't wait to get away. "Not exactly."

"Then let me ask you this, Father." Stella remembered the conversation she heard on the road. "Was the meeting...amicable?"

"Amicable?"

"Cordial. An easy give and take between friends."

The priest looked everywhere but at Stella and she realized the potential value of taking her foot off the accelerator. Could she be her own good cop-bad cop, like the best investigators? "I've had him under my roof for going on two weeks now. I know he can be a bit much. I want to make sure he wasn't as hard on you as he was on me."

Don Arrigo let out a gush of air and put a hand to his heart. "You poor dear. These things are sent to try us, aren't they? Foxes in the hen-house, a drought before olive season, and cantankerous guests. Rest assured, Stella. Our conversation was perfectly friendly. I can't tell you what we talked about, even if it wasn't a confession. It's still his business, and what kind of man would I be if I spilled his words on the street?"

Well, he did have a point. "Do you know where he was going after your meeting?"

He cocked his head in thought. "He didn't mention anything to me, but I heard him ask Cinzia where he might procure a bottle of wine. I rather thought maybe he had plans with a pretty girl afterward."

Frowning, Stella said, "Pretty girl? Was he seeing someone?"

He shrugged. "Not that I know of, but he had that hopeful tone in his voice when he asked Cinzia. Like he was looking forward to a very relaxing evening."

The priest waggled his eyebrows.

Stella forced herself not to roll her eyes. The priest knew more than he let on. She was sure of it.

At her lack of response, the priest went on, "She told him Cristiana's would be the only option, though I don't know why she didn't mention the wine shop—"

"It's closed for the upcoming olive harvest."

Don Arrigo regarded her with what seemed to be admiration.

She shrugged. "Cinzia told me."

"My, that *was* a cozy chat. And here I thought you were just trying to unseat me." Stella didn't miss the accusatory narrowing of his eyes.

"By talking to your assistant?"

He didn't respond but kept his gaze on her until she shifted uncomfortably. Finally, he said, "Severini left, and I reminded Cinzia that Cristiana's would be closed. Not much more to be done about that. My guess is he went farther afield to get a bottle, or showed up empty-handed."

"But . . . showed up where?"

The priest adjusted the collar of his jacket before stepping away. "I guess that is the mystery, isn't it?"

Stella worried the police station would be closed by the time she finished talking to Don Arrigo, but to her relief, the door stood propped open and officers milled about the lit room.

Stella pushed open the door and approached the uniformed woman in a tall hat chatting to the balding man seated behind a desk. Stella asked her, "Excuse me, how do I report a missing person?"

The woman glanced at Stella before turning to the older man whose most significant feature seemed to be the prodigious display of white hair sprouting from his ears. "Good luck, Palmiro. You're in tomorrow?"

The man who must be Officer Palmiro nodded, and the woman rapped on the counter before stepping out into the street.

Stella watched her go and then turned back to the officer. "So. A missing person report?"

The officer said, "And you are?"

"Stella Buchanan."

"Ah yes. Returned from the United States."

"Whatever. Yes, I guess so. Who do I talk to?"

"Aren't you in a rush. No time for pleasantries?"

She gritted her teeth. "Well, as I'm trying to tell you, a person has gone missing and I'm concerned. I'd like to get some help."

He rolled his eyes and perched his fingers over the keyboard. "And who is this missing person?"

"Paolo Severini. A guest at my bed-and-breakfast, Casale Mazzoli."

"You *lost* your guest?"

"I didn't lose him, he, er . . . disappeared."

He sat back in his chair, fingers laced behind his head. "He can't have been missing for that long, I saw him walking with the mayor a few days ago. Hey, Luca!"

A cop popped his head out from behind a partition. Stella instantly recognized his perfectly coiffed haircut and stubbled jaw. She groaned inwardly. "What's up, Captain?"

Oh. *Captain* Palmiro. Not officer.

"This woman says that Severini guy is missing."

Luca glanced at Stella and did a double take. "Well, if it isn't the lurker."

Her heart dropped. *He knew.* Then she remembered their interaction as she loitered around the bar, staring in. She grumbled with an edge of defiance, "I'm *not* a lurker."

He shrugged. "You lost your guest?"

She inhaled deeply, as if praying for patience. "Again. I didn't *lose* him. He just didn't come back to the house and I'm worried."

"For how long?"

"What?"

Luca leaned against the door jamb and said in exaggerated, slow tones. "How long has he been missing?"

She said, "Since last night. Or maybe this morning."

The men exchanged glances, then the Captain burst out laughing.

She stiffened. "I don't see what's so funny here."

Captain Palmiro said, "Little girl—"

"I am *not* a little girl!"

He shrugged. "Big woman didn't seem apt. You're the size of a child."

She was so tired of this theme that she forgot her usual sharp retort and said, "I was a preemie, okay? Sometimes we don't catch up. Can we move on from this very irrelevant detail?"

Officer Luca's grin stretched across his face, even as Captain Palmiro's face darkened with what seemed a thunderstorm of thoughts as he muttered, "Premature?"

"Yes. I came early. Not fully baked. You know."

Captain Palmiro, who Stella finally realized resembled a frog, didn't answer, just continued staring at her. She wondered if he had a premature baby and now wondered if that child would ever gain normal stature. Well, it wasn't her soup to stir. "Look. We're getting off-topic. Something happened to Signor Severini. I can smell it."

"You can smell it." Officer Luca's eyebrows rose delicately.

"Smell it, feel it. Whatever. He didn't come home. No one has seen him since Wednesday evening. His car is in the lot. Where could he be? Something must have happened."

Captain Palmiro turned to Luca and said in mock formal tones, "I'm sure I can't *imagine*."

Officer Luca batted back with, "No reason I can think of for a man not coming home."

"Forget it. Never mind." Stella said aloud before muttering to her toes as she turned around. "Minds forever in the gutter."

"What did you say?" Captain Palmiro's voice hardened.

She looked him in the eyes. "Thank you for your time."

His jaw locked, he said, "That better be what you said. I've given you a lot of latitude with your sashaying in here—"

"*Sashaying?*"

Luca stepped forward and lowered his tone. "It's okay, Captain. She's just—"

"If she knows what's good for her, she'll keep her place." He turned back to Stella. "I know Americans aren't big on respect for authority, but I'd get some if I were you. People may lose their patience and tell you... "

"Tell me what?" She leaned across the counter, her eyes narrowed.

Luca ran his hand through his hair. "Captain? I can take over if you—"

"I'm fine." Captain Palmiro waved his hand dismissively, even as he kept his gaze trained on Stella, a muscle in his cheek twitching. "I'm *fine.*"

He turned back to the computer and Luca shrugged at Stella with a small, apologetic smile before strolling back into his office. Stella had no choice but to turn back into the darkening air.

She wondered if this would be the right moment to make one of her prized boxes of brownies. Right before leaving New York, she'd thrown clothes out of her suitcase and shoved in several boxes of brownie mix. Probably a mistake, but nothing soothed frazzled nerves like a warm, gooey brownie. In her opinion, homemade were never as good, and Italian stores just didn't sell them, for reasons passing understanding.

Stella set off for her home, determined. Yes, if ever a moment called for brownies, this was it.

Stella opened the living room window and leaned out, contemplating the fog settling into the branches of the olive trees. She wondered how winter would be in Aramezzo. She shivered and drew back, clasping the windows shut.

The cold made her more worried than ever about Signor Severini. He'd been gone two nights now. Those towels on the bed hadn't moved, and she'd stayed up almost all night in the living room, listening out for his key in the lock. Nothing. The house had rung with quiet. So quiet she almost went looking for the cat, just to have some other warm body around. But the cat, as obstreperous as ever, had taken this opportunity to absent himself.

Damn beast.

She shuffled to the kitchen and made coffee, breaking off a piece of brownie to pop into her mouth. She wrapped her woolly green cardigan more tightly around herself and took another nibble. Finally, the coffee was ready to pour.

But it failed to focus the fog in her brain. She couldn't even think of what to cook. Her mind kept cycling through the same possibilities.

Maybe he had gotten a ride somewhere with someone.

Maybe he'd gotten an emergency call and taken off, though not having his car made that a stretch.

Maybe he was having a torrid affair with some nubile young Aramezzo woman and was even now holed up in her bedroom, closed off from the world by red velvet drapes. Stella smiled at the image and the expression felt suddenly unfamiliar. She shook her head. No, this wasn't a likely scenario. One thing she'd learned in her questioning of the town was that aside from the mayor, most people didn't care for her houseguest. How he'd wind up in somebody's good graces long enough to land in her bed seemed improbable, no matter what the police captain assumed.

Stella yawned impressively and decided that she needed a walk and she needed to stop in Bar Cappellina for coffee. She pulled on her Doc Martens and tied the bandana to hold back her curls, making sure she had a couple of euros in her pocket for coffee. As she opened the back door, she shivered. Maybe she should switch to a jacket? Nah, she'd warm up as she got moving.

As she stepped onto the *terrazza*, she jumped as a whirl of black and silver shot past her toward the ring road. Had the cat spotted a mouse? She lost sight of him through a patch of greens that she'd recently discovered were *borragine*, and therefore edible, but then spotted the cat again on the road, nose to nose with an enormous orange tabby. The silver-spotted cat turned its head to stare at Stella, ignoring the tabby, who lifted its paw as if to strike. Stella drew in her breath, waiting for it to claw the silver-spotted cat, who sat in the road, bushy tail reaching an all-time pinnacle of bushiness as it flicked erratically. Just as the orange tabby's paw reached an apex, the spotted cat turned its glare to his fellow feline and the orange cat seemed to reconsider. It leaped lightly away, under a tractor and into the surrounding fields.

"Looks like you won that one, eh?" Stella said as she approached the spotted cat.

He lifted his black chin and looked away, as if embarrassed by her sudden flattery. Primly, he trotted down the road, waving that bushy tail like a flag. Perhaps he was headed to wherever he got fed. She followed him, curious and having no better destination in mind. She'd walk for a bit and head back to Bar Cappellina. Maybe Marta would be there again. The last time Stella went to Domenica's, she'd noticed Marta's sheep grazing in the back field hedged with meticulously pruned lavender. So Stella hadn't been wrong about the scent, but she wanted to ask Marta what she did with the herb. It must be something. She wouldn't carry the scent with her into a coffee-drenched bar simply by drifting her hand through the blossoms.

The cat had disappeared again, but no matter. Stella walked along the road that circled Aramezzo, tilting her face to the sunshine. She wrapped her arms around herself, holding in her warmth. For a moment, thoughts of Signor Severini vanished and she let herself sink into the smell of earth, of olive leaves, of tomatoes shriveling on the vines.

That's when she tripped over the body.

At first, Stella assumed it was a tree limb. She righted her balance with a jump, suddenly realizing that the tree limb *gave* in a way tree limbs just *didn't*. It took her a moment to recognize the body for what it was—a body. Wrapped in a kind of open-weave mesh that mottled the skin and torqued the body into an awkward angle. Stella's heart registered the truth before she did. The eye, the eye prodded her understanding, peeking out from the mesh with a kind of silent scream.

Almost without meaning to, Stella knelt to stare at that eye. Wide, the pupil huge, no color or shape that announced the eye as even human, let alone someone she might know. Nonetheless, whispers of thoughts, recently pushed to the side, rose to the surface. It *couldn't* be . . . could it?

Holding her breath, she followed the shape of the reddened face with her eyes, searching beyond the mesh.

Paolo Severini.

Definitely.

She exhaled and turned away, but not before she caught a whiff of something on him, like the forest. What was that? She leaned over the body. Sage. Rosemary. Was the man out rolling in an herb garden? No, there was that other smell, something she couldn't quite place, but something that didn't come from a garden. She shook her head to free herself of the irritating catch. What did it matter what scent hung on this man? The point was, he was dead. *Dead.*

Wait, he *was* dead, right? He hadn't blinked. That wasn't a good sign, but maybe he was paralyzed? The thought prompted her into action, and she plunged her hand into her pocket to pull out her phone before remembering she had no service. She shot one more glance at Signor Severini before she took off running, yelling, "Help! Help me! He's dead!" She realized she was yelling in English and switched languages. "He's dead! And caught in a . . . a . . . fishing net!"

As she followed the bend in the road that surrounded Aramezzo, she caught sight of a man feeding chickens up the hill on the left. She sped up, waving her arms above her head. "Help me, please help me! Call the police! Over there! My . . . a body! All wrapped in fishing nets! Dead, I think, or maybe not, please, help me!"

She wasn't sure if the old man heard her, but he unzipped a fanny pack fastened around his waist and pulled out a phone. An old-style phone, with buttons, not a touch screen, but any phone in a storm, right? And why in the world was she thinking in adages? This was an emergency!

Out of breath, she approached the man and heard him talking to what must be the police, giving them directions. He hung up and with a grim face said, "Show me."

She nodded and ran back down the hill, resisting the urge to tug him along. Instead, she babbled, no doubt incoherently, "I went for a walk. Because of the cat. Or no, not because of the cat, but I followed the cat. It left, it went—it doesn't matter where. And then I tripped, and I thought I tripped over a tree limb, but then it wasn't a tree limb, it was a person limb, but not a limb, a person." She heard herself laugh as if from another universe. Who laughed in these situations? A person out of her gourd, that's who. The man stared at her as if she might snap, which indeed appeared perfectly plausible. "He's all wrapped in fishing nets. Why is he wound in fishing nets? Maybe he got caught?" Her eyes pleaded with the man.

He shook his head. "I don't know, Miss. Where is...he...the body?"

"Right there!" She stopped on the gravel road and pointed at the edge, where the grass sloped down into the valley.

For a wild moment, she didn't see the body, only a blur on the edge of the road. Maybe she'd made it up! Maybe too much stress and caffeine and not enough sleep made her delirious, and she'd made up seeing that wide eye, smelling that scent like skiing through a forest.

But no. An intake of breath beside her, and she knew that the man saw the body, too.

In a gentle voice, no doubt so as not to startle her into more babble, he asked, "You know him?"

She nodded. "Yes. I own Casale Mazzoli. He is staying in one of my rooms. I've been looking for him."

The man nodded and then approached the body. He got down on his knees and worked his hand through the mesh to touch Severini's wrist. The wrist, oh, of course, the pulse. Maybe...

The hope was short-lived, as the man stood quickly and backed away, shaking his head. "He's gone. For a while, it seems. I'd guess since yesterday morning."

She stared at him with wide eyes. How could he know that? And more importantly, how could he access this information from within himself at a time like this, when she who read murder mysteries hadn't even thought to check for a pulse?

At her questioning look, he shrugged. "Chickens. You learn to judge when the fox came."

His words made no sense, but it didn't matter because at last she heard a siren wail as it crested the hill and then descended toward them. She shivered, waiting, her eyes glued to the police car. She groaned when she saw Officer Luca climb out from behind the wheel. Though thankfully, his face held no trace of that teasing expression that so infuriated her. And his partner wasn't Captain Palmiro, but a tall man with an impressive mustache affixed genially on his long, horse-like face that made Stella wonder again why in the world she fixated on irrelevant details at a time like this.

Stella stood back, allowing the officers to approach the body. They stood for a moment, the four of them, in silence. Finally, the mustachioed officer said, "How in the world did he get caught in nets?"

Stella said, "I don't know. And we're so far from the ocean."

The officers looked at each other and then at the farmer, whose mouth tugged up slightly in the corner as he explained, "She thinks they're fishing nets."

Luca's dimple flashed over his stubbled cheek before he and his partner broke out into cackles of laughter.

"What?" Stella demanded. "What's so funny? I get that this probably isn't your first dead body, but it's certainly mine. I don't see what could be so amusing about it."

Chuckling, Luca pushed his hair off his forehead. "Olive nets. Not fishing nets."

"Olive nets? Why do you need nets to catch olives? They're right there in the trees. Don't people pick them?"

The farmer shook his head. "We spread the nets. On the ground. The raked olives fall into the nets, and we funnel them into buckets to take to the *frantoio* for pressing."

Her cheeks flushed. She should have known that. No, she'd never been involved in the harvest, but she must have seen one in a movie. She couldn't remember anything specific, but she must have.

Luca frowned. "Olives aren't ripe yet. How in the world did he get tangled in them?"

Stella's eyebrow furrowed as she gestured to the body. "He's not tangled, he's wrapped."

Luca turned to her. "Wrapped?"

"Wrapped! Look at him. He looks like a sausage in a casing. There's no way he just got tripped up in the nets."

Luca knelt to get a closer look at the body, while the other officer said, "So, what do you think went down, Detective?"

Ignoring the sarcasm in his voice, she said, "His eyes, see how wide? Like a poisoned rat, and believe me, as a New Yorker, I should know. Then there's that...smell hanging on him that doesn't smell like death. Well, it does, he definitely smells like death, but there's this other odor that's off. And he's rolled in the nets. See the knots? He didn't get caught. Someone did this to him."

Luca stood up. His heavy eyebrows furrowed for a moment and then in a playful voice, he turned to his partner and said, "Salvo, looks like someone has been reading too many *gialli*."

The partner, Salvo, chuckled and turned to Stella. "This is Aramezzo, Signora. Not your big American metropolis. Accidents are far more likely than murder."

"Who cares what's more likely? There's only one scenario here. *Someone did this to him*." Stella seethed, even though she knew it was unlikely to help. She'd never been good at catching flies with honey. She always preferred a tart home-cured vinegar.

Luca caught Stella's gaze and said in reassuring warm tones, "Stella, I know this is scary. And confusing. But, see, when we hear hoofbeats, we think horses, not zebras."

Salvo added, "Everyone knows everyone in this town. There's not room to turn up your music past midnight, let alone murder anyone."

"Not everyone knows each other," Stella said through gritted teeth. "I don't. *He* didn't."

Luca and his partner shrugged at each other before Luca said, "It's been a taxing day. I suggest you go home and rest."

"You expect me to return to New York?"

Luca furrowed his right eyebrow. "New York? No, your house, of course. Or perhaps you need company? Bar Cappellina has doughnuts in, the kind with cream—"

"I don't need you to rescue me."

He softened his voice. "Death can be unnerving. It's okay to need a minute."

"Arg! What is with all the assumptions!"

He cocked his head to the side and grew serious, though she noticed his deep-set eyes still lit with merriment. "Assumptions? What assumptions?"

She gathered her irritation and said, "Look, please tell me there will at least be an autopsy." She sent up a prayer of thanks that her reading tastes tended toward murder mysteries or she never would have known the Italian word for autopsy, and would have had to describe it in a fumbling way, no doubt giving these men more fodder for entertainment.

Luca said, "Of course there will be. He's wrapped in nets, but given the dilated pupils and flushed skin, that's not the likely cause of death."

"So you *do* think someone killed him."

Luca shrugged. "I didn't say that. But we need to know what killed him—heart attack or maybe he was allergic to bees and got stung while trapped in the nets."

"That seems far-fetched."

"It happened last year on Subasio. Remember Salvo?" Luca turned to his friend for affirmation. "When Don Carlo got stung at his church picnic? Died before they could get him to the hospital. Everyone thought it was a heart attack, but the autopsy showed different. It's not likely in this case. Two bee stings in a year, around the same mountain. But anything is possible."

"Anything except murder, you mean."

Salvo gazed at her levelly. "No one said it wasn't possible. Just not *probable*. If the cause of death is suspicious, the Captain will order an investigation."

Stella supposed this was the best she could ask for from such a backwater town. In New York, of course, murder would have been the instant conclusion. Then again, if someone turned up wrapped in olive nets in New York, that would be a lot more suspicious.

A voice greeted them from down the road. "*Buongiorno*, officers! What did you find there?"

Stella sighed at the sight of Mimmo. From the looks the officers exchanged, they weren't thrilled with his presence either. But maybe that was for reasons more relevant to securing the crime scene than personal distaste for Mimmo. Or maybe it was because Mimmo was filthy, his boots encased with mud and dirt lining his clothes up to his collar.

Mimmo let out a low whistle as he approached. "Oh, boy. This guy is dead."

Luca groaned. "Thank you, Mimmo. Very helpful."

Mimmo nudged the body with his toe. "I wouldn't expect spoiled fellows like you to recognize a dead body. But I'm a hunter. I see it all the time. He's dead."

Salvo snapped, "Mimmo, kindly refrain from molesting the remains, okay?"

Mimmo shrugged and then peered down before recoiling back like a surprised cartoon character to stare at Stella. "This is your guy!"

The men looked at her. She quickly said, "He's not *my* guy. Mimmo means he's staying at my place."

Mimmo shook his head, chuckling. "Well, I'm glad I got out of that business when I did."

"You mean when I fired you."

Mimmo leered at Stella. "You probably fed the guy wild boar that had been eating poisoned rats. That's why he's dead. Just wait until future guests find out. Bet nobody will book with you anytime soon."

Luca protested, "*Ma dai*, Mimmo. Relax. This guy probably had a heart attack. That's hardly on Stella."

"You tell it your way and I'll tell it my way," Mimmo shrugged before gazing levelly at Stella. "I told you you'd regret it."

Luca stepped in front of Stella, blocking her from Mimmo's glare. "Mimmo! Cool it!"

Stella peered around Luca to see Mimmo smiled broadly as he stuck his finger in his ear and twisted it. "You fellows need help with the body? He looks pretty heavy. Can't know for sure, of course, but he's got to weigh almost as much as a young deer."

The officers sighed in unison. Luca said, "No, Mimmo. We've got it."

"Suit yourself." Mimmo walked away, whistling.

Luca watched him for a moment before shouting out as he walked forward. "Hey, Mimmo! That's an awful lot of mud on your clothes. What have you been up to?"

Mimmo turned slowly. "Camping."

"Alone?"

Mimmo glared at Stella as if she'd asked the question. "No. With friends. You wouldn't know them."

Luca's gaze dipped back to the body before he asked, "Just last night?"

Mimmo paused and then turned to walk away.

Luca recalled him, "Mimmo! How many nights were you camping?"

Mimmo seemed to hitch his shoulders back before turning to say, "I left Tuesday morning."

Stella watched as Mimmo walked away. "You can't believe him. Nobody that dirty has been up to anything decent."

Luca leaned back and regarded her carefully, one dark eyebrow lofted.

Stella looked down at the chocolate swipes on the bottoms of her shirt where her chef's coat didn't reach. "That's chocolate!"

Luca shook his head, tutting.

Stella seethed, "Look. If you must know, I don't have a washer, and I didn't bring many clothes from New York."

He cocked his head to the side and glanced at Salvo who snickered. "Who only brings one suitcase for a move across the ocean?"

Stella muttered in English, "This is what I get for sacrificing suitcase space to boxes of brownie mix."

"Pardon?" Luca asked.

"Nothing," Stella said. "Will you tell me? About the results of the autopsy?"

Luca almost grinned again. "Are you family?"

"Obviously not."

"We don't release the records except to family."

"Oh, come on. You're telling me that everyone doesn't know about that priest dying from a bee sting?"

"Sometimes news gets around," Luca admitted.

Stella sighed in exasperation. "And when it does, can you make sure I know?"

Luca ran his hand through his hair in what Stella was realizing was a nervous tic, which made her begrudgingly like him when she didn't want to. "He was staying with you?"

"Yes."

"Do you have information on who we can contact? Family, I mean?"

"No. But he has his stuff at the house." Should she mention Danilo Crespi? No, she'd let them figure it out. "I'm guessing there's something in his briefcase that would help."

"After we deliver him to the morgue, we'll come by to pick up his things. If we know anything pertinent by that point, we'll let you know."

"Well, okay," she said. She gave the body another look, pressing her lips together before saying. "I didn't like the guy, but he deserves better than this."

Stella trudged home, pausing every once in a while to turn and watch the officers who were now taking photos of the scene. Soon after she got home, she heard a truck rumble past. She ran to the window in time to see the ambulance round the corner and continue to where she found the body.

Just saying the word *body* in her head made her close her eyes.

Without thinking, she pulled out the flour, sugar, measuring cups, and bowls. Ignoring the mostly full pan of brownies from the night before, she flicked the oven on and ran through her ingredients. The sight of the pine nuts she'd impulsively purchased decided it. She'd make mini pine nut cakes. She'd seen little fluted pans in a drawer somewhere, ah! There!

Perfect.

Her hands occupied sifting, measuring, scooping, and beating, her mind flew free to examine the events of the morning. Signor Severini was murdered, no matter what the police said. She only hoped they didn't botch the investigation in their need to have it be some bizarre accident. But why was this important to her? Did she value justice being served that much?

Well, she did. Very much, actually.

But perhaps more than that, a murder needed a *murderer*. And unless someone killed Severini somewhere in the countryside and then dumped the body back in Aramezzo, it meant the killer was local. Severini was hardly popular, except with the mayor, but did anyone hate him enough to want him *dead*?

Her hands stilled at a sudden thought. Signor Severini was staying with her. What if the motive behind his killing had something to do with her? She bit her lip, running through all the motives for murder she'd ever read in her mystery books. Money, love, revenge, power.

Ridiculous, she decided. She and Severini weren't related by anything other than residence.

Nobody would be after her.

But knowing the murderer could be someone she passed on the

street, or purchased goods from, or sipped coffee next to . . . she shuddered.

The police *had* to investigate. And soon. Before the murderer fled or
evidence became corrupted. If she knew one thing, it was that the longer
a murder went unsolved, the less of a chance it would ever be solved.

Stella poured batter into the little cake tins and realized what else
had been bothering her. Mimmo assumed that the death of her guest
spelled the death of her business. Was he wrong? Would rumors spread
about Casale Mazzoli? People wouldn't even have to believe the gossip.
She could very much see the tale becoming one of those humorous anec-
dotes that lodged in people's minds and shed a creepy veil over her business.

She couldn't have that, she decided as she sprinkled pine nuts on the
cakes. She couldn't have people joking about her guest dying. No.

As she slipped the cakes into the oven, she pondered. Men had dic-
tated her life for too long—chefs in one kitchen after another, the editor
of the *New York Times*, the financial backers of *her* restaurant concept.
Could she leave her future, her reputation, in the hands of a few police
officers and *Mimmo*?

No, she could not.

Stella washed her hands, still thinking. She dried her hands off and
walked to the living room, plucking the photograph of the house off the
mantle. Her eyes scanned its now-familiar angles and curves, the illuminated olive trees.

She had never felt better than when she took her future into her
hands. When she chucked college for culinary school. When she packed
her knives and moved to New York, without a job or even prospects. And
when she stepped on the plane to come here. For the most part, aside
from the frustrations of hosting this guest (which, she acknowledged,
was not a great sign), she felt good about her decision. She liked it here
in Aramezzo. It might not have been her mother's choice of brew, but

Stella *liked* it. The people were warm and interesting, they all seemed to care about food as much as she did (more than most chefs she'd met), they didn't engage in indignation for indignation's sake like a lot of New Yorkers, they seemed constantly aware of the natural world—the crops, the weather, both the flora and the fauna. It made her more aware, too. And that felt right. It felt centering.

Yes, she liked it here.

Coming here had been the right move.

Now it was time to take her life into her own hands again.

If the police wouldn't figure out who killed Severini, she would.

How hard could it be?

PART THREE

As Stella pulled the cakes from the oven, steaming with the scent of vanilla, sweet wine, and toasted pine nuts, she remembered Luca's words. They'd be coming by, maybe even today, to pick up Severini's things. What if they wound up suspecting murder and dusted for fingerprints?

She thought as she slipped the tarts onto the rack. It was her house, no one would look askance at her fingerprints on the dresser. Her thoughts hitched on the briefcase. Grabbing a clean cloth, she dashed upstairs. Expecting a knock at the door at any moment, Stella rushed to the chair, lunging for the briefcase. In her haste, she knocked a wedge of brownish-red concrete off the dresser.

Stella paused. Why did Signor Severini have a piece of concrete? She picked it up, examining it more closely. It didn't seem like regular concrete. She knew concrete formed from an aggregate of rocks, but these rocks seemed on the large side. And the material holding those rocks together had an odd, brownish hue. The baseball-sized piece felt heavy in her hand, heavier than she would have expected. As she put it back down, she noticed a receipt, or rather, a yellow carbon of a receipt. She frowned. Italians were old school, but they used printed receipts now. Not like olden times when a shopkeeper wrote out a receipt, keeping the yellow copy and giving the customer the white.

She struggled to read the spidery handwriting, but finally made out

"Blood concrete, Temple of Cybele (Magna Mater), Aramezzo c. 200 BC".
Blood concrete? What in the world was that? And the shop name at the
top of the receipt, *Foro Antiquariato*, it looked familiar.

Something about Cybele tickled her memory.

The chapel! That old man, what was his name? Cosimo!

She read the receipt carefully this time, noting that it appeared
Severini had only put half the price down on this piece of blood concrete.
He still owed Cosimo half the purchase price. She staggered backward.
The other half added up to four hundred euros. Judging by his car and
his clothes, she had figured Signor Severini had money. But apparently
not enough to pay for this bit of antiquity outright. Why would Cosimo
let him take it for only half down? And how come this piece of rock cost
as much as a refrigerator?

She shook her head. Cosimo seemed a bit of an innocent. She supposed she could believe he trusted Severini to pay in full. Or maybe it
didn't matter to him one way or another.

Stella frowned. Wait. She'd asked Cosimo if he knew Severini and
he'd denied it. Why would he lie about it? Could he have some sort of
dementia? Unlikely, he seemed awfully lucid. Maybe someone who
worked at the shop had sold it to Severini? But no, she couldn't make out
the entire signature at the bottom, but enough to read "Cosimo."

As she wiped down the briefcase, she decided to bring a plate of tarts
to Cosimo. She shivered again as she put the brown concrete and the
receipt in her pocket. No doubt there was a reasonable explanation and
the old man should get the piece back, since he certainly wouldn't be
getting the rest of his money. It was time to pay a visit to Cosimo.

Foro Antiquariato's locked door greeted Stella with an abrupt denial.
She peered through the window, hoping to see Cosimo shuffling about.

Maybe he would let her in, considering she bore a platter of pine nut cakes. But no, nothing moved within the shadowy shop.

Stella rubbed her eyes. Caffeine. She needed caffeine. And as much as she didn't want to agree with Luca about anything, finding a dead body did lead to wanting to connect with live ones. She jogged around the middle street and pushed open the door of the bar.

Even though she'd girded herself for a reaction, her heart still paled at the sudden quiet. Her smile wavered, and she moved to the counter as if through water.

Romina paused her conversation with a villager and walked around the bar to greet Stella, her eyes swimming with sympathy. "Stella. We've been worried. Are you okay?"

Stella nodded.

"*Caffè?*"

Stella nodded again. "Make it a double."

Romina swept her snow-white bangs off her lined forehead. "What's that?"

"Never mind."

Romina nodded and Roberto ground beans for her coffee.

Stella glanced around the bar, hoping to find Marta, but the butcher's face was the only one she recognized. Romina announced to the room, "Everyone, this is Stella. She's taken over her family's Mazzoli place, trying to draw in a better crowd than Mimmo did."

At the mention of Mimmo's name, the butcher let out a hiss of disapproval. Stella looked at him curiously.

A thin woman in a faded corduroy jumper clarified. "He's not our favorite, is he?"

"Mine either, I fired him about twenty minutes after I got here."

"Was he stealing from you?" The woman asked, stirring her coffee.

"That's the measure of it."

"Not surprising. But no less unfortunate, right?" The woman nodded to herself. "I'm Flavia. I run the flower shop. Around the corner?"

"*Piacere*, Flavia," Stella said, accepting her coffee from Roberto. She breathed it in, muttering, "Mmm. Better than Prozac."

Roberto chuckled, and Stella looked up with a smile. She took the napkin off the plate and gestured to the assembled villagers to help themselves. "Pine nut cakes."

Romina murmured in a worried voice, "You're baking at a time like this?"

She shrugged. "Baking calms me."

The butcher, probably remembering the *sfogliatelle*, took a bite of cake and his eyes widened. He put another in a napkin and said to nobody, "For my wife."

"Hard luck," Flavia went on, as if their conversation hadn't been interrupted. "To have your first guest die like that?"

The butcher stopped his conversation with the old man Stella recognized as Cristiana's father, from the *alimentari*.

Stella sipped her coffee. "Not exactly how I like to start my day, that's for sure. I just wish I knew what happened to Severini since I last saw him Tuesday evening. Any of you see him?"

They looked at each other.

"No," said Flavia. "But my guess is he died of spleen, you know?"

"Spleen?" Stella asked, looking at Flavia over the rim of her cup. The coffee had filled her with warmth until she felt almost normal.

Flavia shrugged. "Those sorts don't live long, do they?"

Cristiana's father spoke so softly, Stella could hardly make out his words. "Like *istrice*, pushing everyone away until they die alone."

It took Stella a moment to remember the meaning of *istrice* . . . hedgehog? No, porcupine. She had little call for the names of forest animals.

To her perplexed expression as she worked through the definition, Roberto added, "Severini would try the patience of a saint."

"He *did!*" said the butcher, surprising Stella. He seemed a man of few words. But he looked agitated now, and maybe that prompted speech. "Didn't you hear about that fight he had with Don Arrigo?"

"You mean when Severini compared the church to a barn stall that needed to be cleared of manure?"

The butcher shook his head. "No, not that. But remember when Don Arrigo heard that, he just smiled. He *never* loses his composure. He could find a way to excuse a mosquito. But Orietta heard them *shouting* a few days ago."

Stella put down her cup. "Don Arrigo was shouting?"

"They both were."

Flavia leaped in, "You'd expect that from Signor Severini, right? I heard him at the *alimentari* whining about his *panino* being too cold and in here fussing about his coffee being too hot. No pleasing that guy." Tell me about it, thought Stella. Flavia continued, "But for Don Arrigo to lose his cool. It just shows what a difficult man Signor Severini is. Or, was?"

Everyone looked down as if in sudden realization that they were speaking ill of the dead. Cristiana's father made a gesture with his fingers and Flavia touched the cross at her neck.

"I wonder what they fought about?" Stella mused aloud.

"Does it matter?" said the butcher. "The point is, only a demon in human clothing could have gotten under Don Arrigo's skin."

"See? Spleen," said Flavia.

Stella put down her cup. "Where could I find the person who over-heard Don Arrigo and Severini arguing?"

"I'm right here," said a woman at the coatrack, unwinding a scarf from her neck and taking off her coat, revealing a white smock. Stella recognized her as the woman who ran the pharmacy. Stella had been so involved in the conversation she hadn't even heard the door open.

The woman turned to face Stella. "You're Stella Mazzoli?"

"Buchanan. My mother was Stella Mazzoli."

The pharmacist nodded and stepped briskly to the counter to raise a finger, indicating her normal order before turning to Stella. "Any relation to the Mazzoli family in Santa Lucia, southeast of here? My cousin moved there and mentioned a Stella. Married to the mayor."

"Probably." Stella frowned in thought. "There's a Stella in each generation, and I know my grandfather's family originated close to Le Marche."

"Well, Stella, it's nice to have some of the family back. I'm Orietta."

"*Piacere.*"

The woman smiled. "So you're wondering about your ill-fated guest?"

"Yes. I'm trying to piece together what happened to him."

"The police are on that, surely." The butcher harrumphed and the rest of the villagers nodded.

Stella hesitated, not wanting to malign the police to villagers who probably valued them as individuals, if not as a force. "Yes," she thought quickly. "But they have a lot on their plate."

"And you're curious," Romina said with a smile.

"Well, yes," Stella admitted.

Orietta grinned and accepted the coffee from Roberto. "I'm afraid I can't be terribly helpful. I didn't hear much."

Stella sat on the stool and leaned toward her. "When, though, did you hear this?"

"Let's see." Orietta drummed her fingers on the bar in thought. "It must have been Tuesday night. Right, it was. That's the night the pharmacy is open late, and I stopped in the chapel on my way home to light a candle for Marta and her little boy. He's been sick and that's stressful on a single mother. So, let's see. That must have been seven o'clock. Or quarter to, actually."

That time coincided with what Cinzia had told her, though Cinzia hadn't mentioned the raised voices. Not that Stella would have expected her to volunteer this information, but she asked Don Arrigo point-blank about their meeting, and he had said it was perfectly amicable.

"Did you hear what they were arguing about?"

Orietta stirred sugar into her coffee, and Stella felt every eye in the bar upon her. She rushed on as casually as she could, "I mean, it must have been something to anger Don Arrigo. I don't know him well, of course, but I've never seen him without a smile."

A rush of air, and Stella wondered if the assembled villagers had breathed a collective sigh of relief. Orietta took a delicate sip of her coffee and shook her head. "I'm afraid I don't know. He was speaking so quickly. But I did hear Severini answer him in a low tone, and I made out, 'death certificates.'"

"*Death* certificates?" Stella's voice went up an octave. Flavia shot a curious glance at her, and Stella managed to get her voice under control enough to say, "How curious."

Flavia helped herself to another pine nut cake and said, "What's curious to me is Enzo. Did you hear what happened when the police came knocking on his door?"

Everyone nodded and Flavia looked crestfallen until she saw Stella shaking her head. "Oh! Well, you know that Signor Severini, he was found on Enzo's property."

Stella shook her head.

Flavia narrowed her eyes. "Didn't you find him?"

"Yes, I just don't know whose property is whose."

Orietta laughed. "She just got here, Flavia. Give the girl a minute."

Flavia laughed, too. "Well! Enzo . . . you must have seen him around town—"

The butcher grumbled, "Always drunk as a monkey."

"I know Enzo," she said carefully.

Flavia nodded, "Cinzia's father."

"*What?*"

At her elevated voice, everyone stared. She cleared her throat. "I don't . . . I didn't know they were related."

"Right," said Flavia. "So. Severini was found right across the ring road from Enzo's. So, the police went to question Enzo and Cinzia, right? See if they heard or saw anything?"

Roberto added, "Especially since Pia said she heard a kind of strange moaning sound when she walked home from the parking lot early Wednesday morning."

Stella could hardly breathe. "She did? Who is Pia?"

"She owns the *fruttivendolo*." Roberto nodded to himself. "She was bringing up chestnuts and thought she heard a cat having kittens. It seemed out of season, but she didn't think any more of it until she saw the police on the road yesterday."

Orietta shook her head. "Poor Enzo. He didn't understand what was happening."

Stella frowned. "What do you mean?"

Flavia rushed on before Orietta could. "He laughed! Can you imagine?"

Tapping her spoon on the side of the saucer, Orietta added, "Well, he didn't just laugh, Flavia."

Flavia ignored her. "Laughed. Already so drunk at nine in the morning that he couldn't understand people telling him about a dead body on his property."

Cristiana's father shook his head. "That poor family."

Flavia shook her head. "Sure his wife's death was tragic, but he should have pulled it together for Cinzia."

"She hardly made it easy," Cristiana's father sighed.

Flavia let out an exasperated sigh. "But look at her now! Perfectly respectable, right? Enzo has good property and a daughter who looks after him. No need to resort to drink."

Stella decided to stay out of this one. From the sound of it, it was a common debate, and she hardly knew the players, let alone the particulars. So she let it play out while nibbling one of the pine nut cakes.

Which really were quite tasty.

Stella walked home in a daze. Why would Severini and Don Arrigo argue about death certificates of all things? And what to make of Severini dying, or at least being found, on Enzo's property? Could this be a coincidence? Enzo couldn't be responsible, could he? Despite his strange reaction to being questioned? Honestly, the man looked like he couldn't manage a shower, let alone a murder. Besides, what motive could he have? They hardly moved in the same circles.

She blinked as she came out of the tunnel. It looked like the morning's fog had burned off.

Matteo pulled up in his street sweeper, threw it into park, and leaped out, curls springing free from his ponytail. "Are you okay?"

She frowned. "Yes. Why?"

He pulled at his face. "It must have been such a shock!"

"Oh. You know about Signor Severini."

His shoulders rose to indicate the obviousness of the statement. "Of course. Everyone does."

Sighing, she shook her head. "And I thought I'd be able to ask some questions without having to explain what happened."

"You don't have to explain what happened. Everyone knows."

She considered his words. "I suppose that's one advantage of gossip."

"Ha! One of the few, you'll find. But now tell me," he said, his face growing serious as he placed his hands on her shoulders, his large eyes fixed on her. "Was it gruesome? Are you okay?"

"It was awful."

He watched her eyes, waiting for more.

"Really awful. His face—I'll never forget it. I . . . I don't think his last moments were peaceful." She stared at the ground.

Matteo let out a low whistle. "*Cavolo.* I'm so sorry you had to go through all that."

She nodded dully and said, "And did you hear about the nets?"

"The fishing nets?"

She looked up to catch a trace of a smile whisking across Matteo's face, the gap between his front teeth disappearing in a flash.

"So you know about that, too."

"Ah, don't worry about it. Anyone could have made that mistake."

"Any outsider, you mean." She shook her head. "I'll never live it down."

"I think you'll be surprised how short villagers' memories are."

"You're kidding."

"Okay, yes, I'm kidding. They'll remember it for years. Under normal circumstances, it would make you the butt of a thousand jokes. Good-natured, of course."

"Of course."

"But these aren't normal circumstances. A man is dead. It's a bigger gossip fish to fry."

Stella thought about it. "I'll have to trust you on that. I've never been at the center of a murder situation before."

He blinked. "Murder? I heard—"

"The police are ruling it an accident, but I can't believe that. His face, Matteo—" her voice broke.

"But...but...in *Aramezzo*?"

She shrugged. "I think so."

"But...*who*?"

Her face grew grim. "That's what I need to find out."

Stella knocked on the door and stepped back, wondering who would answer. She smiled to see Cinzia.

"Stella!" Cinzia didn't bother hiding her astonishment. "What are you doing here?"

Stella lifted a pot, wrapped in a towel. "Where I come from, we bring food when there's a death. I know Severini was hardly family, but I'm sure having him found on your property—"

"By you," Cinzia supplied.

Nodding, Stella went on, "By me. I don't know. I guess I felt guilty. Like I tracked mud onto your clean floors."

Cinzia regarded her levelly "Well, that's silly. It's hardly your fault."

"I know, I know, he's the one with the ill manners to wind up on your lawn." She tried for a grin and was rewarded by Cinzia's answering smile.

"Why don't you come in?"

Stella nodded and stepped into the house. It was darker than hers, maybe because the windows were smaller. Or perhaps because it faced the crease in the mountains, whereas Stella's house looked out over the expansive, sunlit valley. "Thanks. This is getting heavy. And a little too warm for comfort."

"What is it?" Cinzia asked, closing the door behind Stella.

"Lamb stew." She put it on the table and looked up. "I hope you eat lamb?"

"Of course."

"Super," Stella breathed a sigh of relief.

"But you didn't have to do this. It was hardly traumatic. The police came and went with the . . . body," Cinzia curled her lip in distaste, "before we even knew anything was wrong."

Stella tapped the lid and tried not to let her gaze wander around. She found other people's homes a never-ending curiosity. She ventured, "I heard your father got a little . . . upset, though."

Cinzia rolled her eyes. "So that's why you're here. For gossip."

"No!" Stella protested. And in that moment she almost meant it, but she had to admit that it occurred to her as she seasoned the stew that maybe she'd be able to find out a little about what had been happening on the property before she found Signor Severini. "I'm sorry I said anything. Forget it, I'll go."

Cinzia pulled the stew toward her and lifted the lid, inhaling the savory flavors. "No, I'm sorry. Sit. I'm a bit edgy. And I know everyone is going to make a big stink about this."

Stella nodded in commiseration. She also wished she could snap her fingers and have this event be a speck in the rear-view mirror. "I put artichokes in it. The stew."

"My favorite," Cinzia said, with a faint smile, lifting the pot with some effort to place it on the stove. True, the pot was quite full. And Cinzia's arms looked like toothpicks.

"Mine, too," Stella said.

Cinzia collapsed into a straight-back chair and leaned her chin on her hand. "My father did have a hard time when the police came. I was in the shower, but I caught the tail end. He's had an instant dramatic reaction to police ever since a pair of them showed up when I was eight to tell him a tour bus hit my mother outside of Assisi."

"Oh, Cinzia," Stella breathed. "I'm so so sorry."

Cinzia waved away her sympathy. "It was a long time ago. And I didn't deal with it particularly well. I'm guessing you heard about my misadventures?"

Stella was glad she could honestly shake her head, no. "But you don't have to tell me anything, Cinzia, really."

Shrugging, Cinzia said in a tight voice, "Better you hear it from me. My dad kind of lost it when she died. I never understood why, it's not like they had a brilliant marriage. I don't have many memories of it, but according to my grandmother, he'd been having affairs for years before she died. Afterwards, it got out of control, so to speak. Prostitutes mostly. I was alone a lot."

At Stella's leaning toward her, Cinzia smiled. "People took care of me.

You've met Antonio? The baker? He and his wife looked out for me. The butcher, too. This was back before his wife got sick and he got, well, less friendly. When he smiled from time to time."

Stella wanted to know what happened to his wife, but now was not the moment. Now she needed to listen.

"My father kept bringing these random women home, and I'd run to the butcher or the baker or the bar or anywhere I could. With no supervision, well, I'm afraid I ran a little wild. Got myself into too many scrapes at school, back talking and not showing up to class. Anyway, one thing and another, and my father dragged me to Don Arrigo and told him to straighten me out."

A pause. Finally, Stella said, "And did he?"

"He saved me," Cinzia said simply.

Stella paused, unable to reconcile her version of Don Arrigo with Cinzia's. Finally, she offered a vague, "That's so nice."

"I know it's not cool to say, but he did. He still does." Cinzia offered a tentative smile. "It's funny. People always laugh about how after years of working together, Don Arrigo and I are like an old married couple. They are so limited, they can't understand."

Stella did not know what to say to that. She wondered how different her life would be if someone had reached a hand across the divide of her darkest moments.

Cinzia laughed. "Anyway, I'm not sure why I've gone on and on so much!"

Stella did. It was the stew. Everyone assumed people opened themselves to bartenders. But Stella had noticed that when you gave people a bowl of soup that reminded them of their childhood, they started spilling stories. Stella didn't comment. Instead, she said, "What with all that, I can see why your father would react to the police showing up. He must have thought something had happened to you!"

"I doubt he was sober enough to think that clearly," Cinzia said easily.

Stella paused. "Is he here now?"

"He has a shed in the back where he goes to be alone, as he says, but everyone knows it's a drinks cupboard." She took a breath. "He says he's throwing it all away. All the alcohol. That he wants to turn over a new leaf or whatever. It's a nice thought, but he's said it before."

Stella waited for Cinzia to look embarrassed for her father, as Stella would have.

Cinzia seemed to understand Stella's unspoken question as she said, "When your parent is drunk more often than not, you stop trying to pretend things are okay. I can't let his choices reflect on me. My path is higher now."

Stella decided she should start going to church if it could illuminate her with the beatific light that shone from Cinzia. Stella could hardly look straight at Cinzia and let her gaze wander until it landed on a tumble of books. One dusty text with an etching of leaves on the cover and a pile of books still half wrapped in brown paper. Stella couldn't tell what they were, only that they weren't mysteries. The spines were black and white, rather than yellow. She gestured to the books piled on the table. "Well, looks like you'll have a cozy evening with stew and some books!"

Lame, Stella thought. *Lame, lame, lame.*

"They just came in the mail." She rose. "All right, then. Thanks, again, for bringing the stew. I know my father will appreciate it, too."

As she stood to leave, Stella remembered. "Oh! Can I see your rabbits before I go?"

"Another time, perhaps?" Cinzia said. "I'm already late for work and Don Arrigo will wonder if I'm okay. Especially with all this." She gestured to the world at large.

"Well, we wouldn't want to keep him waiting," Stella added with a note of forced cheer. Seeing how the shadows in the room had lengthened, she added, "You work for Don Arrigo this late at night?"

A true smile lit Cinzia's face, larger and more brilliant than Stella had seen on the woman the whole time she'd known her. "A priest's holy works aren't confined to daylight hours. And so neither are mine."

Stella walked into Bar Cappellina, still thinking about her visit with Cinzia. She wasn't sure she related with the priest's secretary—there were some aspects of Cinzia that were so different from Stella, she couldn't imagine crossing the impasse; their approach to religion being the most obvious. But more than that, Stella most easily formed friendships with people who were frank and unconstrained. Even though Cinzia told her story freely, Stella found her reserved. She paused in the street, considering.

Finally, it clicked. She empathized with Cinzia's story in a way few people could. They both lost a parent, they were both left with an absent one. And yet, Cinzia seemed to have no emotion around it. *Hmm.* Maybe there was something to this religion stuff after all. Could it be better than therapy for getting one through suffering to a place of peace and acceptance?

She shrugged off the question. Anyway, not everyone could be like Matteo, quick to warm. It didn't mean quiet types weren't worth knowing. Stella thought of Martin, back in New York. They'd worked in kitchens together for years before he broke down his walls and confided in her about wanting to break into the world of restaurant design, rather than cooking.

She did like Cinzia, and that was enough for now. She felt like she wanted to feed the younger woman. Soups and stews to thicken her slight frame, make her sturdy in the face of what had to be a complicated time.

With that, she opened the door and smiled to be greeted with familiarity by not only Roberto and Romina, but Orietta the pharmacist and

Antonio the baker. She called the baker "Muppet" in her head because he had a Swedish chef quality about him. Maybe it was just that when she first saw him, he wore that funny baker's uniform of what looked like a white tank top and underwear. Or maybe because of his red-gold hair. But at bottom she thought it came from his cartoonishly sunny disposition.

Stella leaned across the counter and caught Romina's eye. "*Cappuccino* today, Romina. *Per favore.*"

Romina broke into a grin that suggested that perhaps she understood. Stella finally felt comfortable lingering in the bar. Even without an agenda. Even with nothing to offer.

The baker moved closer to her. "*Buongiorno*, Signorina."

"Stella, please." She smiled at him, liking the way he smelled like sherry spiked raisins—warm and a little spicy.

Antonio grinned, making his auburn mustache twitch. "I hear you're giving me some competition."

Stella's heart dropped. *Oh, cavolo,* she thought, blushing instinctively at the swear word.

Antonio must have misinterpreted her blush because he patted her elbow. "I'm teasing you, my dear."

"I didn't mean—"

He chuckled. "Really, I am only joking. I have my hands full making bread and *torta al testo* for local bars and restaurants. Even if you charged for those pastries, which I know you don't, you aren't encroaching on my territory. I limit my offerings to the basics."

She nodded. "Okay, good. I'm glad. I should have thought ahead. Or at least stopped by to talk to you."

"I believe you have had your hands full." He raised his eyebrows to show he knew all about Severini. "But if you want to make it up to me, stop by and bring me one of those pine nut cakes everyone in here raved about. I'll swap you for a loaf of bread."

"Deal!" Stella stuck out her hand.

Antonio took it and pulled her in to kiss her on each cheek. "We're glad you're here, Stella."

Stella's eyes smarted with the tears that came too easily now that she wasn't having to match all that male bravado on the line. "Thank you," she whispered.

Romina set a *cappuccino* in front of Stella, and Stella nodded in thanks.

Orietta said, "Stella, Romina was telling me you weren't part of Severini's...business plan."

Stella shook her head. "I don't even know what the plan is. Or was."

She didn't miss the looks exchanged around the bar.

Orietta mused, "So you weren't working with him to get the right sort of people here? Rich Americans such as yourself?"

"Such as myself!" Stella sputtered.

Orietta turned and eye checked the other villagers, though the baker seemed to have no idea what she was referencing. "Well, yes. I know Americans don't like talking about money—"

"I'd be happy to talk about it if I had any."

A beat. "But you're from New York."

"I'm *from* New Jersey, and I worked in New York. As a chef, hardly a money-making career. At least the way I did it. And anyway, I'm currently without employment."

Roberto asked, concern lacing his words, "Then how are you paying for the renovations?"

"Mostly with pastries." The baker laughed and sipped his coffee and then laughed again even harder. If only she had internet, she could scroll through old Muppet episodes. There had to be a character just like this.

Realizing Orietta was waiting for a response, and in fact, Romina and Roberto were polishing clean glasses in order to listen, Stella said, "Ilaria's family is pitching in between better-paying jobs, and accepting a cut-rate for my flexibility. And they are letting me pay them in tiny installments. I'm going to pay them when Signor Severini…oh. Oh, no. I guess he won't be paying."

Roberto frowned. "You didn't get his payment up front?"

Stella attempted a feeble smile. "You see why I stuck to the back of the house. I can cook, but business isn't my thing."

Roberto shook his head. "This doesn't make sense. You would have gotten his credit card information when you got his identification during check-in. You can run the card, even now."

Grimacing, Stella said, "Identification?"

Romina groaned and Roberto said, "Italian law. You have to see their identification and copy their information."

"Why?"

Orietta said, "So the government can keep track of you. In case you're involved in a crime or disappear or something."

"Well, check and check, I suppose." She glanced at the baker and realized he'd become completely engrossed in the sports page. "Wait. Severini said that he arranged with Mimmo to pay at the end of his stay. Maybe he didn't know he was supposed to give his identification."

"Impossible!" Romina laughed. "Giving your identification is as much part of the process as getting a key."

Roberto thought. "He met with Mimmo to make this arrangement?"

Stella shook her head. "No, this was when he booked."

Roberto and Romina exchanged glances. "Are you sure? Because we heard someone saw the two of them talking in the parking lot."

Comprehension dawned over Stella. "Oh. I assumed when Severini said he arranged payment with Mimmo, he meant over the phone."

Roberto nodded grimly. "The odds are high that Severini and Mimmo met up, and, knowing both of them, arranged a lower rate if Severini paid Mimmo rather than you. In cash. They both stood to benefit."

"I'm going to kill that guy."

Orietta lowered her voice. "I'd watch your words."

Stella's eyes widened. "Understood."

Orietta said, "But you need to find Mimmo. You need to get your money."

Roberto added, "And that paperwork. The police will ask for his check-in information. If you don't have it . . . "

Orietta turned to the villagers walking into the bar. "Any of you seen Mimmo?"

Two of the men shrugged and returned to their conversation, drawing in the baker, who laughingly held out the sports page to the newcomers. The last man put his hands in the pockets of his brown leather jacket and said, "Mimmo? Why do you need him?"

Stella recognized him as the man she'd seen climbing out of his red sports car, the only other car in the parking lot not a beat-up Fiat. He fit the car, too, with his swept-back hair and deep-set eyes, his eyebrows like an artist's scrawl across his forehead.

Roberto straightened his apron. "Stella needs to find him."

The man's eyes flicked over to Stella, who waved awkwardly. "That's me. I'm Stella."

The man hesitated for only a fraction of a moment before he stepped to her and kissed her on each cheek. She knew kissing to be the usual hello, but most villagers had deferred to her Americanness and offered their hands or just nodded. So his assuming her comfort with his custom felt oddly intimate, as did his homey scent of pepper and browning pork. "Leonardo. *Piacere*."

"*Piacere*," Stella mumbled.

He touched the tip of his tongue to his top lip. "What do you need Mimmo for? Does he owe you money?"

Orietta laughed as Stella said, "That's about the size of it."

Leonardo nodded. "I'm at the market tomorrow. With the *porchetta* truck. He's always there at ten o'clock for a *panino*."

"Oh!" she startled. "That explains it."

Everyone looked at her, and she blushed. "Sorry... I just... pepper and caramelizing pork fat. I smelled it on your coat. Makes sense with the *porchetta*."

Leonardo exchanged glances with the rest of the villagers before saying, "You're kidding. You can smell that on me?"

"Well, yes."

Romina breathed, "How extraordinary."

Stella shrugged, "There are better gifts. I'd swap it out for superior patience. I'm terrible at waiting. Instead of waiting until tomorrow, why don't I go to his house?"

"No!" Roberto hissed, his head ducked so as not to attract attention from the villagers at the other end of the bar. "Don't go to his house. Not alone."

Orietta leaned toward Stella. "Roberto's right. Find Mimmo at the market tomorrow. You need to get that identification."

Leonardo and Romina nodded.

Stella vacillated between annoyance at anyone telling her what she couldn't handle and being touched that anyone she knew so slightly should care enough to caution her. Finally, she agreed, "And the money."

Romina nodded, her face uncharacteristically serious. "And the money."

Resignation weighed down Stella's words. "Okay. I'll wait. I have to go to Cosimo's tonight, anyway."

Leonardo's eyebrows raised briefly. "Cosimo? What do you want with that old fart?"

Romina shook a finger at him. "Leo! Show some respect."

Shrugging, Leonardo said with a laugh, "*Ma dai*, Romina. The guy is like a million years old. What could an attractive, young woman like Stella need from him?"

Stella tried not to delight in his off-hand characterization of her. Instead, she patted her bag. "I have something of his I need to give back."

Orietta nodded. "He's sweet, Cosimo is, Stella. Only a bit set in his ways. Don't let Leo prejudice you. Cosimo once criticized Leo's *porchetta* and he's never been able to let it go."

Leonardo muttered, "'Not like your dad made it.' For crying out loud, I make it *better*."

Romina patted his hand. "You do, *tesoro*. That *porchetta* truck is more popular than ever."

Leaning on the bar with a sense of ease Stella wished she had, Leonardo complained, "He talks to me like I'm still in my elementary school smock. I'm a full-grown man."

Romina shrugged. "When you get older, the world seems to move like a runaway horse. Is it any wonder Cosimo wants things to slow down, get steady?"

Leonardo huffed. "The world waits for no man." He gazed around at the female eyes on him. "Or woman! The best we can do is learn how to ride it. For better or for worse. Right, Stella?"

She tucked a curl back into her bandana and grinned. "Right." She had no idea what she'd just agreed to, but wasn't sure it mattered.

Stella breathed a sigh of relief to see the light in Cosimo's shop illuminating his frame as he bustled behind the register. Whatever "blood concrete" was, it filled her with distaste, and she wanted it out of her possession.

A bell jingled merrily above her head when she pushed open the door to a room stocked with candelabras and stone statues and a wall of glittering necklaces. The whole room shone, but in a restrained way, like silver under a veil. Cosimo looked over his glasses toward her. It seemed to take him a minute to place her, and then his face warmed with a welcoming smile. "You came!"

She nodded and suddenly remembered his request when they first met. "Without pastries, I'm afraid."

"Ah, *cara*. What a time of it you've had. You are welcome here empty-handed."

"I'm not exactly empty-handed." Rummaging in her bag, she pulled out the wedge of concrete. "I found this with Signor Severini's things."

A look of fury passed over Cosimo's face as he took off his glasses and rubbed the bridge of his nose. By the time he perched his glasses back on his face, he'd regained his composure. "The blood concrete. Not fully paid, if I remember correctly."

She set it on the counter and then pulled the receipt from her pocket. "You do remember correctly. Given that, I thought you might like it back."

He peered into her eyes. "Did you now? How considerate."

She shrugged. He put the piece on a shelf behind him, one lined with other chunks of the same hued concrete. When he turned back, he smiled and said, "And I'm sure you know about blood concrete, my dear?"

She shook her head. "I confess, it sounds pretty nasty."

"Nasty?"

"Just the name. I'm sure it's not made with blood or anything."

"Oh, but it is."

The sun shifted behind a cloud, and for a moment Cosimo's two different eyes seemed to gleam from the shadows. He went on, "The ancient Romans conquered the known world for a reason. They pushed the limits of knowledge to discover new ways to build, expand, and flourish. This concrete was the cornerstone of Roman domination, the hidden strength behind arenas and edifices and aqueducts that continue to stand the test of time. Their concrete, made up of volcanic rock held together with a mortar of volcanic ash and seawater, was often further strengthened with the addition of blood."

"Blood. Actual blood?" Stella gulped and her voice went up an octave. "Human blood?"

He chuckled warmly. "It's a misapprehension that Romans were wild animals in togas. They were civilized, with deep ways of understanding the world and their place in it."

Stella stared at him.

"No, my dear. Not human blood."

She exhaled in relief.

Cosimo thought aloud, "Pig blood is my guess. At least for these pieces. Given how many pigs lived in these hills. Still do, as a matter of fact."

Her eyes scanned the shelf. "You have a lot of it."

"Indeed. Though the remains of the temple to Cybele lie right at the heart of Aramezzo, we are only allowed to sell what there is in surplus. Coins and concrete."

"So this concrete, it's from here in Aramezzo?"

"Of course. Surely you know the legend?"

She shook her head.

Cosimo's face lit in a smile and he dragged a stool from around the counter to offer Stella a seat, and then perched on one across from her. "I'm surprised. The legend of Santa Chiara and the great mother is one of the few places ancient Roman mysticism and Catholic mysticism come together. You see, Aramezzo's founders settled here long before the medieval architecture would have you believe. Early Romans lived here and built their trademark structures. The forum underneath our *piazza*. And the amphitheater outside of town. You've seen that, I suppose?"

She shook her head.

"Oh, dear, you simply must. It's one of the historical and archeological wonders of our area. In fact, if you walk the trails of Monte Subasio, you'll notice water running through Marchetto canyon. Romans diverted water from that gorge to the arena, filling it with water, where they would stage naval battles."

Stella's mouth dropped open in disbelief. "You're pulling my leg."

Chuckling, Cosimo said, "Certainly not."

"There's an arena outside Aramezzo where ancient Romans staged naval battles? Why isn't that a tourist draw?"

He shrugged, easily. "It brings some travelers, mostly because it's such a different Roman ruin, being built of pink Subasio stone."

"That's why the buildings here are pink!"

"Precisely. We are rather fond of our rosy-hued stone." He went on. "The amphitheater has fallen to ruin over the years, and it takes a bit of imagination to see it as it once was. But, as I said, it's still a marvel." He cocked his head, narrowing his eyes at her. "Not all glorious things are in the public eye. Wonders exist under the surface."

She guessed that as an antiquarian, he would know all about that. She nodded. "Go on."

He watched her carefully for a moment, as if making sure that she had taken in his words. He must have decided she had, because he said, "The Romans built a temple, which lies underneath the current Chiesa di Santa Chiara di Aramezzo, between the modern-day middle and final circular road."

"Close to this shop, then?" She said, her head swiveling about as if looking for evidence.

He waved away the interruption like a mosquito. "Yes, likely. Over the years, it crumbled and villagers used the stones to build a new chapel, right on top of it."

She didn't want to interrupt him again, but he seemed to know her question because he added, "Not our current chapel. This was more modest, as befitting an out-of-the-way village such as Aramezzo."

He eyed her as if waiting for an interruption, but she said nothing. He continued, "Aramezzo's position close to Assisi meant that in the time of Saint Francis, his followers often trekked through on their way to or from the famous priest. One of those travelers was Santa Chiara. You'll know who she is, of course."

Stella grimaced to convey her indifferent Catholic upbringing.

Cosimo sighed, shaking his head. "Ai. All right then. Santa Chiara was born in the 1100s to a wealthy family. At eighteen, she heard Francis of Assisi preach and was so moved, she asked him to help her dedicate her life to God. When Chiara escaped her father's house in the middle of the night, it was Francis's scissors she used to cut her hair. He hid her away in a convent, while her father and uncles stormed the countryside in search of her. But she was adamant that she wanted to follow Francis's preachings, and so she founded the Second Order of Saint Francis, dedicated to serving the poor. The order is known as the Poor Clares, after Chiara."

"Wait, a woman in the middle ages founded a religious order?"

Cosimo nodded. "In a time when men framed religious rules, Chiara was the first woman to compose her own guidelines."

"Wow."

"Yes. Wow." He smiled. "But that's just part of the backstory. In the 1200s, the Saracens attacked Assisi. As they approached San Damiano, where Chiara lived with her sisters, including her biological sister who had by this point joined the order, Chiara snatched up the holy Host. When the attackers saw her holding the Host atop the convent walls, a mortal dread filled their souls, forcing them to flee."

Stella sat in thought. "That is quite a story."

"And now we come to Aramezzo," Cosimo said. "Though this part appears only rarely in niche texts of the time. As I mentioned, the rise of Francis meant more movement of religious people through this area, with hopeful followers crossing the mountain to learn at Saint Francis's feet. Santa Chiara herself walked these hills. Eight hundred years ago, when Aramezzo's chapel was little more than a rough-hewn stone room, a snowstorm closed in and forced Chiara to stop overnight in Aramezzo.

Already, her reputation had grown and villagers, particularly women, visited with Chiara through the night. They asked for her prayers and she gave them freely, blessing babies and the aged alike. Over the course of the evening, she heard story after story of families struck by a strange sickness. Now, perhaps those villagers had deduced that their sickness arrived on an influx of rats, or perhaps Chiara noted the bites like a pox that covered the villagers' limbs. But it is true that while the Black Death hit the Italian peninsula with the wrath of a vengeful god, Aramezzo was spared in its entirety."

Stella, waiting for the punchline, startled. "Wait, what do you mean? The Black Death didn't arrive in Italy until the 1300s."

He nodded seriously. "Yes, and by the time it arrived, no rats lived in Aramezzo."

"No rats?"

"Rats carry the pestilent fleas, you see. And when Chiara heard how the villagers suffered under the tyranny of their sickness, she raised her arms and summoned the wild cats of Subasio. The cats came that very night and wiped out every single rat."

"The cats came. You're telling me that Chiara's miracle is she summoned the cats that killed the rats and saved the villagers."

"Well, my dear, nonbelievers credit the howling storm for guiding the cats to Aramezzo's protective walls. Nonetheless, the cats feasted on the rats, the fleas on the rats no longer plagued the villagers, and in fact, rats never again gained a foothold in Aramezzo. No rats in the 1300s, no Black Death."

"And the cats stayed until the Black Death."

"No, my dear, they live here still. Their line intermingled with the domesticated felines of Aramezzo. There are a handful around that show their lineage."

Stella blinked. "My cat. Or not mine. The enormous, feral beast that came with the house. Its ancestor was called from the mountain by Santa Chiara?"

"So goes the legend, my dear."

Stella ran her bottom lip against her teeth. What a ridiculous story. "And the modern chapel?"

Cosimo nodded. "Good girl. You didn't let me wander too far. Villagers constructed the current chapel in the 1300s. Other than the restoration after the 1997 earthquake that destroyed much of Subbiano, it's essentially unchanged for seven hundred years."

Suddenly, it occurred to her. "Wait, you said this story and stories of ancient Rome blended together."

With a satisfied smile, Cosimo said, "I'd wondered if you'd remember. You see, Chiara performed her miracle of the cats standing on an ancient place of power."

"The Temple of Cybele."

"Just so. And we know Cybele as the Great Mother. As well as the mistress of nature. Her companion? A great cat. Those who believe say that Chiara's divinity awoke the sleeping Cybele, and the women together called the cats that saved Aramezzo."

Stella let the words sink in. Something about this felt very appealing. But it didn't take a shrink or an oracle to explain why. What woman with her history *wouldn't* long to believe a story of a village saved by two women? Two women divided by centuries, but united in love for their people? But, still. Come on. No way.

The cat part gave her pause, explaining as it did the outsized cats in Aramezzo. But there were plenty of likely explanations. Maybe wild cats had interbred with the domesticated ones, but it didn't prove anything. "Well," Stella hopped off the stool. "You have spun quite a story for me. But I've taken up enough of your time."

Cosimo bit his lip to keep from smiling. "You don't have to believe the stories, my girl. They exist whether or not you choose to give them space in your heart."

"Sure thing, sounds good."

He turned away and flipped through a stack of cards next to his cash register. "Did you contact my friend about his olive tree guidance?"

"Oh, that's kind of you to remember. No, the Severini thing knocked it right out of my mind. But I need to get on that. Those poor struggling trees are barely fruiting at all. I think I'll have my work cut out for me."

"You'd be surprised how much healing can happen in a season. Next harvest, I'm sure your trees will groan under the weight of olives."

Stella almost blurted out something ironic about praying to the goddess or saints for extra help, but for once in her life, she held her tongue. Instead, she remembered. "Cosimo. I have a question for you."

"Hmm? What is it, little one?"

She shifted uncomfortably. "When I met you in the church, you said that you had never met Signor Severini and, well," she gestured toward the wall of blood concrete, "I know that's not true."

He sighed. "I hope you can forgive me, my dear. My interaction with Paolo Severini was...unpleasant. He spoke to me about Aramezzo in a way most demeaning. As if my home was nothing but an ore mine to be plumbed."

"Believe me, I get that."

"I thought you might," he patted her hand affectionately. "Those sour feelings lingered, and I stopped in the chapel to find peace and solace at the foot of the Madonna. I didn't want to open the door to them again in that holy space. So I gave you my card and hoped you would stop by and I could explain."

Stella nodded, remembering their meeting in front of the Madonna. She ventured, "But then Signor Severini died. That night probably. If the chicken guy knows what he's talking about." She looked at Cosimo searchingly.

He shook his head sadly. "Yes. The police told me about it when I returned from the monthly meeting of local antiquarians in Perugia.

They were questioning all of us on this side of Aramezzo."

"There's a monthly meeting of antiquarians?"

"Yes," he laughed. "The first Tuesday of the month. I'm sure it sounds frightfully dull to you. But for us, organizing the flea markets, passing on leads for our particular niche, it's terribly important. Plus, it's quite a time. You'd be surprised how boisterous antiquarians can be."

Stella tried to sound nonchalant. "You must get back pretty late with all that carousing. Maybe you heard something on your walk home?"

He laughed. "Oh, no, my dear. I always stay overnight. With my cataracts, I can't drive in the dark. I stay with a friend of mine and come home Wednesday morning."

At her pause, he seemed to come to a decision. Gesturing to the counter, he said, "This month was a lucrative meeting. A colleague had stumbled across this cross that is rumored to have been carried by Chiara herself." He nonchalantly held out the slip of paper from another antique shop, this one in Foligno, with Tuesday's date on it. "Of course, it will take some research to authenticate it, but we antiquarians thrill to a spot of historical research."

Stella breathed a sigh of relief. "Looks like you have your weekend project all ready for you."

He laughed. "This will be more of a season's project."

She supposed he could be fabricating the whole story, but he didn't seem to be. If she could confirm his attendance at the dinner, it would make for an airtight alibi. He was as nice and charming and innocent as he appeared. Thank goodness.

"But if you don't mind my saying, Stella. I feel this event has tangled your energy, disrupted your spirit."

She muttered in English, "Ain't that the truth."

He hopped off his stool and stepped to the wall of necklaces, dragging a stepladder to pluck one off a peg. When they were sitting, she'd forgotten how short he was. He brought down a necklace and turned it over, investigating both sides before nodding to himself. "In these moments, we have to be wary of the evil eye. With our resources low and our souls distracted, negative forces can steal in and make unpleasant situations worse. Here."

He put the necklace into her hand. She'd worked with many superstitious Italians, especially with that stint in Naples, though this necklace didn't look like other charms she'd seen to ward off the evil eye. It wasn't a twisted horn or a piece of coral or rings of color around a black pupil. Instead, the silver pendant featured two raised and intersecting coils. Must be some local version. Pretty as it was, she had an uneasy feeling holding it in her hand. Probably a side effect of Cosimo's stories.

"I can't pay for this," she said.

He shook his head. "Call it repayment for my not being honest with you earlier. Now we can begin on an even footing. But do wear the necklace, Stella. It's imperative that you do." His face grew grave.

How sweet to be so concerned about her. Stella slipped the necklace over her head. She didn't have to believe in any of this. She'd wear it to oblige the old man.

Saturday dawned fresh and clear, and Stella snatched up a few string bags in case she found any promising produce at the market. She frowned as she shoved her wallet into her pocket, realizing the only proper meal she'd made was the stew for Cinzia and Enzo, plus the occasional sausage. Baking had taken up her cooking bandwidth. It was nice, though. Restaurants always had a dedicated pastry chef, so she hadn't been able to try her baking hand in years.

The sun shone warm on her face as she strolled to the tunnel that led through Aramezzo's gate. She turned left along the ring road to the market. She'd been to some pretty major Italian markets and so recognized Aramezzo's as quite modest. Nonetheless, she loved the sight of the farmers presiding over tables of produce that had been slumbering in the earth just the day before. The potatoes felt weighty in her hands, the new little mandarin oranges nestled in wooden crates glowed like Christmas ornaments.

With limited vendors and only one selling *porchetta*, she easily found Leonardo's truck. She caught his eye, and he winked, tilting his head to indicate Mimmo, waiting for his order of sliced roast pork and herbs, crammed in a crusty roll.

She grinned at Leonardo in thanks before tapping Mimmo on the shoulder.

He turned and when he saw Stella, he rolled his eyes and turned away, accepting the bag from Leonardo.

Stella waited for him to give a fall of coins to Leonardo, and then she stepped in front of Mimmo forcing him to notice her.

He rotated his finger in his ear. "What do you want now?"

"Well, my money, for starters."

"Money? What money?" He patted the pockets of his pants and shirt as if searching in vain, glancing over at Leonardo to pull him into this high hilarity. Leonardo, though, was cutting slices off the rolled pork for the next customer.

She set her chin. "You can't fool me again, Mimmo. Signor Severini told me he paid you."

"He did not." Mimmo paused, suddenly uncertain. "He wouldn't."

"He did," Stella lied. "And you know, he's *dead*."

Mimmo regarded her for a moment before setting off down the road.

"Mimmo!"

He whirled around. "I know he's dead. So what?"

She sighed so explosively, an escaping curl lifted away from her face. "So *this*. The police are investigating Severini's movements. What do you think they'll make of the guy who got paid under the table money from a murder victim?"

He sneered. "It was cash, idiot. They won't find out."

A beat. "Mimmo."

"What?"

"You just confessed."

He considered. "Oh. Oh, *cavolo*."

She cursed the instant blush and hoped her extravagant eye-rolling would garner back a bit of power. "Just give me the money, Mimmo. And his identity information. The police will want it and if I send them to you..."

She watched as the gears of his mind moved. Slowly, slowly. *Get there faster*, she thought to herself.

Finally, he turned on his heel.

"Mimmo!"

"I thought you said you wanted his identification."

"And his payment."

"Well, I'm not a moron." Rich, in light of just accidentally outing his misdeeds, but she waited. Mimmo went on, "I don't have it *on* me. Are you coming or not?"

She followed him, Roberto's words ringing in her ears as the two of them walked down the empty country road. Stella dragged her feet as they approached where she had stumbled across the body. As if she'd spoken aloud, Mimmo smirked. "That's where you found him."

The words chafed and Stella blurted, "Do you know where Signor Severini went Tuesday night?"

He stared at her. "How should I know?"

She laughed uncomfortably. "I'm asking everyone. Someone must have seen him, right? He didn't just disappear."

He said nothing and continued staring at her. Finally, he said, "What kind of lunatic are you? Of course he didn't disappear. You found him."

"That's not what I meant."

Mimmo shook his head, muttering, "And Americans think they're so smart."

She sighed. "You told the police you'd been camping Wednesday night."

He sighed in relief. "Yes! Monday and Tuesday, too. Great camping around here. *Really* great."

She didn't know what to say, and it seemed like every step she took away from the market was another step into the bleak unknown. She blurted, "Anybody home at your house today, Mimmo?"

"Who would be in my house?"

"Well, I know nothing about you. If you're married, if you have children. If you live in the village. Or maybe out of it?"

"You didn't seem to care about any of that when you fired me."

"Come on, Mimmo. That wasn't personal."

"Felt personal."

"You did a terrible job. You bled me dry and let the house fall into ruin. What kind of dupe would I be if I kept you on?"

He grumbled, "Blood from a stone, that was. Hardly counts."

She didn't answer.

The road turned away from Aramezzo, and Mimmo took a path that headed into the woods. She stumbled over a rock. "You live down here?"

He grunted his assent.

She thought for a moment and then pulled her phone out of her pocket, punching at the screen before holding it to her ear. He watched her curiously. She hoped he wouldn't be able to hear that there was no ring tone because she hadn't even taken it off the lock screen. "Hey!" she said brightly into what was essentially her calculator and flashlight. "It's me! Yes, finally. Got my Italian number. I know, I know, it took an age. Listen, I'm on my way to Mimmo's now to get the paperwork."

His eyes flicked toward her and she turned away, as if looking for privacy. "Yes, we're almost there. I should have it in a few minutes and will drop it by the station. Want to meet me there? Great! *Ciao! Ciao ciao ciao!*"

She slipped the phone back into her pocket and noticed Mimmo glaring at her.

She shrugged as if to say, "Police, what can you do, right?"

He opened the fence gate surrounding what could loosely be called a house. Dogs of no discernible breed yipped and snorted as they tore around the yard in excitement, leaping on Stella before bounding off to repeat the whole circuit. She tensed. "You must like dogs."

He snorted. "They're working dogs. Mostly hunting for *cinghiale* or deer. Some birds. Those two are truffle dogs." He pointed to the cages against the fence.

"Why are they in jail?"

He shouted at the dogs to stop jumping and they obeyed, instead racing in circles around them for another moment before flopping onto the brown lawn, panting. "We're going truffle hunting tomorrow. I need them hungry."

She looked back at the dogs in the cages. The shadows were deep, but it looked to her like they were plenty skinny. "They look hungry already."

"Delicate Americans. I bet you let your dogs sleep on velvet pillows."

She wondered if he was being metaphorical before deciding he didn't have a metaphorical bone in his body.

He continued his rant. "You forget that if you want your truffles and your wild boar, somebody has to hunt for you and that someone will use dogs and those dogs are stupid by nature. They need a reason to fetch your dinner."

At his voice escalating and the sudden realization that where there were hunting dogs there were guns, she endeavored to soothe him by saying all in a rush, "Listen, I can break down a steer, I'm not squeamish, just ready to learn. I'd love to hunt someday."

He laughed, not at all a nice laugh. "You couldn't handle it."

This was probably not the moment to get into gender politics, so she simply hung her head. "Yes, you're probably right."

He shot a look at her, as if expecting her to be making fun of him.

She sighed. "The truth is, I talk tough, but hunting for sport, I probably couldn't do it. For truffles maybe. I didn't know it was the season."

He frowned at her and said, "It is. For Umbrian black truffles. Most of the world's black truffles come from right here."

This sounded like the same blather he went on about when she used to call him for updates on the property, but it suddenly registered that she'd heard this before, from her truffle agent in New York. She looked around. "And you just find them in the woods? Around the roots of, shoot, what kind of trees? Oh, right! Oaks! Is that right?"

If she hoped for a cookie and a gold star, she was sorely disappointed. All she got were narrowed eyes and a deep grumble.

At his suspicious expression, Stella remembered her mother's long-ago story of how her family would creep into the forest before sunrise, so no one followed them to their secret truffle grounds. Strange, Stella hadn't thought about that in years. At the darkening clouds on Mimmo's face, she rushed on, "Or is it chestnut? I can never remember! Oh, well, it doesn't matter, don't bother telling me because I'll forget in two minutes. Can't keep anything in this head of mine!"

She cursed herself for laying it on so thick, but a moment convinced her she'd laid it on exactly right. His face cleared, and he nodded appreciatively. "I just hope I get to the truffles before the *cinghiale* clean me out."

"*Cinghiale*? Wild boar? They eat truffles?"

He guffawed and shook his head at her dimwittedness. "Of course. You didn't know that? What kind of chef are you?"

"Not a good one, clearly," she smiled.

"But you must have eaten *cinghiale* salami."

"Yes, back in Florence—"

"Tuscany!" He laughed dismissively, waving away her stage at a three-star Michelin restaurant. "Not the same. *Cinghiale* taste of what they eat. And only Umbrian cinghiale eat truffles. So only Umbrian salami tastes of truffles."

Stella completely forgot why she was here and that she was supposed to be on her guard. She mused aloud, "Oh, that makes sense. I never thought about it. So, in a way, Umbrian wild boar must be like the kings of wild boars, with their royal diet."

He shot a look of begrudging respect at her, and his voice lost its roughness. "What good is Tuscan salami that tastes of dry nuts?"

She nodded, still lost in thought. "Right. What good is that?"

She made eye contact with Mimmo and recoiled at the sudden recognition that she had gotten carried away. Mimmo seemed to have come to a similar conclusion. He cleared his throat and found his voice's gruff timbre. "The documents."

She agreed with a cheery, "Gotta get to that appointment at the station!"

He strode through his front door.

Stella hesitated for a moment before stepping across the threshold, allowing her eyes to grow accustomed to the dimness. His house smelled dank. Piles of clothes and plates scattered on every surface, walls streaked with smoke, and what looked suspiciously like dog feces in piles around the floor. Wow. Maybe he had been doing the best he could for Casale Mazzoli.

She was saved from feeling guilty about firing him by remembering that he cooked the books. Maybe in his warped perspective, he felt entitled to her money, sort of equalizing the perceived income gap in his scrappy way, like an Umbrian Robin Hood. She could sort of understand it, but she didn't have to keep him on only to have him continue to steal from her.

Stella ventured into the house and attempted to hide her discomfort at the mess with false cheer. "I hope you have pleasant weather for the hunt tomorrow!" She stopped. Was that blood on the rag on the table beside her? Or could it be liquid from that dark bottle beside it?

He caught her staring and said in clipped tones. "That's elderberry extract."

Seeing her eyes slide to the wadded-up towel, he hurriedly added, "I spilled. When pouring it from the bucket to the bottle."

"Okay!" She laughed, taking a step backward into the feeble light drifting across the floor from the open door.

He frowned and stared at her as if taking her measure.

She offered up her best prom queen smile. "Elderberry is great when you have a cold, right? Cures me right up! Good idea to sock some away for the winter."

He harrumphed and handed her an envelope from the cluttered dining table. She opened it to find a wad of cash and a copy of Signor Severini's identity card. She lifted the photocopy and held it out. "How did you make a photocopy of his identity card?" This hovel didn't even look like it sported electricity, let alone a scanner or printer.

He shrugged. "Just like I always do with guests. We stop by the post office on the way to Casale Mazzoli. We make a copy."

"But this time you didn't bring him to Casale Mazzoli."

"Sure I did. I told your aunt I would bring all the guests I booked straight to her door. And I did." He leaned toward her until she smelled the wine on his breath that he must have had with his morning coffee. Pointing at the envelope, he growled, "I took some of the money."

As he drew closer, she whisked the envelope into her purse. "Good! Good! Seems only fair. You're the one who got Signor Severini to me. Whatever you've left is fine!"

"And he's your problem now."

"Yes," she babbled. "Totally right. You can wash your hands of the whole affair."

"No matter what's in those papers."

She paused. "What's in these papers?"

Mimmo's laugh followed Stella as she hurried through the yard, shoving the frenzied dogs away. Once through the gate, the memory of Mimmo's breath and the steeliness of his gaze hurried her footsteps even as she opened the envelope.

There was quite a bit of money in it. Close to 500 euros. She supposed the advantage of being taken for a ride by a man who lived in squalor was that he didn't have expensive tastes. He probably spent the hundred euros or so on wine and dog kibble.

One more glance over her shoulder and she raced toward the road. Once she got there, she'd be safe. There would probably be farmers who lived on the outskirts of town out in their fields, tending to crops and trees and chickens.

Why had Mimmo bothered copying Signor Severini's identification? It wasn't like he wanted to be on the up-and-up, legally speaking. Maybe it was force of habit. Or maybe he thought Signor Severini would be more suspicious if Mimmo didn't follow the usual procedures.

She shook her head in frustration.

Something shady had gone down between them. Did that make Mimmo a suspect? He fit the profile of a killer. Or maybe not the profile but the horror movie ideal—the squalor, the loose morals, and she couldn't forget the rag with smears of what looked like blood in the half-light. What were the odds he was really making elderberry extract?

No, he was probably up to something. Just as she had the thought, she banged into Domenica, putting the white long-hair cat outside. They both reeled back, and Stella reached to grab Domenica's hand. The cat yowled and took off. Domenica watched it run down the street with a sigh. "Well," she said, "I won't be seeing Attila until dinnertime."

Catching sight of Stella's face, Domenica's eyes widened. "Oh, goodness, dear. What's happened to you? You look petrified!"

Stella could only shake her head.

Domenica led her into the shop, saying, "I should have known. There is nothing more disorienting than finding a dead body. I know when I found my first one—"

"Your *first* one!"

"Yes, dear. In Argentina. Let's see now...thirty years ago? No, more. I was still with Charles. So forty years ago."

"*Charles?*"

"Yes, that's what I said. He hated to be called Chuck. Always Charles." Domenica chuckled at the memory. "So silly and formal of him. But one must indulge the talented in our midst. And Charles had more than his share of gifts. The things he could do with the tip of his—"

"Domenica!"

"His brush dear. Charles was a painter. And also a bush pilot. So many dimensions to that man." She winked as she settled into her chair.

"And you found him dead?" Stella hung up her coat on the rack and moved to the desk in front of Domenica, the envelope still clutched in her hand.

Domenica laughed and pulled a cat onto her lap. "No, no. Charles and I found the body of a man trampled by his herd of llamas. So sad."

Stella stared at the ground. "Well, my life seems pretty boring right about now."

"Don't be silly," Domenica soothed. "I'm sure you've had loads of adventures."

Stella thought about the time she made a really good roast chicken for the attorney general of New York. Did that count? She made a face.

Domenica patted her hand. "There's time. I mean, look at you now!"

"What? Finding a dead body?"

"It's a start. Well, not finding the body, but figuring out who killed him. I've heard you've been asking questions. Tell me what you know."

"I know nothing."

"Well." Domenica stared hard at Stella. "I'm sure that's not true."

Stella shifted her weight.

"Stella?"

"Okay, I have some ideas."

Domenica patted her arm. "There you go! Good on you. Now tell me all about it."

Stella bit her lip. "I think Mimmo is suspicious."

Domenica nodded in a satisfied way. "He is, indeed. A bit hapless. But suspicious. And what do you suppose is the motive?"

"That's where I'm stuck." She paused in thought. "I found out Mimmo met with Signor Severini. Took his payment. So I know they have a connection. But if he got money from Severini, I'm not sure why he'd kill him."

Domenica nodded in thought. "Unless there is more to that than we know."

Stella nodded. "I went with Mimmo to his house—"

"You did *what*?"

"I had to get my money. And the copy of Severini's identity card. I'm sure the police are going to be asking for it."

"You couldn't have met him at the bar? Or somewhere else in broad daylight and two or three witnesses and maybe a security camera?"

Stella shrugged. "I took my moment. It was fine, he didn't... it was fine. Only, when he handed me the papers, he said something strange about it being my problem now."

Domenica stroked the cat. "What does that mean?"

"Heck if I know. Also," Stella debated. "I saw something at his house. Probably nothing."

"Spill it."

"It was hard to tell, but it looked like blood. On a cloth."

"Blood? Could it have been from hunting or something? You might not know that Mimmo enjoys a spot of —"

"Yes, I know he hunts. I met his dogs," Stella said grimly. "He got weird when I noticed it. Said it was from making elderberry extract."

"Which is possible. It is the season." Domenica thought about it. "Was there blood on Signor Severini?"

Stella sighed. "Not that I saw. Which is why that doesn't track. But *something* killed Severini. I don't buy that he got tangled in olive nets."

"Fishing nets?"

Beat. "You, too?"

Domenica grinned. "Sorry. I couldn't help myself. Who else?"

Stella shrugged. She knew the priest was hiding something, but didn't feel comfortable accusing him out loud. She might not want to be best friends with the villagers, but she didn't want social suicide, either. Instead, she said, "Enzo. I found Severini on his property. Cinzia's, too, I suppose, but Don Arrigo was with her when Severini left the church. And anyway, have you seen how frail she is? But Enzo, he's strong. He could have wrapped Severini in those nets, no problem. Plus, Cinzia said he stopped drinking. She said because of the shock, but before that she'd said that the police got rid of the body so quickly that it hadn't been a problem for them. So maybe it's guilt making him babble like that?"

Stella paused. Something about Enzo as a suspect didn't feel right, but she couldn't place what it was.

Into the silence, Domenica said, "Listen, I know you believe Signor Severini was killed, but is it possible that he just had a stroke or something?"

"Ask the police."

"I'm asking you."

Stella spoke slowly. "I've worked in kitchens all my life. Every kitchen has its method for clearing out vermin. Usually traps, but early on, in kitchens of lesser repute, they used poison. The rats—they were twisted, with bulging eyes. Signor Severini, that's how he looked. His pupils... they looked like marbles."

Domenica shivered. "And nothing amiss on the identity document?"

Stella opened the envelope. "I didn't check. I was racing down the path, trying to avoid being gored by dogs—"

"Dogs don't gore people, dear. That's *cinghiale*."

"So I only counted the money." Stella scanned the document. "No, it all looks fine. I mean, maybe the license plate registered here doesn't match his actual license plate? I can check later." She handed the sheet over to Domenica and then snatched it back. "Wait a second."

"What is it?"

Stella stared at the paper in her hand. The photo looked like Signor Severini, but the name on the passport read "Danilo Crespi." She handed it to Domenica. "Take a look at this."

Domenica accepted the document and then did a double take. "His name is Danilo Crespi?"

"Apparently." Stella frowned. "That name sounds familiar."

Domenica stared at the paper as if it might reveal an answer to a riddle.

Stella startled. "Danilo Crespi! He—Severini...Crespi...whatever—had all these contracts in his briefcase, the name on them was Danilo Crespi. I didn't think much of it, but now..."

Domenica watched as Stella's thoughts ran.

Stella seemed to be tasting her words before she spoke them. "Severini was trying to get foreigners to come to Aramezzo, only not on tour, like he told me. He wanted them to buy up real estate—"

"There isn't much real estate in Aramezzo. People pass down property to relatives and tax structures don't motivate people to sell."

"Exactly! But how about in Subbiano?" Stella remembered Cosimo's story. "An earthquake. It destroyed much of Subbiano, right? And the houses fell into disrepair. Abandoned, even?"

"Subbiano?" Domenica frowned. "If Aramezzo is off the tourist trail, Subbiano is another planet. What would draw an American to buy a house there?"

"Because," Stella said, the words falling into place with her memories of what she'd assumed were boilerplate contracts, "Severini was bringing them in on one-euro house deals."

"One-euro house deals?" Domenica mulled. "What's that?"

Stella blinked and seem to come back to herself. "You don't know about them? No, I guess that makes sense. They're only a handful in southern Italy, and the ads probably target foreigners. I can't count how many times I've seen articles about them making the rounds on social media."

"But what are they, dear?"

"Well, you know how in these old towns, the young people leave and the town dies out? Some town councils sell off the abandoned houses for a dollar, or a euro, or whatever."

Domenica thought about it. "Seems like a good way to get cheap real estate. I wonder why they don't market these in Italy where we can take advantage of it?"

Stella shrugged. "I think the towns want to draw people to live in their villages. How many Italians do you know who would uproot to another town, even if the house was a euro?"

"That's true. Not many."

"Besides the fact that these houses are in terrible shape. As part of the contract, buyers agree to rehabilitate the homes in a certain amount of time."

"How long?"

Stella frowned. "I don't know. I think it depends on the town. A couple of years at least, I think."

Domenica leaned back and considered. "I have to tell you, this sounds fishy to me. Are you sure these are legit?"

"Totally," Stella answered. "Everyone thought they were fake at first, but then more and more Americans took a chance and wrote up their experiences in *Forbes* and the *Washington Post*. It doesn't always go well. I mean it's pretty hard for an American to navigate the overhaul of these crumbling homes. And sometimes towns have extra rules about how much time the owner has to spend in the town, or how to prove they can integrate. But it works, mostly. Some towns are coming back to life."

Domenica shook her head. "I'll have to take your word for it. But why do you think Severini was involved in one of these schemes?"

"I found these contracts, but most of the amounts listed were one euro. I thought they must be templates for contracts, but now, I wonder if this was how he'd planned to get Americans to Subbiano. By offering the houses for a euro."

Frowning, Domenica said, "But . . . why? What does he get from that?"

Stella shook her head. "Knowing Severini, he had an angle."

"And that angle might just have gotten him killed. " Domenica nodded slowly. "You need to take this to the police."

But Stella was already out the door.

Stella pushed open the door of the police station and tensed at the sight of Captain Palmiro again at the front desk. Well, there was nothing for it. "I have some information. About Signor Severini. I need to talk to whoever is working the case."

He rolled his eyes. "I know you think your opinions are precious because you stumbled over the body, but please, let the men in charge—"

"Captain?" said Luca, appearing in the doorway. "I asked Stella to stop by. I thought she might have information about his next of kin."

Captain Palmiro looked chastened for only a moment before his eyes flashed darkly. "It looks like Luca would be more than happy to entertain your American crime drama theories."

Luca held the door open. "Stella. Right this way."

She clutched her envelope to her chest and hustled into his office.

He closed the door. "You'll have to excuse him. The Captain is a year from retirement and thought he could skate to the finish line. Then all of a sudden, this happens. He means well. But it's a lot."

"If you say so."

Luca gestured for Stella to sit down. "Looks like you found out quickly."

"I did?" She sat in the proferred chair.

Luca leaned against the edge of the desk, arms crossed over his broad chest. "I didn't figure anyone would loop you into the gossip train for at least another half day."

"But it's not gossip."

He waved his hand. "Rumors. Speculation. Idle talk. It's all the same."

She looked down at the papers in her hand and then looked up at him. "What are you talking about?"

"The chemicals in Signor Severini's system." He frowned. "Isn't that why you're here?"

"No."

"Oh." Luca considered. "I was going to come by and check the meds he left behind. I figured you'd come in to save me the trouble."

She lowered her voice. "You think someone poisoned him?"

"I didn't say that."

"Then what are you saying?" she asked, frowning.

"Wait." He frowned back and ran his hand through his dark hair. "If you didn't come by because you heard about the elevated atropine, why are you here?"

Stella bit her lip for a moment. "Signor Severini."

"Yes?"

She decided she needed to go for full honesty. "I didn't do the check-in.

Mimmo did."

"Mimmo."

"Yes."

"But you fired him."

"Yes."

"Go on."

She hesitated. "This is my first time doing all this, I didn't even know there was a rule about getting copies of identity documents. Once I realized, I asked Mimmo about it. Well, you should see this."

He accepted the paper and his eyes bulged. "Danilo Crespi?"

She pressed her lips together and said nothing.

"This explains why we found no identification or even credit cards on him. Nothing in his wallet but two thousand euros."

"Two thousand euros!" And the man hadn't paid Cosimo the rest of the payment for the concrete?

"That and the sports car. The guy was loaded." Luca pressed his lips together. "Anyway. We tried to locate a next of kin. There aren't many Paolo Severinis, but we came up empty." He stared at the document. "Mimmo must not have reported his check-in to the government."

"Well, that fits since he also didn't give me the money."

"Copy that." Luca leaned back and gazed at the corner of his office in thought. "So Mimmo pocketed the payment for the room and didn't report his check-in. To fly under the radar."

She nodded. "That's my guess."

"But he still copied the identity card?"

Stella said, "That I can't figure out. He looked at me like I'd buttoned my pants on backward when I asked. I think he always makes a copy of the identity card, so for him, it's part of the process."

"Perhaps he wanted to hold something over Severini's head."

"Anyone reading premeditation into Mimmo's actions doesn't know him very well."

Luca chuckled. "Fair enough."

For a moment she considered telling him about the one-euro houses, but decided it was all conjecture and she'd have to admit to snooping, which she didn't think he'd be a fan of. She stood. "Anyway, I thought you'd want to know. Should I bring you his belongings?"

He leaned over his desk, shuffling papers. "No, I'll collect them. Chain of evidence and all."

Stella paused, considering. "One thing you should know. I guess you'll know soon enough. He had a gun."

Luca looked up. "A gun? Are you sure?"

"Quite," she said, grimly.

"Did he," Luca's stubbled jaw worked, emphasizing his high cheek-bones as his eyes flashed darkly. "Did he pull it on you?"

"Oh, no!" Stella said, almost laughing. "Not at all. I saw it when he was unpacking. I'm not sure if it's legal."

"We'll find out," Luca nodded.

They walked out of the station into the early afternoon light, and Luca paused to put on aviator sunglasses while Stella squinted until her eyes grew used to the brightness. Just then, her stomach rumbled and she blushed. "I haven't eaten lunch."

Luca chuckled. "What kind of chef doesn't keep herself fed?"

She scowled. "One with dead guests to chase around."

Luca laughed. "Good point." Without the distraction of his direct eye contact, she noticed how one front tooth slightly overlapped the other. He gestured to the *alimentari* as they passed. "Do you want to pop in? Get a *panino*?"

"No," she said, flatly.

"Suit yourself." He jammed his fists into his pockets and whistled as they began walking.

She cast him a curious look.

He leaned down, close enough to her that she smelled his aftershave, like woods and leather. In confidential tones, he murmured, "Don't want anyone getting the wrong idea."

Stella's thoughts raced—*he doesn't want people thinking we're on a date*. Why would that even occur to him? Did he think of her that way? As a woman, rather than just an annoying American with chocolate smears on her jeans? She hated how her stomach swooped.

But the thoughts burst like a soap bubble when he said, "Can't make it look like you're wanted for questioning. I figure you've got enough on your plate."

As he grinned at her, she saw herself reflected in his sunglasses—the dark smudges under her eyes, the hair springing free from her ill-tied bandana. Was that flour across her cheek? She tried to wipe it off in a casual way before realizing she hadn't answered. Clearing her throat, she said, "I appreciate that."

He nodded and they continued walked down the street.

Impulsively she asked, "There weren't any knife marks on the body, were there?"

He looked at her as if she'd sprouted salami for hair. "No. Why?"

"Just wondering." All in a rush, she asked. "No bullet holes? No nicks or pricks or punctures?"

"You read too much."

She gazed at him levelly.

"None of that. Looks like he hit his head, maybe enough to knock him out, but not enough to kill him. The medical examiner thinks he died hours after that head injury. Some lacerations from the nets, some bruising. But that's it for trauma."

"Do you honestly think he died of natural causes?"

He cocked his head to the side. "Nothing natural about getting tangled in olive nets."

"You know what I mean."

"I don't know, Stella. His levels of atropine were elevated, so they're sending the blood on for further evaluation and doing a full autopsy. But really, antidepressants could explain the elevated atropine, or hell, even herbal remedies."

"Herbal remedies? You think *tea* killed him?"

"Not tea. But some of those so-called healthier alternatives to medicine contain more toxins than you'd think. Especially if he also took prescription medication. Anyway, my money is still on an accident. Maybe even an accidental overdose. That got him so disoriented he wandered around and got caught in the nets."

"You've got to be kidding me. How in the world could a person get *that* tangled?"

"If he were lucid, sure. But drunk? Or in the throes of a heart attack or overdose? I've seen stranger things."

"Well, I haven't," muttered Stella as she withdrew the keys from her pocket. She unlocked the door and gestured for Luca to enter, but he took off his sunglasses and waited until she crossed the threshold first. As she stepped in the house, she continued, "And anyway, the fake name. The fight with Don Arrigo. Something's off."

The smile vanished from Luca's face and his eyes narrowed. "What does Don Arrigo have to do with anything?"

"Nothing."

"Then why did you bring that up?"

"I'm just saying, Severini was up to something. Don't you think Don Arrigo would know about it? Maybe someone should ask him."

Luca pressed his full upper lip against his lower one until they paled. Coldly, he asked, "Severini's room?"

Stella nodded and gestured for him to follow her up the stairs. She pointed into the bathroom and Luca ignored the toothbrush and shaving cream on the sink, opening drawers until he found a black leather case. He took it out and rooted through it until he pulled out a prescription box. "Huh."

"What? What is it? Could it cause the elevated atropine in his blood?"

He shrugged and gave her a cold look. "How should I know? But at least I have something to bring the medical examiner. Anyplace else we can look? His bedroom?"

She led the way and opened the door, gratified that the cat was nowhere to be found. Though the towels showed a depression and a few short, dark hairs suggesting that he'd been there. Stella slipped into the second bedroom and got an empty cardboard box. "He has a suitcase, but this might be easier?"

He nodded his thanks before opening drawers and placing Severini's clothes in the box. Stella pointed at the bureau. "The gun. It's in that one."

Luca nodded and opened the drawer. He pulled out the gun and examined it. "It's a Beretta."

"Is that a kind of gun?"

He looked at her with a smirk.

"What? How should I know?"

"Beretta is a gun manufacturer. Italian. The kind of gun is a revolver." He spun the chamber. "No bullets."

Stella let out a breath. She hadn't realized how tense it had made her just imagining a loaded gun in the house. "Maybe the bullets are in another drawer?"

Luca finished placing all the items in the box and then searched the nightstand. "It doesn't look like it. Either he stashed the bullets elsewhere, like in his car, or he had the gun for intimidation."

Stella nodded. She pointed out the briefcase and then picked up Severini's car keys. Stella handed them over carefully, avoiding the warmth of Luca's hand. He nodded and then, hefting the box onto his shoulder, he jogged down the steps and out the door. She watched his silhouette fade into the waning light until he disappeared.

Stella's stomach moaned again. She really needed to eat. Luca was gone, Severini's things handed over. Snatching up her keys, she trotted to the butcher, wondering what kind of sausage she'd find today. She nodded at Cinzia waiting in line behind an older woman dressed in a navy blue skirt and sweater with navy pumps. Stella grinned. She loved Italian old lady fashions and amused herself by imagining what she'd be like if she somehow wound up living here forever.

Cinzia smiled at her entrance. "Thanks for the stew. It was wonderful. Even my father ate two bowls full, which is the first I've seen him eat proper food in a while."

Stella nodded. "This all must have taken a toll on him."

Cinzia waved her hand. "Not really. I meant he usually prefers to drink his calories."

This seemed like a sad statement, but Cinzia didn't seem sad, so Stella didn't know how to respond. Instead, she turned to the meats in the display case and asked, "What looks good today?"

Cinzia said, "I'm getting a roast for tomorrow's dinner. I like putting it in the oven on my way to evening services and when I come home, it's ready for me and whoever I can convince to come and eat with me."

"Don Arrigo?"

Cinzia shrugged. "Sometimes."

Stella peered at the roast. "Is it filled with something?"

Cinzia looked at her curiously. "Have you not had it?"

"I've been sticking to sausages."

"Ah, well, this is his other claim to fame. Bruno pounds the meat and then rolls it around mortadella, sausage, and prosciutto."

Stella took a step toward the counter, ignoring the lady in navy who stopped her monologue at the butcher about wild asparagus to stare at her for a moment. Stella stepped back and said, "And that's why it's tied that way. It's holding all that filling in."

"*Esatto*," said Cinzia.

Deep in thought, Stella murmured, "Tied with knots."

"Pardon?"

"I don't know. Something about the knots reminds me of something, but I can't think of what."

Cinzia shrugged and pointed to the pendant hanging from Stella's neck. "That's pretty."

Stella looked down. "You think so? I think it looks a bit creepy, myself, but Cosimo seems to think I need help warding off the evil eye."

Cinzia laughed. "That sounds about right. What a sweet man, that Cosimo. And what an impressive collection for a small town, right? You should see his ancient books, too. He's always handing me texts he thinks might interest me."

"Kind of like a lending library."

"With a librarian who is an expert in everything." Cinzia smiled. "This reminds me, Cosimo came round last night and left his card. I need to pop in to say hello. And see that cross of Chiara's."

"You heard about that?"

"Sure, it's a major acquisition for him. Then again, he always comes back from those Tuesday functions with something interesting."

Stella nodded.

Cinzia lowered her voice. "Maybe I should get one of those pendants myself. Any protection from the evil eye right now would be welcome."

Stella raised her eyebrows. "What do you mean?"

Cinzia's laugh felt brittle in Stella's ears. "Well, you must have heard the rumors."

Stella shook her head. "I'm not exactly in anyone's inner circle."

"You and me both," Cinzia confided. Stella couldn't help but flick her gaze over Cinzia's perfectly soft waves and perfectly pink lips. Why wouldn't Cinzia be a sought-after prize to anyone's group? Cinzia continued with a faint blush, "Well, people are saying now that Severini and I had a little thing going."

Her eyes wide, Stella said, "You're kidding." Whoever said this had never seen Cinzia and Severini together. The woman had nothing but contempt for the man.

"I wish." Cinzia sadly shook her head. "Apparently, it's suddenly coming out that my father yelled at Severini, in a way that suggests that Severini looked at me inappropriately. So of course everyone leaps to conclusions."

At the sight of the tears in Cinzia's eyes, Stella put a hand on her arm. "Hey, it's idle chatter. Don't let it bother you."

Cinzia wiped the tears angrily. "No matter what I do, everyone still thinks of me as that wild teenager. I can't ever get beyond it."

Stella didn't know how to comfort Cinzia, so she just continued to pat her arm and murmur nonsense about how it would all be okay.

Cinzia shook the glossy waves off her shoulders. "I can't let the daily nonsense sink my soul."

Stella nodded uncertainly.

Cinzia went on. "That's what Don Arrigo says. I need to focus on who I am in the eyes of the Lord. If I do that, someday they'll see that I'm no one's victim and I'm no one's whore."

The words set Stella back, but just then the navy woman walked out, casting a curious glance at Cinzia's face, pinched in fury. Cinzia's face cleared and she stepped to the counter to order her roast.

Stella looked out over the starlit olive trees and inhaled deeply. She wondered if she'd ever grow immune to their beauty. She startled at a knock at the door. "Matteo! What a surprise. Come in."

"I haven't seen you around lately." He held up a bottle of wine. "So I thought I'd invite myself to supper."

Was this usual Italian behavior, to pop round uninvited? She remembered Cinzia's assumption that Stella's offer of stew had a hidden agenda. Had Matteo shown up hoping for gossip?

As he stepped in, Stella realized Matteo wore sharply creased jeans and a tailored blue striped button-down shirt in lieu of his usual sanitation uniform. Rather than his usual ponytail, he had his curling hair swept away from his face before falling to his shoulders. "You clean up nice," she laughed in English without thinking.

"*Come, scusi*?" Matteo asked with a frown, what's that?

"Nothing," she switched to Italian. It had become second nature to her now to speak and even think and dream in Italian, so it surprised her when English words fell out of her mouth. "I was saying you look good."

"I didn't think you'd welcome me in a trash worker's outfit."

"I would if it meant you'd cart this away." She gestured to the bags heaped in the corner.

"What's with all that?"

"Construction debris. We found out the source of the bathroom stink— mildew in the walls, which encouraged some unspecified animal to climb back there and die. Which did nothing for the mildew problem. We've been tearing it out."

"When I get home, I'll check the calendar for when you can leave that curbside."

"Thanks, I'll need that," she said as she walked to the kitchen. "Now, I hope you aren't hoping for something top tier for dinner."

"Nah. Just a baked pasta, like lasagna. With fresh pasta, of course. Or lamb chops. I do love a lamb chop."

She spun around to see if he was serious.

He held his hands up, grinning, his voice lilting higher than usual. "Kidding! I'd settle for a plate of cookies."

Opening cupboards, she said, "I think I can do better than that.

Though lately, most of my cooking has been of the 'open a can of beans and pour it on top of a salad' variety."

He stared at her. "Now *that* is embarrassing. You thought the fishing net story would make you a pariah. I'd make sure you never lead a conversation with that anecdote."

She laughed and moved cans in her cupboard, trying to find ingredients. She held up a can of tuna. "How about pasta with tuna and tomatoes?"

"Do you have any anchovies to fry up with the garlic?"

He clearly didn't care about how his breath smelled. She smiled to herself. "Of course." She didn't either.

"Fabulous. And it will go so well with my six euro bottle of red wine."

"Ooh, big spender, eh?"

He shrugged with a grin. "What can I say? I thought tonight was too special for my usual four euro bottle."

She laughed and pulled a box of short pasta, shaped like ruffled shells, onto the counter. Meanwhile, Matteo scrolled through his phone and set it against the flour canister as it began playing Italian pop music. She bopped with the beat and handed him the wine opener and turned to take out two glasses. Opening the bottle, he asked, "Has it been hard? Not cooking?"

She thought about it as she filled a battered pot with water. "I've been baking. And I made stew for Cinzia. Cooking settles me down. I need that."

"Yes, because you are right unhinged."

She took the glass of wine he handed her. "If I'm not on the outside, I am on the inside. I can't get my thoughts to settle."

"Well, finding a body can be traumatic." That's why he came. He was worried about her. There was no greater statement of how the last years had killed off her humanity than her inability to recognize simple human kindness when presented to her with a gilded bow.

"There's that," she said. "But also, it's raised so many questions."

"What do you mean?"

"Do you know about one-euro houses?"

"Sure. Every few months they make the rounds on social media."

She filled him in on the contracts she'd found as she lit the burner under a pot of water and pulled out a frying pan to heat on the adjacent burner. To the pan, she poured a glug of local olive oil, which she had to admit was pretty fabulous, and a fraction of the cost she'd pay in the States. While the oil heated, she tossed a head of garlic up and down, freeing the papery skins. "I can't help but think those one-euro houses are connected with his death."

Matteo listened intently as Stella chopped garlic and anchovies. She filled him in on Severini's real name, skipping the part about getting his documents from Mimmo on her own. "But why would he have two names? That's strange. Plus," she paused delicately. "There's that fight with Don Arrigo."

"You can't think Don Arrigo had anything to do with this." She flipped the garlic in the pan with a practiced motion and didn't notice Matteo's eyes bug out until he said, "Wow, you know what you're doing."

"They don't pay me the big bucks for nothing," she said wryly, adding anchovies, stirring them as they melted into the oil.

"It's just surprising."

"Surprising? Why?" She added a can of tomatoes to the pan and broke them up with a wooden spoon.

"Because you look about twelve."

She rolled her eyes. "Don't start. Anyway, whether Don Arrigo is culpable here isn't the point. Why were they fighting so loudly people could hear it from the street?"

"I'm not sure I believe that, by the way."

Stella shrugged as she sprinkled oregano, red pepper flakes, salt, and pepper over the bubbling tomatoes. Seeing the water boiling in the pot, she poured a palmful of salt and the box of pasta, stirring to keep the pasta from sticking. "There was tension between them. I saw it myself."

"I saw that, too," Matteo admitted.

She spun to face him. "What?"

"What? Aren't we talking about the same thing?" he asked.

"I don't know, you tell me." She couldn't tell him about hiding in the chicken coop.

"When I was sweeping the parking lot earlier this week, I saw Don Arrigo pull into his spot, and then Signor Severini pulled in right after him. Severini ran up to Don Arrigo, shouting right in his face."

"And did Don Arrigo yell back?" She stirred the sauce with more vigor than strictly required before tossing in the tuna.

"No, that's why I don't believe the bit about them yelling on Tuesday night. Don Arrigo didn't say a word the whole time Severini was practically spitting in his face."

"He didn't react at all?" She tasted the sauce.

"I didn't say that."

"Matteo."

"He turned pale, okay? He looked like a schoolboy caught turning in someone else's homework. But anyone would turn pale or something when someone yells at them. That's normal."

She tasted the sauce and added a few grains of salt. "Still, why was Severini so angry with him?"

His face grew grim. "I don't know. Maybe Don Arrigo got caught up in something bigger than him. But he is a good man. Really."

Stella set a strainer in the sink. She stirred the pasta and didn't need to taste it to tell by its bounce that it was ready. She poured it into the strainer, before tipping the cooked pasta into the sauce, tossing it to coat all the pieces. As it cooked for another minute in the sauce, she pulled out plates and silverware. Matteo rose from his seat to set the table. Their rhythm felt curiously comfortable, as if they'd been buddies sharing meals for years.

She spooned out a serving of pasta on each plate. Matteo grunted in protest, and she added an extra spoonful to his serving.

As they sat down to eat, Matteo said, "Fine. Add him to your list of suspects. But then you have to add yourself."

She lowered her fork. "You're kidding."

"Would that I were." The gap between his front teeth winked merrily with his smile before he popped a bite of pasta into his mouth and his face stilled. "Wow, this is fabulous."

"You know I didn't kill Signor Severini."

Matteo chewed another bit appreciatively and said, "Listen. You had opportunity—he was staying in your house. You had motive—it's no secret you didn't like him."

"Nobody liked him! And what kind of opportunity? He died on the other side of town. You think I drugged him up and rolled him in nets—"

"Conveniently calling them fishing nets to make yourself look more hapless than guilty."

She stared at him.

His lips twitched and he burst out laughing.

"You shouldn't even joke about this, if rumors start flying—"

"Don't worry!" he clapped his hands together and rubbed them in anticipation. "So, who else had a relationship with Signor Severini?"

"Mimmo."

"Mimmo." Matteo considered. "Unprincipled. Happiest with a weapon. Yes, that adds up. Though it begs the question of why."

Stella leaned back in her chair and tapped her fork against her plate. "I found a rag with what looked like blood at Mimmo's house."

Matteo placed his hands on either side of his plate and looked at her seriously. "What were you doing at his house?"

"I—"

He shook his head and put his hands out to block her words. "You know what? I don't even want to know."

"I already heard it from Domenica." The thoughts in her head picked up speed.

"Good. Secondly . . . *blood*?"

"Yes. Maybe."

He considered for a moment, taking another bite. "Well, I'm not sure what that proves. The guy hunts."

"And according to Luca, the body was relatively clean." A blustering whirlwind of thoughts. She sipped her wine.

"Clean?"

"Yeah, no wounds."

"Which means what, exactly?"

She stood up. "I need to bake something."

"What . . . *now*?"

She picked up her half-empty plate, but he gently removed it from her hands. "I've got you."

She nodded. As if in a trance, she flicked on the oven. Matteo watched her silently for a moment.

As if from far away, she heard his voice. "So, is this an American thing or a chef thing? To just get up from the table when you have a guest over for dinner?"

She flushed in embarrassment. Being with him felt so regular, it was akin to being alone. "I'm sorry. No, we're not all this rude. I . . . well, I think better when I'm cooking. Do you mind?"

"Depends. What are you making?"

"I'm not sure yet." She got out the sugar, salt, a wedge of chocolate, and an envelope of leavening agent they sold in Italy instead of canisters of baking powder. Then she turned to him. "There were no marks on him and something suspicious came back on the tox screen. So it must have been poison. So whoever did it had access to a deadly poison, an opportunity of getting it into him, and a motive for wanting him dead."

She turned back to her bowl and measured in two cups of flour before she turned back to him. "It still could have been Mimmo. Next to the bloody rag, there was a bottle of something, elderberry extract, he said. But he got weird when I saw it. I honed in on the rag, but maybe… maybe there was something else in that bottle. Something more sinister than elderberries."

Matteo stayed quiet as Stella turned her attention to measuring sugar and then rustling through her drawer of extracts until she found the vanilla. "According to the villagers at Bar Cappellina, not everyone was a fan of Severini bringing in tourism, and that's without knowing about the one-euro housing. Any one of them could have invited Signor Severini over after his appointment with the priest Tuesday night and offered him a nightcap laced with rat poison."

She took butter out of its silver packet and plopped it into a saucepan over low heat. "Or, not rat poison. I'm sure that would leave a taste. But something."

She cracked three eggs in a bowl and whisked them until they frothed. "It comes back to the priest."

Now Matteo opened his mouth, but before he could say anything, she said, "He may not have done it, but I bet he knows who did. Nobody other than the mayor had that kind of contact with Signor Severini. Don Arrigo had to know where Severini went after their appointment."

Matteo nodded slowly as Stella added sugar to the eggs. "Or maybe he knows but can't say, because of confession rules."

Stella ripped open the leavener and added the powder to the flour.

Matteo grinned. "Do you still not know what you're baking?"

She didn't answer. "We need two things, as far as I can see. We need to know what Don Arrigo knows and we need to go to Subbiano."

"Subbiano?"

"He spent an awful lot of time there. Maybe someone there will have some idea of his whereabouts on Tuesday night or who might have hated him enough to kill him. Though the real information will come from Don Arrigo. Blondies, by the way. Brown butter blondies. With chocolate pieces."

She added the wet ingredients to the dry and mixed them gently, pausing to sip her wine. "I have to tell you, though, Matteo. If the police get evidence that Signor Severini was killed, Don Arrigo will have to be their prime suspect. Unless we find another one."

Nodding slowly, Matteo breathed in the smell of melting butter and the sound of Stella now chopping chocolate. "I'm not saying I would do this, but maybe I can detour next time I pick up the church's trash. Bring it here."

She turned to him, astonished. "You would do that?"

He shrugged. "Not because I think he's guilty. But because I think he's innocent."

She nodded and turned to face the browning butter, sending the scent of caramel into the air.

The thin morning light drifted across Stella's pillow. Ugh, her head ached. How much did she drink last night? It was hard to tell since she'd sipped as she baked. She sat up, clutching the coverlet to her chest. Blondies. Had she given them all to Matteo to take home? No, she'd left herself at least a few. A solid breakfast.

Stella scarfed them down with a mug of milk and then got dressed as she brushed her teeth, too impatient to get going. She practically ran to Domenica's but stalled at the sight of Don Arrigo making his way toward the town exit. Pausing, she considered.

She made up her mind and called out to Don Arrigo as he slipped into the shadows of the town entrance. Her voice rose loudly enough that windows banged and old women peered out to catch the commotion. Yet

Don Arrigo continued striding away from her.

Stella hurried, still calling him, but he moved even more swiftly around the ring road to the parking lot. Running now, Stella arrived just as Don Arrigo reversed his car. She flagged him down—how could he ignore her calling in this obvious way? He gave her a quick flap of a hand before throwing the car into gear and peeling away.

Watching him race up the road, Stella wondered what the townspeople saw in this guy. She sighed and retraced her steps to Domenica's. As she opened the door, Stella couldn't help the feeling that Domenica had been expecting her.

"*Buongiorno, cara.*"

Stella smiled in greeting, enjoying the light streaming across the floor, making the space snug against the foggy morning. She plopped into the empty armchair set at the end of Domenica's desk, blessedly devoid of cats at the moment, though a calico glared at her as if Stella had stolen its spot. "I've been thinking about those one-euro house programs."

Domenica chuckled. "You don't waste time, do you?"

Stella shook her head as she took off her jacket, hanging it over the back of the chair. "I realized last night, all those one-euro house schemes, villages sponsor them to bring new life to underpopulated areas. The only profit is warm bodies spending money. Why would Severini get involved in a town that's not his? If I can untangle that, figure out what Severini would get out of it, maybe I can figure out why someone would want to kill him."

Domenica nodded. "That's true. Though the motive could just be that someone didn't want him bringing foreigners here."

"I know, but Severini got something from this. I want to know what."

Stella sat back, thinking. The calico cat took this opportunity to stand on its hind legs, a questioning white paw pressing against Stella's thigh. She stared at the beast, wondering what it could want. She didn't have kibble. The cat lowered for a moment and Stella thought it would whisk away, but it leaped nimbly onto her lap. It must have deemed her lap inadequate compared to Domenica's because the cat glared momentarily at her, as if accusing her of refusing seconds of *panna cotta* one too many times. But then it turned twice, slipping off her spare lap a bit before catching itself, and curled into a patchwork ball of white and black and orange. Stella touched it on the back and looked up at Domenica. "It *likes* me."

"She. And don't get a swollen head. Ravioli likes everyone."

"You named your cat Ravioli?"

"And you named your cat something so much better?"

"I don't have a cat. I have a squatter."

Domenica held out her hand. "Not now. Not just when I was beginning to like you." Her smile belied the iron in her words.

Stella let her hand linger above Ravioli for a moment before tentatively stroking her fur. The cat emitted a kind of chirp at the touch and opened one eye to study her before settling deeper into Stella's lap. A soft rumble sounded, softly at first, until it filled the room.

Stella smiled at Domenica, her face radiant.

Domenica shook her head. "Where did you get the idea that you don't like cats?"

"I just never have." Stella thought for a moment. "Wait, that's not true. After my father and sister died, I wanted to keep a kitten I found in the street. My mother said no, but I smuggled it in anyway, thinking she wouldn't know. The cat peed everywhere and yowled when I was at school. My mother kicked it out and I got a beating."

Domenica shook her head at the story. "You haven't loved a cat since then?"

"What's to love? Cats are aloof and reserved and I got enough of that at home."

Domenica said nothing and looked pointedly at the cat, who could by no means be described as aloof.

"Not all cats are good," Stella protested.

"Not all people are good either, and yet we persevere." Domenica shrugged. "Now. The case. You're right, there isn't a ready answer to what Severini sought to gain from the one-euro houses."

"We need Severini's backstory. Or Crespi's, I guess. Both, since we don't know what he's doing with an alias." Stella sighed. "But the cops don't seem interested in thinking outside the box."

Domenica shrugged. "Why wait for them to do the work when we could do it ourselves?"

"Right." Stella paused. "Wait, what? What do you mean?"

"Look, the police are a good sort and are far more intelligent than their lack of literary prowess would indicate—well, Luca is surprisingly well read, if you count historical romance, and as I am no purist, I certainly do."

Stella looked up. Luca read? *Historical romance?*

Domenica ignored Stella's gaping mouth. "But they think in a straight line. They will do what they are told by their commander, who unfortunately is as old and set in his ways as the stones holding up the roof over our head." Domenica gestured into the air.

Stella let out a short laugh, causing Ravioli to lift her head, the fur on her face matted where she'd pressed into Stella's lap. The cat glared at Stella with one open eye. Stella patted Ravioli's head and the cat dropped back into slumber. "So I should somehow convince the cops to find out more about Severini? I mean Crespi?"

"What cops? Like I said, until a superior orders them to search Severini's backstory, they won't bother. Why waste your valuable time trying to convince them when I can do it right here?"

Stella's heart sank. Domenica didn't look that old, probably in her sixties or early seventies. But maybe she was a bit touched in the head? If she thought she could find answers to today's problem in her dusty old books...

Domenica leaped up. "Well, it's worth a try, right?"

"Domenica..."

Fussing with the shawls piled on her desk, Domenica answered her over her shoulder. "Listen, even if our officers wanted to investigate Severini's background, they don't have an expert on staff who can do anything more than a simple internet search. If we want this done, we'll need to do it ourselves."

Domenica's generous girth blocked Stella's view of the desk, but Stella heard the unmistakable hum of a computer coming to life. "You have a computer?"

Rapping the top of the now uncovered computer, Domenica said, "If you can call it that. I don't make enough to get myself a new model. Have to content myself with getting a junk one and refurbishing it."

Stella's mouth dropped open. Again. "How do you know how to do that? I can't make an Excel spreadsheet."

Domenica tossed a reassuring smile toward Stella as she sat down. "You're a chef, why should you be technologically savvy?"

"But you run a used bookstore in a medieval hill town!"

"I didn't always run a bookstore, *cara.*" Before Stella could formulate her scattering thoughts into some semblance of a question, Domenica turned her attention to the screen, her fingers flying across the keyboard. "All right, Severini...Crespi...what have you been hiding?"

Stella shook her head, still floored by the sight of Domenica, at least five scarves wound around her neck, peering intently at the screen.

"Aha!" Domenica clapped her hands.

"What is it?" Stella straightened while trying not to budge Ravioli, now snoring lightly.

"Fascinating." Domenica's face bathed in the computer's blue light as she silently read the screen. Finally, she said, "Nothing on Severini. But Danilo Crespi is wanted for questioning. Looks like Subbiano was not his first one-euro plot. He convinced a village in Calabria to kick start the program."

"That still doesn't resolve the question of what he got from it. I mean, the town gets foreigners to bankroll the town's rehabilitation, but what does he get?"

"That's where this gets interesting. Crespi advertised his services to Americans, offering to broker the transaction as a liaison between the buyer and the town, to make sure everything went smoothly. He charged them €10,000 for his services."

"Wow."

Domenica's eyes skimmed the page. "And that's just the starting point. He also told potential buyers that the housing deal had grown so popular, there was a bidding war for each home. So they needed to bid on at least three houses, at €5,000 a pop, and they would be guaranteed to get one of them. He promised them their money back on any house they didn't get, and the town would hold their €5,000 for the house they did purchase, to be returned to the buyer at the conclusion of the renovations."

"So essentially it became a deposit to make sure the buyer followed through on the planned renovations."

"Correct. And it looks like he also offered to negotiate with local construction companies to get the work done. For a fee, of course."

Stella thought for a moment. "Something tells me these buyers didn't get their money's worth."

Shaking her head, her eyes still fixed on the screen, Domenica said, "They did not. He got about €25,000 from each potential buyer, and then he disappeared."

"Why did the village agree to this?"

"It looks like they didn't. They only knew he was offering his services to help English speakers work with the construction companies. They didn't even know about the rest until irate Americans started hiring fluent Italian lawyers to contact the mayor, complaining that they hadn't gotten their final paperwork for the houses. Crespi had stopped answering emails."

"How many people did he fool?"

Domenica adjusted her glasses. "At least ten. There may have been more since the article."

"So I guess we know why he changed his name."

"Huh," Domenica said, flying through screens.

"What?"

Domenica said nothing, her mouth following along as she skimmed page after page.

"Domenica? What?"

Domenica rotated her chair to face Stella. "Well, I found an arrest record for Crespi. Back when he was sixteen, it looks like he was living on the streets. In London, of all places."

"London!" Stella said. "That explains his English."

"He got taken in for pickpocketing. Told the arresting officer he'd recently arrived from Rome with no local family. They kept him over-night and then let him go."

"A thief from an early age, then." Stella thought for a moment. "Back to the houses. The ones that villages offer to foreigners as one-euro homes. I guess they have be abandoned, right? With no owner?"

Domenica pushed her glasses higher on her nose and turned back to the computer. After a minute, she said, "Yes. It's a bit of a controversy, as sometimes a home looks abandoned, but after it's sold, the grandchild of the previous owner comes forward wanting their house back. Doesn't seem to happen often. Most villages do try to make sure that there are no living descendants."

"The dates of death."

Domenica turned back. "What dates of death?"

"In Severini's papers, he had all these addresses listed in Subbiano, with dates of death noted beside them."

"That makes sense. He would need to make sure he's brokering a sale of a house with no real owner."

Stella shook her head. "But why would a thief care about good business practice? Why not post photos of lovely villas and say they're empty and get Americans to give him money? The whole 'I've got a bridge to sell you' approach."

Domenica tapped on the desk with her finger in thought. "The houses would be listed by the village, or in this case by Aramezzo since Subbiano falls under Aramezzo's jurisdiction. Nobody would bid on a house that's just free-floating on the internet. It would have to have the stamp of approval of the village, complete with the rules for participation."

"Severini had to bring houses to the mayor to list. So those houses had to be at least conceivably abandoned." Stella mulled this over as she stroked Ravioli's fur. "But, Domenica, how is a house declared abandoned?"

"Well, they'd need a death certificate for the last known owner."

An idea bloomed in Stella's mind as she spoke the words. "And who issues the death certificate?"

"Usually the parish priest."

"Don Arrigo." Stella spoke slowly, "So Severini could have been trying to force Don Arrigo to issue death certificates for those houses."

Domenica said, "Well, not necessarily force—"

"They had that big argument. You heard about that."

"Of course, but—"

"What else could it have been about? From the moment Severini arrived in Aramezzo, he spent all his time hounding Don Arrigo."

"So maybe he got the death certificates from Don Arrigo. What does that prove?"

Stella considered. "Severini doesn't seem the patient type. Waiting to contact next of kin, waiting to close the chain of ownership. I wonder if he asked Don Arrigo to fake the death certificates."

"Fake them?" Domenica's voice scaled up.

"Sure. It explains why they argued."

Domenica stared at Stella. "You can't think Don Arrigo killed Severini?"

Stella shrugged. "I can't think why no one is asking the question."

Stella interrupted her work ripping out plaster with Ilaria to answer the phone. She returned with a spring in her step. Ilaria smiled. "Good news?"

"The best. Internet will be installed on Tuesday!"

Ilaria concentrated on a particularly crumbling bit of plaster, tearing it away to toss it onto the floor. "You know that means Thursday, right? At the earliest."

"Who cares? I'm *in the system*. You have no idea how much this means to me."

Ilaria backed up from their work, brushing her hands on her pants. "I think this is as far as we can get today."

Stella peered into the gap between the floor and the stone of the outer walls. No more carcasses. No treasure, either, which she hadn't confessed aloud, but she'd secretly hoped to find. She pulled out a handful of rotting insulation and something caught her eye, a piece of paper. "How would this get behind the wall?"

Ilaria shrugged. "People used whatever they could for insulation. Sometimes newspaper if they couldn't get horsehair. Easy enough for debris to get swooped up with the rest."

Stella nodded and unfolded the paper.

Never forget
The goddess sees
Sunlight and your dark reflection.
Your beauty and your wickedness.
And she can spell them all.

Ilaria asked, "What's it say?"

Stella handed her the note. "It doesn't make sense."

Ilaria's eyes widened as she read. "What does it mean?"

"Who knows? Toss it in the trash with the rest." As Ilaria opened a garbage bag, Stella said, "Wait. I'll add it to my pile of artifacts. Maybe I can turn it all into a display someday. So far, it's only my photographs and some farm equipment from the shed out back. A handwritten note about a goddess seems like a worthy addition."

As they crammed plastic garbage bags with the removed plaster, Ilaria chatted about her husband's improvement. Last night he'd walked one circuit around Aramezzo, and they were feeling positive about him returning to work next week. Ilaria said he'd offered to take Stella to the TIM store in Assisi to get her phone operational. Without Ilaria saying anything, Stella knew that she and her husband were grateful for Ilaria's extra hours at Casale Mazzoli. Stella felt glad that her arrival in the village coincided with a time they needed the income, and also glad to think that soon she'd share a link to the outside world.

Stella frowned as she tied the bag. Without internet or cellular, New York City, indeed the rest of the world, felt like somebody else's life. She sort of enjoyed the cocoon of surrounding herself with her own days, rather than the grind of emails and social media and the relentless march of news stories.

Ah well, she'd adjust. She had to list Casale Mazzoli on websites with her email address if she was going to turn a profit.

She dragged the bags of refuse outside, stopping at the sight of a man a few doors down, walking toward the town entrance. The set of those broad shoulders seemed familiar. As he turned to walk back toward her, she noticed the uniform. Oh! Luca. Stella wondered if he'd been walking the street for a while.

"What's up?" she asked as he approached.

He said nothing, but continued toward her, hands deep in his jacket pockets. He stopped, quiet, staring at the ground with eyes that seemed deeper set than usual.

She shrugged and continued dragging bags of plaster to the street. Finally, Luca caught her eye as he ran a distracted hand through his hair. "He was murdered."

"Who?" It dawned on her. "Oh."

Luca lowered himself to sit on her stoop, and after a moment's pause, Stella sank beside him. Feeling the confusion and discouragement coming off of him in waves, Stella had to stop herself from putting a reassuring hand on his arm. "How do you know?"

Luca studied his hands clasped between his knees. "The medical examiner. Further bloodwork showed elevated hyoscine in addition to the atropine. It's not consistent with his medications. It looks like poison. Probably injected, since there wasn't any sign of anything suspicious in his digestive system."

"What kind of poison?"

He shrugged. "Does it matter?"

Frowning, Stella said, "Well, yes."

Luca stared at her, surprise in the raise of his dark eyebrows. "I'll know when the medical examiner completes the autopsy, okay? So far, we just know he had signs of anticholinergic toxic syndrome—the elevated atropine, dilated pupils, flushed skin, and it looks like cause of death was respiratory failure."

"Listen," she considered her words. "I understand how you wouldn't have wanted to assume—"

"It was a lucky guess." He blinked and looked back at his clasped hands. "Don't puff out your tail feathers."

Stella craned her neck to check her back pockets. "I didn't think I was."

He didn't laugh. Instead his voice rang with resignation. "It's all a game to you, like the Captain says. You're just passing through. I'm the one who had to arrest him."

"Arrest him? Who? Who did you arrest?" Her voice scaled up.

"Enzo, of course."

"*Enzo?*"

He dropped his head to watch his thumbs flick over each other.

"*Enzo?*"

"I know it's a lot to take." His voice softened. "Look, Stella. It happened on his property. You yourself found Severini wrapped in Enzo's nets. Several villagers reported hearing Enzo yelling at Severini the day he disappeared. Unless we get disconfirming information, we're considering the case closed."

She set her chin. "So you're not even considering other suspects?"

He sighed. "Like who?"

"I have some ideas."

"Of course you do." He cast his gaze heavenward, as if praying for patience. "Look, I appreciate the information you provided. I do. You've been helpful."

She barked out a laugh.

"I'm serious. Thanks to you, we know his name. But we interviewed everyone in town about where they were Tuesday into Thursday. Enzo is the only one with motive and means."

"Enzo couldn't have done it." She grumbled. "I don't know how I know, but I know."

His voice pleaded, "Do me a favor? Don't be a cliche and decide to take on the investigation because you can do it better than anyone else. It's so American."

She couldn't decide if he was teasing her and she grew frustrated keeping up with his shifting tone. Sure, this new information shook him. But that wasn't her problem. "Seriously, Luca? Is this what you think of me? That I'm in it for the points?"

He hesitated. "I thought you'd be pleased I came to tell you. I'm trying to work with you here, Stella."

"Begrudgingly," Stella muttered.

Luca ignored this. His voice bristling, he said, "I mean it. I heard you've been asking questions. This isn't your beat."

She sighed and rose to standing. No good getting into it with this impossible man.

Ilaria stepped out of the house with the last bag of plaster. She dropped it on the street and looked from Stella's serious face to Luca's serious face. "What happened? Did someone die?" She gasped. "Madonna mia, *did someone die?*"

Stella took her arm and started walking back into the house without saying goodbye to Luca. "No more than usual. I'll fill you in."

After showering off the plaster dust and scarfing down a lunch of bread slathered with Nutella (why did it taste better in Italy than it did in the States?), Stella set off with a determined step back to Domenica's.

Domenica glanced up from a video of Siamese cats cavorting on a beach. Apparently, she no longer felt the need to hide her technology from Stella. "You heard about Enzo?"

Stella nodded. "How could the police think that man did it? Enzo couldn't kill a houseplant unless he watered it with alcohol."

"Just because he's drunk doesn't mean he can't fly into a rage, or—"

"It's more than that."

"What?"

Stella paused. "I don't know. I can taste the answer on the tip of my tongue, but can't get there."

Domenica smiled. "Let me pour you some coffee. You look like you need it."

Belatedly, Stella realized that the air smelled like toasting coffee beans. A moka burbled on the hot plate. Domenica poured a cup and then lifted a drowsing grey tabby off the overstuffed armchair. Stella dropped into the empty chair, accepting the cup of coffee with thanks.

"Milk or sugar?" Domenica's voice sounded like an order, not a question.

"Neither."

"Good girl."

Domenica settled in her seat with her cup. "The thing you have to know is that Enzo was a loose cannon for a lot of years. Since his wife died, according to the stories."

"You didn't see it play out?"

Domenica took a sip. "I arrived after she died. I never got on with him, but then no woman could, the way he talked about our bodies or joked about sex in a way that was never funny. It was like his wife had muzzled his bad behavior and without her, he was all over the place. And not in a good way." Domenica took a breath before continuing. "There was talk of him picking up those prostitutes that loiter on the road to Norcia, but that could be speculation."

Stella said, "I heard all this from Cinzia. Or a version of it."

Domenica shook her head sadly. "Poor Cinzia. I guess it was only a matter of time before she went off the rails, too. Failing in school, dressing in a way that made the villagers nervous. Maybe it was the influence of all those women coming and going from her mother's old bedroom. Or maybe because she had no one to discipline her."

"Or maybe she was trying to get the attention of the only parent she had left."

"Huh. Maybe." She regarded Stella with new respect. "Nice analysis."

"Plenty of poor parenting and probably not enough therapy." She waved her fingers in a "gimme" gesture. "Go on. Cinzia didn't say what happened next."

"I'm not surprised. She fell in with an older crowd. Some people say she found herself pregnant, which could be true. It's not like there's a lot of talk about safe sex in a town like Aramezzo."

"Even if there were, it sounds like she wasn't in a position to advocate for herself."

"Exactly. All of a sudden, her father was yelling at everyone in Aramezzo, as if the baker or the florist bore responsibility for failing his daughter. She disappeared for a bit and when she came back, her father got her a job working for Don Arrigo."

"You think she had a baby somewhere?"

"No, she didn't go away for long. Just a week or two? Maybe longer, time runs differently when you get older. Long enough that I figured Enzo had dumped her with some relative, but then she came back and graduated from high school after all."

Stella considered this story. "When did she start raising rabbits?"

Domenica frowned. "I can't remember. Why?"

"I don't know. I guess I wonder if she used them to fill the hole left by her mother."

"Ah, more psychoanalyzing." Domenica smiled. "I hate to shatter your fascinating theory, but her mother gave her the first one. According to stories, she and her mother both doted on that rabbit. The baker once told me about a purse Cinzia's mother made for Cinzia to carry the rabbit about town like a baby."

"So one before her mother died. The rest later?"

"I think so. I know the baker gave her one. So did the butcher. Though

I think he intended her to raise them for meat."

"Which she's against."

"Always has been. Those rabbits are her babies. When one dies, she grieves. Everyone drops by with food. It's like a death in the family."

"That's too bad. Rabbits don't live long, do they?"

"No."

"That's a lot of grieving, then."

Domenica nodded slowly. "I hadn't thought about it, but yes. It is."

"How many rabbits does she have now?"

"Six."

"Six!"

"Yes, for sure. Six. Why is that surprising?"

"I don't know. It feels like a lot."

"I have six cats, dear."

Stella decided not to comment. Perhaps a change of topic was warranted. "I got us off track. What happened to Enzo?"

"He never forgave Aramezzo. He doesn't speak to anyone. Barely even to Cinzia even though they live together. You never see them talk. I've watched them pass each other in the *piazza* without a word."

"Have you ever seen Enzo not drunk? Like on Sundays or in the morning?"

"No. I mean, yes, when I first got here. Back then, he drank most evenings, but that was it. But for the past few years, it's been constant."

Stella thought for a moment. "Luca said that the medical examiner suspects poison. Do you have any books on local poisonous plants?"

"Plenty," Domenica said before gesturing to the computer. "Or we could, you know, enter the digital age."

"Oh, right. I've gotten so used to doing things the old-fashioned way. See if any cause anticholinergic toxic syndrome." Stella looked around until she found Ravioli curled up on a bookshelf. She picked up the drowsing cat and settled back into the chair with her coffee. Ravioli beeped in protest, but then got to work kneading her legs. "She's making pizza!"

Domenica glanced over her shoulder and smiled. "You are so cat backward."

"Am not. Just wish my misfit could borrow some of Ravioli's charms."

"Have you tried being charming with your misfit?"

"That seems entirely beside the point. Now, what are you going to search for?"

"I thought 'poisonous plants Umbria' would be a good start. And I'll put in the ... what kind of shock syndrome?"

"Anticholinergic."

"Right. Got it." Domenica started typing and then asked, "Why plants, by the way?"

"A hunch I guess. There was a smell on Severini I can't place. Mixed with common herbs—rosemary, sage. I thought for a hot second it was mastic—"

"What?"

"Mastic. It's a resin used in Eastern Mediterranean cooking. It smells like pine, but that's not quite right. Mastic has a kind of anise edge to it. This didn't."

"So you're looking for a poison that smells like mastic. Or pine, I guess?"

Stella shrugged. "Feels like we might as well begin there. I mean, maybe there's some common poisonous flower that also happens to grow in the chapel garden."

Domenica turned to look at Stella. With emphasis, she said, "Sometimes our view of another's guilt can be colored by our own histories."

"Your subtext is mostly text."

Domenica snorted.

"Anyway, I know you don't agree about Don Arrigo. But I promise he's mixed up in this somehow."

"You are a dog with a bone, aren't you?"

"You say it like it's a bad thing."

"Well. I am a cat person."

Stella considered. "You've never had a dog?"

Domenica tucked her grey hair behind her ears. "Aside from the sled dogs, no."

Stella's eyes widened. "Now you're teasing me."

Domenica's fingers paused and she grinned at Stella. "Am I?" She turned back. "Those were good dogs. But it takes time to train them to compliance. So, cats for me."

Stella stroked Ravioli's neck until the cat left off her pizza making and curled into a tight ball. Stella's mother hadn't been against dogs the way she was against cats, but with her work schedule, they'd never been able to have one. She wondered for a moment, if she stayed here, maybe she could get a dog. Maybe it would prompt the cat to leave. That would be a bonus.

Though she had to admit, something about the purring cat with the warm bookshop and the fragrant coffee made her feel that all was right with the world.

"Bingo," Domenica breathed.

"You found it!"

"Well, not *it*, precisely. Nothing with a pine scent. But there are a couple of poisonous plants that grow in Umbria that can cause that kind of syndrome. Mushrooms, of course. And belladonna."

"Belladonna. I've heard that name before."

Domenica sat back, satisfied. "Sure, it shows up throughout literary history. Emperor Augustus's wife used it to murder his grandson, thus assuring her own son would rise to the throne. Shakespeare often referenced belladonna."

Shaking her head, Stella said, "I never read Shakespeare."

"I suppose not. Since your predilections trend more toward pulp."

"Hey!"

"It's not an insult. Everyone has their tastes. But if you read historical romance like Luca—or actually Cinzia reads it, too . . . or she used to, lately she's just come in for religious texts—you'd know that Renaissance women used belladonna to widen their pupils and bring color to their cheeks."

Stella pulled a face. "Why would they want that?"

Domenica shrugged. "Who can say why people do what they do? For fashion. The doe-eyed, rosy-complected look was 'in', I expect."

"Oh . . ." Stella's voice faded. "Oh. Domenica. Severini. His eyes, did I tell you about that?"

"You did. And his cheeks."

"But it kills people? In real life? It doesn't just . . . dilate their pupils or make them fancy or whatever?"

"It definitely kills people." Domenica adjusted her glasses and leaned closer to the screen. "One of the more toxic plants worldwide. The berries, leaves, roots, all of it is highly toxic. Up there with arsenic. It can take time to kill. Sometimes a day or more, depending on the dosage."

"Someone heard a moaning early Wednesday morning. Close to where I found him."

"Which tracks. After belladonna poisoning, the victim is confused, disoriented. Then they fall into a coma and eventually die."

"Belladonna."

Domenica nodded and continued reading, her mouth moving slightly with the words.

"Where is it found?"

"Kind of everywhere. It's commonly found growing over ruins. We've got plenty of those." Domenica read a few more moments and then said, "I wonder what the odds are that Severini found a belladonna plant in Subbiano or something and ate a handful of the berries."

"No, Luca said they thought the killer injected the poison since the stomach contents didn't show he'd eaten anything suspect," Stella said. "Anyway, he couldn't have tied himself into the nets on his own. The man looked like—"

Suddenly Stella gasped.

Domenica spun around. "What? What is it?"

"The knots. I just realized why Enzo couldn't have killed Severini. The knots on the nets were tight, precise, like the kind on a roast pork."

"I'm a vegetarian."

Stella sighed. "But you've *seen* a tied roll of pork."

"Of course."

"Well, the first time I ran into Enzo in the street, he couldn't tie his shoelaces. I'm not saying he didn't tie them well, I'm saying he could not tie them at all. He gave up and stumbled home with them flapping."

Domenica said slowly, "So the knots prove it couldn't be Enzo."

"Right."

"But remember how Enzo was so strange when they questioned him?"

Stella frowned in thought. "I've had more than my share of conversations with drunk customers. They make no sense, they laugh when nothing is funny, and they'd admit to assassinating JFK if it meant another round."

Domenica mulled this over. "So what do we know?"

"Definitely poison, possibly belladonna."

"And I heard the police say there wasn't evidence of the poison in the stomach, so they're assuming an injection."

Stella nodded. "Making it even less likely to be Enzo."

"Exactly. Making it less likely to be anyone in town who doesn't have experience with syringes."

The women sat thinking until Stella broke the silence. "Unless...."

"Unless?"

"I know this sounds weird, but can you *juice* belladonna?"

"Juice it?"

"Right. If it was a liquid, it would have moved through the body more quickly and might not have been found in his stomach contents."

Domenica went back to clicking the computer. "It looks like you can. The berries are sweet. See the photo? They're shiny and black, a danger for hungry children."

"Black?"

"Well, you know, a kind of purple-black."

Stella stood, her voice shaking as she said, "Do they look like elderberries?"

Domenica looked back at the screen. "I suppose so."

Stella stood so suddenly Ravioli fell to the floor with an aggrieved yowl. "See you, Domenica."

"Where are you going?"

"I'll tell you later," Stella called over her shoulder. To herself, she muttered, "If I have anything to tell."

Stella ran through Aramezzo until she found Matteo sweeping cigarette butts out of the cobblestones in an alley latticed with the shadow of overhanging grapevines. Out of breath, she panted, "Did you hear the news?"

"About Enzo?"

"Dang! I'll never get any news first."

He shrugged and poked at a stubborn bit of trash with the end of his straw broom. "Well, you were the first to know Signor Severini died."

She shivered. "I would have been happy to be further down the gossip chain for that one."

"Beggars can't be choosers." He grinned, his long face bright in the waning sun, which lit his curls from behind like a halo.

"I don't think Enzo did it." Before he could protest that she should let the police do their business, she added, "I've seen him drunk and he couldn't even tie his shoelaces. There's no way he could tie the nets in those tiny knots."

"Huh. I suppose that makes sense." His eyes narrowed.

"I think it was Mimmo. Remember, I told you about the elderberry juice I saw at his house?"

Matteo frowned, trying to figure out where this was going.

"Well, Domenica and I just figured out that belladonna causes anticholinergic toxic syndrome, the very thing that killed Severini. And the berries of the belladonna plant look a lot like elderberry."

He blanched. "You think Mimmo gave Severini belladonna in liquid form?"

She shrugged and half nodded. "I have to find out. I'm on my way now."

"You can't!"

"I have to."

"Alone?"

"Unless you want to come with me?"

"Well, I can't let you go by yourself."

She tried to smile. "I admit, I counted on your chivalry."

On the walk to Mimmo's, they rehearsed a story. Creeping toward the gate, they whispered it through one more time. At the entrance, Stella called over the sound of dogs barking, "Mimmo! Mimmo, are you there?"

Howling and panting greeted her words, and she called again, "Mimmo!" before she heard him shuffling to the gate.

He threw it open and glared. "What do you want now? I told you, Signor Severini is your problem."

She gave her brightest, most innocent smile. "I know, and that was so helpful, thanks heaps! I'm here because I remembered your elderberry extract."

His face stiffened. "What about it? It's just elderberry extract."

Her laugh sounded false even to her ears, but it's all she could do while shoving the dogs off her chest, and did that one even nose at her shoulders? Mimmo shouted, and the dogs scattered, heads low. In the sudden quiet, Stella said, "My friend Matteo here is getting that cold that's going around. He can't afford to miss work."

Matteo coughed helpfully.

Mimmo glowered suspiciously at each of them. "What's that got to do with me?"

"Well, we wanted to see if we could buy the bottle? I know it would help him!"

Mimmo's face lit up. "You want to give me money for it?"

Out of the corner of her eye, Stella noticed Matteo sag in relief beside her. "Absolutely!"

Mimmo's face clouded over. "You should have asked me when you was here before."

She ignored the mistaken grammar. "He's only been down for the last day or two."

Matteo nodded helpfully and gave a little sniff.

"He's not down, he's right here." Mimmo scowled.

Stella and Matteo locked eyes.

Mimmo didn't notice. "Anyway, I already gave it to Marta."

"*You what?*" Stella and Matteo yelped together.

"She was going on about how she needed it for her son. Going on and on about how sick Ascanio is. She gave me this sob story about how when Ascanio heard Severini died just a few pastures over, he freaked out, ran off, stayed out in the cold for hours before she found him hiding in a chicken coop. That kid was always wired up too sensitive and always sickly. She talked like it was my fault, mean in her eyes. You tell me, how that's my fault? The guy wanted to check in with a fake name and I said okay as long as he paid under the table so I could skim—"

He stopped with a grimace, suddenly realizing who he was talking to. Then he continued. "Whine, whine, whine. And the boy, staring at me with those drippy eyes. So I told her I'd give her the bottle. But she shouldn't come crying to me if it didn't agree with him."

"When did you give it to her, Mimmo?"

"I dunno."

"Think!"

"Why?" The suspicious look returned to his face. "What's it matter to you?"

Stella and Matteo looked at each other. Stella adopted the look of wide-eyed innocence she'd found softened Mimmo, at least a little. "Well, if it wasn't that long ago, maybe she has some left."

"Oh." He squinted his eyes in thought as he scratched his belly. "Yesterday, I think."

Stella groaned inwardly. If that little boy had taken that extract, extract his mother tipped into his mouth, it would be a way for Mimmo to have gotten rid of the evidence. And if that was indeed not elderberry but something more sinister and it killed Signor Severini, what would it do to Ascanio?

She grabbed Matteo's hand. "See you later, Mimmo!"

"Hey, wait, do you want a truffle? Prime quality. I got all sizes—"

"Maybe later."

He grumbled and turned away. "They always say later."

Stella and Matteo bolted up the road and then up the stairs into Aramezzo. Matteo panted, "If I didn't know better, I'd say Mimmo likes you."

"What do you mean?"

"He hardly snarled at all."

Stella thought as she tried to keep up with Matteo. "We shared a moment."

"Must have been some moment."

"I wouldn't have thought so. But I'm not sure what it says about me if I can endear myself to a murderer."

The words propelled them to greater speed, as they turned left at the first inner ring to wind around to the other side of town, to Marta's house. Stella's vision blurred with images of arriving just as Marta spooned a dose of the purple liquid into Ascanio's waiting mouth. Though she knew Marta wouldn't wait to give Ascanio a tonic she believed would help her little boy. She could only hope that maybe Ascanio had improved on his own, so Marta had never given the tonic. Maybe the full bottle would be there and they could get it analyzed. Maybe Stella could even tell by smelling it if it was indeed elderberry.

They didn't bother to catch their breath as they approached Marta's door, both knocking vigorously until Marta opened it, eyes wide as she dried her hands on her apron, a white dog with long, coarse fur at her knee, ears pricked forward.

"Ascanio," Stella panted as Matteo doubled over. "How is he?"

Marta cut her eyes to the side with a nod and a pajama-clad Ascanio appeared like a waif. Pale, but very much alive. "Ascanio!" He said nothing, just popped his thumb into his mouth and ran a hand through his dog's fur. The dog sat, his eyes fixed on the visitors.

Marta tussled Ascanio's dark curls, a mirror of his mother's, only his floated around his head and Marta wore her hair plaited and wound like a crown. "Isn't it nice of our friends to check on you, Ascanio?"

Stella's knees weakened in relief. "You didn't give Ascanio the elderberry?"

"Elderberry? Oh, you mean Mimmo's tonic. Yes, I gave it to him."

Matteo peered into Ascanio's face as Stella said, "He's okay?"

Marta laughed. "As you see. It worked wonders. So kind of Mimmo to insist on giving us a bottle. Poor man can't stand to see Ascanio under the weather."

Stella adjusted the bandana holding back her curls, sure she had misheard Marta.

Matteo must have been of the same thinking. "Mimmo? Are we talking about the same guy?"

Marta laughed. "How many Mimmos do we have in Aramezzo, Matteo? I know he's not to everyone's tastes, but he's been a big help to Ascanio and me. Always bringing me *cinghiale*, or salami. And he helps out at sheep-shearing time."

"For a price, you mean," Stella clarified.

Shaking her head, Marta said, "He gets the same lunch we give everyone at the sheep shearing."

Stella muttered, "It must be an incredible lunch."

Matteo asked, "Can we see the bottle of tonic?"

"Sure," Marta turned into the house and then stopped. "Why?"

"Oh," Stella improvised. "Thinking about making my own. Want to get a sense of thickness, viscosity, color, that kind of thing."

Marta nodded and stepped into the house, Ascanio and the dog trailing behind. Stella mouthed to Matteo, "Why?"

He shrugged. "Maybe it's a different bottle than you saw?"

She nodded. "Good thinking."

Marta returned and handed over a bottle, still mostly full. "He's only had a few spoonfuls. It seemed to work right away. Mimmo adds some botanicals. You'd have to ask him about that."

Stella opened the top and breathed in the bright aromas released into the air. Tart, fruity, a little earthy. She realized she was looking for that scent she'd caught at the scene of finding the body. That kind of forest smell . . . pine sap? She still couldn't place it. But no, that wasn't anywhere in this. This smelled fresh, like a cool breeze through a sunlit fruit orchard. Definitely elderberry. She handed it back to Marta, and in reverent tones, she said, "This is something special. I'll ask Mimmo about it."

As Marta capped the bottle to put it back, Matteo whispered,

"Nice hyperbole."

She whispered back. "It's not hyperbole. He knows what he's doing."

Marta turned back and said, "I'd invite you in for coffee, but I was about to feed the sheep."

Stella and Matteo protested against her politeness, holding out their hands and backing up, saying they wished Ascanio a speedy recovery, which was in no doubt, given how well he looked. As the door was about to close, Stella had a thought. "Wait! Mimmo said he went camping last week with some friends. You don't know who those friends are, do you?"

She tried to telegraph to Matteo her intention of checking his alibi.

Marta leaned on the door, and the dog sat beside her, watching Marta's face. "He wasn't camping. He was goose hunting. I know because he brought us some goose meat over the weekend."

Stella frowned. "Then why did he say he was camping?"

"Let me guess." Marta laughed. "There were police around when he said that."

At Stella's reluctant nod, Marta went on. "Mimmo is good to us, but I cannot deny he is a bit of a rascal. He hunts geese out of season. He could get in trouble, so please don't tell anyone."

Marta's face suddenly grew pale and Stella assured her, "Don't worry, I won't."

Marta sighed. "He's been so good to us."

As the door closed, Stella whispered to Matteo, "Okay, I don't know Mimmo well, and my image is embittered by him treating my family property as a cash machine. But does what Marta said square with what you know of him?"

Matteo chuckled. "I've heard your grandfather got on with Mimmo. They hunted together, and maybe that's why he's been the property manager. And your aunt let no one say a bad word about him. But as for the rest of Aramezzo, no. People know him as rough. Not just rough around the edges. Plain rough." He thought for a moment as he ran his hands down his long face. "But Marta could charm a polecat into purring."

Stella grumbled, "Maybe I should have her work her magic on the stray cat living on my premises."

They walked in companionable silence until they reached Matteo's mini-truck.

"I'm sorry for that," Stella apologized. "What a wasted effort."

"Oh, I don't know. I think we can rule Mimmo off our suspect list. That's useful, right?"

"I guess. I mean, he could have used some other poison, but it seems like he was gone at the time of the poisoning. Anyway, I can't think of why he'd kill Signor Severini. He doesn't seem to be in on any of Severini's business dealings."

"So you've ruled out Mimmo and Enzo." Matteo nodded to himself.

"We need more information." She paused. "It would help to get Don Arrigo's trash."

"Oh, I love it when you talk dirty."

She laughed uncertainly.

Matteo said nothing.

So Stella prompted. "I know you don't think it's him. I'm probably crazy for thinking he has anything to do with it. But the police have figured out it's murder, and soon enough they'll have to realize it couldn't be Enzo. We need more information before the trail goes cold."

He muttered to his shoes, "I wish I'd never said I'd bring it. I must have been high on the promise of blondies."

She shrugged. "I'm not saying we'll find something making him a suspect. But I'm pretty sure that Severini was trying to get death certificates. Maybe there's someone else on the trail that connects them. I need more information."

Matteo paused.

"What is it?"

"Well, I don't want to tell you this because I know you'll make a big deal about it."

"Try me," Stella said, leaning toward him eagerly.

"It's Don Arrigo." Matteo took a breath. "He's disappeared."

PART FOUR

I cannot believe you went to Mimmo's yesterday." Domenica glared at Stella over her glasses when Stella pushed the shop door open, releasing a merry tinkle of bells.

"I didn't go alone!" Stella protested.

"I know. I got the whole story from Matteo this morning when he picked up my glass bottles. But, Stella, you can't go flying off half-cocked that way."

Stella muttered to herself.

Domenica smiled. "I don't want anything happening to you, *cara*. I've grown fond of you."

This brought Stella up short. Her shoulders unknotted, and she dropped into the seat beside Domenica's desk. "A fat lot of good it did me. It's now a week since Severini disappeared, and we're nowhere near figuring out what happened."

Domenica retied her scarf and said, "Well, that's not strictly true. You've ruled out Mimmo and Enzo."

"Which just leaves me with Don Arrigo, and everyone seems alarmed at the notion."

Domenica pressed her lips together. "Stella, you aren't sharing this theory with anyone, are you?"

"No. I mean, only you and Matteo. Why?"

"Well, Don Arrigo is a bit of a hero in these parts. It wouldn't get you off on the right foot to accuse him publicly."

Stella picked lint off her sweater. "Yeah, I've gotten that vibe."

Domenica turned back to the pile of books on her desk, but stopped in thought. She glanced at Stella. "And I'd be cautious about involving Matteo into lines of inquiry involving the priest. Their relationship is special. He won't take kindly to you reading into things when it comes to Don Arrigo."

Stella opted not to tell Domenica that she'd convinced Matteo to look through the priest's trash. She just nodded vaguely. "What are you doing there?"

Domenica patted a stack of books. "A windfall! Orietta just dropped off—"

Her words cut off at the sound of raised voices. Stella leaped up and moved toward the window. From her vantage point, she spotted Salvo, the long-faced police officer with the mustache, flanked by a strange pair—Cinzia and the mayor.

"What's happening?" asked Domenica.

Stella waved her hand, "Wait."

Cinzia, tears streaming down her face, touched Salvo's elbow. "Come on, Salvo. You know my father. He's not a great man, but he's never been violent. You can't keep him—"

The mayor started speaking even before Cinzia finished. "Don't you dare let him out of jail. Everyone knows that man is a menace."

"He's not! He's—"

"Bumbling around all the time, and with all that strength leftover from his wrestling days. How are we ever supposed to improve the economic life of Aramezzo with this drunk guy crashing around!"

"But he—"

"Last week I saw him knock over a tourist! Just barreled right into her! Do you think that woman is going to go home and tell her friends about Aramezzo's lovely views and warm-hearted people?"

Salvo stopped walking and put his arms out, beseeching peace. "Look, I only asked you both if you'd ever *seen* Enzo harass the victim. If you had any sign that they had a rocky relationship of any kind."

"That's what I'm trying to tell you, if you would let me get a word in edgewise!" sputtered the mayor. "Enzo practically *attacked* Severini! Rambled on and on about how he didn't want Severini sniffing around his daughter!"

Cinzia cried harder.

Salvo's face grew more serious. "But, if you'll forgive me, Signore, did you hear this yourself?"

"Yes! That is, not when it happened, but the whole town was talking, so I heard all about it. Anyway, you know Enzo as well as I do. He killed Severini, and, with that, ruined our chance of putting Aramezzo on the map."

Cinzia's hands dropped from her face. "You keep saying that, but you've never told us your plan! You're so busy scheming—"

"Scheming!" the mayor yelled. "So now I'm some cartoon villain! Do you hear this, Salvo? Do you hear how she talks to me, the *mayor*? Questioning my efforts to enliven our economy? As if she could understand them!"

Salvo refused to acknowledge the mayor's words, "Cinzia, you haven't been able to provide a useful alibi for your father Tuesday night."

"I told you, he came home about midnight and passed out."

Salvo shook his head. "But you also said you went to bed, so we don't know if he got up after that."

"I said he was *passed out*. How could he murder someone while passed out? Anyway, you said the murderer administered poison, so—"

"Shhh!" Salvo craned his head in all directions and then lowered it again. "I told you, that part is not public knowledge."

Stella had to laugh. She had heard at least three clutches of old women talking about it in the street. Even now, she counted four heads peering out of second story windows.

The mayor drew himself to his full height. "Salvo, that's enough. We need to let Cinzia get home to her rabbits. Tell her you'll keep her father locked away in Aramezzo until we get him transferred to a state prison."

Cinzia's tear-stained face stilled, and thunder passed over it. "Don't talk to me like I'm a child. My father is innocent, and I'll find a way to prove it."

The mayor laughed gaily as Cinzia stormed away.

Salvo shook his head and clucked to the mayor, "You shouldn't have been so gruff with her. She's a good girl. Can't help who her father is."

"She's not the only crying woman in Aramezzo! Why should she get special treatment? My wife won't step outside, petrified she'll be murdered in the street!" Stella could not picture that statuesque woman with two frilly dogs feeling fear of anything. The mayor blustered on. "I need you to assure me that you and your compatriots are gathering evidence to keep Enzo locked away."

Stella could hear Salvo humming as he turned his back and walked toward the station. The mayor followed him, gesturing wildly and keeping up a running commentary.

"Well!" Stella turned back to Domenica. "That was bracing."

"Are you going to tell me what happened?"

Stella walked Domenica through the conflict.

Domenica nodded along and then said, "You have to tell the police. About the knots."

"Come on. You know as well as I do how kindly they take to my interference."

"You'll have to make them listen. I'll come with you, if you want."

"Will they listen to you?"

"No."

"See then."

Domenica leaned toward Stella. "But if there's a chance that we could help Enzo, and help Cinzia, don't you think it's worth trying?"

"I hate it when you talk sense."

Domenica chuckled. "Go on, then."

"Okay, okay," grumbled Stella.

By the time she got to the station, the mayor had stopped to talk to a group of men playing cards in the open area in front of the *alimentari*. At least she wouldn't have to face Salvo with an audience. She groaned inwardly when she noticed Luca and Salvo talking just inside the glass door of the station.

Well, what must be done, must be done. She felt terrible that the information she'd been sitting on might have let Enzo out sooner. Then again, she assumed the police would have considered the knots without her.

Luca arched an eyebrow as she opened the door. "Well, if it isn't our favorite American detective."

Salvo's mustache twitched in amusement.

She took a breath. "I found a body, that's hardly being a detective."

"Ah, but you have so many *opinions*," Luca's dimple flashed as he grinned, and she couldn't tell if he found her opinions a little amusing or plain annoying.

Well, it didn't matter now. With her horning in, she'd be giving new life to their view of the interfering American. "I wanted to talk to you about Enzo."

Luca's smile froze as Salvo looked over his shoulder at Captain Palmiro, chatting with another officer. Stella stiffened, but went on, "I know he couldn't have done it."

Salvo laughed and started to interrupt, but Luca stopped him. "Stand by." He turned to Stella and drew close enough to her so he could almost whisper, "Go ahead."

"It's the knots." To Salvo and Luca's confused expressions, she went on, "In the nets."

"What about them?" Luca asked.

"I haven't lived here for long—"

"You can say that again," Salvo said.

"I haven't lived here for long." She waited a beat. Salvo's mustache twitched again, and Luca's dimple reappeared. She went on, "But I've seen Enzo, his coat hanging open because he can't button it and his shoelaces untied—"

"Because he can't tie them," Luca finished, comprehension dawning.

"Exactly," said Stella. "And those knots. If you've tied a roast, you know knots like that require a lot of precision."

Was it her imagination, or did Luca's eyes glow with admiration for a moment before he ducked his head?

Captain Palmiro appeared at her side. "Ah, excellent. Leave it to the little American girl to solve crimes with macramé tips. How delightful."

"Not a girl," muttered Stella. "The rest I can't argue with."

Hesitating, Luca said, "She has a point, Captain."

Captain Palmiro widened his eyes. "Luca! You surprise me. Did you forget that Enzo already confessed?"

Stella turned to Luca. "He confessed? For real?"

Luca touched the tip of his tongue to his lip. "He did, yes. Last night."

Captain Palmiro chuckled warmly. "And we did it all without your 'help.'"

"Except," Luca ventured, "Cinzia reports the shock made him delirious. That he wasn't talking about Severini when he apologized, crying. That he was lost in his memories."

Captain Palmiro glared at Luca, who stared at the floor.

Almost to herself, Stella said, "Cinzia said he stopped drinking the day I found Severini."

Palmiro's jaw worked. "So? That means he was sober when he confessed. You're only making this worse for your buddy Enzo."

"I've worked with a lot of addicts," Stella went on thoughtfully, as if Palmiro hadn't spoken. "It comes with the territory when you're in kitchens as much as I am. I'd check with a doctor, but it sounds like Enzo could be in alcohol withdrawal."

Salvo opened his mouth, but Stella put out her hand to stay him. "Hear me out. You won't be used to seeing this because in Italy, well, people here have a healthier relationship with alcohol. Italians don't drink to get drunk. I remember one place I worked in Milan, Italians complained the appetizers were too light to drink wine alongside them."

The men stared at her.

She regarded each of them, lingering on Luca, the only one who seemed inclined to give her words any weight. He nodded, as if encouraging her to keep going. "If you drink responsibly, like most people in Italy, you don't get things like alcohol withdrawal. But when people drink heavily—without eating, to get drunk, to block out the world—when those people stop drinking suddenly, like when they decide to get clean for a job interview or New Year's Day or whatever, their behavior changes. Hallucinations. Delirium. In short, they get a bit crazy. That confession you got can't be admissible."

Palmiro regarded Stella silently. Finally, he turned to Salvo and Luca. "Ready for lunch?"

Salvo spoke with hesitation. "All right. I guess so."

Stella and Luca held eye contact and the moment stretched. Finally, he dragged his gaze away from her. "But, Captain. Shouldn't we at least consider this?"

Palmiro tossed his parting shot over his shoulder. "Trust us, Signorina. Let us do our work. And you do yours. The fewer guests die on your watch, the less clean up we'll have to do."

Stella shot a quizzical glance at Luca. "Please, Luca..."

He shrugged irritably. "I told you. It's all a bit much for him right now. And he's never worked a murder case."

"Have you?"

217

"No. But I'm not quite as set in my ways." His brown eyes, the color of deep forest, searched hers. "I'll do what I can."

She nodded and watched as Luca followed his captain.

Stella pulled the tray of sweet buns out of the oven and inhaled. She'd added a dash of the *fiori di Sicilia* extract she'd found at the *alimentari* and liked the faint aroma of flowers, citrus, with a gossamer thread of almond scent. She impulsively brushed the buns with a bit of honey butter before getting ready to drop them off at Marta's house on her way to Bar Cappellina. Stella pulled a bun apart, enjoying its stretchiness and the release of yeasty goodness. Plopping a piece into her mouth, she chewed with a smile. Perfectly sweet and lightly floral.

Piling the buns into a basket lined with a clean napkin, Stella checked the clock. Matteo wouldn't arrive with the bag of paper recycling for another hour, at the earliest. Plenty of time. She straightened her bandana, tied a scarf around her neck three times, shrugged on a jacket, and swore at the cat darting past her legs in a race to who knew where.

Impulsively, Stella added a few more buns to another basket for Domenica. After Stella's conversation with the police officers, she'd been so rattled she went home and started the buns for an overnight prove in the refrigerator. Domenica needed to know that the police had been about as amenable to her observations as Stella had expected.

She strolled the circular road to the other side of town. Now that she'd lived in Aramezzo for over a month, she'd started to notice details. Like her neighbor, Luisella, the trim woman who had still not said one word to Stella, owned that house where the second floor spanned right over the road. A bridge that served as a room! Stella wished she could invite herself over for tea and check it out from the inside, but that didn't seem likely and she couldn't even peer in those windows with the curtains always firmly drawn.

Stella rapped on Marta's door, hoping it wasn't too early for visitors. But no, Marta threw open the door, fully dressed, with Ascanio in her arms, still in his pajamas, and the white dog at her side. Stella held out the basket. "I brought breakfast."

Marta's eyes widened in pleasure. She accepted the basket and raised it to her face, inhaling. "Ascanio, do you smell that?"

He leaned into the basket and closed his eyes, breathing deeply. Stella noticed that his breath came and went easily. She smiled. "Good with jam, or on their own."

"We have a lavender jelly that I think would be perfect. Right, Ascanio?"

He bucked and turned until his mother rested his feet on the ground and then he dashed away, the dog at his heels. Marta watched Ascanio fondly as Stella said, "Lavender jelly?"

"Mmm. Yes, I'm making a line of herb jellies to sell at the market. The lavender is so far our favorite, but bay is getting there. And also tarragon."

Stella couldn't think of any Italian recipe that called for tarragon. "How unusual. Say, do you make any jellies with a pine scent?"

Marta cocked her head to the side as she considered. "Pine? No. Rosemary would be the closest."

Ascanio came running, his socked feet slipping a little on the stone floor, a jar lofted over his curly head. He held it out to Stella, who looked at Marta with the question in her raised eyebrows.

"Go ahead," Marta smiled. "Open it. Tell me what you think."

Stella unthreaded the decorative mason jar lid and popped it off. She didn't need to bring it to her nose to be knocked back by the aroma. "Wow, this is spectacular. I expected it to be a bit ... soapy. But it's not."

"It's tricky. You want enough lavender to be lavender but not enough to get chemical."

"I can tell. You cut it with lemon?"

"Just a touch." Marta grinned. "Bruno told me about your incredible sense of smell."

"It comes in handy." Stella shrugged. "This is dreamy."

Marta shook her head to refuse Stella's attempt to give the jar back. "Keep it. We have plenty."

Stella tucked it into her coat pocket. "Thank you. Here I planned to bring you something and somehow I wind up with more."

Marta laughed easily and Stella got a glimmer that this may be the Umbrian way. She pondered this as she walked to Bar Cappellina. Food came as easily as breathing to these people. She was forever seeing women handing bundles of freshly harvested greens to other women perched on their chairs in the street. Or she remembered those men pouring round plastic thimbles of what looked like homemade *amaro*, the bitter digestive common for a nightcap. Even as much of an outsider as Mimmo was, he, too, shared his bounty with Marta.

She wondered if her DNA had soaked in green olive oil and red Umbrian wine and that's what made her so attuned to flavor, to scent, to food. Or if it was as simple as her mother, who she resembled in few ways, passing on a love of creating tastes from simple pantry ingredients.

Stella resolved that when her next guests arrived, she'd offer a jar of Marta's herb jelly with morning rolls. A bit of local flavor and perhaps a spot of advertising for Marta.

She dropped a bundle of buns at Domenica's sunlit book shop, filling her in on yesterday's conversation with the police. However, Domenica was so absorbed by a BuzzFeed article on Captain Jack Sparrow trivia, Stella assumed the woman only got the broad brushstrokes. The police knew about the knots, it was in their hands now; and apparently, it was much more important for Domenica to learn how Johnny Depp created that accent.

Pushing the bar door open, she unwound her scarf, nodding at the faces that had become familiar. Bruno the butcher, Leonardo the *porchetta* guy, and the farmer on the far side of the ring road who very much enjoyed her gift of a loaf of experimental sourdough. Out of the corner of her eye, Stella also spotted her neighbor Luisella, as decked out as ever, at a side table sipping espresso on her own. Talking to nobody. Maybe she avoided more than just Stella.

"*Ciao*, Stella," Roberto called, already moving to start her espresso. Romina beckoned to join her at the counter.

"I'm glad you're here," Romina said in a low voice. "I'm guessing you heard the news?"

Stella sighed. "Probably not, no."

Romina said, "Bruno was just telling me about Signor Severini."

Everyone waited for the butcher to spill the story, but he just looked around blankly before saying in a gruff voice. "I told you once already."

Leonardo sighed and filled in the story. "Bruno heard the police officers talking when they came in for sausage at the end of the day."

"Yesterday," the butcher supplied. Everyone stopped to see if he would add more, but he returned his attention to his coffee.

Leonardo rolled his eyes. "They got information on our Severini, aka Crespi."

Romina added, eyes alight with interest. "The police had an officer in Perugia run a check on Crespi. Apparently, he worked with a Calabrian town to bring Americans into a one-euro home scheme. What they didn't know was Severini had the applicants wire him money to bid on the houses, and then more money to serve as a go-between. He got about a quarter of a million euros, then he disappeared!"

Stella was unsure how to respond. Maybe Domenica didn't want the town knowing she moonlighted as a hacker. "Those poor people."

Roberto added, in case Stella had yet to catch on. "He was probably trying to do the same thing here."

Romina shook her head. "Cosimo always said that Severini was up to more than he let on."

Stella looked around the room. "I wonder if anyone else knew about his past. Someone who would have wanted to stop him at any cost."

Instantly, everyone in the bar started looking around the room, studying bar menus and white cups they couldn't possibly be interested in. She sighed and dug out a euro from her wallet, saying, "Thanks for filling me in."

Romina touched Stella's hand. "They won't all be like this." To Stella's look of confusion, Romina added, "Your next guest will be easier, I know."

Leonardo chuckled as he watched Stella wrap her scarf around her neck. "Can't well be harder. I've known some shady guys in my line of work, but this Severini is world class."

Stella paused to tie her scarf. "A lot of villains in the *porchetta* industry?"

The bar broke into laughter, and Luisella looked up from her coffee with a look of scorn. Leonardo said, "I used to race cars. You'd be surprised how many drivers were on the take."

Nodding, Stella said, "The boys in my hometown watched a lot of American wrestling. So I'm not sure I'd be all that shocked by professional cheating."

Leonardo laughed and waved goodbye as Stella stepped out into the street, leaving the door open to let the florist enter.

As the door closed, Stella heard the villagers discussing conversations each of them had with Signor Severini, and how they all guessed him to be a scoundrel, through and through. Stella estimated how long they'd stand there rehashing the same information with every new customer. She shook her head, wondering how long the sameness of a small town would prove charming, and how long until she itched for novelty, for something to *happen*. After all, one couldn't count on murder mysteries on the regular in a town like Aramezzo.

She arrived at her house just as Matteo pulled up with two bags of trash beside him. He glanced around furtively before hustling through the door she propped open for him. Once inside, he took off his coat and plopped the bags in the middle of the living room.

Clapping her hands together, Stella said, "What have we got?"

Matteo said, "If you set your trash out today like all your neighbors somehow remember to do, you'd know that it's compost and paper day."

"I've had a lot on my mind!"

He shook his head. "Garbage waits for no man."

"Will you take it on your way out? I have it bagged and ready."

"Nope, no special favors for friends. How will you learn if I keep saving you?"

She muttered incoherently, wishing he wouldn't take refuse so seriously.

Matteo lifted the larger bag and said, "I figured we'd start with paper. I can't imagine banana peels and coffee grounds will be all that illuminating."

"What if there's poison?"

"We've had three compost days since the murder. Don't you think Don Arrigo would have gotten rid of the evidence already?"

"But you don't believe he did it," she said with a grin.

"I don't. I want to help you rule him out so we can move on to other suspects."

Stella grumbled. "I wish I had some. If it's not Don Arrigo, I'm going to have to assume it happened out of Aramezzo and someone dumped the body. People didn't love Severini, some people loathed him, but nobody seemed to need him dead."

"You don't think anybody in Aramezzo stood to lose money with his one-euro house scheme?"

"Not that I can figure."

"But Severini stood to gain a lot."

"I heard he scored about 250,000 euros last time."

"What!"

"At least."

Matteo considered. "What could he have spent it all on?"

"Whisky and cigarettes is my guess."

Frowning, Matteo said, "What's that mean?"

She waved away the question. "So we're looking for anything suspicious. Probably documents related to getting homeowners declared dead. Whether or not they are."

She sat down by the fireplace and Matteo settled his long form next to her, setting the bag on his lap as he said, "I don't feel good about this."

She waited.

"Stella?"

"Look. Don Arrigo was Signor Severini's single-minded focus. The man must have some evidence, even if he didn't know it was evidence. Something in this bag might point the finger at a suspect. It could give us information. Paper hasn't been picked up since the murder, right?"

"Right."

"So if Signor Severini gave Don Arrigo something incriminating that Don Arrigo tossed out, we'll find it here."

"Theoretically. Unless he burned it."

She smiled. "But why would Don Arrigo do that if he's innocent? You see, all this can do is give us some leads, and maybe exonerate Don Arrigo."

"You think so?"

"No, of course not. I think Don Arrigo killed Signor Severini." She ignored Matteo's gasp. "But if I'm right and he did, he wouldn't be the man you thought he was, right? Wouldn't you want to know that?"

He stared at the bag. "I guess."

"And if you're right and he's innocent, don't we want some clues to point us to more suspects?"

He nodded slowly, his large eyes gleaming. "For sure."

"So, are you ready now?"

He opened the bag and tentatively pulled out a receipt. He let out a rustle of a sigh, which confirmed Stella's suspicion that he'd been holding his breath. "It's for communion wine."

Patting his hand, she said, "I think this will go faster if we don't comment on each piece of paper. Let's do my system when I'm coming up with a new dish. I put all flavors that don't work in one pile, everything that could work with another element in another pile, and everything that shines in the last pile. Let's do the same thing here—make three piles: innocent, suspicious, and guilty."

He nodded.

For the next fifteen minutes, Stella and Matteo barely exchanged a word, except when she handed him a piece of paper to ask what a word meant because she didn't know the Italian word for vestry and couldn't have defined it in English either. With each piece of paper, she willed words to appear that would necessitate adding it to the guilty pile. But in the end, she only found a series of receipts for the convenience store outside Subbiano and a list of names that rang familiar. She was pretty sure the names matched the list of names with addresses she'd found in Severini's briefcase. Everything else was for basic food and office supplies and ATM withdrawal slips.

The recycling bag lay empty. Stella stared at the piles, mostly of innocent papers, and a smattering of suspicious ones. She'd been so sure she'd find a smoking gun. The last batch of papers lay on Matteo's lap, and she saw his mouth move as he silently read through the contents before placing yet another slip of paper in the innocuous pile. She flipped through the papers in the suspicious pile and noticed the dates were months old. Why would the withdrawal slips and the shop receipts going back months be in the trash *now*? Did something prompt Don Arrigo to clean out his pockets and desk drawers all of a sudden?

She organized all the receipts and laid them out like a *mise-en-place* before dinner service. She noticed a pattern. Every Friday, Don Arrigo withdrew €200 and then stopped at a convenience store outside Subbiano.

Only one bank slip didn't match. She drew in her breath. There was a cash withdrawal, not an ATM receipt, on Tuesday, November 4th. For 2,000 euros.

November 4th. The night Signor Severini had a meeting with Don Arrigo. The night Severini went missing.

Lost in her thoughts, and wondering if maybe she should bake something, she forgot about Matteo's presence until he spoke, holding up a piece of paper. In a shaking voice, he said, "I'm not sure what pile this goes in."

She held out her hand, and he paused for a moment before placing it on her palm. A crumpled card, on fancy paper. The scrawl inside didn't match the heft and finesse of the paper. She could hardly make out the words—*I'm done with your threats. You know how this ends.*

She looked up. "Threats?"

Matteo said nothing, just ran his hand over his face over and over.

Her voice went up an octave. "*Threats?*"

He covered his ears and cowered. "I don't know, okay! I figured Severini was threatening Don Arrigo, not the other way around. I figured if Don Arrigo did anything, it would have been out of self-defense. But maybe, maybe the note wasn't written for Don Arrigo. Maybe he just found it . . . or maybe . . . he was writing song lyrics. Let's put it in the second pile."

"Matteo," she made her voice as firm as she could. "You know very well this isn't song lyrics. You're reaching. Besides," she shuffled the innocuous pile until she found an envelope and held it up, "identical cardstock, written in the same hand. Addressed to Don Arrigo. Someone wrote that note to Don Arrigo, and it had to be Severini."

She softened when she saw his eyes fill with tears. His voice muted to a whisper. "When my brother stole cigarettes back in middle school,

Don Arrigo stood up for him. Kept my parents from beating him, kept the manager from pressing charges. He spoke with my brother every day after school for a month. After that, my brother worked harder at school, got new friends. He's at university now, because of Don Arrigo. Don Arrigo saved my brother. Saved my family."

"I didn't know that. Why didn't you—"

"I don't like to talk about it, okay?"

Stella realized with a clap of clarity that Matteo never talked about his life at all. She didn't know if he, like many young single Italian men, still lived at home or if he had more siblings than that one brother, or even who his friends were. Even though she saw him daily talking to someone in the street for what seemed an in-depth conversation, now that she thought about it, those snatches of conversation were about the weather or soccer or the Communist party. Stella knew his sense of humor and his kindness, but she didn't know *him*.

"Matteo—"

He stood suddenly, the papers falling off his lap. "I don't know why I let you talk me into this. It's a sin. We can't pry into people's business, especially a priest. We can't decide we understand someone based on, what, a handful of *paper*?" He wiped his eyes angrily with the back of his hand. "This is all fun for you, and you sucked me into it, but it's not fun. It's *not*!"

She looked at the papers scattered around her, the leavings of a man's life. "I know it's not."

"I can't do this anymore," Matteo whispered, before grabbing his jacket and running from the house.

Stella ran after Matteo, but he hopped in his truck and anyway, what could she say?

No, what she needed was to find Don Arrigo. Preferably not alone. Mimmo had seemed too bumbling to be dangerous. But Don Arrigo—his very affability made him sinister. She couldn't figure out why no one in Aramezzo saw underneath his genial bravado. No one could be that open-hearted.

First things first. She had to figure out where he'd gone. And for that, she needed Cinzia. The woman valued a hard day's work, so she could likely be found at the church. Stella would go and innocently ask how to find Don Arrigo.

If she got information, she'd bring it by Domenica's. Maybe her friend would be doing something sensible and could pay attention. Captain Jack Sparrow. *Please.*

Stella jogged up the stairs to the chapel and almost crashed into Cinzia at the door. "Oh! Stella, what are you doing here?"

Stella peered into Cinzia's wan face. "Are you okay?"

Cinzia bit her lip, nodding. "It's a trying time. I'm sure you heard they arrested my father." Stella nodded and took a breath to explain about the knots but then Cinzia went on, "They are letting him go tonight."

"Oh, thank God."

"They searched our house, the entire property, and found nothing connecting him to the murder. And they said they got some evidence that he couldn't have done it." Cinzia bit her lip. "It's been terrible. He's not been the greatest father, but I couldn't stand him being behind bars. He doesn't deserve that. And, the police...I hated not knowing what they were saying or doing to him."

"Do you think he's okay. Medically, I mean?"

"You heard about the alcohol withdrawal? Yes, he said such crazy things, I got a bit freaked out." Cinzia laughed uncomfortably at the memory. "There's not a doctor on staff. Nobody took it seriously."

"I'm sorry you had to go through that. Can I bring you dinner tonight?"

"Oh, that's awfully kind. But I haven't even gotten your stew pot back."

"I'm in no rush, I'd be happy to bring you something."

Cinzia shook her head. "I'm out of rabbit feed, so I'm heading out now and I'll pick up a lasagna at the pasta shop. Or maybe a *parmigiana* of cardoons since they're finally in season. That's my father's favorite. Now that he's not drinking, I bet he'd love it. And that always lasts us several days."

Stella had a zillion questions, but this hardly seemed the moment. "Soon then. Count on me leaving something on your doorstep."

Cinzia pulled Stella in for a hug, and Stella smelled the scent of herbs and the slight muskiness that must come from the rabbits.

As Stella squeezed Cinzia's hand in farewell, she remembered. "Oh, quick question if you have a moment."

"Of course," Cinzia said, flipping her waving hair over her shoulders.

"Don Arrigo. Can you tell me where to find him?"

The smile fell from Cinzia's porcelain-doll face. "What do you want with him?"

Casual, Stella, stay casual, Stella thought to herself. "I wanted to find out if the church still has my mother's baptism records."

Cinzia's smile didn't reach her eyes. Did something happen between Cinzia and the priest? Did Cinzia, like Stella, suspect he might have been responsible for Severini's death?

Stella noticed Cinzia's gaze flick over Stella's shoulder. "Ask him yourself."

Stella turned around in time to see Don Arrigo leaving the chapel, his face uncharacteristically stern. Cinzia's voice seemed so icy it was in danger of chipping. "Don Arrigo, Stella has a question for you. Do you have a moment?"

"Certainly." Don Arrigo's voice echoed Cinzia's frostiness. What had Stella interrupted?

Stella reached out for Cinzia. "You don't have to leave."

Cinzia shook her head. "I have to get to the pet supply store before they close or my babies will go hungry tonight."

Stella watched Cinzia hurry down the tunnel and then plastered a smile on her face as she turned to Don Arrigo. "You're back! How was your trip?"

"What do you want, Stella?"

Damn. That bait went untasted. She considered trying the same line on Don Arrigo as she had on Cinzia, but she didn't know why anyone would need baptism records, so she'd have no answers to any follow-up questions. Her mind raced and landed on the receipts. "Um, I wanted to know...about Subbiano."

His eyes narrowed and his handsome face turned to stone. "What about Subbiano?"

"I heard you go there a lot," she said, shooting in the dark. "And I wondered if you could tell me anything about it. Good restaurants, what to look out for."

He turned away. "I don't have time to play tour guide, Stella. I'm sure you'll find what you're looking for."

He swept away and disappeared down the tunnel before Stella could come up with anything better.

She stood for a moment, considering. So Don Arrigo hadn't disappeared. In that he'd come back. But he seemed to have left his mask of cheerfulness somewhere that wasn't Aramezzo.

Stella's heart leaped every time she saw one of the sanitation department's mini-trucks. But each time she peered into the window, her face fell. No Matteo. She thought she'd caught a glimpse of him last night outside the trattoria when she'd gone for a walk to clear her head after the confrontation with Don Arrigo. At first, she hadn't immediately recognized him dressed in smart jeans and a crisp shirt, his hair brushed back from his forehead, bringing attention to his Roman nose and expressive eyes. By the time she'd finished her double take, he'd vanished. Stella would have assumed she'd invented his presence except the two women he'd been standing with looked around like they'd misplaced their drinks, suggesting that they registered his absence as Stella did.

He was avoiding her. That was the only answer.

Why couldn't she keep any friends? A culinary school boyfriend once told her she was "too much." She'd laughed it off at the time, telling him maybe he was "too little." But the words still stung.

"What's wrong with you?" Domenica asked bluntly when Stella entered the bookstore.

Stella shook her head without answering. There suddenly seemed so much wrong, she didn't know what Domenica could be referring to. Instead, she stared at books without seeing them.

"You do know that's the agricultural equipment maintenance shelf?" Domenica asked, her voice threaded with humor.

Stella blinked and read the title of the book in front of her, *Maintaining Your Small Farm*. She sagged.

Domenica took a noisy slurp of her coffee and settled down, adjusting her scarves and sweaters. "Now, tell me what's going on."

"Nothing."

Domenica's eye roll would have befitted a sarcastic twelve-year-old.

"Nothing!"

"*Cara*, you aren't fooling me, and you aren't fooling you, either."

Tears sprang to Stella's eyes. She picked up a slumbering Ravioli from a chair and sat down, dropping the cat onto her lap. The cat looked like she might protest the intrusion but thought the better of it and curled up into her now-familiar ball.

Stella's eyes felt heavy. Was there some sort of relaxant that emanated from cats when they purred? She only ever felt like this after cooking a particularly satisfying meal. Struggling to sift her thoughts, she said, "Yesterday I found out that Don Arrigo threatened Severini."

Domenica pushed her headband back on her iron-gray hair. "I'm going to need more information."

"We...I...found a note Severini wrote to Don Arrigo where he said threats wouldn't work. I also found out Don Arrigo made a pretty big bank withdrawal the last day anyone saw Severini alive. For the same amount the cops found on Severini."

Quiet filled the shop. Finally, Domenica said, "I expect I shouldn't ask you how you know all this."

"Correct."

Her lips pressed into a thin line, Domenica said, "Fine. So what's next?"

At Stella's lack of response, Domenica drummed her fingers across her desk for a moment before swiveling to uncover the shawls from the computer. She began clicking on the keyboard, muttering, "Don Arrigo. What do we know about you?"

Stella stroked Ravioli's fur as Domenica flew through screens, typing, staring, changing screens, and typing again. She didn't even know what Domenica was looking for, and she felt too tired to care. She just wanted this to all go away.

Domenica pushed the keyboard away from her and huffed. "Nothing."

"What did you think would be there? A history of assaults?"

"Maybe," Domenica said. "Or something that connected him with Severini. Or a bloated bank account that suggested shenanigans."

Stella's voice squeaked, "You got into his bank account?"

"Of course. But there's a modest sum. Less since that withdrawal you mentioned." Domenica straightened her glasses and leaned toward the screen. "Here's something peculiar, though. Every week for the last year, he's made a withdrawal of 200 euros. "

"Yes, I know."

Domenica cast a glance over her shoulder, but said nothing.

"Listen, what you're doing isn't exactly on the up and up, so you have no cause to judge."

Domenica laughed. "Too true."

"Anyway, I didn't know it's been a year. That's odd. I figured it was maybe an allowance or how he pays Cinzia...but why would he start a year ago?"

Domenica shook her head, studying the screen as she flew through pages that Stella now registered as bank records. "No, that would come out of the church coffers. This is out of his personal account."

"Maybe so he has spending money?"

"Unless he's spending somewhere other than Aramezzo, I don't think so. He doesn't pay for coffee or pastries anywhere—no one will let him. His entertainment is sitting with mothers in the park to help them with their children or playing bocce with the men at the court. I'm pretty sure Cinzia even buys his groceries. She certainly does his cooking."

"She cooks?"

"This is Italy, dear. Everybody cooks."

"Okay, okay. So he has no expenses."

"Few."

"Huh."

Domenica clicked off the computer and began covering it with shawls and scarves again.

"Why do you do that?"

"Oh, well, no sense in suggesting my shop is an internet cafe. Besides, I hate electronic racket. I haven't been able to hush old machines, those fans are monstrous."

Stella nodded before her eye snagged on a flash of black outside the window. "Speak of the devil. Did you know he came back yesterday?"

Domenica glanced out the window, leaning to watch Don Arrigo's receding back. "Yes."

"Where was he?"

"Nobody knows. Or nobody is talking."

With a sigh, Stella lifted Ravioli, who meowed piteously and hung like a loosely filled bag of flour. "Nobody found out?"

"It's not polite to ask, *cara*."

Stella stood. "I've always had problems with manners. It's my worst quality, my mother liked to remind me. At least, when my impulsiveness wasn't my worst quality."

Domenica raised an eyebrow.

Stella went on, "Anyway, the point is, yesterday I asked Don Arrigo about where he disappeared to."

"And?"

"The big brush off. And a scowl that did not befit his cherubic face." Stella put on her coat. "I don't get it. Why am I the only one who seems to care about finding the killer?"

"Oh, that reminds me! Enzo was released last night."

"I know. Cinzia told me. I'm sure everyone will be talking about that, but won't be investigating new avenues." She frowned. "You Italians. You want to do nothing but talk, but don't care if you get anywhere."

"You are Italian, my dear."

"Argh. You know what I mean. Don't you want an answer?"

"Sure. In due time. I'm in no rush. You Americans with your impatience."

"I am *not* impatient." Though the words trailed off at the memory of her childhood garden planted solely with radishes because they went from seed to fruit in the shortest time. Little Stella still pulled them up far too early, until her garden was a wasteland of radish slivers she tried in vain to replant.

Domenica regarded Stella over the rims of her glasses.

"Okay, fine. I'm impatient. But remember, the longer it takes for them to find the killer—"

"The lower the chance of them finding him, yes, yes, I know. You've mentioned that once or a dozen times."

"So maybe you also remember that I said—"

"If the trail runs cold, and the mystery is unsolved, people will always wonder about your role."

"You remember."

"I do have an IQ in the triple digits," Domenica muttered.

The bile in Domenica's words recalled Stella. "I'm sorry, Domenica. My foot seems to be living in my mouth nowadays. I really am grateful you tried."

Domenica patted Stella's hand. "It's a challenging time for you, *cara.* I know that. Don't worry."

Stella breathed a sigh of relief. She wished it could be as easy to settle her tension with Matteo. "And thanks for looking up Don Arrigo's transactions. I imagine that's a piece of the puzzle. Another piece is finding out if he has access to belladonna."

"Remember, everyone has access to belladonna."

"Right. I mean, if he has a way to deliver it in liquid form. I know the police were thinking injections, but I still think perhaps Severini could have drunk it." Stella thought for a moment. "Also, I have this gut feeling that Subbiano holds the key."

"Because of the one-euro house scheme?"

"That, and the way Don Arrigo looked at me when I mentioned Subbiano. If looks could kill, I'd be as dead as Severini."

Stella sat on the steps outside her house with a bag of plastic bottles at her feet and a plate of warm cinnamon rolls on her lap. As the sanitation truck rolled up the street, she pleaded with the heavens to see Matteo at the wheel. She closed her eyes so tightly in wishing that when she opened them to see Matteo's familiar curly head behind the wheel, she briefly assumed she willed him into existence.

He hopped out and tossed plastic bags into the back of the truck. She remembered how he once said he loved plastic days. So light, less stink. She shifted the plate of rolls, restraining herself from leaping up. He caught sight of her as he walked back to the cab and studiously looked away. Though he must have seen her. His steps slowed.

Sliding behind the wheel, he paused, the engine idling. Finally, the truck rolled to her house, and he unfolded his lanky body from the cab. He crossed his arms and studied her for a moment. Gesturing with his chin toward the plate on her knees, he said, "That for me?"

At the familiar hint of playfulness in his voice, relief loosened her shoulders. She stood and with knees shaking, she answered, "Yes."

He nodded and took the plate. "What is it?"

All in a rush, she said, "I blew it, I know it."

"We don't need to talk about it."

"I owe you an apology."

His eyes widened. "That's unnecessary."

"You gave very clear cues that you didn't want to be a part of my meddling, and I not only ignored those cues, I bulldozed you. It wasn't fair to you, and it wasn't kind of me."

He cut his eyes away and ran a hand down his face, lingering over his eyes as if to block out her words.

She went on, "I do that. I run like a horse with the bit in its teeth, and I'm sorry. I'm working on it. I promise, I'll be way more careful in the future. If you give me a chance?"

He moved his eyes back to her face, as if trying to figure out if she was pulling his leg. "It wasn't a big deal."

"I pushed you to do something that didn't feel right. That *is* a big deal."

With caution, as if feeling out the words, Matteo said, "Maybe it was. But I let it happen."

Impulsively, she put a hand on his arm. "Can you forgive me?"

"It depends. What's under that napkin?"

The laughter burbled out of her. "American cinnamon rolls."

"Because you want to push me from my Italian tastes?"

She smiled. "Because I know you love cinnamon."

"That's true. I do." He looked at the plate and then into her eyes. "Thanks, Stella, for this, and ... thanks. You didn't have to."

"Sure," she said awkwardly. Not sure if he was referring to the rolls or the apology. Hadn't anyone ever apologized to him before? He sure made it difficult. "And you know what? Up until now, our friendship has been entirely about me. No more. I want to hear about *you*."

"Oh," he laughed uncomfortably. "That's unnecessary, right?"

She started to press him, to explain that expanding intimacies formed the basis of friendship. That it was a crime that she didn't even know he had a brother, let alone know the backstory that still obviously hit him deeply. Then she remembered. No pushing. Instead, she said, "Heard. But if you ever want to tell me anything. If you want to talk about your life, about *you*, I'm here for it."

He looked at her curiously, as if she'd invited him to discuss the fate of phytoplankton. He lifted the rolls. "Better eat these while they're warm."

She nodded. "I hope you like them."

"I'm sure I will. Catch you later, Stella."

She watched him drive off. No, she didn't know a lot about Matteo. But she knew enough to know that she wanted to protect their friendship. He was a good egg—kind, funny, thoughtful, and he didn't take himself too seriously. She trusted him. That's all she needed to know.

As she turned into the house, she thought about Domenica. Could she trust the older woman?

She liked Domenica, for sure. But when she talked with Domenica, the ground under Stella's feet felt in motion, like flour in a sifter. She never knew when it would fall away altogether. Stella shook her head.

It would take time to fully trust Domenica. But she could tell that Domenica looked past the traits Stella's own mother had found irredeemable. She even somehow looked past Stella's distaste for cats. Well, for cats who weren't Ravioli.

Stella stepped into the house, then spun around and walked back to the street. After the evening and morning of baking the rolls, she felt calm and clear. She needed information about Don Arrigo and there was only one place to get it. Anyway, Stella hadn't had any coffee yet today. She'd sat on the steps since the sun barely peeked over the mountains to not miss Matteo.

Her step quickened at the thought of the warm bar, the hot coffee, and the hotter gossip. Well, it wasn't exactly sexy, she smiled to herself. But it was served fresh. She stopped to press the needles on a rosemary bush that lined the *piazza*, releasing the spicy fragrance. Her fingers smelling of rosemary, she waved at a cat perched on the arch over the alley. The cat yawned and nestled into the stones. She laughed to herself. Amazing how everything felt better, more manageable, now that she and Matteo were friends again.

It occurred to her that if she let the mystery go, allowed the police to solve the crime or not as they wished, her life could fall back into a predictable pattern. Things could proceed as normal. She didn't exactly know what normal looked like, but she had a feeling it may be worth pursuing. Maybe it wasn't any of her damned business.

Except . . . it *was* her business. This murder needed a resolution or it would never be put to bed. She stopped outside Bar Cappellina, her hand on the door. A murder without a murderer would always cast a pall. Over her, over her B and B. No, she had to persevere. She had to keep working to find the murderer. She may have been wrong about Mimmo, but the police had been wrong about Enzo. Maybe making mistakes was part of the package. Anyway, with all that evidence, the priest couldn't be blameless.

She set her chin and opened the door, easily greeting the baker deep in conversation with a young man Stella didn't know, who looked like he might be foreign. He almost looked Italian, only with a coppery cast to his skin and hair a bit fuller and straighter than locals. As Stella slipped off her coat, she overheard their conversation and noticed the stranger's accent had a slight blur to it, as if he'd been speaking Italian almost all his life, but not quite.

Stella spotted Luisella, the trim lady in the corner of the bar. Stella realized she'd hardly ever passed the bar without seeing the woman, lingering over coffee in the morning or a glass of wine in the evening. It never seemed to occur to anyone to introduce them, and Luisella herself studiously avoided eye contact. Instead, she perched on her chair, her handbag just so beside her, keeping to herself.

Romina beamed when Stella settled onto the stool, as if she'd been waiting all day for this moment. Stella fought the impulse to look behind her to catch sight of the intended recipient of Romina's greeting. By now she'd reconciled, though still didn't understand, the woman's boundless warmth. "*Caffè?*"

Stella nodded and leaned back to investigate the contents of the display case. *Cornetti*, of course. A selection of focaccia and *tramezzini*, the sandwiches on white bread that Stella always had an irrational fondness for—what made white bread, tuna, and artichokes so crazy delicious? And something new. "What's that?" she asked Roberto, standing by the display case as he pulled her shot of espresso. He glanced at the case. "I told Romina you'd be interested in that. It's *pan di mosto*."

"*Mosto?*"

At her confused expression, Romina added, "*Mosto* is the first pass at winemaking, the hardly fermented juice from crushing the grapes. It's popular here after the harvest." As Romina explained, Roberto took a piece of the bread off the platter with tongs and set it on a saucer beside Stella's coffee.

Stella settled in, almost forgetting the reason she'd come. She lifted the bread and sniffed, noting the scents of fennel and raisin. Huh. Who would have put those flavors together? She took a tentative bite and closed her eyes. Sweet, earthy, with a hit of green from the fennel. What a lovely, balanced flavor.

The baker gestured to the young man he'd been talking to. "I was just telling Lasho about how they released Enzo."

Lasho? Oh, he must mean the young man Stella didn't recognize. His name gave her pause. She wondered if he, like Ilaria, hailed from the Balkans. There seemed to be a pretty well-trodden Balkan to Umbria pipeline. Or maybe he came from somewhere else in Eastern Europe. One thing was certain, Aramezzo turned out to be a lot more cosmopolitan than she would have guessed.

Lasho added in soft tones, "I never thought Enzo could have done it."

Stella regarded him for a moment before reaching out her hand in a gesture she had not quite learned to quell. "I'm Stella."

He nodded as if this was the third time they'd been introduced, but she would have remembered if she'd met him already. "Lasho. *Piacere.*"

Romina regarded Stella with teary eyes. "Luca told us you were the one who convinced the police to let Enzo go. How good of you."

"Oh! Well. It was nothing."

Romina reached for Stella's hand to squeeze it before she turned away to blot her cheeks.

Stella turned to the rest of the customers. "How is the mayor taking Enzo's release? I know he felt . . . strongly."

Lasho smiled a little into his coffee as the baker answered, "Ha! I heard he's blaming Cosimo now."

Roberto dried his hands on a dishtowel. "How does he figure Cosimo?"

The baker shrugged and said, "Because Cosimo was so against the one-euro houses. Said it would wreck the 'historical threads of Aramezzo'. Whatever that means."

Lasho shook his head and put his spoon carefully alongside his cup. "It couldn't have been Cosimo. He was at the antiquarian meeting and didn't get home until Wednesday."

Roberto frowned. "Are you sure he went this month?"

The baker said, "He never misses it!"

Lasho nodded, adding, "I was on a job in Perugia Wednesday morning and saw Cosimo leaving with his colleague. According to the police, Severini was poisoned Tuesday night."

Stella grinned to herself. This was great. All she had to do was drop a conversational tidbit and let everyone else go through the machinations. She listened as she tore a corner off the bread and popped it into her mouth. Wow. She wondered if she could replicate this. Where did one get wine must? New York was one of the biggest wine-producing states in America, and she'd never heard of it. With effort, she tuned back to the debate.

Roberto was saying, "Well, they know it's poison, but they don't know what kind."

The baker leaped in. "It's got to be rat poison. I've worked at enough bakeries over the years with rat problems. It's easy to get, and it gets the job done."

"That's what I said!" Stella crowed.

The baker nodded appreciatively. "Yes, those of us who work with food probably assume rat poison first."

Stella started to mention the belladonna, but realized she only guessed this to be the culprit. If it was, and the police didn't know this yet, they likely wouldn't find her foreknowledge charming. And if they did know and were keeping a lid on it, they wouldn't thank her for spreading the news. Instead, she hedged, "But we don't know, right? I mean, it could be an industrial cleaner or even something botanical. Like mushrooms."

Romina said, "I wonder if they considered mushrooms. That's a thought." She grew still and straightened, putting down the towel she'd been using to buff a spot from the counter. "Wait. Maybe he foraged mushrooms and ate them. Maybe no one murdered him!"

Lasho cocked his head in thought before saying, "But the knots?"

Stella nodded along. "Exactly. And they would have noticed mushrooms in his stomach contents. It comes down to who had a problem with Severini."

The baker laughed, "Everybody!"

Roberto chuckled and said, "Too true. Except the mayor."

Romina added, "I'm sure the police will ask everyone questions again. They'll get to the bottom of it."

Stella turned back to her coffee. She wished people wouldn't accept police judgment as truth. They hadn't even thought it was murder! She wondered if this was an Italian thing, this blind adherence to authority's party line. Talk around the bar turned to smaller conversations—if the coming rainstorm would keep the bikers away, the local soccer league's chances, which elevation had olives ready for harvest.

Stella paid for her coffee and left, the door closing behind her with barely a sound.

"What do you mean you haven't been to Subbiano?" Matteo demanded, as Stella sat on the wall that divided the *piazza* from the view over the terraced olive groves.

"Me and what car?" Stella grumbled. "I'm adding wheels to my endless shopping list."

"But it's right there!" Matteo waved his hand toward the hill as if Stella had stupidly missed the geographic location of Subbiano. "You have feet, don't you?"

"Uphill? I think not. There are better uses of my time." Stella inwardly cringed at her allusion to her murder investigation. The peaceful place with Matteo felt fragile. She added lamely, "With the renovations and all. And I'm doing a lot of experimenting for when I finally get another guest. Which reminds me, do you know of a source for wine must?"

"My uncle makes wine. Cousins, too."

"Fantastic! Do you think I can get some must?"

"For a price."

"Ugh."

Matteo smiled before a shadow crossed his face. "Everyone has a wine-making cousin. Offer to swap must for bread. You'll figure it out."

Did he regret his almost-offer of speaking to his family on her behalf? She sighed. Maybe it would take time for Matteo to feel comfortable with her again. Her heart sank, but then lifted when he put down his broom and sat beside her on the wall, his legs wide apart in a posture of relaxation. He tipped his chin back until they both faced the light like sunflowers. Out of the corner of her eye, she saw Matteo's long face grow still as he soaked in the warmth.

The quiet moment broke as Matteo, his eyes still closed, murmured. "It won't be warm for much longer."

"I know. And I want to see Subbiano before winter. Romina said the trees in the *piazza* are beautiful right now."

Matteo smoothed out creases in his pants that, being essentially made of plastic, didn't wrinkle. "We could go now. If you want."

"Now?"

"Sure. It's a nice afternoon. I was about done anyway, after emptying the trash in those cans." He swept his hand to indicate the *piazza*. She wondered if he remembered that she suspected a clue to the murder lay in Subbiano. She imagined a lit-up square in the ground with an arrow hovering above it. Her imagination boiling away again.

"I'd love to." She stood up and walked to one of the trash containers. "I'll get this one."

"You don't have to." He rose as well.

"Happy to help. Besides, we'll want to head off so we can be back before dark."

He nodded, suddenly looking uncertain. They dropped off the trash and then made their way to the parking lot before they piled into Matteo's car. She pointed at the air freshener hanging from the rearview mirror. "Pineapple?"

He shrugged. "What can I say? I'm a tropical guy."

She rolled her eyes and said, "Is that so?"

"Mmm-hmmm." He yanked the car into reverse, prompting Stella to yelp."Can I get my seat belt on first?"

He paused in apology and she clicked in.

"Okay, I'm buckled."

Matteo said nothing as he backed out of the spot and pointed the nose of the car up toward Subbiano. Silence bloomed, and Stella wondered why he didn't turn on music. She thought about asking, but decided she should sit tight and appreciate the gesture. If only Matteo didn't seem so closed off.

His eyes fixed on the road, she noticed the muscle in his cheek twitching. She couldn't endure the silence anymore. "Is everything okay, Matteo?"

His eyes flicked toward her. "Why wouldn't it be?"

"I don't know. You seem . . . tense?"

He didn't answer for a minute, and she thought maybe he didn't hear her over the sound of the engine, but eventually he said, "It's all good."

The road turned into the creases of Subasio mountain. A parade of cypresses marched up to what must be the Americans' villa, peach-colored and massive, flanked by vineyards. Matteo sped along a straight stretch of road, and Stella glimpsed what must be the amphitheater. She wanted to ask about the stone columns, but they flashed by too quickly. Trees rose high above them, creating a shifting canopy of shadows. A glare on the side of the road alerted Stella to a desultory creek, the water sliding darkly like oil in a cold pan.

The car wound high into the hills. "I thought Subbiano was just a half-hour walk from Aramezzo?"

"It is. There's a trail that connects them. It goes straight down the mountain, without all the zigzags of the road." He waited a beat and then added, "We're almost there."

She rolled up her window as a chill wind blew in. The light shifted, darkened, and Stella noticed the sky's edges dulling to purple, like the corner of paper crumpling to ash at the touch of a match.

Finally, they pulled into a parking lot outside Subbiano's walls. The sound of Matteo's slamming door reverberated into the cold stillness. He stood next to his car, staring up at the top of the wall, his hands plunged deep into his pockets.

"Matteo?"

He didn't answer, but pulled his phone out of his pocket and lifted it to his ear. She hadn't even heard it ring. In tones far too loud for the lonesome mountain air, he said, "*Pronto.* I see. I see. Okay. I'll be right there."

He turned to Stella and said, his voice like stone, "Listen, I have to leave."

"Leave? Now?"

"It's an emergency."

"What kind of—"

His voice hardened further. "It's none of your business."

Stella paled.

The corner of his mouth lifted in an approximation of a smile as he leaned across the car hood toward her. "I can't explain now. But I have to go."

She swallowed. "That's fine. We can come another day. Or I can walk here on my own later this week, if you're busy." She opened the car door.

"You can't come with me."

She stared at him with wide eyes. "What do you mean?"

"I'm going to . . . I'm not going to Aramezzo."

"That's fine. We can detour—"

"No! You'll need to walk home. There's the path, there, see?"

Her gaze followed his arm to the trail marked by a small yellow arrow nailed to a rusting iron gate. The gate swung slowly, sending a creak into the air.

"Matteo, please," she entreated.

"I'm sorry," he whispered.

She watched as he climbed into his car and pulled back to the road, a cloud of dust chasing him back down the mountain.

Well, that seemed clear. He hadn't forgiven her as much as he claimed. He kept his emotional cards close to his chest, maybe he wasn't able to articulate his lingering anger. And this was his punishment? It seemed over the top, leaving her in this town that seemed to grow spookier by the minute, with the trees stretching up into a bruised sky. Then again, perhaps to him, Subbiano didn't seem lonesome and woebegone. He had probably never been abandoned.

She stayed a moment longer, watching Matteo's dust cloud disappear over the white gravel road. Stella shifted her weight in thought. She would have to tell him in no uncertain terms that this little prank or punishment or whatever didn't fly with her. And if that conversation cost her their friendship, then maybe that friendship wasn't much worth having. The sigh that escaped her lips clashed with the resolve in her thoughts.

Briefly, she considered heading back down the mountain. But she was already here. Might as well look around. A crow landed beside her, cocking his head as if to study her more closely. "Scram, bird," she said colorlessly. The bird opened his mouth to caw, but no sound came out.

Stella shivered. She turned on her heel and strode through the town arch. Quickly, she realized it would take ten minutes to walk all of Subbiano. It dropped steeply from the entrance, down the hill. From where she stood, she could trace the streets with her eyes. No wonder the residents abandoned this village. Old people must hate it. No stores for their daily shopping, no community as far as she could tell from the pressing quiet, and, above all, steep steps and angles, which must be a challenge for aged hips and knees. Besides, something in the air—and maybe this had more to do with the circumstances of her arrival—felt derelict in a way that couldn't be comfortable for those leaning into their sunset years.

As she set off down the street, she noticed that though many homes were in disrepair, they had what her builder friend back home called "good bones." Whenever he'd said that, she'd quipped maybe she should toss the building in her stockpot. But the words made sense here. She could see what would lead Americans to bid on one-euro houses in Subbiano. Though some buildings looked burned out, the homes themselves were spacious, with loftier ceilings than the houses she'd seen in Aramezzo. The scale of Subbiano lent it an air of former grandeur, and the proportions added a bit of poshness, even as roof tiles trembled like autumn leaves and fallen beams gave way to crumbling walls.

Behind her, a door banged. Stella jumped backward, clutching her heart. The wind. It must have been the wind. The door seemed to have no lock, or, on closer inspection, no knob at all. A cat the color of pencil lead blinked at Stella from a window frame, before turning its attention to another door, now opening down the road.

Stella followed the cat's gaze. A figure, clad all in black, stepped out of a house, smiling and laughing, in defiance of the leaden stones all around. As the figure bent to embrace a woman in a drab housedress, Stella caught sight of whiter than white teeth and hair with more than usual shine. She gasped aloud.

At the sound, Don Arrigo turned. His eyes widened at the sight of her.

Stella's glance flicked between him and the woman. Suddenly, all the details clicked to make a whole, just like when she got the proportions of spices and fat and acid just right to make a transcendent bearnaise sauce.

Matteo set her up. He'd never been her friend. He only wanted to know what she knew. How could she have been taken for a ride, *again?* Anger bloomed in her chest, like a dusting of cayenne pepper. At Matteo. At Don Arrigo. At every man who had taken advantage of her. But most of all, at herself for finding herself at the mercy of men's whims and men's schemes.

She was alone once more. That whole novel sense that maybe she could belong here? Vanished. She'd deluded herself. It seemed all the therapy in the world couldn't get her to figure out how to spot danger.

Stella spotted it now, though. She had to get out of here.

Ten meters away, Don Arrigo seemed to be making a similar calculation. Plastering a welcoming smile across his face, he cast his arms wide.

She wouldn't let him pretend. "I saw you," Stella said as he approached. Her knees shook, but she straightened so he wouldn't smell her fear.

His smile faltered. "Saw what, *cara?*"

"I'm not your *cara.*" She retorted with more bravery than she felt. If he wanted to hurt her, he would. She might as well say her piece. "That woman. She's your wife? Girlfriend?"

"What?" Don Arrigo's laugh rang like a tin bell. "Stella, I know you've been out of the church for some time, but you must know that priests live in celibacy."

"And as usual, you assume that rule, like others, doesn't apply to you."

He shook his head, his brow furrowed. "You don't understand."

"What's to understand? Given how much time Severini spent here, he must have seen you. It seems you hardly take the trouble to hide your little tryst. He blackmailed you. That's why you withdrew the money from the bank the day he died. To bribe him. That's why you killed him. Because he still threatened to expose you."

"No," Don Arrigo whispered.

"I think yes."

"You are so sure you know everything, city girl, but there are truths beyond your comprehension."

"Is that so?" At the implied insult, her fear vanished, a drop of water in a hot pan. Anger strengthened her voice. "Or are you just surprised that a little girl like me figured you out?"

He drew close to her, his eyes flashing. "You—"

But before he could finish the sentence, a little boy clattered down the street to arrive at Don Arrigo's knee, holding up his hat. "Your hat, Papa! You almost forgot it!"

"Thank you, my son." Don Arrigo smiled and tenderly cupped the boy's chin before the boy ran back to his mother, watching with wide eyes from her doorway.

"I guess I'm not so wrong after all," Stella shrugged. She turned to go, wondering if she could get a big enough head start to beat him down the hill. His priestly loafers did not look made for running. She bolted just a few feet before she felt jerked back by the elbow.

"You have to listen to me!" Don Arrigo's haughty glare transformed to a frown of entreaty. "Please, just listen to me."

"Or else what?"

He looked at her blankly. "Or else nothing. I just need you to listen to me. I'll tell you everything."

Was this one of those things that villains do in stories, where they feel the need to explain their process before they kill the main character? Stella had always assumed that to be an artifice of the storytelling process. She never would have guessed murderers did this in real life.

Stella didn't want to listen to him. She wanted to get away. But maybe if he relaxed a bit, trusted her not to bolt, he'd let go of her and she could slip away. More stealthily this time. She realized now that proclaiming she was getting away had probably been an error.

Controlling her breath, her heartbeat, Stella said, "Go on."

He furrowed one brow as if to assess her sincerity. "That's not my child."

"You called him 'son'."

"I call everyone son. I am a priest."

This was true, Stella conceded. Still. "He called you Papa."

At this, Don Arrigo chuckled. "Stella. The meaning of the word depends on the accent. Children call their fathers 'Papà'. The boy called me 'Papa'. What we Italians call the head of the Catholic Church. He is young and thinks all priests are the pope."

She narrowed her eyes. Was he pulling her leg?

"Papa Francesco," he added. "You've heard of our current pope, I expect? There is no stress on the last syllable. What did you call your father?"

"Dad," she said flatly.

"Ah, yes. But you must have heard children in Aramezzo calling their fathers."

She hadn't. But she had heard of fellow chefs talking about their families. And Cristiana calling her father. Grudgingly, she realized Don Arrigo was correct about the accent. But did the child put the stress on the second a? She couldn't remember.

"Stella," Don Arrigo said in softer tones. "I did not sin with that woman. That is not my child."

She looked at him with challenge in her eyes.

"But my brother did."

Her mouth fell open, and she sat on a step, bringing him with her, his hand still on her arm.

He nodded at her incredulity. "Carlo. Not my literal brother. My friend from childhood. Friend, actually, is not a strong enough word. You see, when he was a baby, Carlo's mother left him and his father, and so when his father died a few years later, my parents took Carlo in. We went to seminary together. Joined the Franciscan order together. Carlo and I were brothers in every sense but the biological one."

Stella snagged on the word. *Were.*

He sighed heavily. "We are none of us perfect, Stella. Not you. Not me. Not Carlo. He fell in love with a parishioner. For years he wrestled with it, wondering if he should leave the church. I can't count the hours he spent in my office, wretched."

Stella's thoughts about escape felt a million miles away. She watched Don Arrigo's face crumple as he spoke.

"He tried to clear his mind of her. But one night, man won over priest. He stumbled. He came to me the next morning, I'll never forget his face. Perhaps you can't know what it's like to live in terror of your own weakness. Carlo, he couldn't escape it."

In a whisper, Stella said, "He didn't quit the priesthood?"

Don Arrigo shook his head. "Perhaps because of his early years, Carlo found it difficult to leave anything. He couldn't leave the church, he couldn't leave Giovanna. Instead, he lived a tortured existence."

Stella hung her head. Briefly, it occurred to her to wonder about the veracity of Don Arrigo's story. He could be making it up, trying to lure her into a false sense of security. But a brief look at the woman still in the doorway, her son clutching her apron, Stella felt the story must be true.

As if in answer, Don Arrigo said, "You can ask her. She keeps to herself. It's why she lives here. So few villagers to question her son's paternity, so few eyes to avoid when Carlo would visit."

She considered his phrasing. "Would visit."

"Carlo died a year ago. A bee sting, of all things."

Stella's heart lurched. Carlo, saddled with grief since his birth, divided between the church and his love of a woman and their son, the family he didn't have. What a tragedy. She stared at her hands, open on her knees. Don Arrigo withdrew his hand from her arm with a pat. The place his hand had been now felt cold. She said, "It's a stupid rule, you know. That priests can't marry."

"Don't I know it."

She looked at him with a start.

He blinked at the unasked question and understood. "Celibacy is not always an easy road, but I had enough...experiences...as a young man to have taken up this mantle with full understanding of the trade-off. What I get by being a priest is worth everything. But for others, with different histories and backgrounds, well, why should they have to choose between love of a partner and love of a church? Isn't love, love? Doesn't more of it feed the universe?"

She didn't answer. Just sat in thought for a moment. The bee sting. Something fell into place. "Wait, he's *that* Don Carlo?"

"You've heard of him?" He sounded pleased, whether to have his story borne out or to have his friend remembered, she didn't know. She simply nodded. He went on, "On his deathbed, he asked me to take care of his family. I accepted."

A chill breeze wandered past. Stella wrapped her sweater more fully around herself. She wondered aloud, "So you've been withdrawing money each week to bring to Carlo's family. Because you promised."

She missed Don Arrigo's look of surprise. "And I'll continue until Giovanna's son starts school. Giovanna can't work. She has no family support, since she never named the child's father, so they still believe him to be unknown from a multitude of lovers. When nothing could be further from the truth. Giovanna loved Carlo. As much as one can claim any two people belong together, they belonged to each other."

"What a sad situation."

He nodded. "Signor Severini, prowling around here all the time, it didn't take him long to discover Giovanna and to make the same mistake you did."

"Why didn't you tell him what you told me?"

"On little information, he threatened to expose me. I have to believe he wouldn't care about the truth. And even if he was more scrupulous than I gave him credit for, if he saw how seriously I take my duty to Giovanna, he'd threaten to expose Carlo. Which would ruin his name and further marginalize Giovanna and her son. I couldn't risk it."

"But you told me the truth."

He gave her an appraising look. "He sought gain. You sought truth. Only one of those leads to a resolution worth pursuing."

She considered his words. "So Severini blackmailed you. To make you sign death certificates."

"He did."

"And you tried to bribe him with a stack of money to get him to walk away from the one-euro house scheme."

"Yes." He sighed. His gravely voice grew soft. "But there's more . . . that I'm not proud of."

Stella tensed, waiting. She couldn't help but admit she had misjudged the priest, coloring his generosity and his attention to her with a brush of ulterior motive. Maybe because her mother had always spoken so poorly of the church. Maybe because he was too handsome to be a priest, so she doubted his sincerity. Maybe because she always doubted sincerity. There would be time later to figure out the source of her prejudice. Right now, all she wanted was for him not to have killed Signor Severini. She needed him to be good. Because she needed to believe in good.

She hadn't realized she spoke the last of her thoughts aloud until he said, "The thing is, Stella, there is no such thing as good and evil. We humans are a cozy, curious, irascible blend of good intentions and sour desires. I am not excepted."

He sighed, and she waited for him to go on. "I did try to pay Severini off. You learned about those bank withdrawals from Domenica, I suppose?"

Stella regarded him with wide eyes.

253

He chuckled. "That woman's gifts are not as hidden as she'd like to believe. In any case, Signor Severini was not after my money, though I admit I tried to distract him with as much as I could offer him."

"He took it, though?"

Don Arrigo nodded. "Oh, he took it. I think he would have taken money out of a beggar's cup. But it didn't distract him from his objective."

"To get you to falsify those death certificates."

"Exactly. He'd been trying to convince me for months by phone, offering me a portion of the take, as if that could persuade a virtuous man to falsify a person's death. When I continued to refuse, he arrived in person. He upped the stakes when he discovered Giovanna."

Stella leaned back against the steps, watching the bottoms of the scudding clouds blur violet. She remembered the note she found. Should she ask about it and risk implicating Matteo? No, she couldn't do that. Then she realized that he'd left her an opening. "You said you did something you weren't proud of."

His eyes also followed the clouds meandering above them. Finally, he whispered, "I told him he risked eternal damnation if he continued to press me."

Stella sat up, staring at him. "You threatened him with *damnation?*"

He hung his head. "I know. A terrible misuse of the collar. I am ashamed."

He looked ashamed too, his cheeks flushed pink and his hands clasped so tightly between his knees she could see the veins building in his wrists.

Casually, she said, "I can think of worse crimes."

His gaze flicked to her.

"Blackmail, for instance. Falsifying documents. The guy was a bastard."

"His sins don't justify my own, I'm afraid."

"Whatever," she waved away his shame like so much leftover steam from boiling pasta. "So you did go home after that argument with Severini."

"I did."

"And you remember nothing else about that night that could help us figure out where Severini would have gone? He didn't tell you anything?"

"No, not a thing. He threatened me with exposure until I snapped and yelled at him. You heard about that, I expect."

She nodded.

"I figured." He smiled. "He said he'd be back the next day with the death certificates, and if I didn't sign them, he'd tell everyone about Giovanna. Then he left. Oh, and he stopped to talk to Cinzia. I think I told you that. About where he could get wine."

"And you're sure about the timing? He left close to seven?"

"Positive. I remember clearly because I ran headlong into Mimmo."

"You ran into Mimmo?"

He laughed. "Cinzia keeps telling me I shouldn't wear my Bluetooth headphones when I'm walking through Aramezzo, but I admit it's my one indulgence. The kids turned me onto hip hop, marvelous stuff, and I love listening to it as a soundtrack. I crashed into Mimmo, but he was unharmed, thank goodness. I took my headphones out to apologize and heard the church bells. That's how I know."

Something about this tugged Stella. Could it be the headphones? "Is that why you didn't respond when I called to you the other day? You were wearing the headphones?"

"Guilty," he laughed, holding up his hands.

They sat in silence for a few moments, as a dove cooed in a nearby olive tree and the cat in the window continued to clean his charcoal fur. Finally, he stood. "Did you want to meet Giovanna?"

"What? Why?"

He offered her a wry smile. "You've suspected me of murder. You wouldn't trust my story based on my say-so alone."

Her turn for red cheeks. "You know about that."

"Well, your talents don't extend to discretion, I'm afraid."

"Matteo told you."

"Matteo? No. He mentioned he wanted to talk to me, but we haven't had a chance." His eyes trained on hers. "Is he all right?"

"How should I know?" she said bitterly. Matteo might not have been trying to put her in Don Arrigo's path, but he still abandoned her here. "He brought me here and then took off."

Don Arrigo nodded, placing his hat on his head. "I was afraid of that. His grandfather must have taken a turn for the worse."

"Grandfather?"

"He didn't tell you?" He looked at her curiously. "I shouldn't be surprised. He does hold back, which makes sense given his history. But it does mean that those who love him are left outside his heart."

His words washed over her, eerily familiar to her own assessment of Matteo. "*Grandfather?*"

"Practically a parent to him, really. Since Matteo's father died in that freak farming accident when Matteo was small. Giuseppe stepped in to help his daughter raise her children. A good man, with an unfortunate cigarette habit that has caught up with him now. The cancer, it seems there's little they can do. He was taken to the hospital in Foligno last night, unable to breathe." He rose. "I need to be with them. You are welcome to stay with Giovanna. I know she has a ragù on the stove. It's simple, but as you know, there's a beauty in simplicity."

She stood. "Can I come with you?"

Don Arrigo stopped buttoning his coat to look at her.

"I won't get in the way. But I can fetch everyone food, coffee." She couldn't explain that picturing Matteo, who so carefully guarded himself in ways awfully familiar, shattered her. A flutter of memories cascaded like photographs—sitting on those hard hospital chairs with her mother three seats away, refusing to look at her. Being taken into the harsh-smelling rooms with unforgiving lights, seeing her father with the tubes coming out of his mouth, her sister so weirdly quiet and eerily small.

"Absolutely, *cara*."

This time, she didn't correct him.

The next morning, Stella blinked at the sun hanging heavily above Aramezzo as Matteo pulled his car into the parking lot. He and Stella climbed out, noting Don Arrigo's car already parked. The priest had had to leave at sunrise to prepare for Sunday services.

Matteo yawned impressively as they climbed the steps into Aramezzo.

Stella walked silently beside him. Finally, she said, "I wished I'd known him. The stories you and your family told..."

Matteo ducked his head, tears standing in his eyes. "He was a good man."

"That's exactly what Don Arrigo said."

He put his arm around her shoulder and pulled her against his side. "I was so surprised when you walked in together."

She noticed the scent of hospital still clinging to his jacket. She wondered how long until it dissipated. "Don Arrigo. I missed the mark with him."

Matteo cast her a curious glance. "I've never met anyone like you, Stella. You are so ready to be wrong."

She shrugged. "I hate feeling at the mercy of the universe. If I take responsibility, then it's like I get some power back."

He looked like there was more he wanted to say. More he wanted to ask. She could see the questions in his eyes—about where this came from, her desperate need to be author of her story. But the sun's rays were still warming up for the day and they had been up all night. They walked in companionable silence through the tunnel to the first road. As they stepped out of the tunnel's shadow, he said, "Headed home?"

She shook her head. "I'll get a coffee first. You want to come?"

"I'm not ready for the questions. I'll wait until everybody knows first." His voice trembled, and she squeezed his hand.

"Get some sleep."

He nodded and turned toward his house. She had never been there, but their friendship had shifted in these last twelve hours. She had a feeling she'd be invited soon.

Stella wound her way around the ring road, stopping to pet Ravioli on the step outside Domenica's shop. She continued to the *piazza*, lifting her nose to catch the scent of pork fat, melting. Must be the *trattoria*. She remembered Matteo had suggested they go together next week. Maybe with Domenica. He said Adele made a sinfully good *cinghiale* stew when a hunter brought her a wild boar—

Wait.

Something clicked. *Cinghiale.*

Mimmo.

Mimmo hadn't been camping the night Severini disappeared. Don Arrigo had seen him.

Mimmo lied. She stopped, her heart racing.

Cinghiale.

She suddenly remembered. When she found the body, Mimmo had said maybe she had fed her guest wild boar that had been eating... what was it... poisoned rats. Wasn't that specific? Maybe he had lured Severini to his house, had fed him tainted meat. Not tainted with poison, the autopsy results would have been clearer, but Mimmo practically lived in the woods. He'd know another way.

Stella frowned. The only way this made sense was if Mimmo had something to gain. Like what? Well, it had to be financial. Lost in thought, she moved away from the bar, through the quiet streets. She stopped at the town gate. She couldn't approach Mimmo alone. An idea dawned on her, and she reached for her phone before remembering it didn't work. She jogged home, opened the door, and ran through the house to the kitchen. She found Mimmo's number in her phone's contacts and pressed the landline's buttons, praying for him to pick up.

"*Pronto?*"

"Mimmo?"

"Who's asking?"

"It's Stella."

"Oh. *Ciao*, Stella. Change your mind about that truffle?" His voice warmed.

She warmed hers to meet him. "Definitely, definitely into that truffle. But I'm short of cash, so maybe the next one?"

"Then what do you want?"

"Can you meet me? Outside Bar Cappellina?" She hesitated, fingers crossed that the fish would bite. "I think I owe you money."

He paused, and she heard him shifting. "For what?"

"Can you meet me? Like in five minutes?"

"See you." He hung up.

Stella wiped her sweaty hands on her jeans. It would be okay, she told herself. The upside of her impulsivity was her ability to think on her feet. She'd wing it, trusting her ability to pick up on his cues to direct the conversation. Then again, she'd been up for twenty-four challenging hours. Her ability to navigate the situation may not be up to par.

Well, no use worrying about that now. Her mind raced as she fast-walked up the stairs to the second level of Aramezzo. It would be fine. She'd be in full view of the bar, even if she messed up, what could he do?

A voice whispered, *but later, if he's angry . . . he knows where you live.*

She set her jaw. Then she'd get the information without making him angry. She held her arms to keep from shivering. From nerves or the sudden cold, she wasn't quite sure. Outside Bar Cappellina, she waited.

Was it only a quarter of an hour ago she stood here, a smile on her face, contemplating a meal with friends?

Mimmo appeared in his stained shirt with buttons once again misaligned. He smiled when he saw her. Or was it a leer? She almost couldn't tell with him. Being a potential murderer aside, he was simply a weird dude.

She lifted her hand in greeting. "Thanks for meeting me."

He shrugged.

She hesitated, the words forming a second ahead of her speaking. She flashed him a winning smile and said brightly, "So I heard you met with Severini last week. You convinced him to pay ahead for his longer stay?"

The smile fell from his face. "What are you talking about?"

She fake frowned. "Didn't you meet him last Tuesday? I'd heard you had."

"Who said that?"

Stella gestured airily. "Oh, you know. People."

"People should mind their own business. Or they'll get what's coming to them."

"It's not true?" She cocked her head to the side and tried for the half-lie thing she read about in murder mysteries. "He was in debt all over town. Only paid Cosimo half what he owed him. I figured he owed you money."

"So what if he did?"

She nodded in pretended understanding. "I get it. I do. He stiffed you. Like he stiffed the rest of Aramezzo. It's okay that he scared you, with that gun and all."

"Scared?" Mimmo pushed his chest to the sky. "My gun is bigger than his gun!"

Ugh. She'd erred and prompted him into a pissing contest with a dead man. "I understand. I found him intimidating, too. No wonder you couldn't get what he owed you."

Suddenly, Mimmo snickered. "Yeah. 'Cause he died. Idiot."

She didn't know what to say to this abrupt change of topic.

He went on, "Did you hear what he was trying to do? With the one-euro houses?"

"Yes," she said, slowly, trying to keep up. "Did he tell you about that?"

He ignored her question. "Can you imagine? Trying to fill our woods with Americans tromping around?"

He misinterpreted her wide eyes.

"No offense," he grumbled.

"None taken," she whispered.

"He tried to ruin everything." Nodding at her conspiratorially, he added, "He got what he deserved, right?"

She shivered. Here it was. Mimmo's motive. Slowly she said, "The police found money on Severini."

His eyes widened.

"I figure if you convinced him to pay what he owed, the money is yours."

He put his finger in his ear and twisted it. "All two thousand euros?"

So he did know about it. "Whatever the two of you agreed on."

"You keep it." He grinned. "I have everything I need."

She watched dumbfounded as he crossed his arms to stick his hands in his armpits and stroll away. Did Severini have more money on him when he died, and Mimmo left some behind? But why would he leave the exact amount the priest withdrew as a bribe? Maybe it was in a different pocket of his jacket? Or in an envelope Mimmo didn't want to mess with?

She made her way to the bar, mind whirring. She'd have her coffee, then go to bed for a few hours. When she woke up, it would be afternoon. She could organize her thoughts until they made logical sense. Then she'd go to Luca. He'd listen. Even if he got mad for not heeding his advice to stay out of it, he'd listen. Probably. Maybe. She was too tired to decide.

Pushing open the door of Bar Cappellina, she greeted Romina behind the counter. "Roberto not in?"

"He's picking up wine in Assisi."

Stella nodded. "*Cappuccino* today, if you don't mind."

Romina replaced the tiny cup she'd picked up with a larger version. "Feeling okay?"

"Late night last night. I'm hoping the milk settles my stomach."

The sound of milk frothing filled the bar, and Romina set the cup in front of Stella, nudging the container of sugars within her reach.

"Well, I hope you didn't come for quiet." Stella followed Romina's gaze to a group of people entering the *piazza*.

The group sounded like a gaggle of geese as they entered the bar. Stella noted the butcher and the florist among unfamiliar faces. A few nodded at Stella. The rest cast her a curious look, but then went back to their conversation.

Stella rubbed her eyes and sipped her coffee. Maybe coffee was the wrong idea. She should nap. Her limbs felt heavy, her mind felt heavy, as if she could fade into unconsciousness right here in this bar, warm and cozy with the chatter of locals swirling around her, the sunlight warming her back, and the persistent rumble of grinding coffee. Her eyes drooped.

And then flew open.

Severini.

Someone mentioned Severini. She cocked her head to the conversation.

"Lamb scottadito. Definitely. That would be my last meal."

"Could a last meal be *dolci*? Because I'd happily go with *tiramisu*, *panna cotta*—"

"You guys. That's not the point. He didn't *choose* his last meal. I'm saying Severini was lucky to go with a belly full of pasta."

Before she could stop herself, Stella interrupted. "Pasta? That's what was in his stomach?"

The florist answered her. "That's what the police said. And I'm saying that going with ragù in your belly? If you have to die, that's the way to do it, right?"

"Ragù..." Stella mulled this over as the conversation wandered off. Something nagged at her, like that time she'd forgotten to put baking powder in her orange cake and realized something was wrong even before she pulled the gloppy mess out of the oven. She'd known, the whole time. The mistake niggling her like a feather, even as she folded in the chopped oranges.

The conversation now sounded like it was happening in another room, down a hallway.

"My grandmother makes a lasagna with pesto. That's what I would choose."

"She's from Liguria, your grandmother?"

"Yes, Genoa."

"They do like their pesto there."

"My cousin, he works at a hotel in Camogli, and he said they had to add eggs scrambled with pesto to the menu for tourists who demand more and more pesto."

Laughter.

"What is it about Americans and their eggs?" The voice trailed off as people darted looks at Stella, the one person who could explain the vagaries of American culinary sensibilities. It took her a beat to realize everyone was waiting for her to answer. She said in a distracted voice, "It's the protein. More staying power for long days in the coal mines and car factories. Are you sure they said pasta with ragù? In Severini's stomach?"

Everyone exchanged looks.

She went on slowly, "Because he didn't smell like tomatoes. Not even a little bit. Could it have been a northern ragù, with a lighter tomato hand? No," she answered her own question. "The herbs are still all wrong. The sage, for one."

One of the villagers laughed. "You think you can tell who has eaten tomatoes by their *smell*?"

The rest hooted with laughter, but the butcher put up a hand to quiet them. "She can tell."

She thought aloud, "But if it wasn't a traditional ragù on that pasta, then what...?"

She stood suddenly, the press of a thought nudging her brain. Flinging money at the wooden plate at the register, she said, "Thanks for the coffee, Romina."

"You didn't even finish it!"

"I can't. I have to bake."

The florist called across the bar, "What are you going to bake?"

She shook her head and hurried out of the bar, calling over her shoulder. "I have no idea."

Soon, flour arched through the air as she scooped it into a bowl. Sugar crystals dusted her nose like freckles. As the oven clicked to the proper temperature and she beat almond paste into submission, her heartbeat slowed, her thoughts fell into place. She could feel knowledge pushing against her brain.

As she dragged her hand across her forehead, she turned to find the cat drowsing in the armchair she'd moved to the kitchen for reading cookbooks. Eyes closed, the cat seemed at peace. Still, for the first time. What could have tempted him to drop his omnipresent guard and stretch across the cushion? Perhaps the patch of sunlight warming the chair. She smiled, admiring how the sun pinked his ears from behind even as it illuminated the tips of his fur until his flanks gleamed a metallic sort of silver.

But maybe it was more than the promise of warmth that brought the cat to the kitchen. She remembered his other appearances. Maybe kitchen noises and scents drew him the way they drew her. He certainly seemed comfortable, even though she'd been banging tray pans and clinking measuring cups.

She moved toward him and then stopped herself. Biting her lip, she crept closer and put a hand on the top of his head. She expected his fur to be bristly and coarse, but it was silky, compacting until she could feel the firm hardness of his wee skull. Holding her breath, she scratched behind his ear. The cat leaned into her touch for a moment before his eyes flew open. He recoiled, hissing, and then jumped, back arched like a Halloween cartoon. He dashed away, tail whipping behind him, down the hallway to some exit she still hadn't found. Stella watched him vanish with a strange sense of loss. Shrugging, she reminded herself he'd be back. If vitriol and ire couldn't get rid of him, no way a reckless moment of kindness would do the trick. And if he left for good, insulted at the presumptuousness of being petted like a common domesticated animal, well, wouldn't that be for the better? Didn't she want nothing more than to be rid of the beast?

Turning back to the counter, she imagined him running down the street to the edge of town. Past chicken coops and rabbit pens and chestnut trees and evergreen bushes. Stella reached for the butter.

And then put it down.

Evergreen bushes.

The scent, it clicked into place.

She stood, her eyes open wide as she let the last weeks run through her mind.

It couldn't be.

With a gasp of recognition, she bolted to the door, pulling on her jacket as she ran down the darkening street.

PART FIVE

iao, Stella," called an old woman putting her newly sorted greens in a colander to cook for dinner. Dinner time already?

"*Ciao!*" Stella panted for breath. She couldn't spare a moment to figure out if she knew the woman.

She rounded the corner and barely noticed Marta and Ascanio out in the field with the white dog now herding the sheep. As she approached Domenica's shop, she closed her eyes and willed it to be open. She wished so fervently, it felt like she'd summoned the lights on within the shop.

She flung open the door. "Thank God."

Domenica looked up from sorting books. She straightened her glasses with a grin. "Why, I'm happy to see you, too."

"It's not that, I mean, I am..." Stella fumbled.

Domenica smoothed it over by asking, "Big epiphany?"

"The biggest."

Domenica lowered her glasses to regard Stella over the rims. "Spill it."

Stella shook her head, taking off her jacket to get to work. "Not yet. It sounds too wild." She hurried to the cookbooks and pulled out volume after volume until she found the one she wanted. She read silently, nodding to herself, and then appeared at Domenica's side.

"Point me to a book on belladonna."

"If you tell me, I'll look it up—"

"I can't. Not yet."

Domenica nodded. "Follow me." Domenica stopped in front of a shelf with books adorned with images of flowers and leaves. She ran her finger along the spines, until, "Ah. This should have something."

She placed the book in Stella's hands. "Godspeed, *cara*."

Stella fell to the floor in a heap, flipping to the index and turning pages. As she read, the color rose in her cheeks and then faded to ash. She took her time getting up. Hooking her finger on the page, she walked to the front of the shop with deliberate steps. Hearing Stella's footsteps, Domenica spun around, stepping backward at the sight of Stella's pallor. "You found something."

"I think so, yes. Who poisoned Severini. And how."

The moment stretched like taffy, quiet filling the shop.

Finally, Domenica said, "I hope you aren't expecting me to guess."

Stella shook her head. "I can't even get my mind around it. It makes no sense and yet it all fits together."

They stood in silence.

"Domenica, I have to check something out."

"If you have information, you need to tell the police."

Stella's bark of laughter splintered the last of the shop's silence. "It's too wild. I'll check out my hunch and if it's right, I'll go to them."

"Stella."

"I promise."

"*Cara*, I can read you like a book. Whatever you're considering is dangerous. I don't want you putting yourself at risk. I've grown rather fond of you."

"Thank you, Domenica. That means a lot." Patting her pockets out of habit, Stella added, "Wish me luck."

"Would luck mean you find something or you don't find something?"

Stella shrugged and turned to the night air waiting outside. "I wish I knew."

"Stella... "

But the door had closed.

Stella ducked into the town's exit tunnel, holding her breath as the darkness pressed against her, filling her ears. She shook her head when she emerged back into the open air. Hurrying along the road, she listened for sounds of people, but only silence roared in her ears. She crouched low, running below the level of the windows, wincing when she stepped on a brittle stick with a snap that sounded like the shot of a gun.

Stella slowed her pace, her eyes on the windows. She inhaled sharply at light moving across glass, but she blinked and it disappeared. She glanced over her shoulder and caught sight of a car in the distance. It must have been the headlights, reflected in the window. She exhaled slowly, avoiding making a sound.

She pulled up at what she figured must be the right spot. Practically crawling now, she listened carefully. A rustling sound pulled her and she leaned forward, counting what looked like thickened shadows. With a start, she remembered her phone and pulled it from her pocket, switching on the flashlight.

She strangled out a gasp as a burst of flash exploded into her eyes. With fumbling fingers, she brought down the intensity to a low glow. Turning the light out in front of her, she counted to herself, once, twice, and three times, to be sure. A voice screamed in her brain to get out before anyone caught her, but she had one more task.

Her ears pricked at a noise that began like a faint wind whistling through pines and then grew into a haunting melody. She remembered that sound from the day she met Don Arrigo. The music lifted and floated above her as she crouched, her light shining on the grass until she found a pile of animal droppings. She reached for a stick and then lost her balance at a splintering sound above her. Holding her breath, her eyes widened as the sound intensified into a crackling. A light thud, followed by the sound of small footfalls, an animal running. She saw the cat out of the corner of her eye as it streaked past her and leaped nimbly to the roof of the woodshed beside her. It cast an annoyed glance as it ran by.

A cat. That's what she'd heard. It *must* be.

With the stick, she poked the droppings. Gross. They squished under the prodding stick and with her knees protesting the uncomfortable position she considered abandoning this fruitless exercise when the stick rebounded off something. Something... *bouncy*.

On her hands and knees now, Stella crawled until her nose practically met the pile, shining the light where her stick had felt resistance. There, so dark she wouldn't have noticed it, but now she saw a kind of sheen, a reflective quality missing in the droppings.

She poked her stick to work it free until it rolled toward her.

A belladonna berry.

She fell backward and then scrambled up, plucking up the berry before dashing along the ring road. No longer troubling to be quiet, she tossed a glance over her shoulder as a light clicked on.

Running full tilt now, she raced up around the road, up the steps, through the tunnel, and to her house. Her thoughts raced. Should she call 911? She gritted her teeth in frustration. Of course not. The emergency number in Italy was 112. But was that who she should call? She'd have to explain it all. No, she should call the local police. The office would be closed, but they would have someone managing the phones. Wouldn't they?

She gripped the berry and then ordered her fingers to relax.

As she approached her door, she felt a prickling at her neck. Was someone following her? She looked over her shoulder. Nothing but shadows. She pulled out her keys and spun the ring around, looking for the right one. The bundle slipped from her fingers, landing on the cobblestones with a tragicomic clank. She swooped up the keyring, careful to cup the berry in the crease of her palm while she found the key. Her first attempt failed. She felt like she did on the Jersey shore as a child, when she watched an overwhelming wave approaching but couldn't move out of the way fast enough.

"Nobody there, nobody there," she muttered to herself, though she couldn't help but peer over her shoulder again into the darkness.

Finally, she threw the door open and slammed it closed behind her. Stella pressed her body against it for a few breaths before racing to the kitchen. She flung open the drawer, muttering, *the number, the number.* There was a card somewhere with the number of the local police, along with the numbers for the electric company and the town governing board to report loose cobblestones. Written in spindly old-lady hand-writing, she assumed her aunt's.

She rested the belladonna berry on the counter and pulled out a handful of cards and papers, flinging them to the side until she found the paper printed with the emergency numbers along the top. With shaking fingers, she picked up the landline phone and pressed the first three numbers.

A sound behind her.

She gripped the receiver, her eyes darting from the numbers on the paper to the numbers on the phone. Her finger slipped on the buttons. She had to finish. She had to finish.

"You know, it's rude to keep a guest waiting."

Stella whirled around to find Cinzia standing in the doorway. Her hand leaning on the butt of a rifle.

"Cinzia."

"You were expecting me?" Cinzia gestured with the gun barrel to the belladonna berry on the kitchen counter. "Looks like you have something of mine."

Her mind racing, Stella attempted an air of casualness, as if Cinzia had complimented her gown at a ball. "What, this? Just a berry I found. You know how I experiment. With cooking."

Cinzia laughed to herself. "Is that so? What's that berry taste like?"

Stella's mind went blank.

"You talk a good game, Stella. I'll give you that. You might have fooled this town into thinking you're some innocent little transplant. But I know where you come from."

Stella's shoulders seemed weighed down with bags of flour as she lifted them to her ears. "I come from New York. Everyone knows that."

"Again, with the pretending. You can choose to ignore the rumors about your family, but believe me, I listen."

"From what I understand, there's been rumors about you, too."

Cinzia picked the rifle back up and hefted it over her shoulder against her effortlessly waving hair. "Mostly true."

Her eyes fixed on the rifle, Stella said, "What do you want?"

Cinzia widened her eyes. "So blunt. To the point. American, I suppose."

Stella didn't answer. Her gaze snagged on the silver-spotted cat as he stepped into the kitchen and stopped, regarding the women. Stella backed toward the window to draw Cinzia away from the cat. Cinzia closed in on her.

Go, she internally screamed at the cat. *Get out of here!*

Oblivious, the cat leaped nimbly to the kitchen counter. Over Cinzia's shoulder, Stella saw the cat nose the berry and recoil. Meanwhile, Cinzia inched closer to Stella. Desperate, Stella babbled, "Aren't you worried the police will track you down if I show up murdered with one of your bullets in my chest?"

"Ah," Cinzia smiled. "But it's not my bullet. It's my father's."

"Your father's."

"His sobriety didn't last long. When he comes to with this gun in his lap, the police will have no choice but to arrest him for both murders."

"Maybe he'll even confess to this one, too."

Cinzia laughed, coldly. "Wasn't that lucky? When I asked Severini over for dinner, Enzo had already passed out. But the poison didn't work right away. These things are hard to control, dosages and such, especially if you're working through an animal." Cinzia's voice trembled. She shook her head and went on, "Anyway, Severini thrashed about quite a bit. Kind of disgraceful, if I'm honest. Enzo came to and didn't understand what was happening. Some scrap of parenting instinct must have kicked in and he pushed Severini outside to the shed, knocking him unconscious."

"So the poison killed Severini. The nets kept him still until the poison finished the job," Stella thought aloud.

"The fishing nets?" Cinzia grinned. "I heard about that. Classic. Anyway, after my father realized what happened, he quit drinking. I have you to thank for getting him back home before he spilled my secrets in his withdrawal delirium."

"You can thank me by letting me go. I promise, Cinzia, I won't breathe a word to anyone about the belladonna."

Cinzia's laugh grated. "Believe it or not, I'm going to miss you. You provided a welcome distraction. But the time for distractions is over. It's time to get serious."

Before she could think about it, Stella said, "Does Don Arrigo know?"

"That I killed Severini?"

"That you're in love with him."

Cinzia shrugged. "It doesn't matter. My feelings for Don Arrigo, they transcend this mortal plane."

"Which is why you couldn't stand by and watch Severini blackmail Don Arrigo."

"Severini forced Don Arrigo to make a choice that would have ruined him. Either betray his deathbed promise or sign his name to forged religious documents. He couldn't do either without dooming his soul."

"So you saved him from damnation."

"As he saved me. I owed him that." Cinzia's voice softened. "He could never have lived with himself, with heaven's gates barred to him. And now we are connected. Tie upon tie."

"And Don Arrigo. Did he thank you for what you did for him?"

"If I did it for the gratitude, my efforts would be selfish." Cinzia laughed. "The strength of our connection lies in what we do for each other without ever saying a word. I'll make sure he never knows. It's the truest, most generous gift."

"Gift?" Stella blurted. "Cinzia. You killed a person." Her eyes darted to the cat, now walking along the counter, his gaze fixed on hers.

"I sacrificed him," Cinzia shrugged, "to save the soul of a righteous man. Only someone stuck in the secular dimension would punish me for that."

The cat cocked his head to the side, as if trying to understand the conversation. Stella sent up a silent prayer that he would stay quiet and not spook Cinzia.

"Have you shot a rifle before? I have," Stella lied. "In America, everyone uses guns. So I know, they have an incredible kickback. If you aren't familiar... You need to know how to use it..."

Cinzia cut off Stella's babbling by aiming the gun at Stella's chest. "I'll learn in killing you."

Stella whispered, "Cinzia, please."

"I have to, don't you see?" Cinzia's voice quavered as she said, "Or killing her would have been for nothing."

Her? Then Stella realized. The rabbit. Cinzia meant the rabbit. Stella's eyes flicked to the cat, now walking again toward her, threading his way around the cooking supplies she'd left out in her haste to get to the bookstore.

She had to get the gun from Cinzia. A thought clicked into place. "I guess you don't love those rabbits as much as you pretend."

"I had no choice. It was part of the journey. Sacrifice is always part of the journey."

"Still. You twisted her neck."

Cinzia's lip trembled.

Stella leaned forward a touch and added in a soft voice, "That rabbit's eyes, right before you killed her, they must have stared at you. Stared into your soul." A flash of memory of Severini's staring eye.

Cinzia made a strangled sound and lowered the gun a hair.

"You watched the light die in your baby's eyes. You watched her suffer."

Cinzia shook her head with a sob, the gun lowering further, "She didn't suffer, I made sure. I made sure she didn't suffer."

Cinzia wiped her eyes. Stella moved forward to grab the gun, just as the cat rubbed his body against the flour canister. It crashed to the floor with a sound like thunder in the still room. Cinzia startled at the sound, shooting wildly even as Stella yanked the butt of the rifle. An explosion in Stella's ear. Stella's momentum pushed her into Cinzia's shoulder until the two of them collided with the floor. The metallic odor of gunfire filled the room. Where, where did the bullet go? Not into Cinzia. The woman's eyes blazed as she pushed Stella off her, staggering up to steady the gun against her shoulder once more.

Just as the door flew open with a resounding bang.

Luca stormed into the house, catching Cinzia by the elbow and twisting the gun up and out of her hands. Cinzia shouted in protest. The room became chaos as more officers flooded through the door. Was that Domenica? Stella blinked slowly. Why was Domenica coming to her house with a bunch of police officers? Was Stella in trouble? As Stella stared around in wonder, she noticed a bloom of red on her sleeve.

"I'm bleeding," she murmured, to no one in particular.

Though she spoke softly into the uproar, Luca turned toward her, his dark eyes flashing. He passed a handcuffed Cinzia off to another officer and strode across the room in two broad steps. Though he'd barreled toward her, he lifted Stella's arm with surprising gentleness. His jaw working, he carefully slid her sleeve up to examine the wound. "It's just a scratch," he said with relief. He grabbed a clean kitchen towel from the counter and pressed it lightly against the wound as he instructed Domenica, "Make sure she keeps this here. We'll have a doctor look at it."

Domenica nodded grimly as she held the towel against Stella's arm, pulling it off after a minute to check the blood flow.

Stella blinked. "She shot me. Cinzia shot me."

Domenica and Luca exchanged glances. Softly Domenica said, "She caught on. That you knew what she did."

Mute, Stella nodded.

Luca blurted, "But how did you know?"

Domenica tried to shush him. "There will be time later."

"No, it's okay," Stella said. "She must have seen me at the rabbit pen. I went there to count the rabbits, to see if any were missing, any she might have used in a rabbit ragù. I only counted five, and I found a belladonna berry in the droppings. She must have followed me here. With the gun. A *gun*, Domenica."

Luca dragged his hand through his hair. "But Stella, how did you *know?*"

"Severini." Stella's gaze moved from Domenica to Luca. "When I found him. Something smelled strange—the herbs, sage and thyme and rosemary. When I heard his stomach contents, it clicked. If there was a ragù, it had to be a white sauce, no tomatoes. Then the final scent dawned on me. Juniper berries."

"Juniper berries!" Domenica and Luca practically shouted at the same time.

"Juniper berries. Only white ragùs call for them. And white ragù is only ever made with a few kinds of meat."

"Like rabbit."

Stella nodded. "There are others, but rabbit is the most common, yes. Certainly, it made rabbit occur to me. Especially with those herbs."

Luca shook his head, drawing closer, his eyes fixed on her. "But still... how did you—"

"Something I read," Stella said. "Remember the scene of the crime, when Mimmo said maybe I fed Severini tainted meat? Today that came back to me, and it reminded me of a section in a cookbook about how certain animals, like quail and hare, can ingest poisonous botanicals and not be affected, even while their meat becomes toxic."

Domenica checked the wound. The bleeding had slowed. "So Cinzia fed her rabbits belladonna and made a sauce with one of them to poison Severini."

"You worked all that out." Luca shook his head and stared at Stella, his eyes glowing. "I still don't get the motive."

Stella knew there was something she shouldn't say, some secret of Don Arrigo's that wasn't hers to share. She tried to shrug and winced instead. Luca flinched and moved toward her, his eyebrows drawn together.

"I'm okay," Stella said. She continued, "Severini was blackmailing Don Arrigo for death certificates. Cinzia had a kind of warped feeling about Don Arrigo. He took her in after the abortion—"

"What?" Luca gasped.

Stella nodded. "Domenica, you said she got pregnant, then disappeared, and then came back and started working for Don Arrigo. I think in a mixed-up way, those rabbits became the baby she'd lost. And Don Arrigo, he became her savior. She felt they had this cosmic—" Her words cut off at a high, wailing sound.

"The cat!" she yelled. "Where is the cat? The cat saved me!"

At Domenica and Luca's blank looks, Stella said, "He knocked the flour canister over again, this time to the floor! The crash, it distracted Cinzia enough for me to get the gun! *Where is he?*"

She broke free of Domenica's hand on her arm,. The cat wasn't on the counter, or in the kitchen.

Amusement tinging his words, Luca said, "Let me get this straight. The cat does something obnoxious and now you think he saved you?"

"Oh, you wouldn't understand," cried Stella in exasperation. A sob yanked her words, "Domenica, help me find him."

But just then she caught sight of the cat. He'd fled the scene and collapsed in the living room, where he lay in a growing pool of blood. Stella lurched forward, stumbling, and fell on the floor in front of the tabby. The wildness had fled his eyes. He looked up at her, confused and suddenly tiny. Stella smoothed the cat's side, looking for a bullet wound. She glanced at his face, something was wrong. A hiccuping cry escaped her when she realized the cat's ear had been blown off.

"Oh, no," she breathed, the pain in her arm now evaporated. "Oh, please, no."

The cat meowed plaintively in response, his eyes fixed on her.

Stella noticed Domenica standing behind her. "Quick, Domenica, that towel, there on the chair."

Domenica handed her a fresh towel and Stella carefully wrapped the cat and slipped one arm and then another under its body. He was lighter than he looked, but she sagged under the weight. Stella's voice rose frantically, "A vet. Do you have a vet? Can you take me? I need . . . "

But Domenica already had her phone, punching numbers. She spoke quickly; the words lost to Stella as she spoke soothingly to the cat. The cat's eyes, still intent on her, blinked once and it let out another plaintive mew.

Domenica slipped the phone into her pocket. "He's waiting for us."

"Who? Domenica, I can't leave him." Her voice caught. "He's lost so much blood."

"The vet, Stella. The vet is waiting."

Stella allowed herself to be led out the door. She looked over her shoulder and asked, "Can I leave, do they need me?"

Luca appeared beside her, his dimple appearing and disappearing as he endeavored to keep a straight face. "Go. I'll send a doctor to the vet to clear your arm."

Stella stumbled, following Domenica into the night. "His ear, is he going to be okay?"

As they hurried down the road, Domenica studied the cat tucked in Stella's arms, his eyes open, alert. "The ear is beyond saving."

"His ear, Domenica!"

Domenica shrugged. "Cats go on to live happy lives, even with missing parts."

Stella pulled the cat closer to her chest, sobbing.

Domenica murmured, "People, too."

"Stand back, he doesn't like people crowding him," Stella ordered. Matteo and Domenica backed away from the kitchen counter. Stella carefully lowered the drowsing cat onto the stack of folded blankets she'd placed there.

It had been less than twenty-four hours since Cinzia's arrest for the murder of Paolo Severini AKA Danilo Crespi, and the attempted murder of Stella herself. Yet those moments with Cinzia that ended with the explosion weirdly felt like a lifetime ago.

Matteo and Domenica exchanged glances, in silent agreement to not comment on Stella's behavior. She caught sight of the shared moment and grumbled, "You lose an ear. See how you like it."

Matteo laughed, the gap between his front teeth winking merrily. "Do you have a name for him yet?"

"I have to name him?" Stella scooped chicken that she'd cooked down with carrots and rice, tapping the food into an antique saucer with tiny violets winding around the silver rim.

Domenica nodded, trying to suppress a smile. "It is what cat owners do. They name their cats."

The cat hunched over the plate and regarded the assembled humans with gleaming topaz eyes before he buried his muzzle into the saucer of prepared chicken. He looked up, his eyes half closed with pleasure, bits of chicken clinging to his black chin.

"Blackbeard," she said aloud, not realizing she'd switched to English.

To her friends' confused expressions, she switched back. "Barbanera."

Domenica furrowed her brow. "The almanac with proverbs and gardening tips and lunar phases?"

"The pirate," Stella laughed. "His one ear, his black chin. It fits. Though I like him being named after a guide to living, too."

"Barbanera," said Domenica. "I like it."

Matteo asked, "Did you get any sleep last night, Stella?"

"Not much, no. What with the vet visit and then staying up with the cat. Plus, you know."

He nodded. "You were wired."

"Like I'd had a thousand shots of coffee."

Shaking his head, Matteo's voice rang with concern. "And you got no sleep the night before. At the hospital."

She didn't answer as she watched the cat tuck into his meal, the bandage over his ear fresh and white and almost jaunty. A match to the bandage on her arm.

Domenica pulled Stella close. "Go sleep, *cara*. We'll stay and watch Barbanera."

"I need to talk to Don Arrigo. He deserves that. He deserves that much." Her voice trailed away.

Matteo shook his head. "I hope this doesn't disillusion him from his fundamental belief in the goodness of people."

Domenica hesitated and then said, "It might. For a while. Being so wrong about someone he trusted. But there are enough of us to remind him about the good." She murmured to Stella. "He told me to tell you he sends his love and he'll be by tomorrow."

Stella nodded.

Matteo added, "I think he'd started to doubt Cinzia. He told the police that he asked her questions the other day and found the answers disturbing. She didn't deal with it well, which concerned him more."

Stella thought for a moment. "That makes sense. I saw a tense moment between them."

"And did you hear?" Matteo asked. "The police arrested Enzo. He'll serve time as an accessory to murder. Though his altered state and his attempt to confess should lighten the sentence."

Stella let out a grunt of irritation.

Her friends studied her.

She grimaced. "Once again, a woman suffers for the sins of a man."

Domenica nodded in thought. "Her father failed her, yes. But she's the one who held the gun."

Stella shook her head, but said nothing.

Matteo took a beat and then said, "The cops also found Cinzia's books, the kind Domenica would never stock."

Domenica shuddered. "I am no arbiter of taste, but books that focus on the deflowering of priests? No."

"I saw those books," Stella remembered. "When I was at her house. But I didn't know what they were, just that they'd arrived by mail. Only later, when I was putting the pieces together, did I remember. That, and she had another book with them, with a plant on it. She'd been doing her research."

Domenica nodded. "You don't need to think about it anymore. It's behind you. It's all behind you."

Stella frowned. "I still don't understand why the police showed up. How did they know?"

Matteo glanced at Domenica. "Someone called Officer Luca at home."

Domenica shrugged. "I told him that if he didn't go to your house and check on you, he'd have to go to Perugia for his historical romances. And that I might let it slip to his mother that I saw him flirting with an Australian tourist in Assisi last month when he was supposed to be home for Sunday supper."

Stella chuckled and stroked the cat's back. Barbanera hunkered down and leaned toward her touch. He closed his eyes, letting out a rumbling purr that sounded as rickety as a long-unused Ape just starting up. Stella smiled and caught a glimpse of an unfamiliar tea towel on the counter, stained and wrinkled. "What's that?"

Matteo grinned. "*Cinghiale* salami. Mimmo dropped it by this morning."

Stella's eyes widened. "Mimmo brought me salami?"

"Word travels fast, even to Mimmo's house," Domenica laughed. "And I'd ignore the indifferent wrapping, my dear. His salami is legendary in these parts."

Matteo touched Stella's shoulder. "Go to bed. We've got this."

"But what if something happens?"

Matteo grinned. "This is Aramezzo. What could happen?"

I HOPE YOU ENJOYED YOUR VISIT TO UMBRIA, THE GREEN HEART OF ITALY!

More mystery is already brewing in Aramezzo; check out *Bread and Murder in Aramezzo,* available now! Don't want to miss a clue? Sign up for the Grapevine, at *michelledamiani.com/grapevine,* and you'll be the first to know when the next book is available.

As a welcome to the Grapevine, you'll receive *Seasons of Secrets,* a free novella set in Santa Lucia—where, you may remember, Stella has a great aunt who is married to the mayor. The books will cross at some point, so now is the time to discover Santa Lucia!

Along with top-secret book news and deals, and your exclusive copy of *Seasons of Secrets* (not available in stores), every month you'll receive expert travel tips, delicious recipes, and books reviews for your next wanderlust read.

Hope to welcome you soon!

Ciao for now,

— Michelle

ALSO BY MICHELLE DAMIANI

Bread and Murder in Aramezzo:
Book Two in the Murder in an Italian Village *Series*

Il Bel Centro: A Year in the Beautiful Center

Santa Lucia

The Silent Madonna

The Stillness of Swallows

Into the Groves

The Road Taken: How to Dream, Plan, and
Live Your Family Adventure Abroad

Find out more at michelledamiani.com

Made in the USA
Coppell, TX
22 June 2023

18411430R00173